TRUE COLOURS

TRUE COLOURS

BY

ALARIC BOND

Fireship Press
www.FireshipPress.com

ISBN-13: 978-1-935585-30-5

BISAC Subject Headings:
    FIC014000   FICTION / Historical
    FIC032000   FICTION / War & Military

Address all correspondence to:
Fireship Press, LLC
P.O. Box 68412
Tucson, AZ 85737
USA
Or visit our website at:
www.FireshipPress.com

1.0

To Kitty

Acknowledgements

Thanks are due to Keith Watkins, David Hayes, Richard Spilman and Fireship's senior editor, Tom Grundner for their constant support, encouragement and critical comment; also to my family for doing what they do best. The remaining errors are mine, but without their attention, there would have been far more. I would also like to recognise the understanding and patience shown to me by the guests and staff at Scolfe's, and members of HFC; I won't mention individual names as most already know theirs, and it would only serve to confuse the others.

CHAPTER ONE

HE had been asleep for less than an hour and in his mind Lieutenant King was many miles from his cabin in *Pandora* when the call awoke him. He lay for a moment as the sound of running feet and bellowed orders reverberated about the small enclosed space. It was one he shared with a locker, a washstand that turned into a narrow desk, and a sea chest that doubled as a chair; the shirt and duck trousers he had been wearing lay casually across the latter. He had gone below just before dawn; presumably the onset of daylight had revealed some new and extraordinary problem that only someone of his astonishing intellect, ability and courage would be able to solve. He pulled a face to himself and sighed. *Pandora* was clearly manoeuvring; and heeled slightly as he swung out of his cot, his bare feet hitting the cold wooden deck that was still a little wet from the previous night's storm. It was too dark to see, but his chin felt tolerably smooth. His beard was several shades lighter than his short auburn hair and hardly needed the attention of a razor two days out of three; it would certainly suffice for an early call.

The ship's bell rang four times; by rights King had two more hours of precious sleep due to him, two more hours after the nine he had spent in the very teeth of a Biscay tempest. His mood did not improve greatly as he reached for his trousers, and found them still heavy with damp, and he cursed mildly as he remembered the other pair were badly torn. He had two pairs of britches in the sea

1

chest, although these were only worn when uniform was specifically required. On a small ship like *Pandora* uniform rules were inclined to be relaxed and Lieutenant King was rarely seen on deck in anything other than blue jacket, white shirt and seaman's trousers.

The shirt was equally moist but now King was fully awake, and gave it little thought as he hunted for his boots, snatched at his hat and jacket and opened the frail deal door that led into the gunroom and, in this instance, the bulk of Adam Fraiser. The sailing master turned his stocky frame and smiled at the younger man. "Seems they canna' do without us, after all, Thomas."

"Trouble, gentlemen?" Marine Lieutenant Newman looked up from where he sat in his shirtsleeves at the gunroom table, and beamed at them both with the humour of a man who had not spent the previous day and night fighting a storm. King and Fraiser squeezed past him.

"Och, it's probably little more than one of the convoy sailing under the water for a bit of a change." Fraiser assured him genially.

"Nothing trivial, then?" Newman was a man who smiled easily, and despite his own bad temper King found the act infectious.

"Nothing that should deny a man his sleep," he agreed, and collected his stiff, brown watch coat from Crowley, one of the stewards.

Outside the gunroom, the berth deck still held the damp, sleeping bodies of the watch below. Clearly it had not been a call for all hands, or even both watches, and so the two officers made their way up, and into the fragile dawn light on the quarterdeck a little more at ease. There was no sign of the captain; Caulfield, the first lieutenant, had the watch. He stood hunched over the traverse board, also wearing a heavy brown coat, although his was dark with moisture and, its owner being relatively short, hung down to well below his knees.

"Sorry to disturb your caulk, gentlemen," Caulfield's smile took most of the sarcasm from the remark, although he appeared every bit as weary as King felt. "Seems we have company, and the captain thought it better that all shared the sport."

"The captain?" King went to ask more, but a poignant look from Caulfield made him glance upwards. The captain was directly above them, in the crosstrees of the mizzen, with one arm wrapped about the topgallant mast, and the other focussing a glass on the horizon.

"Masthead sighted a strange sail to leeward." Caulfield explained, removing his hat and running a sleeve across his slightly balding head. "Probably no more than a stray merchant, but in view of our friends we thought it better to take no chances."

King's gaze swept around to the small group of ships that had been their constant companions since leaving the Tagus. There were only five; barely enough to justify a frigate escort although, considering the trouble they had caused, there might as well have been fifty.

"Behaving themselves, are they?" Fraiser asked, and Caulfield snorted.

"If you mean in the hour or so that you two have been resting none have collided, sunk nor raised the French flag, then yes, you could say they were behaving themselves. As to the future; I would not care to commit."

No convoy containing ships manned by merchant seamen, men used to choosing their own course and speed and who would instinctively keep as much distance between themselves and their brothers, could ever be easy to escort. But this particular collection were apparently commanded by officers eager to compete in both independence and originality, and the last few days had been frustrating for all on board *Pandora*.

"Make more sail, if you please," Captain Banks had finished his inspection and was passing the mizzen top on his way down.

"Shake out the reefs and add forecourse and jib," Caulfield ordered, in a voice barely louder than conversational. The hands stood ready at their stations and swarmed up the shrouds, encouraged by the squeal of boatswain's pipes. The wind that had plagued them throughout the night had dropped to a strong breeze and was now reasonably steady. It came from the south, across their starboard quarter, and *Pandora*'s heel increased only slightly as the new canvas began to fill and her stem dug deeper into the crested waves.

The captain joined them on the quarterdeck, replacing the glass on the binnacle and retrieving his hat. At twenty seven he was younger than all the senior officers bar King, and had already established himself as a rising star in the navy. A knighthood had been acquired into the bargain, although the distinction, along with the captaincy of *Pandora*, had been produced by favours and nepotism; a system known as 'interest' that was customary in a navy that thrived on tradition. As unfair as it was widespread, interest could be blamed for countless potential commanders currently stuck on the beach, or in the lower ranks on dead-end commissions. In this instance a worthy man had been promoted and honoured, but Banks was a rarity, and it was slowly becoming obvious to all that the practice was ripe for change.

"Merchant, I'd say, and like enough British, but we'll know more in a while." Banks glanced at King. "Better make to the convoy to maintain present course and speed."

"That would be a first, sir." Fraiser's dour Scot's tone brought a smile to the faces of tired men, although each felt a mild disappointment that the sighting had proved so mundane. King walked across the deck and caught the eye of Dorsey, the signal midshipman, who was already thumbing through his book, and returned his nod. *Pandora* was a small ship with a relatively young crew. During her commission the officers and men had melded themselves into an efficient team, helped in no small way by the mutual trust that had grown from shared experiences. At twenty eight guns she was decidedly inferior to most other ships with a Captain in command, but despite her size she had seen a fair amount of action and the respect and understanding which had evolved allowed for a relaxed, almost casual, atmosphere that would be quite out of place in a larger, or less competently manned, vessel.

Dorsey's signal flags were run up by the halyard and broke out. The storm that had been brewing for several days had passed completely, and soon the decks were steaming as the spring sunshine reasserted itself.

"Deck there," The lookout called down to the expectant officers. "She's hull up now and I can see her lines. A brig, or m'bee a snow, couldn't rightly say. She's not showing much sail but flying British colours, an' there's another flag, but I can't make it."

"Chance is she's in difficulties." Caulfield commented. Remembering the recent storm it was not unlikely.

"Perhaps, but I have breakfast awaiting," Banks informed them, brightly. "Give the watch below as much sleep as you can, but call them and me if our friend turns out to be anything out of the ordinary."

With the captain gone the three officers relaxed into a companionable silence. The temporary release from the convoy's constraints, an increase in speed, and this delightful spring sunshine were enough of a contrast to be quite therapeutic, and each was alone in thought as the sighting became visible from the deck, and gradually began to form into a merchant brig. The captain had returned, crisp, fed and refreshed, by the time they were drawing close enough to inspect her properly.

"She's flying the fever flag," King muttered when it became clear. "Fortunate we're well to windward."

"And all ahoo aloft, fore topmast's damaged." Banks was inspecting the ship's rig minutely as *Pandora* spilled her wind and began to slow. "Might well be the storm, but I'm not happy. Give her a hail, Mr Caulfield, and we'd better have the men up."

The first lieutenant collected the brass speaking trumpet. "What brig is that?" His voice boomed across the water, accompanied by the pipes of boatswains mates as they summoned the off duty men. There was no sign of hands on the brig's deck, although she was being steered into the wind and was now almost stationary.

"Take her in, if you please," Banks murmured when no reply was forthcoming. Slowly the British frigate closed with the merchant, until the brig lay comfortably in range to leeward.

"Brig ahoy!" Banks this time, his voice was lighter than Caulfield's although the distance was not great and the clatter aboard *Pandora* had lessened. "I wish to speak with your master."

A man appeared amidships and began to walk almost reluctantly back and on to the short quarterdeck. "Master's below. We've two men sick with the fever, an' one died in the night."

"What brig, and where from?"

"*Katharine Ruth*. Last touched at St Helena," the voice replied.

The officers looked at each other. St Helena was a month or more's sailing away. Longer was needed for most of the exotic diseases to reveal themselves although Typhus, commonly known as ship fever, was always ready to strike when conditions were right.

"You have damage aloft, do you require assistance?"

"No," the voice was far more ready to reply this time. "We can manage, thank'ee."

Banks took a pace along the quarterdeck, before turning to his officers. "I don't like it," he said. "A topmast shaken in a wind, yet the rest of the rig appears in order. And hiding behind a fever flag; that's a Frenchman's ruse, no mistake. Mr King, take the cutter and a boarding party, if you please. Mr Manning may accompany you in case there is illness, but be on the alert; I have an uneasy feeling."

King touched his hat, Crowley was there with his sword and pistol, he took both and exchanged his watch coat for a boat cloak and made towards the starboard cutter. Boarding a fever ridden merchant was not the ideal start to his day; as far as uneasy feelings went, the captain did not have the monopoly.

* * * * *

Manning appeared as the cutter was about to cast off from *Pandora*'s hull. King held his hand out as the assistant surgeon stepped into the boat, already crowded with seamen and marines, and seated himself in the sternsheets. His face was rosy with sleep, and he yawned easily as the coxswain pressed them away and ordered the oars out.

"Wake you, did we?" King asked his friend, who had begun to rummage in the small leather bag he held by his side.

"Happily with Morpheus when I gets the call; tell me, what is there about the world of a seaman that is so contrary to normal living?"

King's grin faded as he looked across at the brig. Two further figures had appeared on deck, and there seemed to be some sort of altercation amongst them. With six strong men at the oars the distance would soon be covered and as the boat swept closer, the panic apparently increased. Then one of the group broke away and glared down.

"We tolds you, we don't need no 'elp" It was a different voice, and clearly not an educated one. King raised his hands to his mouth in an improvised speaking trumpet.

"Brig ahoy, we are boarding you."

"You keep off," the first voice again. "We got the fever, it - it ain't safe."

By now they were almost alongside, and King could clearly see fresh damage to the wales. Paint and splinters had been torn from the strakes as if she had grazed a quay. The coxswain brought them level with the gangway port and, ordering the oars in, reached out with a boathook. King was the first up and through the narrow gap. Two seamen blocked his path. Large men, with dark brown tattooed hams for forearms, they were dressed in

6

checked shirts and seamen's trousers, and he was clearly not welcome.

"Nothing for you on this ship, mister," one said. "Best you leaves us to mend the barkie an' we'll both be on our ways."

"My name is King, I am a King's officer," he swallowed, not for the first time, at the clumsy repetition. "And I have orders to inspect your vessel."

"Let him through boys, let him through." A new and more cultured voice cut in and the two men stood to one side. Behind them a smaller, older man, possibly in his late forties, stood dressed as a senior merchant officer.

"Forgive me, Mr King, you are more than welcome aboard this ship, we are merely concerned for your well-being." He stepped forward and proffered his hand. King took it, mildly relieved to hear his seamen and marines as they formed up behind him.

"Fever struck us a few days before that storm and, being short handed as we are, there's been much for the well amongst us to do, as you might surmise. My name is Boyle, I'm the mate; I'm afraid the master is laid low with the flux, but I have our papers here if you would care to inspect them." A small canvas covered package was handed to King.

"Flux? Fever?" Manning sounded confused. "What are the symptoms?"

The mate considered him. "You are a doctor, sir? Do you have a physic that might help?"

"I will need to examine your patients; take me to them, if you please."

Again a moment of reluctance, then Boyle turned and walked toward the stern. "The captain is in his quarters, follow me."

* * * * *

Roused from their rest an hour early, the men of the starboard watch were not content.

"Three hours sleep, and they turns us up again," Jenkins, a seasoned hand, grumbled. "Be glad to get back to Pompey; this is a lark, an' no mistaking."

"What makes you think it'll be any better in England?" Scales asked. Scales had only recently joined *Pandora*. Educated, and with assumed authority, he had quickly established himself as one of the major figures on the lower deck. The kind the men listened to, even though they did not always agree with what was said. "Supposin' we do stay more than a night in Spithead, the only way any of us will set foot on land is if we desert."

"Aye, he has you there," an anonymous voice agreed. "Spithead's all well and fine when the Weddin' Garland's up, but there's little chance of a spree ashore."

Jenkins attended to his hammock. He supposed they were right, but he had far more than the prospect of a couple of drunken nights waiting for him at Portsmouth.

"Never mind," Cribbins, an ordinary seaman, patted him on the shoulder. "Even if we are bound for England, even if we land at Pompey, and even if you get a spot of shore leave, it won't do you no good."

Jenkins eyed him warily. "Why's that then?"

"Cause you ain't got no money!" Cribbins roared delightedly. "An even what they owes you, you owes me!"

The other men laughed good-heartedly, although it was clear that Jenkins did not find the situation amusing. He had been transferred to *Pandora* in a draft of twenty men from the Channel Fleet. They had been sent to make up her numbers just after the recent battle off Cape St Vincent. At first he had thought it a good move, as quite a few of his old shipmates from *Vigilant* were aboard but both Scales and Cribbins, nasty pieces of work in Jenkins' mind, had more than redressed the balance.

"What ails thee, Clem?" the latter was asking him now with elaborate concern. "I won that money fair an' square, you cannot question."

"Aye, you won it, an' you'll get it, but I still yearns for England, an' knowing I'm skint don't change that."

"Yearn for home, or someone at home?" Cribbins asked, a little more softly.

"Ain't no shame in that." Jenkins replied defiantly.

"I should say not," Scales spoke with quiet authority. "Why, it is feelings such as that which separate us from the animals."

"Old Clem's got a fancy piece on the quay, ain't that the truth?" Jehue, a forecastleman, laughed as he pushed his way past.

"That right?" Cribbins beamed. "Doxie, is she?"

Jenkins shook his head. "Not no more, she ain't."

"What's her name?"

"Rosie," Jenkins admitted, smiling slightly. "Rosie Wells, though we're makin' it Rosie Jenkins, soon as I gets my way."

"Rosie Wells?" Cribbins pondered elaborately. "Why she still be a workin' girl. Or was, last times I hears."

Jenkins swung round. "Not my Rosie," he said.

"Is that right?" Cribbins grinned maliciously looking about for support "Well, one thing's for certain; you'll gets your way, an' no mistake. Mind, you might have to wait your turn, an' make sure you have your money ready!" His eyes flashed about, eager for laughter from the other men, but finding only an iron hard fist that landed square upon his jaw and sent him spinning to the deck.

"What's going on here?" A boatswain's mate pushed through the tight body of seamen, and stood over Cribbins' recumbent figure. "This would be a fight then?"

"No fightin'," Jenkins said firmly. "We was just having a talk, and Cribbins here falls from 'is 'ammock."

The petty officer eyed the two, he had served with Jenkins on previous commissions and knew he could be trusted whereas Cribbins was known for three things: skiving, gambling and causing trouble; all of which were likely to make him unpopular with a boatswain's mate.

"Well, take more care in future," he said to Cribbins, who was now clambering up on to all fours.

"You might watch your words, as well," Flint added as the boatswain's mate departed. "Folk round here don't take kindly to blabs and pickthanks speakin' 'bout their women."

Cribbins slowly rose to his feet, pressed his bruising face with care, and examined his hand for blood. "Well if it ain't her," he said doubtfully, looking across at Jenkins with renewed respect. "Then it must be another with the same name."

Jenkins nodded and moved on.

"And in a similar line of business," Cribbins added in a much lower tone.

* * * * *

King looked about as Manning was led away. There was a sharp clattering noise from the foremast that repeated each time the brig rolled with the swell. He looked up to the mast, then across to *Pandora*. The convoy had almost caught up; it would be wise not to delay too long inspecting the brig, although there were more than a few things about her that disturbed him.

"Ford, Wright and Thompson," He said suddenly, turning to three of his men and pointing up to the foremast. "Get aloft and see if you can take care of that." The three topmen made for the shrouds as he switched his attention to the canvas package. He untied the cord and pulled out a sheath of documents. Most referred to the cargo, a mixed lot of rice, spices and fabric, but he could follow the ship's progress by the ports she had visited. The mate had gone, but the two seamen remained.

"Why did you not wait for a convoy?"

One of the men shook his head. "Not down to us, that sort of thing. Master said it weren't worth the trouble, so we didn't."

"In a rush to get back, were you?" King addressed his question to the other seaman, who showed no change of expression as he shook his head.

King turned to Jarvis, the corporal of marines. "Search the ship, and be quick about it. You men," he nodded at the remaining seamen. "You can help, but I want a thorough inspection."

The first merchant seaman started. "We ain't got nothing hidden."

"I am very glad to hear it," King smiled at him. "So you will have nothing to worry about."

* * * * *

There was no light in the master's cabin apart from that which filtered through the shutters blocking the stern casements and skylight. A body lay in a half-curtained cot that swung from the low deckhead. Two sailors stood to either side, neither spoke, although Manning noted that one was carrying a small pistol in his waistband.

"Expecting trouble?" he asked as he entered the room.

"Can't be too careful," the mate replied for him. "We're sailing independently, and these are hostile waters."

"Well you may dispense with that, if you please." He pointed at the pistol. The seaman said nothing, but slowly drew the gun from his belt, placing it on the table next to him. The two men eyed each other for a moment, then Manning broke away and, turning to the cot, swept the curtains to one side and regarded the patient.

"I'll need a light," he said. A candle in a sconce was found and lit for him. He held the amber flame over the man's face, moving it from side to side, the shadows playing strange tricks across the cold, still face.

He was heavily comatose, his breathing shallow and irregular with no sign of dialectic movement, although one eye was heavily bloodshot. Manning found only a feeble pulse and the body was clammy and quite without life.

"At the onset of the illness, what symptoms were exhibited?" he asked. The mate stepped forward, looking uncomfortably about him.

"He was groggy, slurring his speech like. And he seemed to faint," he replied, uncertainly. "Bashed 'is head when he did. We took him down here to rest, and he is as you see him now."

"How long ago was this?"

"Couple of days," the mate answered more positively.

"And the other patients?" Manning had pulled back the blankets and was examining the man's body.

"'bout same time."

"And the symptoms?"

"Pretty much as the captain." There was an air of awkwardness about the conversation that was not lost on the surgeon.

"I'll need to see the others of course, and the body of the man who died."

"He's over the side," the mate replied. "It's the fever, we didn't want to take no chances."

"If it is the fever you would have done better to keep all in one place, rather than spreading them about the ship."

The mate nodded but said nothing.

"Conversely, with this particular case, I don't think you need worry." Manning replaced the blanket over the master and stepped back. "He has no fever."

Even in the poor light the mate's look of surprise appeared forced.

"There are no symptoms of known maladies," Manning continued. "But what he does have is a wound, probably caused by a severe blow to the head; certainly far harder than would be expected had he simply fainted. That is what knocked him senseless, and might well still account for him." The mate looked away as Manning turned to face him. "Now I suggest you explain exactly what is going on here, and believe me, I do not have the time nor energy for any further japes."

* * * * *

The convoy was now passing *Pandora*; King could see the officers on the frigate's quarterdeck pacing back and forth. They had spent longer than a routine inspection would warrant, and found nothing. He was still not happy, and yet had no solid ground on which to base his suspicions. So far all the cargo inspected had proved to be completely legitimate, and noises from the foremast told how the topmast was being secured and would soon be solid and functional once more. The marines had rousted out the rest of the crew, who now sat gossiping in an untidy group on the brig's tiny forecastle. All was completely as he would have expected it, but the feeling remained that there was something missing, or rather something that he had missed.

Ford, one of the topmen, approached him now, knuckling his forehead. "All set to rights, sir," he said. "Topmast had sprung and the housing was strained, sure enough. Maybe too much sail, maybe something else, but we've partially struck her and secured to the lower mast; she'll take a reefed tops'l and see them back to port."

King nodded. "Very well," Ford went to turn away when he stopped him. "And if it hadn't been stressed through wind and sail, what else would have accounted for the damage?"

Ford paused and sucked at his teeth. "That's the funny thing, sir. Thompson found some fresh marks further up, just below the crosstrees. It was as if it had been struck, like. A glancing blow."

"Round shot?" King asked.

Ford considered this. "Aye, I reckons; certainly weren't chain, an', as I says, not a direct hit."

King nodded; it was all falling into place. He turned back to face the two seaman who had first greeted him, and was about to

12

speak when an instantly recognisable sound cut through, silencing all around and chilling the very air.

CHAPTER TWO

THE noise of the scream reached Manning in the cabin; instinctively he grabbed at the pistol that lay on the table. He was beaten by a fraction of a second, and found the weapon turned on him by its original owner.

"What goes here?" he asked, of no one in particular.

The seaman with the gun brought the hammer back to full cock with a deliberate double click, then waved for him to move towards the far bulkhead.

Manning took two steps back and away from the mate and the other seaman. "Cat got your tongue?" He peered at the man in the half-light.

"He's French," the mate replied softly. "Can't speak a word of our lingo." A stream of shouted instructions cut off further explanation from the seaman.

"And I can't speak a word of his," Manning said shrugging, and holding his hands palm upwards in incomprehension. The Frenchman looked from one to the other, clearly undecided.

"You might have spoken earlier," Manning all but whispered. "Given a sign or a signal; we're both on the same side, don't you know?"

"They're holding the master's daughter." The mate said crisply. "That would have been her what screamed. We couldn't take no chances, we just wanted you on your way..."

15

The Frenchman shouted once more, clearly calling up to his colleagues, although no sound came from the deck. It was a classic stand off, but with a single barrelled pistol, the gunman had limited options. Manning shuffled slightly further to his left, stopping as soon as the muzzle swung round to point directly at him. He looked across to the other British seaman, expecting to see a similar move, but the man was either too dense or frightened, and remained where he was.

"This cannot last forever," Manning spoke directly at the Frenchman, who stared back. "You only have one shot," he held up a finger. "Can't kill three men with a single round."

Something of the surgeon's meaning must have got through. The Frenchman's expression changed, his eyes rolled from one to the other and the hand that held the pistol wavered. Again he shouted for assistance, and again the call went unanswered. Manning held out his hand and nodded. The barrel was raised uncertainly until it was aiming directly at his face. Then the Frenchman suddenly turned his head, as if frightened of the explosion, but rather than squeeze the trigger he let the weapon fall away, until it pointed directly at the deck.

A sigh was breathed as one by the three men watching. Manning stepped forward and reached for the pistol, which was given up without protest. Gently easing the hammer back, he nodded at the Frenchman, who had visibly shrunken in the last few seconds.

"Right," he said, the relief obvious in his voice. "Now that's in order, we'd better see how Lieutenant King is faring on deck."

But at that moment the cabin door was kicked violently open and two marines with fixed bayonets thundered in. They were followed by King, a little more sedately, who beamed readily at Manning in the gloom of the cabin.

"Ah, Robert; no trouble here, I see?"

Manning smiled in reply and shook his head. "No trouble at all. Why, 'tis fortunate you came in the nick of time."

* * * * *

On deck the scene had changed dramatically. Momentarily blinded by the strong light, Manning could just about make out the group standing in line facing Corporal Jarvis and four of his marines. The red coats and white pipe-clayed webbing stood out in contrast to the shabby clothes of the men, and as the early sun glinted off the steel of the bayonets, it was clear that there was no fight left in the French.

"Prize crew," King informed him, as the last prisoner was pushed forward to join the rest. "Fellow here's in charge, he's got a bit of English," he indicated a rather sorry specimen who was dressed no differently to his companions. "Found them in the cable tier; took four to hold a young girl hostage – fancy that?" The prize officer raised his top lip in a sneer as King continued. "Seems there's a frigate in the area, snapped up this brig yesterday morning, an' it don't sound like the first. They would be well on the way to France were it not for the damage aloft. With a rig like this, the fore topmast is pretty essential when carrying any sort of sail; they must have been crazy thinking..."

"Excuse me, gentlemen," a feminine voice cut in. "But who is seeing to my father?" They turned, and Manning was struck by the delicate face and penetrating green eyes of the girl who addressed them. Perhaps woman would have been a better description: she appeared in her early twenties, slightly below average height, with long, jet black hair tied loosely back, and a poise and confidence well beyond her years. There was also an intensity in her gaze that both men found quite disconcerting.

"Your father, m'am?" Manning asked awkwardly.

"He's below," the woman persisted. "I had assumed you were looking after him."

"Yes, of course; you will excuse me, sir?" Manning flashed a look at King.

"Carry on, Mr Manning; I'll be in touch with *Pandora* directly; let me know if there is anything you require."

* * * * *

It was a shallow, ovoid wound, not more that three inches across, although the bone felt tender and weak under Manning's gently probing fingers.

"One of them hit him with the butt of a musket," the girl explained. "They shot another man dead, and wounded two others."

Manning looked up.

"They're below; cutlass wounds, but nothing too bad. I have attended to them."

"You?"

"That's right; before I ventured to sea, I spent some time as a midwife, and have also worked as a physician's orderly. Cuts and abrasions I can handle, but I fear my father's condition is far more serious."

Manning returned to examining the master's skull.

"Well, I believe this to be badly fractured and possibly depressed," he said finally. "There are methods of dealing with such a condition, but beyond me, I'm afraid."

"You are not a doctor?"

He shook his head. "No, I too am only an assistant, but Mr Doust the surgeon might have more idea."

"If there is a doctor on your ship my father must be taken there," she said simply.

Manning smiled. "He will, be sure of that. But first we must secure him. Really a man with such a head wound should not be left to swing in a bed; if you will help me release the stays, we will settle him on the deck."

"Of course." She broke away from Manning's gaze and examined the lines that held the cot. He watched as her long, capable fingers began to unravel the knots.

"We'll let this end down first," he said, moving past her. "You undo the lines, and I'll take the weight." Together they lowered the foot of the cot to the deck, both strangely conscious of the other's proximity. The opposite end was dealt with in a similar manner, and as soon as the job was done, and the cot laid safely on the deck, the two moved quickly apart.

"You have been caring for your father?" he asked.

"As much as I can," she was looking at the patient as she spoke and Manning took the chance to study her face more closely. They were of a similar age, he guessed, and probably not from vastly differing backgrounds, although she had a natural grace that was certainly lacking in him. "The Frenchmen gave me full access and anything I needed, but he has not stirred nor spoken since he was struck."

Manning reluctantly returned to the figure in the cot. The surgeon might do something with a depressed fracture, but he doubted that much could be achieved in a ship on a rolling sea. "We'll get him back to *Pandora*," he said finally. "I'm sure Mr Doust will do all he can..."

18

She turned to look at him, and Manning felt the breath catch in his throat as those eyes sought his. "Thank you," she said, and a faint smile lit up her face. "I would be so grateful."

* * * * *

The prisoners were secured below, Midshipman Dorsey had been transferred to the brig, with five topmen to assist him, and the injured master was safely in the clutches of the surgeon. Mr Doust had examined him briefly, before rousting out his trepanning equipment, although he was clearly in no rush to put it to use.

Apparently it was quite a bad depression. The bone was badly crumbled and a build up of fluid was putting pressure on the brain, but with the ship rolling and pitching there was no hope of carrying out a successful operation. Banks had returned to his quarters and now considered the matter again. Being brutally blunt, one merchant captain more or less was of little concern; what bothered him, and inevitably the entire ship, was the introduction of a woman.

Officers' wives, female passengers, even the occasional sick-room assistant, all of these were relatively common aboard the larger ships of war. But *Pandora* was a light frigate with a crew of roughly two hundred and the addition of one solitary nubile female amidst such a crowd of healthy men could cause problems beyond measure.

The obvious course would be for her to remain in the brig, although with her father ill it was natural that she should wish to be with him, and Mr Doust was adamant that the patient must have the most stable platform available. He supposed that she would be safe enough tending to her father in the sick bay, but what about other times? Should he make provisions for one of the petty officer's cabins to be made over for her use? Some thought should be given to her privacy, and the hands took their ease in the open; she would have to have only limited access to the forecastle. But that still wouldn't alter the fact that the men were used to exposing astonishing amounts of bare flesh; something that could only offend a young woman.

Banks was barely twenty-seven and freely admitted his experience of the feminine gender was limited, and mostly consisted of examples from his own class. He had two older sisters who he supposed he liked well enough. They, in turn, had many female friends, some of whom he had come to like very much indeed, although the relationships always proved to be one way. Apart from them, other officer's wives, and the occasional encounter with the more raucous females that he normally associated with the lower deck, he had very little contact with women. It was not something he would boast about to his peers, although he also felt no shame. The facts were plain; from an early age he had been at sea, spending many months of most years in the company of men. The only exception was a prolonged period in his second ship, a third rate that had lain three months at anchor with the Wedding Garland hoisted, and all manner of women running riot throughout the crowded decks. He had been a volunteer with no official rank, and barely free of puberty; a fresh page on which the more experienced could practice their art: the memories remained with him still and had certainly left a healthy appreciation for the celibate life of a seaman. One day he would marry, there was no doubt of that, and the idea of raising a family was quite appealing. But at that moment he was the captain of a light frigate, and his country was at war. It was a position he had attained by not a little effort. The time for domestic affairs was some way in the future, and this woman, with all her associated problems, was not welcome.

He looked up from his desk as the clump of a musket and a shout announced the first lieutenant's presence outside. Caulfield entered and gratefully took the seat that Banks indicated.

"We're catching the convoy, sir," he said. "Should be back on station by noon."

Banks nodded. "How's Dorsey faring with his new command?"

"Fine, a little slow in making sail, but he'll soon get the measure of it."

"As he will the knowledge that the entire ship is watching." Both men smiled, Caulfield was a few years older than his captain but neither had been at sea so long to have forgotten their first temporary command.

"I've allocated quarters for the young lady. Carpenter's given up his cabin an' moved into the cockpit. She'll be comfortable enough in there – and safe, if we goes into action."

"Very good, Michael; thank you."

"Crowley, one of the gunroom servants, has the lingo; I've had him speak to the prisoners," Crowley was an Irish hand who spoke French fluently. Originally a volunteer from a French capture,

Banks had reserved doubts about his loyalty at first, although the man had proven himself to be solid and dependable.

"The frigate's a thirty six; not much bigger than us, and she's certainly been active in this area for the last three weeks or more. Taken at least five merchants, not counting the last."

Banks nodded. "That's a fair number needed for prize crews; she'll be light in her men."

"Yes, sir."

"Well, there are no convoys due from the south for some while, and we are several day's sailing from the nearest blockading force. I cannot divert or stall, but we must make every effort to detect this ship and, should we do so, take her."

Simple words, but Caulfield could not help himself from smiling at the captain's certainty. Banks caught the expression and grinned back. He was the captain of a warship. Two hundred fighting men and a powerful weapon were at his command and he knew himself to be more than equal to the task. It was one he had chosen and, he believed, had been born to carry out. Certainly it came naturally to him and, when all had been said, was so much easier than dealing with the difficulties and requirements of a young woman.

* * * * *

"Tells you what, I can see you're in a bit of a fix," Cribbins had cornered Jenkins, just before 'Up Spirits' was piped and was now smiling at him in a good hearted, conciliatory way. "What say we sorts this money problem out, once an' for all?"

Jenkins paused in the act of stuffing his second best hat into his ditty bag. "What you sayin'?"

"Sort it out; then there's nothing in the air between us. An' you can look forward to Pompey, and a run ashore to see yon' girl, however unlikely that might be."

"Go on."

"Toss you, double or quits," Cribbins beamed.

Jenkins looked about but all the other men were bursting with chatter. The noon issue of rum was the first of two and taken as it was after a busy morning and before a non-banyan day, when meat would be served at dinner, everyone was too filled with expectancy to take notice or give advice. Certainly the memory of the losses he had made at Crown and Anchor the previous weeks were very much on Jenkins' mind.

"Toss a coin, lands heads, you owe me double, lands tails, we cancel the debt."

"Cancel it, like it never happened?" Clem Jenkins wasn't the fastest at logical thought, and yet the prospect of solving his problems on an even chance was appealing.

"Here we are," Cribbins produced a coin and threw it up, plucking it out of the air overhand with practised ease. "What say you, heads or tails?"

"You'll let me toss," Jenkins said firmly.

"Just as you like, but don't lose it," he threw the coin across. "Though it were probably yours to begin with."

Jenkins weighted the coin in his hand, and looked again at Cribbins. He probably hated him more than anyone he had ever met, and yet there was no real reason for it. Certainly you could not blame a man for being smarter; or beating you at a game of skill, come to that

"All right you men, I wants you to watch this," he shouted suddenly. The hubbub of voices and laughter lessened slightly as he went on. "Mr Cribbins an' I are having a discussion on this coin. I say it'll land heads up, and he says tails. You want to watch who's right?"

A crowd soon gathered round, well knowing that a gamble was afoot, and loving it both for the crime, and the second hand tension it created.

Jenkins looked at Cribbins again. "What we agreed?" he asked.

"What we agreed," Cribbins confirmed. "You can throw."

"An' if it be heads, I win?"

"If you like: heads it is."

"Hurry it up, then," Greenway, a seasoned hand who liked his rum, muttered. "Pusser an' stewards are on the way; you don't want no one stagging you."

Jenkins took the coin and placed it on his thumb. There was silence. Then, with a flick, it spun up into the air, catching the strong spring sunshine in a fiery blur as it traced an elliptical course, before landing loudly on the deck.

"Make way, make way there!" Jenkins pressed forward, head extended to see the fall of the coin, and there was mutterings and whisperings amongst the men.

"So tell, Clem." Cribbins said, softly. "How did she land?"

"Tails."

A sigh travelled throughout the group; slowly men went back to their work, and conversations were taken up once more.

A steward announced the rum mixed and quartermasters began to call out mess numbers, but Jenkins had no taste for grog, and remained looking at the coin for some time. He picked it up and examined it more closely.

"I think you'll discover that to be mine." Cribbins smirked, extending a beckoning hand. Jenkins ignored him, turning the coin over and over as he looked at each face in turn before, eventually, passing it back to the rightful owner.

* * * * *

Mr Doust returned to his chair after examining the patient and shook his head sadly. The storm of the previous night might have passed, but the ship was still riding high Atlantic rollers, and there was no possibility of an operation in such unstable conditions.

"I'm sorry, lassie," the old man said, his hand patting her forearm paternally. "If it were on dry land an' I had a room set aside, I would attempt it, but even then the chances would not be good."

"How long before we reach a harbour?"

Manning, who had been silent since delivering the patient to Mr Doust, sat back and spoke in a soft voice. "At least a week, probably a fair while longer."

"Will he last so long?"

The surgeon shook his head again. Her eyes shone back at him in the lanthorn light and they all knew that she was close to tears. Then she nodded, and raised her chin.

"So be it; I thank you, gentlemen for what you have done. I'm sure my father could not be more comfortable in the circumstances."

The surgeon shifted in his seat. "If you wish me to try, I will," he said. "But, I'm telling you now, an operation such as this on a ship at sea would not be a success."

"No, doctor; I do understand, really." She looked again at her father. "But you won't mind me staying with him?"

"Of course not, my dear." The surgeon looked around. The sick bay was quite empty. Even the seamen wounded from the merchant brig had elected to stay with their ship, rather than risk impressment on board *Pandora*. The noontime grog had been taken and the hands were now at their dinner. The sound of eating and conversation was quite loud, although all in the sickbay remained quiet. Then the noise outside subsided and there was a stifled silence. Someone spoke, and there was a gentle ripple of polite laughter, but no more. Manning looked at Mr Doust doubtfully as the door to the sick bay opened, and Captain Banks walked in.

"Please remain, gentlemen," he said to the officers, who had started to rise. "I have merely passed by to see all is well." He glanced at the patient then across to the girl. "Your servant, Ma'am," he said, extending a hand. "I am captain of *Pandora;* you and your father are most welcome aboard."

She took his hand, nodding politely, and Banks was conscious of a slight thrill at the touch of a woman.

"My name is Katharine Black; my father is the owner and master of the *Katharine Ruth*."

Banks nodded in reply, "I trust he is comfortable?"

"He requires an operation, sir. And I understand we will not be in harbour sufficiently quick to allow for one."

The captain avoided her gaze. "If that is so, then there is little I can do," he said.

"Could you not make for the French coast? I understand we are quite close. Then you might anchor, and the ship would surely be still enough?"

"I need not remind you that we are at war, madam."

"But a flag of truce? In circumstances such as this..." her sentence hung, unfinished leaving an empty, awkward silence. It was an impossible request, yet no one was eager to explain that the life of one man was not equal to the risk to the ship and all on board.

"Madam, I regret we must make for England," Banks finally broke the impasse. "Should the weather ease and the surgeons consider it safe, then clearly they can operate, but unless that happens," he paused, knowing the likelihood of what he had just said. "Unless that happens, I hope your father will remain healthy until we arrive. I can do no more than that."

"Very well, captain," she had clearly resigned herself once more. "Then I am grateful for that much at least and thank you." She finally held him with her glance and he nodded in reply, feeling foolish, incompetent and most uncomfortable under her inspection. Not for the first time he blessed the fact that there were no women in his life, and only wished the same could be said for his ship.

"I believe we have made provisions, whilst you remain on board?" he continued awkwardly.

"Oh yes," the smile was more ready now. "Everyone has been most kind, but you need not worry, I have spent the last eleven months at sea, and have become accustomed to life in a ship. I will be as little trouble as possible; I can promise you that."

* * * * *

It was just before eight bells in the afternoon watch: four o'clock, and the hands were about to be called for their second issue of grog and supper, when the maintop lookout first made the sighting.

"Sail ho!" The words made everyone pause and silenced a dozen separate conversations. "Off the larboard bow." There was a delay as the man, who had been watching the smudge of grey for some minutes, tried to make out more. "Can't say other than that," he finally added weakly.

The captain, who happened to be on the quarterdeck, turned to the duty midshipman.

"Mr Cobb, a glass to the main, if you please. See if you can make anything further."

The lad grabbed at the long watch telescope and, threading the strap over his shoulder and across his back, bounded for the main shrouds. He was aware that every eye was on him as he ran up the ratlines. Banks took a turn or two across the deck, pausing as the first lieutenant approached with a routine question.

"No, Mr Caulfield," he spoke in a loud voice so all nearby could hear. "There will be no spirits issued until that sail is identified and, if she be what I feel she might, supper will be postponed as well." Caulfield touched his hat in response aware, as much as his captain, of his part in the proceedings. "And you may retain the old watch at eight bells," Banks added for good measure. The vast majority of commanders would have been glad of the chance to send their people into battle with full bellies and a dose of spirit, although Banks preferred to have sober, slightly hungry men at his command, especially as a duel with another frigate would probably call for some fancy sailing.

The air was still with an odd mixture of expectation and disappointment. Banks continued to pace; a demon at the back of his mind telling him he had made a dreadful mistake. At any moment a shout from the lookout would identify the sighting as innocent, and him a fool. But he had an odd sense about this one; they were steering a course much travelled by merchant ships, either independently or in convoy and, if the Frenchman had really been as successful as the prize crew claimed, she was likely to be cruising this area. He stopped at the break of the quarterdeck and looked forward; *Pandora* was in good order. Repairs made after the fleet action in February were highly satisfactory, the fresh wood and paint having weathered to the mellowed colour of her original timbers. Much the same could be said of her people. Illness and injury had accounted for a few, but those who had been drafted in as replacements were experienced in the main, and he felt he had a fine and tempered weapon at his command.

"She's a ship; I can see three masts, an' running under topsails," Cobb's voice had lost all traces of adolescence, and could be heard quite clearly. "She's close hauled; course looks to be roughly north east, can't tell more than that for certain."

Pandora was currently heading north-north west, with the wind coming across her starboard counter, and the convoy, augmented now by the *Katharine Ruth*, to larboard. If the sighting was the French frigate he would have to make a few changes.

"Wait, she's tacking – reckon we're sighted!"

Banks snorted; any vessel that altered course towards a convoy was likely to be a warship, although a chance remained that she was British.

"She's round now, on the opposite tack, steering as close to the wind as she can," That meant heading for *Pandora*, even though her course was several points off. "An' she's adding sail," Cobb's voice continued, although the pitch had been raised slightly in his excitement. "Courses, t'gallants, and royals – she's fair packing it on!"

"Very good, Mr King, please make to Mr Dorsey in the brig; 'Enemy in sight, alter course, heading south west'." Midshipman

Rose, now in charge of signals in Dorsey's absence, conferred with his team and in a couple of minutes the flags were racing up.

If what they had gleaned from the prisoners was right, the enemy was a thirty-six; probably what the French called a *frégate de dix-huit*. She would be carrying eighteen pounders on her gun deck, with heavier carronades on her forecastle and quarterdeck; the combined broadside weight would be more than double that of *Pandora's*. In addition her frames were likely to be heavier; certainly more difficult to damage with his puny nine pounders than the eggshell carcass of a jackass frigate.

But, in her captain's mind at least, *Pandora* still had the upper hand: she was fast, and she was his, and he knew how to sail her. Banks turned to look back to where Dorsey, in *Katharine Ruth*, was starting to lead the other merchants away. With the wind as it was they should make reasonable progress, although he found that it mattered little to him what they did or where they went. The two frigates might slug it out for hours, or the action could be over in twenty minutes, either way the merchants would have to fend for themselves; he had other matters to consider.

A ship-to-ship action was a taxing task for any fighting commander; he would need to retain all his wits for the job ahead. And when those ships were frigates; fast, agile and packing a fair punch, it was also the most intellectually demanding; the equivalent of rapier fencing to a swordsman, and probably every bit as stimulating. Banks knew that he was about to fight one of the hardest battles of his life; the next few hours were as likely to see him a prisoner, or dead, as victorious, although he was equally aware that his increasing heart rate was due more to excitement than concern.

Then he remembered the girl, and cursed silently at a distraction he did not need. He supposed some care should be taken to see that no harm came to her. Doust would be setting up his operating theatre on the orlop deck, deep in the bowels of the ship. Presumably her father would be moved down there; well, she could go also, leaving him to get on with what he did best. The anticipation inside him grew; he turned and caught the eye of the first lieutenant, who stood ready by the binnacle.

"Clear for action, Mr Caulfield, and beat to quarters, if you please." Caulfield smiled and touched his hat in response; he was clearly looking forward to the action as much as Banks. The men went about their duties; soon the deck beneath him vibrated to the knocking down of bulkheads in his cabin, and clouds of steam showed where the galley fire was being tipped over the side. The gun carriages squealed as the long nines were cleared away and run out. King was leaving the quarterdeck to take command of the main battery; he passed a remark to Lewis, a master's mate, and they both laughed. *Pandora* was working like a well oiled clock; everyone appeared eager and confident. Really he should congratulate himself: he had a weapon to be proud of: a fine ship and a worthy crew. All on board were wholly focused on the battle ahead, with no thought for anything other than their duties.

But it was strange how penetrating her gaze had been.

CHAPTER THREE

FLINT was the first captain of number three gun, main battery. His team had already cleared away the larboard piece, and were now turning their attention to the starboard. The gun carriage had been released, and Jenkins, the second captain, had supervised it being run back, and the tompion and apron removed. The servers, Wright, Jameson, Greenway, Ford, Lloyd and Thompson were ready with the flexible rammer and swab; the worm, and loader; handspikes and crows of iron. Shot had already been assembled in the garlands, a cheese of wads broken out and the lad, Jack, had checked the salt box for powder, and was ready to get more as soon as it were needed.

A whistle blew, and one of the midshipmen shouted from the quarterdeck ladder. "Captain's orders: trimmers to assemble." There was a muffled groan and a few ribald comments as Ford and Thompson joined the other designated topmen and filed up to the gangways, abandoning their mates at the guns.

"Fine thing," Jenkins grumbled. "Expects us to go into action with half our crew up an' skylarkin'".

"Captain expects more than that." King said unexpectedly. He had been standing, quite unnoticed, in the lee of the galley stove, and his voice made them all jump guiltily. "The enemy's a frigate, and this is a fast sailing wind," he continued. "Be sure, no one will have been idle by the end of it."

"Will it be ball sir?" Flint asked, referring to the shot their guns would be firing.

"Initially, yes and I would say throughout," King strolled towards number three gun; he knew the men well and had served with some in an earlier ship. "Expect long range stuff, so chain would be no good, even if we are shooting at spars. But fear not, we'll give you fair warning." *Pandora* carried a variety of specialised shot for her main armament, in addition to chain or bar to be used against the enemy's top hamper, canister could sweep a deck clear of men although close range was desirable for all. The standard solid round shot was more accurate over longer distances, as well as being faster and easier to load, and on balance it seemed to carry out most purposes adequately enough.

"Reckon we're in for a bit of a scrap, do you, sir?" Flint smiled easily at King. There had already been several scraps in their shared history, as well as one memorable run ashore, when Mr Midshipman King had been in charge of a prize crew delivering a captured coaster to England. Memorable it might have been although in truth, both he and Flint had difficulty in recalling the exact details.

"Oh, I think there might be action." The deck was silent as he spoke. "The other ship's a touch larger than us, but probably a heavy sailer, and certainly not so fly."

"And French," Jenkins added significantly, grinning widely.

"Oh yes, undoubtedly," King smiled back.

"Then there's nout to worry about," Flint smacked the cascabel of the starboard gun soundly. "Ain't that the truth?"

Everyone laughed, as everyone was meant to; these were seasoned hands and this was the expected shared bravado before battle. All were ready to fight, all were eager for the fray and the fact that they would be victorious was accepted as readily as night would follow day. None of them were frightened; none feared death, injury or disfigurement; that was something for other men; for newbies, landsmen and boys. That was something they would only admit to themselves.

On deck Marine Lieutenant Newman watched as Sergeant Bate and Corporal Jarvis stationed the marines on the forecastle and quarterdeck. Of all the fighting men on board *Pandora*, Newman would have the least to do. Unless the call came for boarders, or to repel the same, his job was to stand upright and still, no matter what atrocities were occurring about him. The fact that this must be accomplished whilst wearing a tunic of the most startling red, one that clashed visibly with the white of his cross belt and glint of his buttons, was not entirely lost on him.

But on the orlop deck, Mr Doust was certainly expecting to be busy. Two operating tables had been made up from sea chests covered with canvas, and the surgeons' tools were laid out within easy reach of both men. The loblolly boys were putting a final edge to the scalpels using spit and Arkansas stones as Manning heaved two bales of bandages from the store, placing them with the needles, horsehair and gut that would be needed for sutures.

"Yon lassie will be safe enough," Doust assured Manning and himself. "Carpenter's cabin is well placed, but jus' keep an eye out if we starts to take in water."

Manning nodded grimly. The orlop, being below the waterline, might be out of the range of enemy shot, but the danger from drowning was far higher, and there would be little chance of escape if fire broke out. The older man, who had now tied a fresh black apron about his waist, smacked his hands together and looked expectantly at his assistant. "Other than that, I'd say we were ready."

* * * * *

Pandora still held her course. Banks had ordered the royals and stunsails set, which gave her a dramatic increase in speed. Now she fairly tore through the water, with a cloud of white spray flying up from her bows, as the sun started to dip towards the horizon. The enemy frigate, clearly in sight from the deck now, was still close hauled, and moving far slower. Presumably her captain was gaining as much of an easterly position as he could, although Banks wondered if the true advantage would lie in another quarter.

Fraiser watched the Frenchman with a curious objectivity. He had no hunger for fighting, although he did appreciate the intellectual exercise that was playing out before him. The ambition of both captains was to cross the T, and rake the other ship; to hold her in a position of helplessness with all broadside guns directed at her opponent's bows or stern. According to John Clerk of Elgin, the naval strategist that everyone seemed to be talking about, this could be easily achieved in a fleet action. With rows of lumbering line-of-battleships it needed only a slight change of course, and the courage to maintain it, and a glorious pell-mell of a battle would occur. But for all his novel theories, Clerk was not a professional seaman, and this current duel, set between the fastest of fighting ships, was hardly one that leant itself to armchair philosophising. It was instinct and quick wits that would win the action and the Scottish sailing master watched his young captain with professional interest.

"Take her four points to starboard, and run up the colours." Banks spoke with quiet deliberation. Caulfield shouted the orders through the brass speaking trumpet, and *Pandora* bucked slightly as the braces heaved the yards round to keep pace with the wind. Fraiser nodded quietly to himself. So he wasn't allowing the Frenchman too much to the east; that made sense, and keeping the speed up meant that he was forcing the action, calling the shots, as it were.

"She's showing colours." The call came from the main lookout. An ensign had broken out on the enemy, closely followed by a series of hoots and catcalls from the men.

"British flag, sir," Caulfield said stiffly, casting a sidelong glance at his captain. It was a common enough ruse, although one still likely to shake a hesitant commander.

Banks looked up to where their own tattered ensign was flying. "Snap!" he said, and there was a ripple of laughter amongst the officers. Then the mood became more serious once more.

"Mr Peters, I'll be asking to have the stuns'ls off her directly." The boatswain turned and touched his hat to the captain, acknowledging the warning that would make his men's work that little bit easier. The stun, or studding, sails were set on extensions to the lower yards. Their use greatly increased the total sail area, although by their very nature they were difficult to set or take in. Peters bellowed to the topmen, who were prepared and in position in good time when the captain gave the order. Fraiser watched the Frenchman as their speed started to decrease. She was off their larboard bow, but considerably out of range. Despite the reduction in speed, they would overshoot, and could surrender the windward advantage.

"There she goes!" Caulfield's voice signalled the French ship's change of course. Tacking once more, she was now putting *Pandora* in danger of having her own T crossed.

"Steady," Banks muttered, as much to his officers, as to the helmsmen.

Minutes passed as *Pandora* edged closer; they were almost in range now, although travelling too fast for accurate shooting. The Frenchman had also taken her studding sails in, and the wind was holding strong and steady; both ships must have been showing eight to ten knots on the slightly converging course.

"Prepare starboard batteries, maximum elevation." Banks shouted, taking them all by surprise. By rights it would be the larboard side in use first. "Mr Peters, I want every man ready to take us to larboard on my word. We will hold that for a spell, then hard to starboard. To starboard, do you understand?" Again the acknowledgement, and the tension increased further as every man realised what Banks had in mind.

They were closing fast. The enemy's ports were open and her guns run out. The officers watched as she altered course to starboard by a point, bringing her as close to the wind as she could sail and *Pandora* deeper into the danger position.

"Now, Mr Peters." Banks shouted. *Pandora* swung quickly to larboard, her speed apparently increasing as the enemy moved across to her starboard bow. It was long range, but certainly worth the effort.

"As your guns bear, Mr King!"

King acknowledged from the depths of the main deck, and squatted down to peer through a gunport. The men were signalling their pieces ready, but it would need an accurate estimate of the roll to get the correct angle.

"Fire!" His voice cracked, followed by a harsh staccato chatter as the shots rang out. The smoke was swept forward, revealing the servers as they struggled to swab and load their pieces, although all eyes on the quarterdeck were on the Frenchman and the fall of the broadside.

"To starboard, close as she'll come!" Banks voice rang out even while they were waiting for the result. The braces were brought round and the helmsmen spun the wheel as the ship heeled into the fast turn. Only Newman, Banks and King registered the fact that the blow had been ineffective, and the shots had fallen somewhere unknown.

The Frenchman had seemingly been taken by surprise, and continued on her course, although her British ensign was lowered, to be replaced with the tricolour. With luck, and thirty seconds, they might have a second bite at the cherry.

"Larboard battery, broadside!" King called as it became clear what Banks intended. Men ran to the gun opposite as each of the starboard pieces was secured, and in no time the entire battery was signalled ready.

"Elevation as before," King instructed, feeling mildly guilty following the previous miss.

"As you will, Mr King." Banks held no hard feelings for the lost broadside, it was extreme range and *Pandora* may well be able to send two across without receiving a single in reply.

King raised his hand once more, suddenly aware that the Frenchman was also turning.

"Fire!"

The range was closer this time, and *Pandora*, having crept as near to the wind as she would bear, was sailing more slowly. The men watched as the enemy continued around, clearly intending to wear. She was part way through the turn when the first shots hit her.

A hole appeared in her mizzen topsail that quickly became a split, and the sail turned to ribbons. Another had parted a group of shrouds, or possibly struck a channel as the mizzen topmast sagged slightly. Apart from that, there was no obvious damage.

All the officers drew breath, although no one spoke; two broadsides, and one only partially effective: they would have to do better.

"Here it comes!" The voice of a nearby gunner caught Banks' attention, and he looked up to see bright but ragged flashes erupt along the enemy's hull. The French were taking advantage of the moment and firing as they turned: an ambitious gambit for any but the most highly trained of crews. And they were firing high; again, very unlike the French, although their gunners might not be allowing for the ship being pressed over by the wind. One shot punched a hole in *Pandora's* main topsail, and another parted a mizzen shroud. The ripple fire broadside was slow and measured; again, an indication of a well trained crew. Banks continued to reassess his opponent when an unexpectedly brighter flash drew his eye.

"They've blown a gun!" Caulfield's startled voice: Banks stared hard at the Frenchman's hull. He was right, the sixth or seventh discharge had made a duller sound, and there was no obvious fall of shot. "At the very least they've shaken a vent, but I'd say an entire piece has cracked."

It was a likely explanation, especially in a ship that might not have used her full broadside for some while. Banks had seen a gun explode when a lieutenant, serving in a line-of-battleship. The shards of flying iron had caused mayhem and terror in the confined space of the gun deck. Three men had been killed, and many more horribly wounded, although any injuries the French might have suffered would be nothing to the confusion caused while their ship was manoeuvring. Banks drew breath and set his jaw firmly: however grim, he must take advantage of every piece of luck that came his way; and this was one that would certainly set the odds back to *Pandora's* favour. With each second that passed they were moving out of the danger area, and it was a full half minute before the broadside continued, with the remaining shots being ill aimed and falling very wide.

But now the Frenchman was completing her turn and, whatever their state, *Pandora's* stern would be exposed. Banks had intended to retain his present course and delay in tacking to starboard: it was only now that the manoeuvre had played out that he realised how vulnerable their position had become.

"Take her about, Mr Fraiser; tack to starboard!"

The sailing master started. "Now sir?" They had barely gathered way, and the Frenchman was coming up on their stern. Tacking at that moment was dangerous; should anything go wrong with the evolution, or if the enemy closed faster than Banks had calculated, they would be raked at close range. Then the action would be as good as over.

"Now, Mr Fraiser!" Banks bellowed at the older man as if he was on the forecastle, rather than standing a few feet away. Fraiser spun round automatically and shouted the orders. The quartermaster was eyeing the sail, waiting for the first signs that they had lost the wind before spinning the wheel across, and the afterguard heaved at the braces, while below the gunners fought to reload the larboard battery. *Pandora* met the wind head on, and baulked, her sails momentarily backing as they caught the full force of the Atlantic air.

"Coming up behind," Caulfield's voice: and the entire quarterdeck watched as the Frenchman closed. Sailing fast and under control, despite the lack of a serviceable mizzen, she was eating up the space between them. Already they were far closer than at any time in the action; unless *Pandora* completed the tack and took speed without delay, she would suffer those tremendous guns at close range.

Caulfield continued to watch as two puffs of smoke from the enemy's forecastle showed that her bow chasers had opened fire. One shot whined overhead, but another cracked hard into the bulwark amidships, sending a cloud of splinters across the open spardeck.

The yards were across now, and *Pandora* was moving, oh so slowly, to starboard, although the Frenchman still powered towards them, with spume bursting from her bows.

"Abandon larboard, prepare starboard battery." Kings voice rang out, and the men reluctantly left the larboard guns secured but half loaded. *Pandora* was moving faster now, as the wind found her limp sails and made them hard.

"Keep her turning." Banks watched the oncoming enemy intently. For a moment they were on a parallel course, with the Frenchman less than a cable off her starboard counter then, as the turn continued, *Pandora* began to swing across the frigate's bows, and the big ship rushed down on them.

"Prepare for boarders!" Newman this time. He had seen that collision was likely, and rallied his marines; with the crew stretched between handling the ship and manning the guns it was possible that the thirty or so uniformed men he commanded would be the only defence offered against an attack.

But now *Pandora* was back under full control, and cutting in front of the larger ship. Seconds later she had almost crossed the T, and the enemy's rudder kicked in an attempt to avoid what had become inevitable.

"Fire!" King spoke and the broadside erupted a split second later. Caulfield fancied he could see debris flying from the Frenchman's bows, but that could have been mere imagination. What was real, what could not be disputed, was the scream and crack of the round shot that dug deep into the timbers, followed by the groans from the jib boom as it sagged. Then, tearing guys, bobstays and shrouds, and ripping sails from the yards, the entire bowsprit collapsed into the ocean, dragging the foretopmast with it.

"Too much, too much!" Fraiser shouted, waving at the helmsman. He was right, and the only one to notice. *Pandora*'s turn was continuing to the point where she was coming back on the Frenchman's starboard side, and would soon be facing the battery of eighteen pounders that awaited her. Slowly the ship's course corrected, but they were only saved from an immediate broadside by the damage they had already caused.

"Hard to larboard," Fraiser again, pointing wildly over *Pandora*'s bows. He had instinctively continued to conn the ship although, with a shared dread, everyone realised that the manoeuvre was seconds too late.

The French broadside caught them on the larboard quarter; not a complete rake, but enough to cause a fair amount of damage and confusion. The larboard quarter gallery was smashed in, and number twelve gun larboard side overturned, the shots continuing to take out the majority of the men reloading starboard number eleven. The aim went low, aided perhaps by the wind that was laying the stricken frigate over; no one was injured on the crowded quarterdeck, although screams could be heard from the deck below.

Caulfield ran to the break of the quarterdeck and looked down. "Mr King?"

King was further forward and raised an arm in acknowledgement.

"The larboard battery; how are you set?"

The confusion caused by the broadside had clearly affected only the stern-most guns. King glanced back, and along the entire row.

"We can have most ready in under a minute, if you require."

Caulfield looked back and the captain nodded.

"Do your best, Mr King."

Pandora continued to turn, this time presenting her larboard broadside to the enemy. The range had increased, since the fallen spars had robbed the French ship of all her momentum, and she was now completely stationary. Fraiser muttered a prayer as he watched the enemy seamen frantically hack and slash at the remains of the foretopmast that had collapsed about them in a tangle of wood, line and canvas. A flash of yellow caught his eye in the early evening light. Yes, there was a fire, possibly caused by *Pandora*'s shots or the effect of the Frenchman shooting through the wreckage.

"She's caught ablaze, sir," he turned to the captain, pointing at the stricken ship. Banks nodded but in the same instance King's broadside roared out, pelting the desperate men with a further measure of round shot.

"Back mizzen and fore top'sl, we'll maintain her at that." Caulfield was holding them almost stationary in the water, keeping the French ship, which was now properly on fire, under their guns for further broadsides.

"She's caught alight, man!" Fraiser roared back at him. Caulfield's eyes were unnaturally bright, and Banks was repeatedly smacking his fist into the palm of his hand. Fraiser drew breath. "They canna' fight back, we must lay off!"

Both commissioned officers regarded him with set expressions. For all that the forecastle was burning, the only reason the French ship had stopped firing was that none of her serviceable guns would bear. But she remained far more powerful than *Pandora*, and carried a greater number of men into the bargain. There was no question of suspending their bombardment until she had struck, or clearly could fight no more.

"Carry on, Mr King." Banks ordered. His words were cold and distinct, although meant for other ears.

* * * * *

For Doust and Manning business had begun in earnest. There were already five casualties and as they worked they could hear the sounds of moaning and mumbled requests as more were laid down to await their attention.

Manning looked up and wiped his hands on a piece of tow while his present patient was taken away, to be replaced, almost instantly, by another. He glanced down at the man, already naked, and with a splinter rip that ran nearly the entire length of his thigh. It was Piper, an elderly hand who was known for long and rambling stories as well as his not infrequent grumbles. Manning wiped back the mop of hair that was inclined to fall forward when he worked; Piper would have enough to complain about for some while to come. A blackened tourniquet had been tightened around the top of his leg, which was now quite white and lifeless. After a cursory wipe, Manning peeled back the faces of the wound, ignoring the cries and convulsions from the patient. The splinter had ripped deep into the leg but only a few shreds of dark wood remained. Plucking these out with a pair of iron tweezers, he examined the muscles. They would need stitches to pull them back into shape. Horsehair was ideal although, if the truth be known, the man was likely to die of the poisoning that so often accompanied such wounds.

"Small needles and light sutures," he muttered at Powell, a loblolly boy not noted for intelligence, although he did have an innate ability when it came to dealing with the wounded. The equipment was passed across, and Manning began, tying each stitch individually, and passing the needle back to be wiped and rethreaded while he worked on with a replacement. It took no more than two minutes, although that was still longer than he could allow for a man who was not expected to live. Now he just had to close the wound up, and stitch again. Despite the tourniquet, the bleeding had been steady, and his hand slipped as he tried to bring the two faces together. He wiped his hands on his apron, and tried again, but it was no use, he could not get a purchase on the slippery flesh.

"Spirits," he said, remembering an earlier instance. Powell handed him the pottery flagon of Hollands that was always on hand on such occasions. Manning deliberately trickled a line of alcohol over the leg, wiping the residue off with a fresh white rag. It was becoming accepted that strong alcohol was an excellent deterrent to most forms of mortification. Piper moaned again, although he had long since ceased to struggle. Now with a cleaner subject Manning tried once more. It was better, but the soft tissue continued to slip beneath his fingers. He paused, uncertain; it would be no good if the wound would not close evenly: that was a sure way to let poison in. Again he tried, this time with greater success, but still could not keep the entire length together, and have a hand free to stitch and tie. Then two more hands appeared next to his. He looked across as they held the lesion tight, and gratefully released his hold to grab at a needle and thread. Two stitches, each a third of the way down. It was easier now. Another, in between the two, and two more; then the wound was fully closed, had ceased to bleed, and he could almost relax. Two more, nip out the one that was not quite straight, and replace it with another. Finally those God sent hands began to wipe the spirit soaked rag across the entire leg, cleaning with gentle dexterity.

"I'm going to release the tourniquet," he said, looking straight into her eyes. "Be ready for a bit of bleeding; it will be better to know how bad before we bandage." She nodded, and Manning cut at the rope stricture with a scalpel. A little blood oozed from the lesion, but it was not a major haemorrhage, and would certainly be contained when properly bound.

"Very well, I think we can bandage," he said, almost to himself.

39

"I shall take care of that," she was already reaching for a length of cloth. "See to the other men and I will join you when I have finished."

He had not the time to argue, nor the inclination, come to that. She was a sensible head with a pair of capable hands that were doing a competent job, and that was all he needed or cared about at that moment. "Next, Mr Powell." The loblolly boy already had a waiting patient, and Manning attended to him with no further thought.

* * * * *

The flames on the French frigate had apparently been quelled but her forecastle was still enveloped in a shimmering haze of heat and smoke that funnelled out from below. The wind had caught her stern and taken her about, although *Pandora* had maintained position and remained roughly a cable off, and still athwart the bows as she continued to fire regular broadsides into the stricken ship. Fraiser had taken himself away from the other officers, and stood on his own at the stern.

Banks glanced briefly in the sailing master's direction. "I can do no more until they strike," he said quietly. Caulfield nodded. Twice they had suspended firing, and twice the call for surrender had been rudely declined. Another ragged broadside erupted; the pace was slower now as the men at the guns were growing tired and night was falling fast. Banks looked at his watch, realising with a shock that he had postponed supper over four hours ago. He also felt exhausted, and yet could do nothing until the enemy was seen to be beaten.

Caulfield peered forward suddenly. "There's movement further back, sir; I'm certain of it." Sure enough work was being carried out amidships in the frigate and before long a small boat was seen to be lowering into the water. "They might be abandoning?"

But Banks could think of other, more logical, reasons for a boat to be deployed. He walked to the break of the quarterdeck and looked down. "Thank you, Mr King, that will do for now." King waved wearily from the deck below and Banks turned to the main lookout. "Masthead, there!" he bellowed. "What do you see of the boat?"

"It's a cutter," the lookout replied, hesitantly. "Double banked; twelve men at oars, an' couple of officers, looks like."

"It's no evacuation," Banks said. "They will be trying to manoeuvre."

Caulfield shook his head and swore silently: what did they have to do to finish this accursed ship off?

"Bring her round, if you please," Banks looked to where Fraiser was still sulking by the taffrail. "Mr Fraiser, you are required."

The cessation of noise, both from the firing of the broadsides and the tending to the guns, gave extra poignancy to the moment. Fraiser turned from the enemy to regard his captain, his expression filled with dismay and a certain disgust.

"The ship is ablaze, sir."

Both Caulfield and the captain looked again, but no flames could be seen in evening light, just dense smoke and that same shimmering haze of heat that hung over her like an aura.

"Mr Fraiser the enemy are manoeuvring into a firing position," Banks spoke slowly and with deliberation. "Very soon we will be facing their broadside, and I wish for us to take evasive action." There was no room in his ship for anyone who was not wholeheartedly intent on killing; the sailing master would have to know this. "And I wish for you to conn the ship, Mr Fraiser; is that perfectly clear?"

"Aye, sir," the older man replied. "It is." But his eyes remained fixed on the smouldering wreck, and he gave no orders, and made no attempt to move.

Banks watched, already the cutter was dragging the stern, and the side of the French ship could be seen. If Fraiser did not act immediately, he or Caulfield would have to. The master would be guilty of disobeying an order, and liable for trial under court martial. The offence was being committed in action and in a very public manner; there could be no doubt that Fraiser would be broken, and might even face a firing squad. "Now, Mr Fraiser, if you please!"

Fraiser opened his mouth to speak but whatever he had to say was lost. A small explosion from deep within the enemy's hull made them all turn, and they were in time to see the considerably larger eruption that followed.

Heightened by the darkening sky, a rich tongue of yellow and red flame burst from the very heart of the ship, spreading upwards and outwards in a radiating arc that disappeared almost as instantly as it had come. As the noise of the first explosion reached

Pandora all on her decks instinctively took cover. Splinters of wood, cloth and other matter began to fall about them, raining down on a tired, stunned crew as the second and louder explosion came to deafen their ears. The silence that followed lasted several seconds, before the men cautiously rose up and looked about in disbelief. The captain was amongst the first to recover. Taking a step towards the spot where his enemy had been, he drew a long sigh, removed his hat and ran his fingers back through his hair.

"Both cutters, if you please, Mr Caulfield," he said slowly, his gaze still fixed on the darkening ocean. "There might be survivors."

CHAPTER FOUR

"OF course, there'll be prize money," Cribbins said, thought-fully as the watch below were slinging their hammocks and gener-ally preparing for sleep. "An' a sizeable amount; she were a fair ship, an' there ain't no doubt that we sank her."

Despite the initial exaltation, tinged not a little with relief, that had greeted the annihilation of the French frigate, the mood on the berth deck was surprisingly sombre. They were at war and the French their sworn enemies, although no seaman enjoyed the sight of another vessel being destroyed in such a devastating way, especially when each held a share in the destruction. Of them all only Cribbins showed any obvious pleasure at the outcome.

"And head money," he said, relishing the prospect. "Don't for-get that!"

"Head money?" Jenkins asked. "For them poor devils we plucked out of the brine, an' one of them as near dead as makes no difference?"

"Government pays out head money in cases like this. Five pounds for every sailorman aboard," Scales came in with the quiet voice of authority. "An' we'll be due a fair amount of salvage for that merchant brig we re-took."

"But she were British," Jameson protested.

"She *were* British, yes," Cribbins wagged his finger importantly. "But she was captured by the French, an' we took her from them. There's a law of salvage, and they got to pay."

"Maybe so, but when?" Jenkins was not impressed.

"Captain's a fair one," Flint this time. "Paid us out on the nail when *Aiguille* were taken; did it from his own purse an' all."

"*Aiguille*?" Jenkins had his hammock slung and was arranging the biscuit mattress into position. "That the frigate you took earlier in the year?"

"Aye, big old beast she were too." Flint confirmed. "Only lightly armed, but filled to brimming with soldiers. Captain paid us handsomely."

"That right?" Scales stroked his chin as he considered. "An' did anyone of you see the price she got at the prize court?"

"Why would they want to do that?" Jenkins felt inclined to argue with anything Cribbins or Scales said out of principle, although this time he really was at a loss.

"Well, seems to me a mite slack to sell your share in a capture, just on the captain's say so."

"Captain's a gentleman," Flint again. "Otherwise he wouldn't 'ave extended us the money."

"'s right." Greenway, who had been quiet until now, confirmed. "Didn't have to, but he looked after us. Gentleman, he is; like Flint says."

"An' a rich gentleman, by all accounts." Scales was smiling enigmatically.

Jenkins looked doubtfully at the others. "Have to be, to pay out like that; stands to reason."

"Stands to reason that's how he came to be rich," Scales' smile was now more of a smirk. "It's what comes from riding gullible old fools like you!"

"What you saying?" Flint's eyes flashed in the gloom of the berth deck, although Scales was in no way intimidated.

"I'm saying you all let yourselves be trodden down like so much grass. You treat officers an' gentlemen like they was gods. Don't you ever think how they came to get their high an' mighty positions? It's by climbing on the backs of the workin' man. People like you an' me."

"He's right," Cribbins nodded emphatically. "You know that, don't you?"

"Workin' man?" Jenkins said. "I ain't seen either of you do much work," but Scales was well in to his stride.

"You only have to look at the conditions you live in; the wages you get, when you gets them – *if* you gets them. We've all been plucked from our homes; from our wives, families, an' sent aboard to live in conditions that are no better than sties. You know your rate of pay ain't changed by a farthing since Cromwell? You can say the same for most of the conditions as well, and your victuals. An' if you're in the sick bay, the little you are entitled to is stopped, even if it were the navy what puts you there in the first place!"

There was a rare silence on the berth deck; all knew that what Scales said was quite correct.

"An' if you don't get better quick enough, they dumps you like so much rubbish, without a thought, a pension, or even a thank'ee very much."

"Greenwich gives you a pension," Greenway said defiantly. "We pays our sixpence a month for that."

"Oh you thinks you're going to Greenwich, do you?" he smiled at the others as he dealt with the fool amongst them. "How many sailormen can they take? An' those that don't gets in; they all comfortable, are they? They all living high on the hog an' no complaints?"

The men were silenced once more, although Scales left them no room to digest what he had said.

"An' to top it all, any of us could get killed tomorr'a, then what do our families get?"

"Widows men," Flint was positive. "They deducts money for crew that don't exist, an' gives it out to widows at the end of a trip. Pays for the families of those what don't make it."

"Pays for a month or two's rent, more like."

"An' we has an auction for possessions." Jenkins was troubled by what Scales was saying, and felt strangely eager to reassure himself and the others. "I paid top dollar for O'Connor's knife after he copped it in *Vigilant*. A pretty fair blade it is too, no mistake."

"An' that's what you want? That's what a working man can expect at the end of his days; when he has given everything for his King and country? A couple of months owed wages, and the charity of his friends."

There was silence as the men around the berth deck took in his words. Recognising the chance, Scales moved in with the killer punch.

"But it's all going to change, friends; I can promise you."

Flint eyed him cautiously. "How's that then?"

"I'm not the only one who sees your position, and knows what tis an tisn't right. There are more of us."

Flint was not sure if he wanted any more like Scales but he let him continue.

"I was switched from the Channel Fleet, and there are a measure there what think the same. Folk who ain't gonna stand for no more nonsense."

"Hey, I was with the Channel Gropers," Jenkins again. "An' no one told me nothing about no changes."

"And they wouldn't. You're not the sort to tell. You're the kind what takes the captain's word, and his money, not thinking he might be thieving from you. You're the kind what longs for shore leave, but when it's denied, lays down an' says nothing. You're the kind that let's 'em get away with murder."

"So what are these changes, then?" Flint was still eyeing Scales with caution.

"Ah, you'll have to wait for that. But I tell you brothers – it won't be long."

"Brothers?" Jenkins was clearly disgusted. "I ain't your brother."

"Time will come when we will all be brothers," Scales spoke with his eyes set somewhere in the mid distance. "Time when we will stand shoulder to shoulder and see that we're heard. That, or deal with the consequences."

"You speaking mutiny?" Flint asked.

"I'm speaking our rights, the rights of all men, however they are born, however ill used they have become."

"However much they don't want to change," Greenway added.

"Ah, mock if you want, an' you can stay where you is, an' die like the pack animals you're so keen to remain."

The men were in their hammocks by now and from the depths of his Jenkins let out a mule's bray.

"Scoff your fill," Scales muttered, when it was clear the men had every intention of doing exactly that. "But the time is not far off. There's men aboard this very ship who ain't afraid of taking action." The sound of laughter fell away uneasily as Scales' words registered.

"We're gonna have changes, big changes," he continued in the silence he had created. "British sailors have been messed about with long enough, it's time we spoke up for ourselves, it's time we spoke up for what's right."

* * * * *

The wounded had been moved back to the sick bay when *Pandora* returned to cruising stations, and were now relatively comfortable. There had been no more fatalities since the enemy ship exploded, and the badly injured Frenchman who had surrendered an arm to Doust's saw was progressing well. Manning was making his rounds, checking on each as the surgeon finally took some rest, and it was completely natural that Kate, as the girl had become, should accompany him.

"How's it feeling, Piper?" he asked the seaman who's thigh they had stitched only a few hours before.

"I've felt better, sir," his face was pale in the lanthorn light, although there was no sign of fever. "Leg hurts something rotten, 'but then I suppose it has the right to."

"Have you eaten?" Kate asked.

"Yes ma'm, I took a sip of soup an' some cheese." He smiled at her, clearly pleased at the attention; it was something that Manning had noticed in the others. Most on board welcomed the company of a pretty woman, but when they were ill it seemed that what was once merely a pleasant diversion became a need that went so much deeper. The very atmosphere in the sick bay seemed lighter and consequently more positive because of her presence, and as he glanced at her face in the lamplight while she spoke easily with a man she had seen all but ripped apart, he could not blame anyone for responding to her charm.

She moved easily from one to another, asking the occasional question of Manning or the patient; sometimes there would be a brief discussion, or they would refer to Doust's notes. But each man felt easer when they had left, and Manning was under no illusions that this was due to his attention.

Even the Frenchman who had lost an arm, even with the barrier of language, and the fact that one of his countrymen had all but accounted for her father, even with him the magic worked. She rested her hand against his cheek in a way that appeared affectionate, although Manning knew she was feeling for unnatural warmth. The man gave her a weak, toothless grin, and she smiled in return.

"Rather warm, I'm afraid." She spoke lightly to Manning, although still smiling, as if predicting a speedy recovery.

"He's lost a lot of blood," Manning said. "Unless he drinks more fluid, I fear we might lose him yet." He too was following her example; keeping his tone brisk and positive. Without understanding the words the man might easily think they were envisaging a long and healthy life for him. She reached for a leather beaker and filled it with lemonade from a nearby jug.

"Here, drink this," she offered it to the man who guessed her intent and shook his head.

"You must," she insisted, raising the drink to his lips. "Make you well."

Reluctantly he sipped.

"More," she held it against his mouth. The man swallowed, and took another mouthful, and one more after that, returning her smile when he had finished.

"You must drink lots, lots." She held the beaker up emphatically, before refilling it from the jug and replacing both where he could reach them with his good arm. He smiled again, and muttered something in his own language that sounded like thanks, and was taken as such.

"I think that's all today's casualties," Manning said as they left the final patient to rest. "There's not much else, apart from your father, of course."

"We could take a look; if you're not too tired?"

"No, that would be fine," Manning followed her through to where the master of the *Katharine Ruth* lay recumbent on his berth. The sight of her father made him feel strangely guilty: Kate had done so much for the wounded. Working tirelessly throughout the day, she must have saved several lives, and yet there was little they could do to repay her. The one favour that might have been totally fitting, a successful operation on her father, was the one they would not perform. There were reasons of course, but they all sounded like so many excuses.

"No change, Mr Manning," Powell, a loblolly boy, although he was sixty if he was a day, was attending to him as they approached the bed. "Although if you ask me I'd say the eye was a little more red."

Manning lifted back the lid gently and nodded. The fracture must be depressed; pressure was building upon the brain, and the man would eventually die. The question remained: would they reach a home port in time for an operation?

"Have you a mind to operate?" Powell asked artlessly. Manning shook his head.

"If an operation were possible, it would not be me. But I cannot see anything being attempted while we pitch and toss so."

"But if you had a clear spell, then it might be tried?"

Manning looked at Powell sharply. Everyone knew that the patient was Kate's father, and were equally aware of the efforts she had made on their behalf. If Powell was trying to ingratiate himself with her; give false hopes or even the slightest reason to think an operation could be carried out, he would personally report him to the surgeon or even the captain come to that.

"There is no chance of operating while we are at sea," he spoke firmly, and as much to the girl by his side as the well meaning but misguided old fool that faced him.

"The movement's the problem, is it Mr Manning?" Powell persisted.

"That is correct, the motion of the waves is not conducive to such a delicate operation."

Powell nodded as if in total agreement. "Then it will be the day after tomorrow, first thing after dawn, wouldn't you say, sir?"

"What's that?"

"The day after tomorrow's morning," his tone was completely matter of fact as if they were discussing the allocation of portable soup. "We should have a quiet spell for a few hours after sunrise," he went on. "Would that be long enough for you?"

The girl took a sharp intake of breath and Manning put his hand to his forehead. "Powell, we are in the North Atlantic. Periods of calm are very rare and can not be predicted, certainly not with such accuracy."

"Very good, Mr Manning, I takes what you say," Powell smiled agreeably as his superior was clearly not quite up to the mark. "But I've been watching the weather all my time at sea, and I knows when it's going to change, and I knows when we're in for a break."

Kate moved suddenly, "If he's right, we could maybe try?" Her eyes were imploring, and Manning found it very hard to meet her stare.

"If he's right," he opened his mouth to say more, and looked between the pleading stare, and the earnest expression of the buffoon who had awoken hope inside her. "But, but there is no guarantee," he finished, lamely.

"Guarantee? There's no guarantee that we'll reach England with my father alive." The smile had gone, as had any form of appeal in her countenance; she was simply disgusted with him for not having the courage to try. "Even if we do, and he has the operation, there is no guarantee it will be successful." Still those green eyes fixed him with their painful beauty as she continued with clipped precision. "In fact, if t'were guarantees you looked for, Robert, I fear you have chosen the wrong profession."

* * * * *

Everit, the Carpenter, surveyed the mess that used to be the great cabin and pursed his lips. The main damage was to the larboard side, the quarter gallery was badly weakened where several round shot had entered, punching neat holes in the bulwark just aft of the final gunport. Fortunately the sternpost was unaffected; one of the lodging knees was split, but no more. It would have to be a patch up job, and there was only so much he could do from the inside, and at night, but that didn't mean they should not start now.

"Hanks, roust up some frame timber," he said to one of his mates who had been swabbing down the deck where the gun crew had fallen. "Say four lengths of each. We'll need plankin' later, but that should do for starts."

Another of his team had set up the portable workbench, and the tools were assembled; razor sharp and as individual to each man as any that Doust wielded. Everit examined the entry holes forward of the quarter gallery. There was a full frame and an oak knee, which had survived unscathed, and was still securely locking the side of the ship to the deck. One of the port cills, the timbers running horizontally above and below the gunports, was weakened and would need a fresh piece grafted in. He could do that with a simple scarph; not a difficult job, but one that Everit found oddly satisfying. His mates should cope with the filling frames, just as they could the work on the quarter gallery; it was light stuff, not intrinsic to the structure of the hull, and hardly worth the attention of a proper carpenter. He looked about as the first of the timber began to arrive. Eight hours, he reckoned; nine at the most. With luck they could have the frames done and solid by dawn, giving them first light to start on the outside, and finish off the spirketting: the lighter internal planks that effectively panelled the cabin. The captain would have to find alternative quarters, even his sleeping cabin would be out of commission. Sound travelled well in a wooden ship; there would be few of the crew who would be unaware of his work tonight, and he didn't give much for the chances of any of the officers sleeping in their frail little hutches on the deck below.

But strangely that did not worry Everit, and he picked up a small crow of iron, and began to rip the splintered spirketting away with a half smile on his face and hardly a thought for anyone else.

* * * * *

The noise from Everit's repairs had been continuous, and Jenkins doubted that he had slept more than half of the four hours he had been allocated for the purpose. A stirring in the row of hammocks signalled that it would soon be time to rise, although he had become comfortable at last, and felt he deserved at least another thirty seconds of rest. One of the penalties of sleeping in a hammock was the lack of movement: of late Jenkins had found himself waking up set in one position, and required a few moments of gentle easing before his muscles and joints could be persuaded to work properly. None of this worried the boatswain's mate, however.

"Do you hear below?" The shout cut through Jenkins' nebulous thoughts, and his mind began to clear as the men about him started to rise, cough, yawn and make other, less social, sounds commensurate with waking. Jenkins finally stirred, pushing himself up in his hammock as he looked for the time when it would be safe to swing his legs out, and it was then that he noticed the piece of paper that lay on his belly.

It appeared yellow in the half light, and was printed; the smudgy inked message looked amateurish and rushed, but key words caught his attention, and he snatched at it as if it could have done him physical harm. He yawned and considered the matter for a moment before taking another quick look, but there were men all about, he was not a fast reader, and this needed to be studied properly.

"Ready for the off, Clem?" Ford's voice, and Jenkins hurriedly screwed the note back into his fist and looked at him.

"What's that?"

The boatswain's mate was still prowling about with his knife, ready to cut down any unfortunate who had stopped too long in his hammock and Jenkins was a prime target. "It's out an' down, I ain't taking no holiday!" the man roared, and his voice was closer than Jenkins had thought.

Swinging from the hammock, his bare feet hit the deck and, as he staggered slightly, the piece of paper fell to the floor. Ford, who was wide awake and ready, caught it as it fluttered down.

"Give me that here!" Jenkins all but yelled.

"No need to take on so," Ford said, immediately giving it up. "Just caught it for yer. Come on, we're called on deck."

Jenkins mumbled something that might have been an apology, and stuffed the paper into the waistband of his trousers. It would be safe there, or as safe as anywhere he could think of. He'd get rid of it as soon as he could, of course. Carrying a thing like that could do a man harm; everyone knew that. In fact Jenkins' small piece of paper was probably the most dangerous item on board *Pandora*.

CHAPTER FIVE

SIR Richard Banks sat at his desk and sipped his third cup of coffee. The morning had run smoothly enough; the convoy had been relocated and would soon be under their lee, and his cabin, damaged in the previous day's action, had been roughly repaired, and should remain reasonably watertight and serviceable for the week or so it would take them to make Portsmouth. The one minor nuisance, the loss of his own personal privy, was of trifling significance; he might be a knight of the realm as well as a post captain, but his trade had been learned in the midshipman's berth where far greater inconveniences had been endured.

The ship they had destroyed the day before was the second *Pandora* had accounted for in six months; a good toll for any commanding officer, and one that was also blessed with his excellent connections should soon be moving on to greater things: perhaps an appointment to one of the newer heavy frigates that were now being built; possibly something more. At that moment, however, Banks felt little inclination for change; even a fortunate morning, and the prospect of personal advancement, could not lift the feeling of impending gloom that appeared whenever he thought of the interview that he was about to conduct.

The thump of a musket butt, followed by the sentry announcing his visitor, focused his mind on the inevitable. He pushed the cup of coffee away and called for Fraiser to enter.

"You sent for me, sir?" The sailing master was only ten years older than his captain, although he had a strong personal presence and a strange air of authority. They were rare qualities in one with a non-commissioned rank.

"Yes, Mr Fraiser; take a seat won't you?" The Scotsman sat in the wooden armed chair that Banks indicated, and the captain noted that his back remained upright, in no need of support.

"I must speak with you about the events of yesterday," Banks had already decided it better to come straight to the point. "During the action I gave you a direct order that you did not act upon. I have to know if you had thought to obey me before the enemy ship exploded, or if it was your intention to flout my instruction."

Fraiser looked at him evenly. "I had no intention of obeying your order, sir."

Banks nodded; he had expected as much and was oddly grateful for the honesty. "So, you refused a direct order whilst under fire; you are aware, I am sure, of the severity of such an offence?"

Fraiser continued to regard him with a neutral expression. "I am fully aware of the situation, sir. But the ship had nae fight left in her."

Banks felt a sudden anger rise within him. "Mr Fraiser, she was attempting a manoeuvre that would have placed us under her fire. It was your responsibility to conn the ship when ordered to do so, and you declined!"

"You will excuse me, sir, but ultimately it was your responsibility, and you chose me to act for you. I also have responsibilities: in matters pertaining to th' ship, they are to you, but in other issues it is to a higher power." It was a measure of Banks' irritation that he was momentarily at a loss as to Fraiser's meaning.

"What higher power?"

"I was born a believer, and am sure tae die one," Fraiser continued, his accent growing thicker as he spoke. "At present I serve as a sailing master in the Royal Navy. For all I ken that might change; but my faith ne'er will: of that I am certain."

"You refused a direct order;" Banks said coldly. "You could be shot."

Fraiser's smile was sudden and unexpected. "Aye, that I could, but it nae weighs heavy on ma mind. If I had ordered the ship round, if my actions had kept those puir divils under our fire while a'burnin'; now that would trouble me. But death? Nae captain; death holds no fear for me."

Banks shook his head, sensing depths he would far rather avoid. "But you have been in action before, at least three times in *Pandora* to my certain knowledge; when we fought the *Aiguille* you conned the ship like a true fighter."

"Like a true seaman, sir."

"It is the same thing, you brought *Pandora* into battle, your commands meant that she was in a position to fire into an enemy ship, to kill men; why do you now say you will not fight?"

"With respect, sir, it has ne'er been a secret that I do not relish battle and regard fighting as an evil business, although I do accept that it is at times necessary. My duties as a sailin' master charge me tae navigate, and at times command the ship, and that would naturally include taking her to fight. Yesterday I felt that what you intended was beyond that necessity, and I would hae nae part in it. I would also say, sir that you were well aware of my feelings, and yet you chose me to order the ship round, when there were others who would hae bin quite ready to obey."

Banks nodded; that was completely correct. "Mr Fraiser, we have spoken of responsibilities; one of mine is to show no favouritism amongst those I command. If I had to consider each man's sensitivities before I gave an order I would be in a sorry state. The point remains; the enemy was being towed into a position where she could resume fire. She was bigger than us, more heavily armed, and likely to be carrying a larger crew. Your lack of attention could have accounted for every man in *Pandora*."

"Well there, if you will excuse me, sir, is where we differ. As a fighting man you see an enemy being towed around and take it as a threat against yourself and your ship. As a seaman, I see a ship on fire and assume it is to prevent the spread of the peril."

Banks was aware he was in danger of losing his temper. "Are you saying I was wrong; are you questioning my order?"

Fraiser recognised that he had worsened his situation with a slight nod, in the same way that a duelist might acknowledge a minor wound, but still continue to fight.

"Sir, I dinna believe they were towing the ship in order ta continue the action against us."

The captain sighed. "Do you not?"

"No sir. From where I stood I could see the men were still engaged in fighting the blaze."

"The fire was all but out."

"Forgive me sir, but the fire had a good hold below. From the taffrail I could see a red glow deep within, I believe they were attempting to tow the ship's stern inta the wind. That would have been the most sensible course of action, I'm sure you would agree."

"The most sensible course of action would have been to surrender."

"I canna account for that, sir, although I believe that when a vessel is afire men's minds might become a mite preoccupied. It is a terrible thing, a burnin' ship."

"A terrible thing indeed, but I believed the fire under control." Banks spread his hands out wide, and gradually the tension relaxed. "You could have warned me."

Fraiser's head lowered slightly. "I could, and for that I am deeply sorry. It was my intention, but my mind wisnae thinking correctly."

"We had been in action a fair while."

"Yes sir, we had."

There was silence for a moment. Fraiser had made a fair point and one Banks had not expected: he had been certain the Frenchman was intending to continue the action, and not considered the possibility that she was merely fighting the fire. They had been given the chance to surrender, but who could be sure that the offer had been heard by an officer; had there even been one alive, to accept it?

"I take what you say, Mr Fraiser, but still cannot tolerate a subordinate who will question my authority. I must consider that *Pandora* is a ship of war, liable to be in action at any time, and I have to draw my own conclusions as to your position aboard her."

"I understand, sir. And if it helps, nothing has changed as far as I am concerned, and I certainly meant no disrespect to yourself. I will continue to carry out ma duties; to navigate and command this ship when called upon, and take her into action, should that be necessary."

"But in the same situation as yesterday?"

"In the same situation as yesterday, I would do no different." The man was totally unmoved, and Banks sensed that nothing he could have done or said would alter his resolve. In the face of such certainty he felt further progress to be unlikely and relaxed into his chair before reaching for his cooling coffee.

"Very well; I will consider the matter again before we raise Portsmouth."

The master made to leave when Banks stopped him.

"There was just one more thing, Mr Fraiser."

"Yes sir?"

Banks noticed that Fraiser was once more as composed as he had been at the start of the interview. "You make a study of the weather, I fancy?"

If the change of subject surprised him, Fraiser did not show it. "Yes sir, I take regular observations and keep a log."

"I have spoken with Mr Doust and Mr Manning this morning. They have a mind to operate on the captain of the merchant we recaptured. Apparently Powell predicts an easing of the motion some time after dawn tomorrow, would you concur with that?"

Now Fraiser's smile was warmer, and with just a hint of mischief. "I could not concur, sir; such accuracy is beyond my powers which, after all, are merely scientific. But Mr Powell has a fair gift when it comes to predicting the elements. I have been known to consult with him myself on a number of occasions. If he thinks there might be an easing, then I would say that there probably will be."

Banks also smiled slightly. "And you have no evidence?"

"No sir, it is a talent that Mr Powell has, and we should all be ready to benefit from any such gifts."

"A talent?" Banks could not help himself, although once more he had the odd sensation that he was drifting into an area where he could not talk on an equal basis with his sailing master.

"Yes sir."

"But Powell is a simple loblolly boy."

"Forgive me, sir; Mr Powell is certainly a loblolly boy; that is the rank that men have given him. But simple? Now there I would disagree with you. He has an uncommon knack when dealing with the wounded and the sick. He might not be skilled as a physician, but they say he can tell when a man will heal, and when he will die; it is an aptitude that Mr Doust makes service of I hears. Not all learning comes from books, nor intelligence, come to that. I would submit that Mr Powell's sensitivities contribute greatly to the working of this ship, even though his rank might be low, and his responsibilities, apparently few." Fraiser paused, his face softened and the mischievous glint returned. "And after all, he can predict the weather and that is something that we, with all our fancy titles, can not."

* * * * *

"It will be a small burr hole," Doust announced. Powell's promised lull had occurred exactly on schedule; Kate's father was brought up on deck at first light and now lay in an improvised bed on the quarterdeck. Space and light were more plentiful and the position, just abaft the mainmast, was considered the best to minimise the ship's motion, although in truth the ocean was almost completely flat and the wind hardly more than a breeze. *Pandora* eased through the water making only slightly more than steerage way, with barely a ripple from her bows.

"You're not going to attempt to raise the depression?" Manning asked.

Doust shook his head. "Others may later, and welcome to it," he said. "I intend to relieve the pressure on the brain that he might live for long enough to let them try." He turned to Kate. "I will not ask you to leave, my dear. But please do not interfere; we might have complications, I am sure you understand."

She nodded silently, and Doust, aided by Powell, began to arrange the body to lie face down, the head turned to one side. About them the crew waited expectantly; although there was no crowd and the mizzen and main tops, probably the finest vantage points for the ordinary hands, were strangely unoccupied. No one gathered to watch, but that was not to say the decks were deserted. Men carried out their normal duties in rare silence; even the officers who had reason to be on deck were subdued and thoughtful. And the others, those from the watch below who sat quietly on the forecastle, indulging in scrimshaw work or embroidery, had not come on deck to witness an operation, and possibly a man's death. There was nothing ghoulish in their presence; most would have readily admitted that the very idea did not catch their fancy at all, but the fact that it was being carried out in their ship, their home, made them attend. It was the same way that a man might wish to be present at the birth of his child; not actually in the room, which was naturally unthinkable, but in the general vicinity. To attend; in a strange way to show support, but not to watch.

Doust felt the wound again, then moved his hand slowly down the side of the patient's head, stopping just above the ear.

"That will be the place," he said with clinical detachment. "We will make one wee hole through the bone, and see what we find. The smaller of the drills, if you please, Mr Manning. Mr Powell, you will secure the patient in case he decides to move. Now, gentlemen, let us begin."

* * * * *

There would never be a good time, never any real privacy, but that morning the ship seemed unusually quiet, with some talk of an operation on the quarterdeck, and Jenkins decided to lie in wait by the forward companionway. He knew it was Flint's turn as mess cook and he was inspecting the tackle of their larboard gun with laboured nonchalance when Flint and young Matthew Jameson finally appeared.

"What cheer, Clem?"

Jenkins looked up with elaborate surprise at their arrival.

"Keeping busy are you?" Flint guessed that something was up and leant against a Samson post, waiting. Jenkins pursed his lips and reached into the waistband of his trousers.

"Found this, thought you might want a look."

Flint took the paper without comment, and spread it out over the cascabel of the gun so that both he and Matthew could read. The silence that now seemed to saturate the entire ship gave dramatic import to the moment. Then Jameson let out a sigh, and Flint looked up.

"You know what this means?" he asked. Jenkins nodded, almost sadly.

"Where did it come from?" Jameson this time, as Flint was reading the note once more.

"Found it in me hammock when I awoke this morning."

"You've read it?" Flint again, and again Jenkins nodded.

"Most of it, yes. Some bits were a bit beyond my learning, but I know the meaning right enough."

"It says more money," Jameson said, meditatively. "That would be a ripe one."

Flint nodded. "Aye, but money's nothing if it ain't paid."

Jenkins looked at him quizzically. "Money's paid at the end of a cruise, there's no wrong in that."

"Money's paid six months behind, an not at all if you're in sick bay, 'spite what put you there."

"Then there's deductions," Jameson added gloomily. "When we got ours after *Vigilant* paid off, it hardly lasted more'n a couple of days."

"'sright," Flint agreed, his mind wandering agreeably back. "Gone before you knows you've got it."

Jenkins looked at the note again. "Vegetables to be provided when we's in port, an' fresh flour. How's anyone going to promise that?"

"How's anyone going to promise half of it?" Flint sighed. "An' they're being asked to hand out shore leave to all that wants to go. Admiralty'll never agree; everyone would be swapping ships like dogs at a fair. An' there's some, a good few, who don't want to be in no navy; they might 'ave taken the bounty eager enough, but given half the chance they'll be off, with their pockets full, an' never to be seen no more."

"It's what they're asking for. And they're asking in our name."

"Aye, that's the point. We're all gonna be blighted with this one."

A noise astern made them all jump, and Flint quickly hid the note he had been holding up to examine more closely. They looked at each other guiltily.

"We got to get rid of this," Jenkins all but whispered. "Officer catches anyone with it, and we'll be scragged for sure."

"Just for having a piece of paper?" Matthew asked.

Flint nodded. "Not just a piece of paper; it's a proclamation. It's men demanding things that they ain't going to get. Officers will see it as mutiny and anyone who has a hand in it will be liable. I'm not getting my neck stretched because Clem here didn't do the right thing an' use it for bumfodder."

"So, what do we do?"

"We cag it," Flint said definitely. "But that won't make the problem go away. Someone gave this to you, someone who's looking to cause trouble, and they're not going to stop at leaving notes in hammocks."

"Who do you think?" Jameson asked.

"Scales." Jenkins was definite. Flint shrugged.

"That's as maybe. But they'll be more'n one, and probably from the Channel Fleet; we took quite a draft, and they've always been a grousey lot of lubbers."

"I comes from the Channel Fleet," Jenkins said, the hurt evident in his voice.

"Well there you go," Flint rolled his eyes at Matthew.

"Hey, but I don't know about any demands for more pay, nor holidays, nor flour, nor any of it. I'm not behind this."

"No, an' you wouldn't be," Flint was serious again. "You're a regular seaman through an' through, but there's plenty who ain't; both in this ship, and all the fleets. And plenty more are joining them by the day."

"So what happens?" Jameson looked from one to the other. "I mean, we chucks the note away, and it might all stop, right?"

"We chucks the note away for sure, but nothing's going to stop, not now it's gotten this far." Flint said bitterly. "Someone's gone to the trouble of having this printed. There's organisation behind it, not just a simple 'Round Robin' to the admiral, and hope he gives us a 'make an' mend'. These Jimmies are dead set, and it's going to get nasty, mark my words. Real nasty."

"You mean they'll give it to the captain?" Jameson asked.

"Way beyond the captain." Flint began to deliberately screw the note up into his fist. "It goes higher, like as not as high as can be. There'll be admirals reading this afore we knows it."

"Then you'd better hand it over right away." It was a new voice, a voice with command; a voice with authority; an officer's voice and no one moved as the terrible realisation dawned on them that they had been caught.

CHAPTER SIX

THE operation was a success, at least as far as anyone could tell. Certainly the patient hadn't died, and even now, as he lay in the sick bay with diachylon plaster and cotton waste over a surprisingly small wound, he appeared to be breathing more easily. Kate placed an enquiring hand on his forehead.

"Seems cooler," she said. "But then that might just be my imagination."

Manning smiled. "We've only just brought him back to his berth," he said. "You must recall that half an hour ago..." He stopped; neither of them wanted to think too much about half an hour ago. As surgical procedures went it had not been particularly gory, but the idea of drilling into a human skull did not sit well, even with the most experienced of medics. Doust appeared with a small dark bottle, which he handed to Manning.

"If he wakes and appears to be in any pain, you can give him a half measure of laudanum." He peered at the patient with a stern, almost severe expression.

"Wakes?" Kate was surprised and the old man's look mellowed as he turned to her.

"Aye, we drained off a fair amount of the fluid. I expect he's had enough sleep for the time being so you might find he'll be coming round in the next hour or so. But don't expect anything else. We've been lucky so far, I canna tell ye how lucky. It would be an error to assume he will make a full and complete recovery, so kindly do not expect it."

But Kate was satisfied, and as she smiled at them both her face was lit by an energy never seen before. Her gaze returned to her father, as if she was expecting some immediate response.

"He'll be none the worse for a bit of attention," Doust muttered, placing his hand gently on her shoulder, but he looked at his assistant pointedly before leaving. "Don't ye go forgetting your duties, Mr Manning. There are other folk ill who needs a look now and then. Belike they haven't all got pretty wee lasses for daughters, but they're our responsibility ne'theless."

* * * * *

Mr Soames, the purser, was not one of the patients as such, and he certainly did not have a pretty young daughter. Indeed there was little, if anything, attractive about Mr Soames; his face, which resembled a bullfrog's in a surprising number of ways, could never have been called beautiful, and his main social ability; a talent for naming every one of the stores *Pandora* carried, with an estimate of their cost price and an oblique reference to what he might make from them, meant that he rarely mixed easily with the other officers and had virtually no contact with the opposite sex. Which was a shame because, for all his faults, Mr Soames was partial to a pretty face and very much wanted to be loved.

Perhaps part of his problem lay in that he had no love to give in return, in fact the very idea of giving was very much against his nature. As the ship's only professional capitalist, Soames had exclusive rights to all government stock sold to the men. Every piece of clothing, equipment and stores they might require was supplied though his offices, as well as some of the rarer luxuries such as soap, ink, sweetmeats, paper and tobacco. Mr Soames set a high price for all of these, but then he was able to as he had no competition and a captive market. It was a position he had bought: nearly four hundred pounds, a considerable sum of money, had been put up at the start of the commission to guarantee the stores, and it was up to him and his careful ways, to see that nothing was wasted. In this he was helped by an arrangement that allowed meat to be issued at fourteen ounces to the pound, and there were generous allowances for clothing, candles, flints, chalk, rosin, brick dust and other issued stores that helped to keep him on the right side of solvent.

Actually Mr Soames' ambition lay beyond simply staying in credit; he expected to retire a very wealthy man, and in not too many years' time. Then, if his plans came to fruition, he would start a heady social life. With a reasonable sum invested in the funds, and a lifestyle that was both secure and comfortable, it would be strange if attractive females could not be tempted to share themselves with one such as him. He might even get married, although Mr Soames had already decided that to spend all his money with one woman would be something of a waste; far better to spread his wealth, and himself, more generously. A few years working with the Royal Navy and all this would come about; the plan was as solid as any of his business dealings, and it was a pity that one stupid mistake in Gibraltar had almost wrecked everything.

He approached the sickbay now, somewhat tentatively. The surgeon would have made his morning rounds, and it was his habit to shut himself away in his cabin until dinner was served in the gunroom. Mr Soames knew this, and hoped to catch Manning, his assistant. It was a simple matter after all, and he was not one to call attention to himself if he could avoid it. He had thought to call before, although the signs had only made themselves known in the last few days. Since then *Pandora* had been tossed about in a storm, boarded and recaptured a merchant, fought a desperate battle with a superior enemy, and the medical staff had been rather preoccupied with other patients. Throughout that time the problem had grown, both literally, and psychologically, to such an extent that Mr Soames felt it must be addressed without further delay. Such a thing had never happened to him before, but then he was no fool, and knew that it was a problem that could be solved. Solved as easily as adjusting a balance sheet, or altering a return. He simply needed to speak to a person who knew what to do, and the sooner he did so the better.

* * * * *

"As I have said," Banks gave a light smile, "I am not one to ask advice," Caulfield now filled the seat that Fraiser had so recently occupied and even as he spoke he could not help but notice that his second in command made full and ready use of the chair's backrest. "I would not have asked you here," Banks continued. "Except on a purely unofficial basis."

Caulfield nodded. He could understand that the captain was in a difficult position. If Fraiser's apparent disobedience had lead to injury, death or defeat, he would have had no option other than to offer him up for court martial. As it was, nothing had been lost, except perhaps a slight dent in the captain's own personal pride. And the resulting explanation that Banks had just relayed in full seemed to assuage even that. Caulfield did harbour a slight feeling of disappointment that Fraiser had not seen fit to confide in him; they had served together for several months now, and he felt he had the master's confidence. But then friendships aboard ship were delicate and complex; to live in close proximity with other men, both working and socialising with the same limited group, often encouraged as much secrecy as trust.

"Ignoring the fact that he disobeyed, or to be exact, did not obey your order," Caulfield said slowly. "If you had been aware of the severity of the fire still burning below, would you still have ordered *Pandora* to maintain the bombardment."

Banks considered this for a moment. "Yes," he said, eventually. "Yes, probably. I take the point that they might well have been manoeuvring their stern into the wind, but I had my duty to protect the ship and her people, and I must admit, my blood was up. The enemy had declined surrender, for whatever reason, and I had to continue the action until they struck, or be seen to be beaten."

"And it was right to order Fraiser to conn the ship?"

The captain smiled. "No, that might have been a mistake."

"We had been in action for some while."

"We had, nerves are inclined to become frayed, and judgement deteriorates."

"And your blood was up."

"Indeed it was."

Caulfield leaned forward, and pressed his fingers together thoughtfully. "Can I ask, if the incident is forgotten, if your report shows no dissatisfaction in Mr Fraiser or his competence, would you trust him again?"

"Oh yes," there was no hesitation. "Yes, possibly more so. Strange, isn't it? But if anything he has rather risen in my estimation."

The clump of the sentry's musket called attention to a visitor outside the great cabin, and Caulfield sat back in his chair. Both men were suddenly aware how personal the conversation had become; more as one between two close friends than a captain and his senior officer.

"Mr King to see the captain." The marine's voice rang out.

Banks bid him enter, but King was not alone. Three seamen stood slightly behind him with an odd mixture of defiance, embarrassment and fear on their faces.

"I'm sorry to disturb you, sir, but this has just been passed to me." King stepped forward and handed the creased proclamation to his captain. Banks stood and accepted the paper, spread it out on the desk in front of him, and read in silence.

"Where did this come from?" he asked, when he had finished.

"The master at arms found it in the possession of these men," King said, hesitantly. "But I am not of the opinion that they are involved."

Bank's eyes moved from one to the other, examining each in detail until he finally returned to the lieutenant.

"I am grateful for your view, Mr King; nevertheless it is an offence to be in possession of such a document."

"They were to hand it in, sir," King said.

"Or cag it, sir. We weren't..."

"Silence!" Banks' sudden shout stopped Flint's words instantly. "You will not speak again until you are required to do so."

Only the captain could break the awkward pause that followed. Instead he read through the note once more, before passing it to Caulfield.

"Well, there is clearly organisation behind this," he said, returning to King. "Have you more instances?"

"No sir."

He singled out Flint as the seamen's natural spokesman.

"And you obtained it, how?"

Flint lifted his chin and looked straight ahead. "It was passed to Jenkins, sir. 'e found it on 'is belly when he woke this mornin'."

"And no one knows how it got there?"

"No sir, but we 'as our suspicions."

"Indeed." But the captain did not ask him to elaborate. Instead he summoned the sentry with a single shout. The marine clumped awkwardly into the room.

"Ask your corporal to arrange for these men to be taken into custody," he said almost quietly. The marine left and the seamen looked to each other in concern.

"I will be speaking with you later," Banks said to them, not unkindly. "Until that time I want you separated from the other members of the crew. You will understand that this might be as much for your own safety as any concern regarding your conduct." In a small wooden ship rumours could travel almost as fast as sound, and if there was a mutinous faction aboard, men who had been marched to the captain with evidence might be ripe for attention from their peers. Corporal Jarvis along with two marine privates made their entrance and, in a mixture of bewilderment, fear and silent protest, the men were shepherded out. When they had left Banks indicated a chair to King, and the three officers sat.

Caulfield looked at the message again. "This has all the hallmarks of the Channel Fleet," he said, almost meditatively, but formalities must return now that he was no longer alone with the captain, and he hastily added a forgotten "sir."

"What has the fleet to do with it?" Banks asked.

"I spoke with Lieutenant Gibson of the *Fox* when we were last at the Tagus. He'd just returned from Spithead, and there were murmurings then. Rumours were abroad that petitions from Lord Bridport's lot had been handed in to Lord Howe, but all went unacknowledged. Gibson was pleased to get away; there had also been talk of confining the port until the disturbance had died down."

"Confining Spithead?" Banks was taken aback. "But that's where we're bound!"

"Indeed it is, sir."

The three considered the matter for a moment; certainly it no longer appeared that their problems would cease when they sighted England.

"And what of this ship?" Banks asked suddenly, his voice rising. "There are men from the Channel Fleet aboard; do we separate them, make investigations?"

"Sir, Jenkins is from the Channel," King said more softly. "I know how it appears but I have served with him afore and would consider him loyal."

"And the others, from the same draft?" Banks looked at him searchingly, and King's eyes lowered.

"No, sir, possibly not all."

* * * * *

"Really you should be seeing the surgeon," Manning told Soames. "I'm not supposed to prescribe treatment, or even make a proper examination." He wiped his hands on a piece of cotton waste as he spoke.

"Come, come, Mr Manning," Soames smiled ingratiatingly. "We're both men of experience. I don't want to trouble Mr Doust if it can be sorted between ourselves."

"A condition like yours is potentially serious," Manning persisted. "The treatment is not exactly pleasant, and can be quite futile if the diagnosis is awry."

"You mean it cannot be cured?" for a moment Mr Soames was properly worried.

"I would not say that; not exactly. You must understand that complaints of this type are similar, and what is treatment for one, might be ineffective or even dangerous in another."

Soames raised an eyebrow enquiringly.

"Well, for one astringent injections; possibly a compound of Peruvian bark, bistort, balaustines or galls might be prescribed, whereas for another, another that presented in very much the same manner, bleeding, purging or fomentations might be required."

Soames, a man whose vocabulary of facial expressions was limited, found himself using almost his entire catalogue during the conversation.

"And there is not one, one sure found method that might put the condition to rights?"

"Well, mercury," Manning mused. "There is always that."

Soames beamed. "There, I knew you would be my man. Mercury it is, and as soon as you can administer it, the better."

69

But Manning was still not convinced. "Mercury is not an item to be toyed with; it can be a dangerous substance in itself, if handled incorrectly. And it would not be a simple case of a pill and calling it the end of matters. The situation would have to be monitored; belike the dose would be altered, maybe a poultice needed, possibly an infusion, or a cooling purge. I would not wish to undertake any such procedures without Mr Doust's attention; I really feel you should consult with him."

"Very well, if you insist," he sighed. "If you feel yourself incapable of administering a simple drug; one that you would give a regular hand without comment..."

"Were I to give mercury to a hand, it would be under the surgeon's directions." Manning interrupted. "I am considering you, as a patient, Mr Soames."

"Very laudable, I am sure. But when I am prepared to trust you for your diagnosis, where is the trouble?"

Manning shook his head. "I am sorry but I fail to comprehend why you should be so reluctant to see Mr Doust; this can be a serious condition."

"This condition, serious or not, is well under your power to cure, Mr Manning." Soames said almost sharply. Then he sighed and looked resigned. "I do not wish to see Mr Doust on account of his brother."

"His brother?"

"Yes, his brother is my backer." Soames adjusted the waistband of his britches and sat back in the chair. "I was a captain's clerk for seven years; Mr Doust junior was purser at my last posting. It was he who put up the bond money to enable my position in this ship."

"Mr Doust has never spoken of a brother."

Soames nodded. "I fear the two are of the same mould; conscientious, precise and accurate in all their dealings. Worthy attributes in any man, for sure, and ones I was able to persuade were present in myself. Were he to discover my complaint," Soames cleared his throat and looked slightly awkward. "Well, he might require his funding returned, and certainly would not see his way to advancing more, should it be needed for my next commission."

Manning smiled and nodded. "I see," he said, and he did, all so clearly.

"I am prepared to take your medicine, young man," Soames continued. "But I would prefer this to be kept between ourselves, were that possible."

"Let me think on it."

"You will not be long?" Soames was starting to find his condition slightly more than inconvenient.

"I will not," Manning assured him. "We shall speak again at the first dogwatch."

Mr Soames smiled a genuine smile for the first time. "You will have my thanks, my boy; my heartfelt thanks. And were there anything I could do for you in return, you need but to ask."

* * * * *

Banks also had plenty to think about, and needed just the space and time. He mounted the steps to the quarterdeck and made, instinctively, for the windward side. As soon as his presence was noticed the officer and midshipman of the watch retreated, leaving a clear path for him to pace. He was purposely not wearing his hat, an act that formally announced him as off duty and, rather more subtly, indicated that he was temporarily a private person; one who should not be interrupted. The wind had risen slightly, and there was a chill to the air that Banks found quite refreshing; excellent weather for physical exercise, one of many small luxuries that were all but denied the officers.

But it was not to be. Even before five minutes had passed and without the first signs of a sweat breaking, Banks found his concentration start to wander. The girl, the damned girl from the merchant ship; she was on the quarterdeck: he could see her. Wrapped in a long coat slightly shorter than the dress it covered, she was talking with his officers by the mainmast. Whenever he turned to walk forward she was there, petty skirts flapping in the rising wind, and long hair akimbo. To think, with such an apparition appearing every ten seconds, was all but impossible, and after several attempts at forcing his gaze down to the deck, Banks gave up, and came to a halt.

Of course it was pure chance that dictated this should happen at the forward end of his walk, when he had reached the fife rails, and was nearly level with her. She turned to smile at him as he stopped, almost as if she had engineered the meeting herself.

71

"Good day, captain; I am glad to have the chance to talk with you." Banks found he was smiling, despite the fact that the woman had disturbed his precious private time. "I wanted to thank you for your services to my father."

"I have done very little," Banks said, pleased despite himself. "It was the medical team who operated; to reduce sail for a short while was really very little inconvenience."

"That's as maybe, but I am grateful none the less." She held out her hand, and he touched it, feeling the cold skin soft against his.

"I... I am glad, and happy: happy that all went, well, or so it appears, for now." Blasted woman, he found himself stammering and stuttering in reply, and on his own quarterdeck. She bowed her head slightly, and there were those eyes, and that darned gaze, the one that seemed to go right through him.

"I am sure you did not come on deck to talk to me." The truth of her words worried him, it was as if she could read his thoughts, and at that moment his thoughts were something he wished to keep private. "Thank you once more."

He bowed casually, and she made her way off the quarterdeck. As he watched her go he enjoyed the memory of those eyes, and it was only when she had finally disappeared from sight, and he had returned to reality that he realised he must have been staring rather rudely.

* * * * *

"Now's the time," the heavily tattooed man said with certainty. "There ain't no point in delaying, not with them three in jink."

They had been detailed to move stores in the hold. Each day *Pandora* consumed several hundredweight of food, water and other provisions, and periodically the remaining supplies had to be moved to spread the weight evenly. It was a trifling matter as far as the officers were concerned and Fraiser, the sailing master, had things in hand. Every week or so he would make a rough calculation, and order casks of water and meat, and sacks of flour or biscuit to be moved from their berths, and carried, dragged or in any way manoeuvred, to positions that would make them both accessible, and keep the ship slightly down by the stern; her ideal trim. The thought behind the orders took less than five minutes but the effort that followed could last many hours. And it was heavy work;

the casks were large and there was little room for manoeuvre in the dark, airless space just above the bilges. The one advantage that Scales' party had was that their labour could be carried out virtually unsupervised. The master or the purser would inspect at the end, and a steward might pass by while they were half way through, but in general Scales and the other holders had a free rein. As long as it were done in the prescribed time they could take a rest now and then and providing a wary eye were kept, there was even opportunity for private talk.

"We sure they're in custody?" Myatt asked.

"Sure as can be," the tattooed man, who was as bald as he was colourful, remained positive. "Young Billy says he saw t'jaunty take the proclamation off them. Next thing you knows, they're heading with King for the captain, and ain't been heard of since."

"So they knows we're gonna start askin'," Parr, this time, another who had joined them from the Channel Fleet, although less than a year ago he had been earning a reasonable living as a pick-pocket on the streets of Guildford. "Tain't no secret we got demands; sent several letters to Lord Howe, much good that it did us."

"Aye," another agreed a little more carefully. "But that's just it. What good did it do us? We ain't been in Pompey for four months or more; anything could 'ave 'appened. Black Dick might have got some of the grievances attended to; for all we knows the fleet's at sea, and we're heading for an easier life." He turned to the other men. "An' you all wants us to take over this ship? Getting a bit beforehand, aren't we?"

Scales spat on his palm where a piece of hard skin was starting to flake away. "That's as maybe, but I don't see it myself. They were saying nothing when we was taken off an sent down south. All them petitions went unanswered, didn't even admit they'd got them. When we left, the plan was for a protest in April; well we're in May now – reckon if the fleet rose up like they said, it won't be over, and if it is, then we've failed."

"Failed?" Parr looked confused.

"Aye, failed; there wouldn't have been the time to organise all our demands."

Myatt nodded. "Aye, it would not be quick, that's for certain."

"But if they get's Clem Jenkins up before the cap'n, then we're going to be in trouble, an' that won't take no time at all." Parr persisted.

"You think he'd talk?" Another asked.

"Oh, he'd talk all right; who wouldn't to save themselves from a scragging?"

"So what you suggesting?" This time the question came from Harrison, a man who had found himself in the Navy after confessing to poaching; something he had been very ready to do in order to hide his other crimes.

Scales looked at his hand, and spoke slowly. "I'm saying we make a move at the end of this cruise."

The others were quiet as they digested this.

"We'll be off Ushant afore we knows it, and in the Channel soon after," Scales continued. "Can't see the captain taking us anywhere other than Spithead. Mind he'll stay off if the fleet's still in strike, an turn away; probably to London, or back to Falmouth, come to that. But the moment we sees the red flags a flying, we act."

"What, take over the ship?"

"'sright. Be the safest time. We'll have our brothers within sight; only got to hold her for an hour, mebe less, and take her to the anchorage."

"Yeah, but what if the Channel Fleet 'as sailed?" Myatt asked.

"Or what if they're still there," Harrison again. "But there ain't no mutiny?"

"Oh, they'll be there." He looked up briefly. "Most of you are from the Channel Fleet; you know the mood the men were in, an' know what was a brewing." His attention returned to his hand. "Men sick and tired of being treated worse'n animals; men fed up with askin' for what's right, an' being ignored. They'll be there, ready to greet us, ready for us to join the fight for what's fair." He finished examining his palm and clapped his hands together suddenly. "So what do you say?"

The other men nodded or grunted approvingly. Scales smiled in the dim light. "But we got to play this pretty careful. Captain's gonna be worried, what with catching hold of Jenkins and the rest. He's gonna start asking questions, and getting all uppity. We got to be a bit clever; make them think there ain't no problem. Then, when the time comes, they won't know what's hit 'em!"

* * * * *

Powell's predicted calm had lasted just long enough for the operation to take place, but now the glass was falling and the ship began to groan once more as the wind grew. A chorus of whistles signalled that the officer of the watch was calling for topmen, and soon *Pandora* was once more punching broad Atlantic rollers. Manning, having returned from the interview with Soames, found Kate watching her father intently. She stood up when she saw him, but was still slightly bent under the low deckhead, and at that instant *Pandora* chose to give a slight but sudden lurch that threw the girl against him. He caught and steadied her, and they laughed self consciously, although their eyes met and neither tried to draw apart. It was the briefest of moments, but seemed endless to them both; they were silent, until a single word shattered the trance.

"Kate," it was half a whisper, and had not been uttered by Manning. They broke apart and turned to the patient. Nothing had apparently changed; he still lay still, although Kate dropped to her knees and peered close.

"Are you awake?"

"Kate, is that you?" his voice was a little firmer, but the eyes remained closed.

"Yes, it's me." She looked up to Manning and beamed at him delightfully, before returning to her father. "You're safe, you're going to be well, and you're being looked after by the most wonderful man I have ever met."

CHAPTER SEVEN

THE message had been given to Crowley in the gunroom, who had passed it on to Dupont, the captain's steward, who duly delivered it to the captain, and it was no accident that he did so along with a plate of devilled ox kidneys, his favourite breakfast. Banks took the large piece of folded paper, and glanced at Dupont enquiringly.

"From the men, sir," Dupont said, his accent soft and voice low. "Would you be requiring eggs and bacon?"

"No thank you," Banks replied automatically. The bacon they had taken on in Portugal had lasted well, due mainly to the strong flavour that both preserved the meat and made it all but indigestible first thing in the morning. But still there was the note, and he was no more the wiser as to its source.

He glanced at his servant again, but the lowered eyes, and reserved manner gave nothing away. Banks examined the paper closely; a single sheet, folded twice over, but not sealed, and with his name written in ink in a clear, round face. Not the work of a clerk or an educated man, but certainly no simpleton either. He dropped it on to the table and tried to give his full attention to his breakfast.

It would be a 'Round Robin', he knew that, although never, in his life had he seen one, nor had he ever thought to be a recipient. The crew of *Pandora* were organised: each man was in a mess and each mess a division and each division a watch. Officers, either petty, junior, or commissioned, oversaw each segregation and were responsible for the health, efficiency and morale of the men under their charge. In theory any problem encountered was either solved, or passed on to the next senior in rank for attention. For a grievance to be given from the men to the captain, a grievance that, by its very nature, would have been signed or marked by a good proportion of the crew, meant that something had gone seriously wrong with the system. That was cause for concern in itself, without considering the fact that there was clearly a problem important enough for the men to rouse themselves and risk approaching him directly.

Banks paused to drain the last of his coffee from the pot. They had made good progress, and would shortly be entering the Channel. A few more days and they should be in sight of the island, and their Spithead base. If Caulfield was right, when they left Portugal the word had been that the Channel Fleet were unhappy. Apparently their demands had been made straight to the Admiralty, who would have to seek further approval; but even taken at their lowest worth, the men wanted far more than the government would be able to give.

He sighed; there was nothing firm to make his judgement on other than rumours and supposition. The semaphore station at Falmouth would give him more information, and it would take little more than a day out of his schedule, to divert there. If the unthinkable had occurred, and the Channel Fleet had risen up in revolt, it would save him sailing straight into trouble.

He looked at the note again, but still continued to eat. There were problems amongst his own crew, that had been made obvious, but nothing on the scale of a full uprising, surely? But then how would he know?

In the past, when a crew had mutinied, had the officers expected it? He smiled to himself - almost certainly not. Would they have had warnings, other than a rolling round shot during the middle watch? Did they receive notes from the people? And if they did, how long afterwards had the revolt occurred? Was it days? Weeks? Hours? If this note gave demands he was unable to meet, would the prospect of a home port in a few days be enough to contain the uprising? And if, when they did arrive, they found that the Channel Gropers really were in mutiny, would it just be a formality for his people to take over the ship and join them?

Banks laid down his fork. Maybe it was age, or experience, but of late he fancied himself becoming a little more serene; if a question could not be answered, where was the purpose in asking it? He had twenty-eight marines on board, along with their officers; each was a volunteer, and each would think nothing of using force against any seaman, if he were ordered. But twenty eight was nothing when the crew were determined, and even if he could count on a few loyal souls to even the balance, *Pandora* would be taken; there could be no doubt about that.

He collected his fork and finished his kidneys, scraping up the last of the sauce with a mixture of regret and resignation. The coffee was cold in his cup; there really was no point in putting off the moment any longer. He picked up the paper, opened, and read it twice, before folding it once more, and replacing it on the table. A slight smile played about his lips as he breathed out for what felt like the first time in ages. He reached for the coffee pot and found it empty. Suddenly he felt hungry; despite the kidneys, he wanted more, and the idea of strong bacon did not seem really quite so bad. And there were the eggs – it had not been possible to stock up with fresh at Tagus; he had been jealously hoarding the last few. It would be stupid not to eat them now, when they were so close to home. And another pot of coffee, hot coffee, he had drunk the last almost without noticing, and all because he had been worrying needlessly. The smile was full on his face as he roared for Dupont, and more breakfast.

* * * * *

"I'll tell you what, Mr temporary assistant acting surgeon's mate, Manning," she tapped him on his nose with her forefinger playfully. "I've been invited to dine with the captain."

"The captain?" He was surprised, but not as much as he sounded. It wasn't unheard of for passengers to dine with the captain, after all. And when they were as young and lovely as Kate, it would indeed be strange if she were not asked.

"That's right, he sent a messenger just after breakfast; seems we're entering the Channel, and will be home afore we knows it. He's having a dinner at three, and I'm requested to attend. He asked my father as well, but he won't be able."

Of course not. Captain Black had made a remarkable recovery and could speak, eat and would soon be able to walk, although he was still far from well. He tired easily and was inclined to break a conversation with the sudden shout of an irrelevant word if his fragile train of thought were broken. He had also been violent on one occasion; Powell had removed his soup before he had considered it completely finished, and had received a smart blow to the face that had drawn blood. Since then Mr Doust had kept him liberally dosed with laudanum; something that subdued and encouraged sleep, which they all knew was healing, although Manning wondered how many problems were being stored up for the future.

"Captain's table's a grand affair," Manning said, shaking his head ruefully. "A lady's gonna have to make some particular efforts to impress. *Pandora*'s a King's ship: she has high standards."

"Pah!" she tapped him on his nose again, but grinned playfully. "You don't catch me with that one. There ain't no great ladies aboard this little tub, an' the captain's a reasonable cove, he won't expect me to come in grand finery!"

"Captain won't expect you to call him a cove, that's for certain." This time he dodged the tap, although almost regretted the lack of touch. Their recently discovered intimacy was a new experience for Manning. He had had friends amongst women before, of course, but with Kate the stakes had risen dramatically.

"So, you'd be game then?" She asked, toying with the pewter cup that had held her mid morning drink.

"Me, am I invited?"

"Not by the captain, but I'm inviting you. He said I am to bring a guest, and Mr Doust an' Mr Powell ain't available, so it has to be you, don't it?"

The jibes about Kate's apparel came back to haunt him now. He had signed on as a surgeon's mate with just about enough to buy the medical books he needed to read up on his duties. In the six months or so since there had been a small amount of prize money, but that had gone before he'd known it, and he was still wearing the same waistcoats, shirts and britches that he had begun with. Of course there was that open offer from the purser; Manning guessed he could easily obtain a set of fancy clothes with just a word to Mr Soames, although he felt oddly reluctant to presume upon the man.

"Mr Manning?" How strange; Soames was standing at the entrance to the sickbay even as he thought of him. "If you have a moment?"

Manning smiled briefly at Kate, before rising from the table and walking across to the purser, who was apparently unwilling to enter the room.

"I am sorry to bother you so," the older man said, his voice low and his words almost whispered. "The condition has slightly increased, and caused me much trouble in the night. I'd be greatly obliged were we to start the treatment most promptly."

Manning nodded. "I have taken reference and feel an initial dose of a mercurial tablet would be a reasonable opening." He reached into his waistcoat pocket and brought out one small tablet that appeared slightly blue in the gloom of the sick bay.

"I will give you a supply directly," he said, handing the pill to Soames.

"Please do not concern yourself," the purser shot the tablet into his mouth and swallowed it greedily. "A store, or any form of supply, might be discovered; gunroom servants are inclined to talk, don't you know?"

"Very well, if you attend me at the same time tomorrow I will administer another dose. You might not notice a change for the meantime, but one can be expected within a few days. Until then no strong drink or heavily spiced food, and take rest whenever possible."

The man nodded twice, and left eagerly. Manning turned back to where Kate was watching him with interest.

"That would be the purser, would it not?" she asked.

"Mr Soames, yes," Manning replied awkwardly, hoping she would not ask more.

"Well, I don't know him as a man, but as a purser I'd say he were deficient."

"In truth?"

"The stores he buys are not fresh. Believe me, I have victualled my father's ships for long enough and know six week biscuit from twelve."

Manning shrugged. "Preserved food is never the most attractive."

"Pah! He buys old for a lower cost, and passes it off as fresh." She paused to brush her dark, long hair from her eyes in a way that caused Manning pleasurable pain. "Ask me, the man's amassing a tidy sum for himself. And you, and the rest of the officers, are doing nothing to stop him."

* * * * *

Men joined *Pandora* in various ways. Less than a quarter had volunteered, while slightly more than half had been pressed. These came either by the official and highly organised impressment service, the ship's own irregular press gang, or had been taken from other ships. The latter were mainly from homecoming merchant vessels, who had thought themselves safe when entering British waters, only to be stopped, boarded and all but stripped of their crews. They might be returning from several years at sea, but as far as the Royal Navy was concerned, it was day one of a fresh commission. And some came *via* the newly established Quota Act, the law that placed an obligation on every county to provide able men to serve His Majesty. These inevitably were the petty, and sometimes not so petty, criminals that the county was glad to be rid of, glad to see gone to a service who would take what good it could and discard the chaff. Finally there were the foreigners, men who had abandoned their own country, either by desire or chance, and had now taken Great Britain as their own, and her fight as their fight. Of all the methods, Crowley's entry had been closest to the last, though his had an extra cachet that made him more remarkable. Though Irish, he had been taken as a prisoner from the French frigate *Aiguille* that *Pandora* had captured earlier in the year. And he had volunteered, entering the service of a King he did not recognise, and a country he had been bred from birth to despise.

Despite this somewhat dubious start, Crowley was as sound and loyal as anyone with his acknowledged lack of home or beliefs could be. He had formed an immediate bond with King when he, as acting lieutenant, had been placed aboard the nightmare that had been the captured *Aiguille*. With a crew and several hundred soldiers more than decimated by the battle that *Pandora* had ultimately won, it had been King, with Crowley's assistance, that had saved the ship from foundering and kept her, and the remains of her crew, afloat long enough to see Gibraltar. Crowley had volunteered for *Pandora* on arrival there, and was readily accepted by men well versed in converting those unwilling to serve. But Crowley had not been unwilling; he had simply been without a cause. His life to that time had been one in search of a goal, a target for his energy and ambition. He had joined the invasion organised by Wolfe Tone ostensibly to release his birth country from the

82

oppression of British rule, although it had not been lost on him at the time that Ireland would simply be exchanging one master for another. With the capture of *Aiguille*, and the subsequent collapse of the invasion, chance had led him to joining the British, and ultimately fighting for them. Now, after just a few months aboard, he felt more comfortable with the ship and her people than he had anywhere, and with anything, in his life so far.

But one as sensitive to the feelings of his fellow men as Crowley was, could not ignore the dangerous undercurrent he had detected when the draft from the Channel Fleet had been taken on. It was as if saltpetre had been added to sulphur and charcoal; all that were needed was the spark, and there would be an explosion. Now that spark was very readily available, and rapidly growing into a flame.

King had come off watch and was finishing a somewhat bland and totally alcohol free figgy dowdy that had been prepared for the officers' dessert. The gunroom was apparently empty; a rare occasion in itself, although the cabins that lined either side might not be, and all but the quietest of conversations were in danger of being overheard through the thin partitions that separated them.

"I wonder if I might have a word, sir." King always felt strange when Crowley addressed him so, as the bonds of friendship and common service were stronger than any rank that separated them.

"Of course, Michael; what's on your mind?"

Crowley lowered himself and spoke softly. "I delivered a 'Round Robin' to the captain's steward this morning," he said.

"I see," King considered the remains of his pudding. "Sit down, won't you?" Crowley sat awkwardly, and the two men's faces instinctively drew together. "Should you be telling me this?" King asked.

"Possibly not, but I felt I must. It's on account that it's not right, if you see what I mean."

"No, I fear you fail me. What are they asking for?"

"They asked for nothing, that is very much the point." Crowley continued. "There was none of the regular grievances as might be expected. The very mirror in effect. They assured the captain there was no need for concern. That loyal men, who would stand by him, manned the ship. An' it were signed and marked by a good proportion of the people. Not every man; that would never have done, but more than half: a deal more."

"But that is good, surely?"

"It's wrong, Thomas. Very wrong. Those that signed in faith, all well and power to them, but I fear there were many who signed in fraud. Many who are ready to take this ship over. It is only the chance they are lacking, and that chance will soon be coming."

"What do you know of these men, Michael?"

"Nothing for sure" Crowley said simply. "Least, nothing that you or anyone else could take to the captain," he paused. "And I am not a man who goes against his fellows. But then I'll also not see others that I like an' respect turned over for the sake of a few evil, tainted ones. Which is why I'm speaking with you now."

King considered this for a moment. "But the captain, he believes the message?"

"So it would seem. He has released the men he had in custody when the note was found."

"Flint, Jenkins..."

"Aye, an' Jameson, they'll be back in their watch by now; an' no hard feelings."

"Are they sound?"

"Oh yes, they're straight, sure enough. But watch for others."

"New men?"

"Aye, from the Channel draft."

"Seamen?"

"In the main, no; though there be Jacks enough amongst them."

"What are they planning?"

"I couldn't say, and not just because I'm not knowing," he smiled briefly. "But I wouldn't want you to face a problem without hearing something of it first."

"I'm grateful, Michael, really I am. But there is little I can do – the captain will not listen to rumours and tattletale, the more so when it be second hand."

"I had thought you would say as much, but you won't think the worse of me for speaking?"

"No of course not, but there is little I can do, not without some actual evidence."

Crowley nodded, then stood up suddenly as the sound of someone approaching came to them both.

"Very good, sir, would you be requiring anything else?" He took King's bowl and spoon, as Fraiser entered the gunroom.

"No, thank you, Crowley," King replied gruffly. "You may see to Mr Fraiser."

* * * * *

Just how much planning had gone into the choice of guests at the captain's party was impossible to say, but they were a young collection, with Marine Lieutenant Newman the oldest at twenty nine. Banks was there to meet them at the entrance to the great cabin as they filed in and collected a glass of Madeira from Dupont. Kate turned to smile at Manning, who was feeling decidedly uncomfortable in a jacket he had borrowed from Conroy, one of the master's mates. Cobb, a senior midshipman, looked no easier, although the smell of good food from the pantry and the sight of Rose, several years his junior, in a positive state of terror did much to bolster him. The last was Caulfield, who arrived just after Lewis, the other master's mate. Banks beamed at the company with genuine pleasure. This was so much nicer than the twice weekly dinner with a couple of officers, and the presence of a comely young woman, and the young Miss Black certainly filled that role, brightened up the proceedings no end.

"We will dispense with formalities," he said. "Please sit where you will, and be comfortable."

The group moved as a whole toward the table, each member carefully avoiding the temptation to make for the foot and, despite what the captain had said, each avoiding his chair at the head without question. Manning found himself seated next to Kate who in turn, and much to Banks' delight, was at the captain's left hand. Directly opposite, on the captain's right, Newman took his seat, with Lewis next to him. Caulfield was at the foot, with the two midshipmen to either side, well within striking distance, should the need arise. There was a brief silence while the captain muttered a simple grace, then everyone seemed to start talking at once as Dupont led a line of marine servants carrying pea and ham soup.

"Are you not drinking?" Kate asked Newman, in her customary straightforward manner. The marine officer smiled back, and raised his glass of cordial to the girl.

"Yes, but not of the demon spirit," he said affably.

"Are you temperate, sir?" she enquired further, jumping slightly as Caulfield began to choke on his soup.

"That is a description rarely applied to Alex," he said, amidst light laughter from the others. Newman beamed back at her as Caulfield continued. "I have been with Mr Newman on several runs ashore, and can testify that he needs no liquor to enjoy hi'self." The laughter was more genuine now, as slowly the differences in rank and status dissolved, and the party began.

"So you are a midwife?" Banks remarked, enjoying yet again the deep fascination to be found in the green of her eyes.

"Yes, a Mother Midnight for nigh on two years," she agreed. "I've helped give birth to countless children, yet never had one for myself."

Banks cleared his throat silently, dismissing the thoughts that had flooded, unbidden, into his mind. "So how did we find you in a ship on the ocean?"

"Miles away from the nearest pregnant woman, do you mean?" There was more laughter around the table although Banks claimed her gaze with his own. "My father is a brilliant seaman, but of no use whatsoever when it comes to simple matters, such as feeding himself, and his people. After my mother died I accompanied him as a mixture of purser, cook, seamstress, nurse and companion. I have no other family, and travelling the world seemed a likely enough pursuit."

Indeed, she was by no means the first and only seafaring female Banks had met, and certainly did not have the monopoly of spunk and directness; qualities that he particularly valued in the opposite sex. But few combined such attributes with beauty and charm and by the time the soup had been removed, and they were hacking their way through roasted chickens, chickens that really were hens and had been left far too long before slaughter, the captain was totally smitten.

Lewis had asked Manning a question about his forthcoming examination, which he was struggling to answer whilst still keeping track of the conversation to his right. He was due to call on his betters at Surgeons' Hall to have his position confirmed, and truly this had been at the forefront of his mind although he now found the exact details hard to recall, as Kate and the captain were falling deeper into a *tête-à-tête* that was definitely excluding all others. Rose sneezed suddenly, blushed red, and there was general laughter, but as soon as the commotion had died down, the two were back to each other, and Manning found himself playing with his food, while he hopelessly searched for any *entree* or witty rejoinder.

"Wine with you, sir!" Newman's booming voice broke into his mood that was in danger of becoming morose. Manning glanced up to see the good-hearted marine smile at him over a glass of lemon cordial. He nodded in response and raised his glass, although when he drank he was careful just to sip. It was possible that Newman had noticed his dejection, together with the cause, and had taken pity on him. The situation was becoming more dangerous by the minute; if Newman had noticed then others might as well. Kate would certainly not be impressed by what she would take to be nothing more than an adolescent tantrum; Manning had long ago learnt that no human emotion is so misunderstood as jealously.

Spurred into action, he turned to Rose on his left and hurled himself into conversation. The midshipman froze, his fork hardly up to his mouth, as the surgeon's mate began a tirade of observations and questions, many of which he seemed capable and eager to answer himself. Fortunately Cobb, who had not been quite as careful with the wine as he might, was soon lured into response, and in no time their little corner was alive with laughter and comment to the extent that Caulfield, more used to dining in the respectful silence of the gunroom, was quite disconcerted. He glanced up, and caught the eye of Newman, who appeared to be considering his fellow guests with the dispassionate view of an outsider. The two men exchanged a friendly smile, and returned to their food.

Plates were removed and smoothly replaced by empty dishes. Banks tore himself away from the girl to look around expectantly.

"Dupont was talking of Spotted Dog, or maybe a Drowned Baby," he said, almost absent-mindedly. Newman cleared his throat and the captain realised his *faux pas* and hurriedly explained the naval terms for the various types of boiled puddings to Kate.

"All appear sound to me," she grinned. "Drowned, boiled or raw, I mind not!"

The laughter that followed died as a massive lump of carbohydrate was placed in front of the captain, who began to solemnly cut it into sections.

Manning struggled with his dessert. He was growing hot, and the heavy pudding, combined with Conroy's jacket which seemed to be getting tighter by the moment, made him feel self-conscious and foolish. He turned to Kate, but her attention was elsewhere. Newman flashed him a glance, but he knew himself unable to make conversation. There was a lump in his throat; he set his spoon down, and wiped his mouth with his napkin. The room was unbearably hot, the tightness of his collar increased, and his face grew red and swollen.

"Goodness, there's no air in here!" Newman said suddenly, turning to the captain. "With your permission, sir?"

Banks broke away from the girl and nodded at a marine servant, who opened several panes in the stern gallery. The cold afternoon wind swept in, and Manning looked his thanks at Newman. Suddenly a hand touched his; it was Kate's.

"Not eating, Robert?" she asked, her head slightly angled and her lips so deliciously close.

"A pause," he said, hesitantly, feeling the strength slowly return to him.

"Summoning the energy for a final attack, eh?" The captain was smiling at him now, and he was able to meet his eyes and nod in return.

"Splendid fare, sir; I thank you."

"Indeed," Newman was quick to back him. "Finest we have eaten for many a while."

Kate's hand had remained on his, openly; on the table for all to see. And it returned often while they drank a single glass of port, and the party finally dissolved. Then, as they were saying their thanks and goodbyes to people with whom they shared the same cramped space each hour of every day, it slipped quite naturally under his arm, and stayed so as they left the cabin together.

* * * * *

The ship had altered course at noon, and was now beginning to start the steady jolting motion that signalled her entry to the Channel proper. Reassured by the men's message, Banks had not ordered a diversion to Falmouth, and her stem was set for Portsmouth; their home port. Within a matter of days the delights of an English shore would be within the reach of them all. There would be fresh food, fresh water, an end to the constant motion and, for many, the chance to sleep more than four hours at one time. Maybe there would be wives on board: the touch of female flesh, dancing to the fiddle and a tot of 'Sailor's Joy'. All this was so close at hand as *Pandora* punched her way towards Spithead, and the might of the Channel Fleet that lay at anchor there.

But it was a fleet that had done the unthinkable; a fleet that had made unheard of demands, and risen up in rebellion against the Admiralty, and even Parliament when they were ignored. Even now the warships lay under the control of a small group of junior officers and men, men who were willing to risk the noose to see their requests met. And with every moment *Pandora* sailed closer, closer to the red flags of rebellion, and the danger they proclaimed.

CHAPTER EIGHT

THEY raised the island at four in the afternoon, St Catherine's Point just becoming visible from the deck as Fraiser ordered *Pandora* two points to starboard, to bring them to the western approach to Spithead and Portsmouth. For the rest of the afternoon and well into the evening small groups of both officers and men found reason to take themselves on deck to gaze at their home country. All but a few had been on British soil less than six months before although, in that brief period, their ship had seen independent action three times, and actually participated in the greatest fleet battle of the war so far. They had stories to tell, many on shore to tell them to, and even a glimpse of Wight's grey chalk cliffs was enough to awaken dormant feelings of homesickness and longing in the stoutest hearts.

Evening gave way to night, the convoy was behaving itself and, as Caulfield took over the middle watch, lights from the south east coast of the island told him they were making slow but steady progress.

"We'll catch the start of the tide before dawn," Fraiser informed him. "I'll be back when King relieves you at four."

Caulfield nodded, and settled down to the next four hours of peace. Surely there would be little demanded of him, apart from the occasional night signal from a passing ship, or shore base. The watch below should be sound asleep in their hammocks, while the watch on deck huddled in the lee of the gangways, muttering and yarning to each other. He could relax and enjoy the late spring night, with nothing but the promise of England and home in the morning to concern anyone.

Fraiser came on as promised and with King as the officer of the watch, Caulfield knew he would be leaving the running of the ship in capable hands. He made his way from the quarterdeck and was about to descend to the gunroom when the voice of the captain stopped him.

"Too early for breakfast, Michael?" Banks appeared from his quarters in shirtsleeves and without a hat. Caulfield paused, he was suddenly ravenously hungry, and the captain served devilled kidneys and the most excellent coffee.

"That would be most welcome, sir," he said, and wished the fresh marine sentry a good morning as he followed Banks through to the great cabin.

* * * * *

By the time they had rounded the foreland off Bembridge and were preparing to enter the Solent proper the first faint wisps of dawn had begun to appear. Caulfield had shortened sail during his watch, but the incoming tide now held them firmly in its grip, and it seemed likely they would arrive at the anchorage sooner than expected.

"We could heave to, or wear about?" King suggested, but Fraiser shook his head; true dawn was not far away; there seemed little point in disdaining such favourable conditions. Besides the watch on deck were restless; both officers had detected the tell tale signs of minor arguments and grumpy retorts. To have *Pandora* delay on the very threshold of a homecoming would not be popular, and it might also mean complicated, and probably misunderstood, communications with the convoy.

To larboard, in the shelter of St Helen's Bay, a sizeable fleet was at rest. The riding lights stood out plainly, but the darker hues of the hulls could also be seen.

"Channel Fleet?" King asked.

"Aye, like as not," Fraiser replied. "They'll be awaiting a favourable wind."

King stared at the assembled shipping; Crowley's warning was still with him, and he knew that the men might well have mutiny on their minds, but now he could reassure himself that there was little to fear. This was their home, after all; Britain's principle naval base was less than an hour away; nothing so very wrong could occur there. And with the protection of the Channel Fleet so close, there was little reason why they should not continue at this leisurely pace. Surely no trouble could come from them arriving slightly earlier than they had intended.

* * * * *

"I'm leaving *Pandora*," Banks said when they had finished their meal. "I wanted you to be the first to know."

"Leaving?" Caulfield wiped his mouth with a napkin and considered the captain. "Why?"

Banks pursed his lips. "Well, I think it time. This has been a lucky ship, and obviously I will miss her and everyone aboard, but..."

"You are staying with the Navy, though?"

"Lord, yes." Banks waved the crumbs from the table. "This is the only life I could tolerate. I simply feel that a larger ship and a touch more responsibility might be beneficial."

Privately Caulfield recoiled at the captain's confidence; something that, to his mind, was bordering on the arrogant. Banks could not have been in contact with anyone on shore since Tagus, and even then it was likely that letters or news would be some months old. And yet he was planning a career move, deciding to abandon a well set up and successful ship and all because he fancied a different one. Despite the steady increase in supply, few officers could simply name their vessel and station. Banks was either deluded, mad, or had access to interest and influence of the very highest order. But whatever the backing, his behaviour was nothing more than that of a spoilt child.

"And you are certain of a command?" Caulfield could not help but ask.

Banks nodded. "I might have to wait a spell, but something will come up. I have prior assurances; if this commission is judged successful, and I think we deserve as much, it should be a matter of course."

Caulfield sipped at his coffee, which was not quite as good as others he had enjoyed in the captain's quarters; somehow the very atmosphere felt tainted. It would be fine if the commission be allowed to continue, but what if it were decided that *Pandora* required extensive repairs? She might easily be paid off. He was her first lieutenant, and the ship had been successful in action but, even for him, the prospect of re-employment was by no means guaranteed. A period on shore, maybe six months, maybe far longer, might be just around the corner. And the other officers, men he had served with, men he respected, could find themselves permanently on half pay. The image of Fraiser and the problems of the previous week came to him suddenly. The sailing master was currently on the quarterdeck; a few feet above their heads he was taking *Pandora* in to anchor. Depending on the captain's report, it was quite possible that it would be the last time he conned a British ship of war.

"Well, I am sorry to hear of it," Caulfield said somewhat feebly.

Banks nodded. "Then we are both of one mind. Were *Pandora* to be laid off I would hope that you and some of the others might follow me to my next command. However, I think it more likely that another will take my place, and the commission continue."

There was some solace in that, as well as a sizeable compliment, and a man who could pick and choose his next vessel would certainly have some say in his previous command's future. It was also flattering to be considered worthy enough to become a follower; were he to pin his colours to Banks, he would advance at a similar rate. He might yet die a post captain, and could even achieve his flag.

"Let's say no more for now; I have people to meet on shore, and there are the repairs to consider. But I wished you to be aware of my thoughts. As I said, I feel *Pandora* to be a lucky ship, and we have created something good in her people, have we not?" he smiled. "It would be a shame were it to go awry at this late stage."

* * * * *

"Don't want no breakfast: 's too early." The man pushed the spoon away and turned his head in disgust. Manning stirred the bowl of burgoo and offered it again. Looking after Captain Black was not his favourite task; that he was Kate's father made it slightly easier, although the fact remained that he was truculent, objectionable and ungrateful; he could certainly detect little family resemblance.

94

"Come, father," she intervened. "You're going ashore today, an' we have some travelling to do. Eat your breakfast; you'll be the stronger for it."

"This ain't my ship," Black informed them. "My ship's the *Katharine Ruth*, an' this ain't her."

"Your ship is in convoy," Manning told him, soothingly. "You'll see her once more when we anchor, and that will be any time now."

"Anchor? I'll say when we anchor!" Black roared, and Manning took the opportunity of slipping a full spoon of the oatmeal gruel into his mouth. The man coughed and choked agreeably, and Manning loaded afresh.

"He didn't used to be like this," Kate whispered. "It's the injury; he's not himself."

"So I had surmised," Manning tried the spoon again.

"He'll be better when a doctor has had the chance to examine him."

The spoon was knocked back, this time depositing a line of burgoo over Manning's shirt. Carefully he scooped up the spill, and returned it to the bowl.

"Haslar is the nearest hospital," he said almost absent-mindedly. "Not more'n a mile or two away, and they've a fair reputation."

"Yes, but we are to travel to London," she said importantly. "There is an excellent hospital near to St Paul's. One Sir Richard recommended; it seems his family have some influence."

How convenient for their well-connected captain to be able to provide a hospital at the proverbial click of a finger. Manning tried another spoonful, which was unexpectedly received and swallowed.

"And he has a house nearby in Lombard Street where I may stay while father is attended to," she added.

"Rather opportune," Manning said, feeling ever so slightly ridiculous as he spoon-fed the man.

"Yes," she continued, blithely unaware of any effect her words might have been causing. "Richard is a kind and thoughtful man."

"Indeed, I am sure of it." Richard, eh?

"He'll be taking us up to the hospital today. As soon as he can leave the ship, we'll be off in his own carriage." She busied herself with packing, not looking at Manning. "He said it was important for father to see a proper physician without delay. Now wasn't that considerate?"

* * * * *

"No sign of a grey goose," Fraiser muttered as *Pandora* crept slowly towards the anchorage. The moment when a grey goose could be spotted a mile away was the official definition of daybreak. It was then that colours were raised, and signals could be made. That time was still a little way off; *Pandora* had already made the private signal and her number by lights, which had been acknowledged, although there had been no further contact.

"We have company, it seems," King said, looking towards three line-of-battleships and a frigate that sat idly at anchor.

"Aye," Fraiser agreed. "That'll be *London*; we spoke with her in the winter."

King nodded; HMS *London* had been the flagship of Admiral Colpoys, they had met with her and the rest of the Channel Fleet, after running in with a French invasion force. There was a slight dew and he rubbed his hands together to warm them. "Strange, if Admiral Colpoys still has her, why should she be separated from the rest of the Channel Gropers?"

Fraiser pursed his lips. "Who can say; belike they have mutinied after all!"

The two men smiled readily, although King knew his to be false, as Crowley's warning came back to him once more. He looked about; all seemed perfectly normal: no signs of a mutinous horde forming to storm the ship and sail her off to France. Besides, they were well into Spithead now; there could not be a safer place, and nothing more peaceful than the scene that presented itself could be imagined.

"Deck there, boat heading for us," The foremast lookout reported, his voice unnaturally loud in the still of early morning. "It's comin' from windward; from the fleet."

King and Fraiser turned to see a cutter under sail running down towards them.

"No, wait, there's two; one from the land, an' one from the fleet."

Sure enough another, smaller, boat was heading their way under oars. That one was to be expected, it would be carrying customs officials, doubtless with health declarations and a wealth of other formalities to go through. But there was still no rush, and Fraiser decided he would call the captain shortly. The tide was carrying them in beautifully, although the leadsman had been reporting adequate depth to anchor for some while.

"I think we might make to the convoy to shorten sail," he said, almost conversationally. "And do likewise ourselves."

King nodded to Rose, standing in for Dorsey, who started to search through his signal book, muttering for his assistants to help. King then opened his mouth to order the change of sail, when a strange sight met his eyes.

Men were already at the shrouds, a few were even working aloft: he could see them in the gloom of dawn taking in sail unbidden and in eerie silence. In the waist he could just make out Cobb, running to the foremast in what looked like a mild panic. There were shouts and someone was laughing almost hysterically. He turned to Fraiser, but the older man was bounding towards the break of the quarterdeck.

"What goes there?" he bellowed, although no one had a mind to answer. Men were still taking in sail, while some attended to the starboard bower anchor. But there were others interfering, seemingly intent on restoring order, and separate arguments erupted throughout the ship. The quartermaster yelled at the helmsmen, who were turning the wheel, forcing *Pandora* to lurch out of the channel and towards the nearest group of anchored shipping. Light was coming faster now, men could be seen on the deck of the warships ahead of them. A sound, like a pistol shot, echoed through the confusion, and there was a momentary pause and silence. Then the anchor cable roared out, and the tumult continued afresh.

"Master at Arms!" Fraiser shouted, as the hatless warrant officer appeared on deck. "Order there, if you please!"

The man looked back, an expression of total incomprehension on his ruddy face. A gun fired, but from a long way off. King turned to see the colours slowly being raised across on the port admiral's office. His glance switched to the nearby cluster of ships at anchor. They too were hoisting colours. From above the noise of shouting broke out. He looked up to see the yards and shrouds black with men waving and cheering; this was not just the watch on deck, others must have joined and yet it was long before the watch below were to be called. A fight had broken out further forward, then fists were flying seemingly everywhere; by the forecastle a group of men were at each other like bears in a pit. He looked back at the anchored fleet as the cheers continued about him and the awful truth dawned. *Pandora* jerked slightly as the anchor cable bit and found the Spithead mud. Fraiser was shouting from the break of the quarterdeck, and below there came the unmistakeable sound of gunfire from the captain's cabin. Ahead the anchored warships were flying plain red flags; looking back the same red flags could be seen on ships of the Channel Fleet; the entire force had apparently been taken over by the men, or whatever power it was that backed their treachery. It was impossible, unthinkable, totally beyond belief, but a British fleet had mutinied while their country was at war.

* * * * *

"What's that noise?" Banks asked as the cheering began.

Caulfield shook his head. The squeal and clatter of the anchor had startled them both, that and what sounded like confusion and chaos on deck. Banks instinctively checked the time, it was long before the watch would be called, and he could not remember hearing the last bell struck. Both men rose to their feet as a new and separate commotion erupted outside the door. The voice of the marine sentry rang out, but this was no ordinary announcement of a potential visitor. The man's shout, a scream almost, was indistinct. Then there was the sound of two shots close enough together to mark separate weapons. The officers made towards the door as a heavy weight hit the deck. The captain paused; there was someone in the coach outside, he heard heavy footsteps that could never belong to Dupont. He tore the door open, and was struck by the sight of three ordinary seamen advancing towards him.

"Back in the cabin, captain." It was one of the new hands, Banks did not know his name. He was holding a discharged pistol in one hand, and as he spoke he reached for another, loaded and impending, stuck in his waistband. "An' you, Mr Caulfield."

"Scales, what the hell do you think you're about?"

Scales grinned smugly. "It ain't just me, Mr Caulfield," he said. "I got a few friends, an' we have help, help that you can't imagine.

The whole darned fleet is up in arms, an' there ain't nothing you, nor anyone else, can do about it."

* * * * *

On deck Fraiser and King had retreated, and now stood together by the taffrail, with Rose and two hands from the larboard watch.

"Tain't none of our doing," Ford, a topman who had been with *Pandora* for all the commission, assured them.

"Them new draft seemed set on taking us from the start," the other confirmed. "Said it was all being ordered by the Channel Fleet; they knew this would happen; planned it, so they did."

"Well something could have been said." King murmured, turning to keep his eyes on the nearest ships as *Pandora* swung about to present her bows to the oncoming tide. But something had; Crowley had risked much confiding in him, and what had he done? The two small boats were still making for them, although the one from the flagship would arrive first by quite a measure.

"Pardon me, but we thoughts you was awares," Ford continued. "Thought, when you picked up Flint an' the rest, you'd come to realise what was about."

The man was right, Banks might have placed too much confidence in that damned 'Round Robin', but he himself had been equally remiss in discounting the warning of a trusted friend. Crowley had looked to him as an officer to put matters right, and he had let everyone down. Well the cost was before them all now, and for the first time King felt the shame and self doubt that follows failure.

Suddenly the sound of a drum was heard from below. The *rafale* grew louder, and the pandemonium that had seemed to fill the ship slowly stilled.

"The marines!" Fraiser said half to himself, before making his way forward at a pace, with King no more than a step behind.

Lieutenant Newman's hat could be seen rising up as its owner mounted the quarterdeck steps. Then the shakos of his men and the bright polished steel of their bayonets came into view. Newman's face was uncharacteristically serious, although he held himself as erect as ever, and seemed to exude order and reassurance as his men fanned out across the quarterdeck.

"Secure the deck, corporal."

The marine N.C.O. saluted smartly, before turning to bellow at the seamen. "You lot, back in the waist!"

"Those two can remain, Mr Jarvis," Fraiser interrupted. "They are loyal."

The others were pressed unceremoniously down the steps or onto the gangways, until the entire quarterdeck was back in control, with a line of marines standing firm across the break.

"We had better speak with the men." Fraiser muttered to King.

"But the captain?"

"The captain is nae here, and this needs to be done quickly."

King nodded. Officially he was the senior officer, being of commissioned rank, but there was no doubt who had the greater experience and, if it came to it, natural authority. Newman glanced across, clearly ready to take control. As the officer in command of the ship's marine detachment he could order his men to advance, and attempt to quell the uprising with force and cold steel, but something told them all that a more delicate hand was needed.

Without a word Fraiser pushed himself forward until he was level with the mainmast, and stared down at the mass of milling bodies in the waist below. He glanced up, the yards were all bare now, although men still manned the tops, and a few hung to the shrouds, presumably to get a better view of the proceedings.

"So tell me, who'd be in charge here?" he asked, the irony strong in his voice. "Is it your officers, those you hae sworn to obey, the ones you look tae when you need help or support? Or are you set on organising things for y'selves, from now onwards?"

The question elicited roars of defiance and denial that mingled oddly; no man caught his eye but it was clear that the people were not united.

"Ver' well," Fraiser continued, examining the crowd, and gauging his time. "So when I gie ye the order tae disperse, you will do so, and return tae your usual stations." His voice was firm, without hint of waver, and only the slight strengthening of his accent gave any clue to his emotions. King glanced across at Newman, watching respectfully to one side.

"Disperse." The order was delivered at the same volume, and yet the effect was staggering. Men moved almost instinctively, and began to shuffle away. From further forward one man started to speak in an angry whine, but was quickly shouted down by his fellows. Those aloft began a slow decent by the shrouds, and others started to file down the companionways, muttering and arguing as they went. It was clear that Fraiser had regained control; the deck would have been cleared in no time, were it not for another shout that came from the captain's quarters, followed by an ominous sigh from the rest of the crew. Fraiser and the other officers looked down; clearly something was happening on the half deck below. Then the captain could be seen walking from under the quarter-deck, with Scales and another man following close behind.

"You stay where you are, or I'll know the reason why!" Scales pushed Banks roughly forward and King was astonished to see that he held a pistol at the captain's back.

"Och, it's you, Scales," Fraiser said, as both men turned to look at him. "Ah might have known yon waur behind this."

"Not just me," Scales waved the pistol complacently, "We're all together, as I have just been explaining to the captain here."

"Not all!" the captain's voice rose up suddenly. "*Pandora* has more loyal hearts than traitors, what say you lads?"

Scales thrust the pistol into Banks' side, making him wince in pain.

"Captain's right, Scales!" Flint's voice rang out from deep inside the crowd and amid a chorus of agreement.

"Aye, you can put your head into a noose if yer wants, but you ain't takin' us with 'e." Jenkins bellowed, from somewhere further back.

"Let the cap'n, go," another voice. "He never done you no 'arm!"

Scales tried unsuccessfully to spot the defectors, ignoring the murmurs and mutterings that might have been support or defiance.

"It's a dangerous thing for anyone that follows you." Fraiser continued, addressing the entire crew, while his eyes remained set on Scales and the captain. "The penalty fur mutiny is death, as you all are well awares. An' perhaps you also know that, unless this is settled now, I might face the same fate. And I don't intend tae waste mah life on a weasel such as you."

A ripple of gentle laughter came and was gone in an instant. Scales looked about him.

"It ain't only us, *Mister* Fraiser." he said with certainty and more than a hint of disdain. "The 'ole fleet's up, an' 'as been so for a while. We've put demands forward, an' they gone unanswered.

We've made claims, reasonable claims, and they've been ignored. No man's pay has increased for nigh on an hundred an' fifty years, ain't that right, lads?" A mutter of support was starting to grow amongst the men as he went on. "An' we're being short changed even when we gets it." There were more nods of agreement now as Scales got into his stride. "Short changed in pay, and short changed in provisions – who ever heard of fourteen ounces to a pound? Our pusser – that's who! He an' every man like him in the fleet!"

"We are at war," Banks said evenly. "Do you expect our lives to be easy?"

Again Scales thrust the pistol at the captain, although this time Banks caught the barrel and calmly moved it away.

"It will do you no good if I am shot, so kindly remove your weapon."

Scales drew back, but continued to hold the pistol level with the captain's chest. "I mean no disrespect, but it ain't fair, the way we're treated." He looked about, with a trace of uncertainty as the enormity of his crime began to dawn on him. "It ain't that we're disloyal, all are more'n willing to fight for our country, but God help us if we're wounded, 'cause there's no pay when we're in sick bay, an' you're tellin' me that's fair?"

"I'm not saying you have no cause to complain," Banks' voice was low and steady, and gradually the men started to listen, "and I'm the last to deny any man what is rightly his. But this is not the way to proceed, and anyone who tells you otherwise is a fool or a liar." The crowd murmured again, and the theatrical aspect of his position struck Banks. He might be an actor on the stage or, more accurately, a lawyer appealing to a jury. Despite the fact that Scales was holding a gun on him, it was the crew that held the true power. "You say the Admiralty have ignored your requests, well what did you expect?" He turned slightly, sweeping the deck with his glance. "How would it be if a navy were governed by the men, where would be the command?"

Scales opened his mouth to speak, but Banks was too quick.

"Are you Frenchmen? Do ye want to discuss if you feel like fighting: yes or no? Must you be consulted if you wish to put to sea, or as to the course, or the set of the sails? Is that the kind of men we have aboard *Pandora*?"

Again the men began to mumble and argue amongst themselves, although Banks had won a good many back.

"Think how it would be if the Admiralty agreed to whatever you want; some amongst you might be satisfied, but there would be others," his eyes fell back to Scales. "Others who would ask for more; others who would never be happy until they had wrung out every last penny, and then some. So tell me, is that how you want the Navy to be run?"

The murmurs of discussion rose up in a crescendo until once more the men were arguing vehemently; apparently the captain's words had found a home.

"We expect to have our grievances heard!" Scales almost screamed, and then repeated himself in a lower tone almost truculently.

"Then you'd be sadly amiss in your method." It was a new voice, a voice none of them had noticed before. It came from an unknown man in his late twenties dressed in the uniform of a quartermaster's mate. Backed by another, slightly older, petty officer he stepped forward from the ranks of seamen with an air of authority and weight that drew immediate attention and respect from the crowd.

"You'll forgive me, sir?" he turned to Banks and knuckled his forehead. "It appears there has been some misunderstanding, and perchance a little over enthusiasm amongst the people."

CHAPTER NINE

BANKS sipped at the welcome glass of brandy and stretched his feet gratefully towards the fire that burned in the port admiral's office. Sir Peter Parker was well into his seventies, and it was hard for a young frigate captain to detect the vibrant, energetic officer that had been so active during the American wars in the portly, bewigged admiral. The same man who had led the attack against Sullivan's Island now sat comfortably opposite him, belly protruding generously over his britches and powdered wig slightly askew, to the other side of the grate. But then his appearance came as no surprise; Sir Peter had been a family friend and frequent visitor at the Banks household for as long as he could remember and the admiral's image had changed little over the last twenty years.

"Your father sends his regards, Richard; I was with him not three days back."

"Thank you, sir. I hope to call on him directly."

Parker raised an eyebrow. "I'm not sure that will be possible."

"You're thinking of the court martial?"

"Not especially," Parker examined his drink at leisure. "Although there will have to be one, and your fellow, Scales, will hang of course."

"He claims not to have wounded the marine."

"No, blames it on his mate, so I understand, a measure of their fellowship, I would chance. Seems his comrade thinks different, as well he might. It is of little consequence; blood was drawn and authority challenged: we'll string 'em both up, like as not." Parker paused, as a thought occurred. "Mind, it could influence things as far as that other affair is concerned." There was a pause as the old man became lost in thought.

"Other affair, sir?"

Parker returned. "All in good time, Richard. But this is not a good place for *Pandora*, you'll have to take her away."

"She is in need of repair, sir."

"That's as maybe, but still you must be gone."

"Are you worried about my people?"

"In truth, I am worried *for* your people. You saw how easily some were swayed by twenty or so hot heads."

"From what I can tell, our draft from the Channel Fleet was made up almost exclusively of misfits and malcontents."

Parker laughed sharply. "Common enough; when a man is asked to give up some of his crew, he ain't likely to choose top-men."

"No, indeed, but I fear these were the very worst. They had been given the idea for mutiny, but not the organisation, nor the control."

"That's as may be; still, it would be wrong to tempt fate further. I'm afraid a foreign station is out of the question, but there is little reason why you should not be sent to another home port."

"You think the mutineers will let me sail?"

"Oh, no doubt of it; *Pandora* is a frigate, an escort: you may go as you please."

Banks shook his head. "It would seem a strange way to run a mutiny," he mused, sipping at his drink. "To openly rebel, refuse to sail, risk the noose and many lesser punishments, then allow frigates and other escorts to accompany convoys and generally move at will."

"This could in no way be thought of as a normal mutiny," Parker was long past the age for sipping, and drank deep, before placing his empty glass down firmly on the delicate table by his side. "We knew something was a-coming, of course; there'd been no end of petitions and the like. My Lord Howe passed them on to Spencer at the Admiralty, but of course he did nothing."

"No?"

"Well, who could blame him? Besides, there was little he could do, and no one was going to listen, not until something like this blew up."

"They're listening now?"

"Oh yes," Parker picked up his glass and spun it thoughtfully. "They're listening now all right. I said we was aware, but perhaps that isn't strictly just. Admiral Bridport knew nothing, not until I sent word, mid April," he sighed. "Commander of the Channel Fleet, and no one thought to tell him his men were communicating with the Admiralty. Never known Alex to be so angry: wrote to the board directly, but if you ask me it had already gone on for too long and the men were tired of being ignored. I'm not sure if they got his letter and responded out of spite, but with the next despatch my Lord Commissioners of the Admiralty saw fit to order Gardner's squadron to transfer to St Helens; that was on Easter Sunday. We all knew the men wouldn't take it, and we were right."

"They refused to sail?"

"They did. Incredible, isn't it?"

Banks sipped at his drink again. Incredible was the word. In the past, nearly every instance of mutiny had been contained within a single ship; for several to be involved, let alone a squadron or an entire fleet, would have taken a great deal of organisation and enterprise.

"Charlie Pole went to the Admiralty and told them face to face. Spent half the night with Nepean and Spencer. Next day Spencer speaks to Pitt and before you knows it, Spencer's down here himself. Says Billy agreed to everything they asked for."

"Everything?"

"Pretty well; there were a few qualifications of course, but in the main they had it in the bag."

"And that was, when?"

"Oh, we're still talking the middle of April. The delegates met in the *Charlotte*, and by the end of the week it looked like we were getting back to normal, although how anything can ever be normal again, when the men have been shown to have power, I do not comprehend."

Banks shook his head, and Parker signalled for both their glasses to be refilled.

"Last thing they asked for was a King's pardon; no problem there, Spencer went back up to London himself, and I was able to distribute to all who required by the following Sunday."

"Brisk work."

"It was; just a week after everything had started off. Shame our lords and masters couldn't have acted as quickly in the first place: none of this need happen."

"But the fleet is still in mutiny?" Banks prompted.

"Oh yes, it all started to go rather awry, I fear. Proclamation had to be ratified by Parliament of course, but they didn't get that done till a few days back. By then the main fleet had finally moved down to St Helens, where you see them now. A few remained here, *Marlborough, Minotaur,* with Thomas Miller and his son on board, and *Nymphe. London* stayed as well, Colpoys decided he wanted to watch the other ships, as well he might.

"And there we have it, idle ships and idle men; you can imagine the rumours; the people all ahoo from their demands being granted, yet nothing apparently happening. Days went by, then weeks, and the people started to wonder if they'd been sold a pup. Wind turned in our favour last Monday, but it were no good asking them to sail; we could tell nothing was to come of it until they had firm news of the ratification from Parliament, and all appeared destined to blow up once more. And just because our esteemed members couldn't get down to a decent day's work, f'ra change."

Both men paused to drink, before Parker continued.

"The mutineers met again, and came to some sort of a conclusion. Then they set off to Spithead to spread the news there. Colpoys saw them coming and came the high and mighty; ordered their boat off and called up his marines. The rascals boarded in spite and all turned very nasty, we lost several men; *London*'s first lieutenant shot one."

"Bover, Peter Bover?" Banks exclaimed. "Why I spoke with him not six months back."

"And well you might once more, but do not count on it. Men took umbrage and put a noose about his neck; they'd have strung him up there and then, except that some thought better of it."

"I'm glad."

"Indeed, it was that fellow Joyce what swayed things, the one you met this morning; quartermaster's mate from the *George*. I can't say I approve of all this, of course, but in the main the delegates are reasonable enough; certainly not the bunch of revolutionary cut-throats that Spencer and his press would have folk believe."

"You've said they are allowing frigates through."

"Yes, any escorting vessels are excluded from the mutiny, even if they wants to join. *Romney* and *Venus* were due out with a Newfoundland convoy. They tried to come across the day after it all blew up. Delegates told them straight - how did they put it? 'Their desire and earnest wish was that they continued to obey orders.'"

"Extraordinary."

"Extraordinary be damned, it's devilishly clever."

Banks raised his eyes, as Parker continued. "The country depends on commerce, and commerce means ships. The rebels know they need the people behind them, and to try an' starve us out will make them unpopular. As it is, well, you only have to read their demands; fair pay, better food, leave once in a while, 'tis stuff the mob can understand. And if the mob's behind them, as they are, Spencer, Pitt and Parliament really hasn't much of a say."

Parker drained the remains of his drink in one, and peered at the empty glass for a moment. "Mind, they're keeping discipline in the ships; watches are running as normal, officers respected; even saluted."

"Indeed?"

"Oh yes, but not always obeyed, and recently they've been taking to putting those ashore they don't take a fancy to. They've always said they would return to duty if the French look like coming out. I'm inclined to believe them, although I'd rather it not put to test."

"So, where are we now?"

"Now, Richard? Now we are in limbo. Word is my Lord Howe's coming back from London, even as we speak, but what he brings with him, no one can say. Meanwhile we stay in an uneasy truce."

"And *Pandora*?"

"*Pandora* is better off out of here, repair or no."

"I could head back to Falmouth?"

"You'd be no better there, the situation is roughly the same."

109

"London?"

"More chance, though these are troubled times; and anything might occur. Your convoy's bound for the docks, so I believe. We can take the capture here in Portsmouth; but someone'll have to see those merchants through, might as well be *Pandora*."

Banks eyed the admiral warily. "Sir, I was hoping to stand down."

"Were you indeed?" Parker rolled the stem of his glass between his fingers as he considered. "Getting tired of your saucy little ship are ye?"

"Not tired, exactly."

"But wanted a change, eh?"

Banks nodded. "Yes sir, that's about it."

Parker's eyes flashed suddenly. "Well you can forget all about that, if you want to remain wearing a King's uniform."

In his surprise Banks almost dropped his glass, and it was with considerable effort that he replaced it on the table without damage.

"I'm sorry, sir I don't understand."

"Well it's time you did, young man. I'm not saying you haven't done well; few, if any, could have fared better. But to place you in your current position has caused not a small amount of strife for your father. And his friends, if the truth be known."

Banks was suddenly aware of a chilling in the atmosphere that was very nearly physical; the conversation had taken a distinctly dangerous turn.

"Sir, I have nothing but gratitude for..."

"Spare me, sir, spare me. I don't think you know the position you are in. Men crying out for employment, and you thinking it better you should have a bigger ship, and a little more clout, ain't that the case?"

"Sir I..."

"Damned country near on its knees, with nary a friend to help, our own sailors holding us to ransom, and you're thinking of changing a ship, a ship that has proved itself in action."

"I really hadn't thought along those..."

"Then do not, and do not let me hear any more talk of shifting, or moving on." Parker sat back in his chair and signalled for more brandy. The servant came and attended to him. Both men were silent for some time, then Parker gave a tired smile.

"I said these are troubled times, Richard, you must understand that."

"I do, sir."

"You've been at sea for a while; difficult to keep track of politics and the like when you have a ship to manage." He drank from his glass. "We need all the good men, so no more talk of changing ships eh? Not until this little lot is over."

"No, sir."

Parker gave him another smile. "Good, good, I am very glad to hear it. It's stability we want at this moment." He looked at the young frigate captain with not a little affection. They were very similar, might even have been brothers, were it not for the fifty odd years that separated them, although that, to Parker, seemed like no time at all. He drained his glass and coughed sharply. "Next thing I'll be hearing, you'll be thinking yourself in love," he said.

* * * * *

The sick bay was emptier now; Manning retreated to the small desk and checked the ledger. The ink had fully dried on the last discharge so he closed the heavy book, but paused before replacing it on the shelf under the laxatives.

All but three of the patients had been taken off earlier in the afternoon, most would be transferred to Haslar, the naval hospital, although two, suffering from bursten belly, had been discharged ashore. Abdominal hernias were a common ailment, caused in the main by the normal rigours of shipboard life. There was little even a hospital could do, and it would be up to them to fend for themselves from now on; certainly they were of no further use to the Navy.

The marine had been shot just below the right shoulder, the *pectoralis major*. It was not a bad wound, considering the pistol had been fired at close range, and Doust had removed the ball easily enough. The lad was in Haslar now; providing infection did not set in or the joint itself prove affected, he should be back to normal duties within the month. The Frenchman had also recovered well from the amputation; he too had been taken away although in his case it was probably to a prison hulk, or maybe the new gaol they had built in the West Country. Manning had been concerned that he would not receive further medical treatment; there were remaining ligatures sealing his arteries which would have to be removed in due course. Nothing he could say or do would influence the Frenchman's fate however, and he soon forgot about him.

Piper was still there. His wound had responded well, and the ragged scar was healing nicely. He would also have been transferred to Haslar for recuperation, but Piper had refused to go. Despite the excellent chance that no more than a week in the hospital would see him discharged a free man, he seemed convinced that the only way he would leave was as a corpse, and chose to stick it out in *Pandora* instead.

And the wounded were not the only ones to have gone. As soon as the ship had been moved out of the channel, and moored in a safe anchorage, officers had appeared from the shore. An armed marine guard came for Scales and two of his mates; many had witnessed their departure, although little was said. In fact they were manacled up and led from the ship in silence, a silence that was both dangerous and disquieting to anyone familiar with the ways of British seamen. Then further changes were made.

In consultation with Caulfield, all those from the Channel Fleet draft were swiftly removed, apart from one, who seemed to have friends on board. They had not been with the ship for long, and seemed content to leave. There were also others, men marked out, either by their fellows or officers, who considered them as no longer needed. It was clear that they would not be facing charges, or further discrimination, but *Pandora* was no longer their ship, and they were to be moved. This also was carried out in virtual silence, with none of the comments or ribaldry usually considered essential when shipmates departed.

But then the mood of the people had been strained following the mutiny; the mutiny that had hardly happened, the one that all regretted, and were now desperately trying to forget about as the remaining men threw themselves in to settling their ship down to anchor.

Many that were left, indeed most, sympathised with the demands made by the official mutineers, the ones who were still negotiating almost in sight of *Pandora* as she swung at anchor. But that was an organised rebellion; one undertaken with care and planning; undertaken by petty and junior officers and, in the main, reasonable men. Men who knew they had right on their side, and that perseverance and patience were better weapons than intimidation or violence. Scales' rebellion had been totally different; he had taken his followers by surprise, and alienated the loyal hands with the wounding of the marine and threatening the captain.

The young quartermaster's mate from the *Royal George* who had boarded *Pandora* was one of the official delegates, and would be lucky to avoid the noose at the end of matters. Despite this he had spoken well, told the hands that there was no need for Scales' tactics. Told them that the actual mutiny was being run on more civilised lines and that the mutineers themselves were, as a body, loyal and patriotic. He had explained that conditions on the rebel ships had changed little: watches were called, and stores taken on. Officers were still respected, even though some of their orders might be ignored, and even punishments were awarded and carried out in the normal manner. Were the French to put to sea, every Jack would return to duty, and the ships would sail and fight in defence of their country. The meeting that had started with Fraiser's address broke up then, and the men returned to duty, subdued, and shaken by what they had witnessed. They worked without comment, carrying out the usual shipboard routines promptly, and with every respect for every level of officer. But there was a change.

It was subtle; nothing that could be identified, or acknowledged but it stood out plainly for anyone with the time to notice. The men were different; repentant and yet defiant. The joy and swagger that had come from two successful ship to ship actions and a fleet victory at St Vincent had gone, and there was none of the usual banter and supposition about pay, shore leave and wives.

They felt that the action they had taken had disgraced them in some way, yet was also necessary. To challenge authority might have been wrong, but was it right for them to have been placed in a position where the challenge had been all but inevitable? Perhaps the delegates would pound out a resolution; one that would be acceptable to all, and the whole untidy mess could be forgotten; that would be the ideal solution. But it would take time, and until then the men were different, and because of it, the ship itself had altered.

And she had gone; she had been one of the first to go. The captain had left to visit the port admiral before noon, and had sent a message that he was to stay ashore until further notice. There had also been one for Kate. It had just outlined the arrangements for transferring her and her father to the London hospital, although she had been strangely reticent about him reading, or even seeing the note. After knowing each other for little more than a week, and discovering so much more just days after, their separation had been awkward, distant almost and, he couldn't deny it, cold.

"You'll excuse me, sir?"

Manning jerked back to reality to realise that he had been staring at a closed book for some time, and that Soames, the purser, had entered the sick bay and was standing watching him.

"Mr Soames, my apologies; I did not hear you."

"Indeed? Well I wished not to disturb your wool gathering, but thought it time for another dose."

"Of course," Manning extracted the pill he had placed in his waistcoat pocket earlier that morning and passed it across. "The symptoms, sir; are they in any way changed?"

"No difference," Soames threw the tablet into the back of his mouth and swallowed it straight down in one motion. "Apart from a dizzy head, a thick tongue and my guts in such disorder that you would not credit."

Manning nodded, "I fear that is a side effect, but relief should come in time."

The purser nodded grimly and left without another word. Relief should come in time; Manning sighed: with all of modern medical science and potions without number at his disposal, that was probably his best cure as well. A fortnight before he had not known the girl: two weeks hence, who could tell? Although deep in his belly the young man knew he would remember her for always and miss her far longer.

* * * * *

"I think we should keep the people active." Caulfield said to Fraiser as the latter took another bearing to check the anchors were behaving themselves.

"Aye, with no further word from the captain, we can expect to be here a fair while longer."

Caulfield stroked his chin thoughtfully. A fair while was probably right, possibly not long enough to necessitate setting down topmasts, although he knew of few evolutions that were quite so public, or worthy of comment, and consequently likely to encourage the men to give their all.

"The people are certainly listless," he said in a softer tone. "I feel some exercise with the yards to be in order."

"It would not hurt and might bring some spirit back to them."

Caulfield stepped forward and brought his silver whistle to his lips. The men responded readily enough, and in no time the shrouds were black with topmen busily working aloft. Fraiser watched for a moment. They would be bound to take in stores, and the hold would have to be rearranged. Many of the holders had come from the Channel Fleet draft, and had now been removed, but there would be enough left to make a start, even without reorganising the watch bill. Below him the carpenter's crew were at work rigging a stage to inspect the damaged quarter gallery, and the smell of pitch was starting to permeate the air, along with that of paint and marine glue. Clearly every department was taking advantage of the rest and there was no doubt that *Pandora* would be the better for it, in fabric if not in spirit.

* * * * *

"We're to sail on the afternoon's second high, once the people are fed."

They had lain at anchor for three days, for three days the usual routine of a ship of war had been postponed, replaced by a series of light repairs and general maintenance that slowly gave way to more intensive exercise. It was the time when arrangements would normally be made for wives and other followers to be allowed on board, but no such request was made, and even the shore bumboats, the bringers of fruit, illicit drink, exorbitant exchange rates against pay tickets and, often enough, colds and other ailments, did not approach them. Of all the homecomings any on board had previously made, it was certainly the strangest.

The captain had been absent the whole time, and only now stood on the quarterdeck fresh from his gig. He wore a new undress uniform and an expression of detached irritation; it was clear that either his business ashore, or the return to *Pandora*, had displeased him greatly, and his officers responded to both his mood and announcement with quiet deference.

"Single up during the morning watch, if you please, Mr Caulfield," he continued. "I want no delays, no distractions. The *Katharine Ruth* is to stay in Portsmouth to be condemned; we will be escorting the merchants on to London, then continue to Yarmouth and join my Lord Duncan, and the North Sea Squadron."

"Very good sir." Caulfield touched his hat automatically as he took the information in. The posting was just about as far away from the Mediterranean as it was possible to get, and known as the hardest station, both for weather and duties. The entire east coast from Selsey Bill would have to be patrolled, and the standard and quality of the ships were notoriously second rate. Banks caught his eye and relaxed slightly.

"There'll be no sailing for foreign stations, not for as long as this nonsense continues," he looked pointedly at the Channel Fleet still anchored across the water. "They're giving us to Duncan; he's preciously short of fast sailers, and we seem to have won ourselves a reputation in that department with the board."

Caulfield nodded, noticing the captain's slight unbending. "But what of our repairs, sir? *Pandora* needs to be properly set up, maybe a minor refit."

"Sheerness can take us; not a refit, but at least some of the damage we have suffered might be addressed; a patch up job, I fear," he added hastily. "News is not good from the north; I cannot say more. Perchance we can make further repairs later, but more likely all else will wait until we raise Yarmouth."

"Very good, sir."

"And maybe not then; in fact maybe not at all, Mr Caulfield. As I have said, the news is not good; it would be better to expect the worst," he smiled suddenly, and a glimpse of the old captain was allowed to slip out. "That way any surprises we encounter will be of the better variety, if you follow my meaning."

* * * * *

It appeared that surprises were the order of the day, although the surgeon was able to contain his. "You've not given me much of a chance to consider things," he said evenly.

Manning nodded. "Sir, I realise that. To be honest it is something I have not thought greatly about, although you will accept that my intentions are genuine, and I feel myself ready."

"Oh yes, there's none that would be doubting you. But I cannot talk with the captain now, and that is the normal way of things."

"We are bound for the Nore, sir. I could settle my business and meet with *Pandora* there."

"You're asking me to make this unofficial then?" The brow furrowed very slightly.

"I would not put you in a difficult position. I will rejoin *Pandora*, of that you have my word."

"And in the meanwhile?"

"Sir?"

"Should we see action between here and the Thames; not something that is totally unheard of, I fear..."

"You will have Powell, sir, and the other loblolly boys."

Doust smiled suddenly. "I would, and though you might be missed, I chance that a better surgeon will be coming back to me at London than is asking to leave at Portsmouth, and that I would welcome greatly."

"Thank you, sir," Manning smiled weakly

"I will have to tell the captain, of course."

"The captain?"

Doust caught the lad's expression and relaxed suddenly. "Och, it can be no concern for him. I'll tell him if I'm asked, but you go about your business, and return a happier man."

* * * * *

It was two bells in the afternoon watch: one o'clock. The hands were just finishing their dinner, and would then attend to the final anchor that still lay in the Spithead slime. The morning had been busy, with the last of the water being taken on just before 'Up Spirits'. The hands in the water lighter had been laughing and chattering like monkeys, so much so that Fraiser was quite sure that some of them had access to drink. But they were also full of news and, despite the fact that it was mainly good, they seemed eager to spread it.

"Belike they've come to a reconciliation," King told Caulfield when he came on deck. "Strangest thing I've heard in many a year."

117

Caulfield nodded, but then the whole business had been bizarre in the extreme.

"A fleet to mutiny, that's unheard of, surely?"

"Aye, that's as maybe, but they settled it soon enough, so it were clear someone was in the wrong."

"Settled within the month, they're saying, with Royal pardons for all. An' they're taking the delegates for dinner this afternoon."

Caulfield looked at him sidelong. "For dinner? You heard that?"

"The men in the last hoy were adamant," King confirmed.

Caulfield shook his head. "The whole world's gone mad," he said flatly.

They were almost level with the anchored fleet off St Helens, and could see lines of small boats heading for the flagship. Then, with a roar that could be heard across the Solent, the red flags started to be hauled down as further fresh outbursts of cheering broke out. Ships bells were rung and a night signal rocket rose up in a pyramid of yellow from the quarterdeck of a seventy-four. King smiled at Caulfield. "Looks like it be true then."

"Aye, true enough, and let's hope we hears no more of demands and the like. Country's at war; this ain't the time for all to be complaining. Settle our score with the French, then we can address problems at home. I've had my fill of mutinous demands, and am mightily glad we'll be hearing no more of them."

* * * * *

Manning examined the insect with interest, it was dark in colour and far, far larger than the usual pink 'bargemen' that were relatively common in ship's biscuit, although even they were rarely found in home waters. This had taken time to grow, and even if all and sundry might refer to it as a weevil, it was actually a type of beetle; *stegobium paniceum*, or so his reference book told him. Hard, round and relatively heavy; it had grown to a considerable size: according to his source, it had reached an advanced stage of development. He had found it in the hard tack bag he had opened that morning. The sick berth having the choice of provisions, it had come from the most recent delivery, taken on board *Pandora* only the day before. So in theory the biscuit should have been fresh; the freshest available in the ship, but the presence of a large bread beetle told a different story. Her words came back to him as he examined the creature; clearly Mr Soames the purser was not buying, or insisting upon, premium supplies. It might be pure chance, of course, but then he could also be dishonest; accepting stale provisions from the dockyard victuallers for a small, or not so small, personal consideration. Manning bounced the beetle in his hand reflectively as he considered the matter. A noise alerted him and he looked up to see the man himself, furtively entering the sick bay. He rose, still clutching the beetle. The purser and his condition was something Manning had forgotten about in his haste to be rid of the ship. He would have to provide him with a supply of mercurial tablets, if he was to go ashore for any period.

"Ah, Mr Manning, I wonder if I might impose upon you." The purser's bullfrog face broke into a slimy, ingratiating, smile.

Manning unconsciously clutched the beetle in his hand. "How are matters progressing, Mr Soames?"

"Capital, capital. I still have the side effects from your treatment, of course, but the condition itself seems to be accounting well. I cannot thank you enough."

"I am glad of it," he reached out towards the purser with the beetle enclosed in his closed fist. "I wonder if there is something I might bring up in return?"

"Of course, of course, my dear fellow. Did I not say I would be happy to reciprocate in any way I could?"

Soames held his hand under Manning's, and received the beetle into his open palm.

"It is provisions, sir; an item I wanted to raise with you."

Soames accepted the beetle causally. "Anything you wish for, Mr Manning, anything at all" and with a sweep of his hand the purser shot the creature into his mouth. "Just state your needs and I will provide," he said smugly, manoeuvring the thing to the back of his throat before swallowing it whole.

CHAPTER TEN

ONCE more the tide was with them as they approached anchored British shipping, but this time the tension on the quarterdeck was almost tangible. They had left the convoy to continue alone, and collected a pilot off North Foreland. The man was conning the ship well enough, leaving the officers, currently assembled on the quarterdeck, strangely void of responsibility. The leadsman at the forechains maintained a slow, regular chant, marking out the sandy depth beneath *Pandora*'s keel and, unintentionally, counting them nearer to the small untidy group of warships that lay at rest.

They were taking the Queen's, or Middle, Channel, the South being too shallow, even for *Pandora*'s meagre draft, and were just edging past the sandbanks off Minster on the Isle of Sheppey, heading almost directly for the Great Nore anchorage.

"I see flags," King said finally. It was true: they had been visible for some while although none on board *Pandora* had cared to admit the fact. Apart from the lightweight escorts and independent frigates, there were only a few larger vessels. Just a handful of line-of-battleships, the backbone of the fleet, but it was these that helped to make up the North Sea Squadron. Rumours were rife that, barely thirty miles away, an army was gathering intent on the invasion of England. These ships were all that denied them use of the Channel, and they were now blatantly flying the red flag of mutiny.

"But it had been settled," Caulfield muttered, the exasperation evident in his voice. "When we left Spithead, not three days back, all was agreed."

"Belike the news has not reached them?" King said, though he knew that, even without semaphore, reports of the agreement must have been made known throughout England.

They were drawing closer now, and individual ships could be made out.

"That's *Sandwich*," Caulfield pointed at the aged battleship, a participant in a much earlier Battle of Cape St. Vincent, although it was unlikely that she would ever see foreign service again. "Flagship, depot ship, receiving tender; a real jack of every trade."

"I hears she carries more'n twelve 'undred above her standing compliment," Lewis, a master's mate, added.

"Must be a mite uncomfortable." King mused. "I'd wager the only thing they don't suffer from is loneliness."

They stood in silence as *Pandora* drew level with the other rebel ships. Three were liners, including *Sandwich*, together with some smaller vessels. As King watched a crowd began to flow up the shrouds, and soon were waving in their direction. A chorus of cheers and calls came to them. King momentarily held his breath, but there was no response from *Pandora*'s men. He glanced down towards the waist. The watch on deck seemed quietly attentive; a group with the boatswain were replacing a stay that had become worn, and the sailmaker was supervising the stowing of the fore topgallant, which was due to be replaced. Some looked towards the cheering, and a couple gave derisory waves in return, but it was obvious the men did not wish to associate themselves with the mutineers.

Now the cheering had changed to catcalls and shouts of abuse. In *Sandwich* King could see some form of argument was in progress; a group were clearly trying to launch a small boat, while another attempted to stop them.

"Larboard a point, steady." The pilot, a solid man worthy of his profession, was clearly ignoring the diversion and continuing to take them in. Then they were past Cheyney Rock and the dangerous sands and preparing to round Garrison Point; ahead lay the mouth of the Medway. The noise of a gun cracked close by making all on the quarterdeck jump. King turned back and saw a cloud of smoke disappearing from one of the upper deck battery in *Sandwich*. There was no sign of the shot. A chill ran through his body as the pilot ordered them round. One of the seamen nearby swore softly to himself; King empathised totally. *Pandora* was a warship and all aboard were used to being under fire, but for another of her own country to deliberately take aim was disagreeable in the extreme. The ship creaked as she finally turned her stern to the rebel ships and allowed the tide to carry her on to the safety of the Sheerness dockyard. Clearly the mutiny at the Nore was being run on very different lines to that of Spithead.

* * * * *

"Six days, captain," the short and slightly stocky man told him. "Eight at the most." He was commonly known as a Foreman Afloat, and had probably seen and assessed a hundred warships in his time.

Banks stroked his chin; eight days was longer than he had hoped for, especially with the problems across the water. Not only would he have to disable *Pandora*, and submit her to the care of dockyard workers, but there was his own crew to keep happy in the meanwhile.

"I have my people to consider," he said. "We're well below compliment, but there would still be a fair number to accommodate."

The man shook his head. "Can't do nothing about that, I'm afraid. Usual measure would be to use the old *Sandwich*, but there's no tellin' what's going on aboard her at present."

"When did the trouble start?" Banks would normally have avoided discussing a mutiny with an unknown landsman; he could not be sure where his true sympathies might lie, but the man was clearly trying to help, and there was no shame in ignorance.

"'bout five days back. There'd been a court martial in *Inflexible*, trying Captain Savage for the loss of 'is ship. Same day *Sandwich* was ordered to clear before unmooring; most of the officers was at the court, an' the men just took over. Told the number one he 'ad to go, and gave him the choice: by boat or by noose; they didn't care which. Admiral Buckner never went back to his flagship, but Captain Mosse, he were game enough an' faced them. Much good it did him mind, the men were respectful enough, but it were like they didn't know what they wanted themselves."

"They have no leader?"

"Don't seem like it. They got delegates, representatives from all the ships up the estuary, but no one wants to take control." The man's honest blue eyes stared hard at Banks. "There's some on shore what approves of all this. But, after getting things straight at Spithead, there's a fair few what don't," he said, earnestly. "It's a mess, an' no mistake."

It sounded like one. For the people to rise up was bad enough, for them to do so without control or leadership was far, far worse.

"That doesn't solve my problem of accommodation. Would those hulks be of any use?"

Across the water four elderly ships had been dismasted and now lay at permanent moorings, with awnings across the decks and heavy staging to the entry ports.

The man smiled. "There's nigh on two hundred families living there," he said. "My own including; an' they ain't half as bad as they appears; we got rooms on the half deck, an' very nice they are to."

Banks smiled in return. "Well, we won't be presuming on your hospitality. The men will stay on board, they'll keep out of the way as much as possible."

"That would be fine, captain. An' probably the soundest place for them, if you don't mind me saying. Mind you, for as long as they're flying them red flags, I don't see how anywhere is properly safe."

* * * * *

Two days later Manning sat in the Chequers, a large and popular alehouse on the east side of Sheppey, and near to the docks where *Pandora* would be waiting for him. His business ashore had gone extremely well, and he eyed the tankard of dark Kentish ale with pleasant expectation. He had travelled to London on the mail coach, arriving at Surgeons' Hall about the same time as *Pandora* passed Beachy Head. The appointment was made for three days hence; almost exactly the period of time he had hoped for, and he had booked himself in to a nearby boarding house, paying extra for a private room. The days were spent with his head buried in books, eating and drinking little, but sending down for more candles so often that his landlady grew suspicious, and challenged him with all manner of nefarious activities. On the third day he had washed and dressed as well as he could, and appeared for inspection a good half an hour before the appointed time. There were three others to be examined that day and, being the last to apply, Manning had been the last to be seen.

The board had consisted of three physicians and a young surgeon; the latter had done most of the questioning, while his elders and betters flipped through Manning's brief history. It had hardly taken an hour; less time than any of the previous applicants. He had answered on amputation and the preventative measures for gangrene. Venereal disease was also touched upon, and Manning had blessed Soames and his ailment for giving the extra edge that allowed his answers to ring out with confidence. Then there was a little about diet and the measures that should be taken to maintain a strong constitution amongst the people. He had to prove he was familiar with the various returns and reports he would be responsible for, and there were a couple of simple questions about the colour of glass used for different types of medicines.

He supposed he had acquitted himself well enough although the fact that the most of the board were rather keen to adjourn for dinner might have had some influence in the matter. The young surgeon had continued to ask ever more searching questions until the president had told him bluntly enough that they were satisfied, and that Manning should return the next day for his warrant.

It was with him now, in his jacket pocket, as he drank deeply from his beer and told himself the world was really quite a comfortable place. He was now officially a surgeon's mate, a respected warrant officer, and one who might progress to surgeon or even physician, should he be spared, and the chance occur.

From Surgeons' Hall, he had naturally travelled to the hospital where Kate's father had been taken. There he enquired, but they had no patient by the name of Black. His subsequent walk down Lombard Street revealed two lines of imposing, but anonymous houses. There were local shopkeepers nearby; a simple enquiry might have found the Banks residence, but the idea had been repugnant and he had set off for *Pandora* that same afternoon. A man could always be traced by his ship, if she had the mind. And if she had not... well, then he was still a surgeon's mate.

A disturbance as the other end of the room distracted him. Two men had entered, clearly expecting some recognition from the other occupants. He examined them; dressed as sailors, they both carried small canvas bags, and swiftly removed their tarred hats, which he noticed were adorned with red ribbon; not the first he had seen that day on Sheppey, and something he had already wondered about.

"It's MacCarthy!" one of Manning's fellow drinkers shouted, and soon men began to file noisily in from the other rooms to make a crowd about the newcomers.

"What news, Mac?" one asked. "An' where are the others?"

"All in good time, all in good time." The arrival accepted a tankard and drank deep. "It weren't no easy trip," he said, emerging once more and wiping the froth from his mouth. "At one point we had to run from the press – think of that!"

"It were twenty pounds we gathered together to send yon lot to Portsmouth," one said dryly. "Don't tell us what a hard time you had of it, just give the news."

MacCarthy smiled, and placed his pot down on the table. "Well if 'tis news you want, it is news you'll get, an' not of the bad kind, neither. Our brothers at Spithead have been victorious." He paused, smiled, and looked about him before continuing. "Admiralty and Parliament have allowed their every wish; it is a total victory, nothing short."

There was silence amongst the group for a moment, then a lithe, swarthy man who was dressed far better than his fellows, spoke.

"We heard the like, Mac, but could not tell if it be true."

"Why then there is proof here." MacCarthy reached into his ditty bag and pulled out a sheaf of papers. "I have documents from my Lord Howe hi'self. Parliament has agreed, and the King has granted a full and Royal pardon for all. They'll be no scraggin', not for none of us."

The men accepted the papers in silence, and passed them amongst themselves.

"Not quite all the demands," one commented.

"As near as makes no difference," MacCarthy countered, clearly pleased with himself. "An' we certainly won't be needing to carry on. You should have seen Pompey - there was singing and dancing in the street: bands, cheering, and all 'good on you' for Jolly Jack Tar!"

The well-dressed man looked up. "Though it is honest, it is never good to bring bad news," he said; his voice was cold and measured.

"Bad news?" MacCarthy looked genuinely taken aback. "But how could it be so? There's an answer to our troubles, and a pardon for us all. Our brothers have triumphed; 'twere our help they needed, an' now they needs it no more. We can go back to work, go back and serve in a navy that treats us proper."

"Hear him," a voice came from the back. "There speaks an Admiralty man!"

MacCarthy turned in anger. "How say you, were I not a founder an' delegate in *Inflexible*? No Admiralty man would have forced the crew of the *Fiorenzo* to cheer us so!"

"These pardons do not set us free." It was the same educated voice, belonging to the well-dressed seaman.

"How's that, Dick?"

"They refer to the mutiny at Spithead, and are dated for that. We have been in revolt for longer, and cannot gain protection from such a document." Once more silence descended upon the group as the man continued leafing though the pile of papers that MacCarthy had brought.

"There are concessions here, to be sure, but they do not meet our demands."

"They meet those asked for at Spithead," MacCarthy countered.

"I say they do not meet our demands and I stand by it. There is no guarantee of liberty ashore. No amnesty for our fellows who have run in the past, but have now returned to serve. No changes in the laws of prize money that sees one get a thousand times the share of another. What we have is concessions, but they might only last a year, and do you see how this is dated?" He held a document up and the crowd, many of whom could not read, nodded wisely. "This is but an Order in Council, it has no power, and can be rescinded at will." He turned to MacCarthy and tossed the papers down in front of him. "This is naught but three pennyworth of ballads, bought for twenty pounds."

The group began to murmur ominously, and Manning started to feel uncomfortable. MacCarthy picked up the papers defiantly, sorting them back into order, his eyes downcast and lips tightly pressed.

"'spected more of you, Mac," the muttering was general.

"Came to fool us, did ye?"

127

"Belike a stretch at the yardarm will put your thoughts in order."

"Aye," another agreed. "And learn you where your loyalty lies."

The well-dressed seaman stood suddenly, and the noise subsided. "My lads, there might be many of us who take an exit from this matter that will be both boisterous and sudden. But that is not for now, and not for Mac, to be sure." His words were soft but he held each man's attention as if he were speaking to them alone.

"The Admiralty and the Government have listened to our brothers at Spithead and, just as surely, they will listen to us as we will build on their success." he paused, as if seeking inspiration, before continuing at a steadily increasing tempo. "We will state our case clearly, and not waver. We will shame them with our demands, which are just, fitting and deserved. And we will see those demands granted. We will remind them that British seaman are to be respected. Respected, considered, and not ignored. And we will be victorious!" The speech, made in a rousing crescendo, was enough to inspire and unite the men, and soon all in the room were cheering. Cries of 'Parker for president', and 'good old Dick' were heard, while men called for more beer and pipes. Manning surveyed the scene with disquiet; a chill had entered his body, and he felt almost too weak to get up and move. Someone began to thump the table, and soon a further chorus of cheers broke out. More seamen entered the room, and the stool opposite him was knocked sideways and turned over. Taking advantage of the diversion, Manning rose suddenly, and squeezed his way through the mob.

Outside the light was failing, but he could see well enough to find the road that should lead to the docks and *Pandora*. Men were filling the streets and in the distance a rough and ill timed band could be heard playing '*Britons Strike Home!*' The dockyard was in sight now; he could see the grey edifice that was the tower, but still there were seamen everywhere.

A figure rushed towards him, looking behind as he went. Manning tried to dodge, but could not avoid his bulk cannoning into him. He fell sprawling to the ground, but recovered himself almost immediately. Clambering to his feet he felt for his warrant, which was still safe, however the man was now giving him all his attention. "Hey, where's your ribbon, matey?"

Manning looked anxiously about as others began to take notice of him, and made to move away.

"He's an officer, a spy!" The crowd surged towards him ominously, and soon he was breaking into a run. More shouts, cat calls and laughter; he found himself hurtling down the hard and dusty streets, dodging the oncoming revellers. There were yells from behind, and an object was thrown that grazed his shoulder. He quickened his pace still further, aiming for the street that he hoped would take him to *Pandora* and safety, while all the time his pursuers grew in number and determination.

* * * * *

They had all been moved further forward on the berth deck to give the dockyard workers, and *Pandora*'s own carpenter's crew, more space to attend the damaged stern. With the ship operating at anchor watch, and few official duties for the regular seamen, most had fallen into groups that roughly equated to their usual messes. In these they sat and yarned the time away, waiting for the moment when they would be herded back into a true fighting force, and return to their natural element. Until that hour came, each day was an unofficial 'make and mend', where private tasks and general maintenance could be conducted under a brief but welcome relaxation of discipline.

Jenkins was sewing. He had scrounged a piece of cloth from a sailmaker's mate, and been working on an elaborate embroidery for several weeks. There were no lines to guide him, in fact he had not sketched out the design in any way, but simply started to sew, adding letters and embellishments as he went and as they occurred to him. A girl's name, 'Rosie' stood out in glorious detail, along with a naïve picture that was clearly a frigate, and a whale that appeared almost as large. The composition itself was slightly awry, but that was of little concern, as the value to Jenkins lay more in the execution than the finished result. Besides, it kept him away from Cribbins, who was always up for a friendly game of Crown and Anchor, and maybe a little money on the side. Jenkins had already lost all he had, and all he would get, and would never gamble again; of that he was absolutely definite.

"I 'ear's from a dockyard Jimmie we was lucky to get away with it, comin' in here," he said, pulling the thick needle through, and adding slightly to the third letter

Flint was also sewing, although in his case it was necessary work; repairing the seam of a round jacket that had ripped. He looked up when Jenkins spoke, but said nothing.

"*San Fiorenzo* was fired upon, few days back," Jenkins continued.

"We was fired upon," Flint said.

"Ah, but they didn't hit us, an' they hit *San Fiorenzo*."

"Any damage?" Jameson this time. He had been annoying a broken piece of top hamper with his knife, trying to work it into an albatross that was fast becoming a seagull.

"Not particular: cut through the foot rope of her jib boom; no one killed nor nothing."

"No, but a fair few have been," Flint held the jacket up and pulled the seam straight. "And a fair few more will end up dead by the end of it."

"A bunch of them delegates made an inspection of The Old Swan, the place they're using as an hospital," Jenkins again. "They say a surgeon there got so aggrieved he cut 'is own throat rather than face them." Jenkins looked up for special emphasis. "*They say* it was 'im what done it," he added, pointedly.

"All the hospital ships 'ave been inspected," Flint continued after a while. "*Union* and *Spanker* were fine, but they took exception to goings on in the *Grand*, and set the steward and the butcher over the side, an' then 'ad 'em flogged."

"Probably deserved it," Jenkins pronounced, after considering the situation.

"Probably did, but it's not for them to judge." Flint let the jacket drop to his lap. "Ask me the whole thing got out of hand after Spithead. They was reasonable there, asked for what we needed, and stopped as soon as they got it. This lot are from a different kettle."

"Group set upon our Mr Manning," Jameson said. "Chased him back into the yard, they did. Officer of the watch had to call up the marines to restore order."

At that moment the noise of an ill tuned band could be heard from a long way across the water.

"Here he comes again," Jenkins scoffed. "President Parker and his delegates."

"Admiral Parker?" asked Jameson.

"No, Dick Parker," Flint told him. "He's just a regular Jack, though they say he were an' officer once upon a time. Now he spends his days travelling about from ship to ship with his portable orchestra and bunch of toadies, Calls hi'self the president of the mutineers, though I don't know anyone who's voted for him."

"Well no one would in this ship," Jenkins added quickly. "'cause we ain't in on it. No red flag on *Pandora* an' not likely to be, not after Scales an' his lot got what was comin'."

"Think so?" Flint looked at him firmly. "Think we're all going to stay loyal, when half the North Sea Fleet is up in open riot? We're going to have to join them, sooner or later. Can't see Dick Parker and 'is lot leaving us to chart our own course and not having a word or two to say about it."

"But they can't force us to mutiny," Jameson's seagull was now starting to look like a duck, and he pushed it to one side as the conversation warmed.

"They can try."

"What? Come on board *Pandora* and make us? I'd like to see them." Jenkins was also starting to lose interest in his embroidery. "Captain would never stand for it."

"Captain might not have any choice. There's not one of them rebel ships that's smaller than us; most could sink a jackass like *Pandora* with a single broadside."

"They'd never do that." Jenkins and Jameson spoke together, but Flint was not to be swayed.

"They've already fired on us and *San Fiorenzo*; nothing to stop them doing it again. They been turning officers ashore, an' marching round Sheerness armed to the teeth, shoutin' the odds. There's no one who can stand against them, an if they did, if the military was called up, then there really would be trouble."

"Yeah, but that ain't going to happen, is it?" Jenkins asked in a voice eager for reassurance. "They won't let it get that far."

"Who, the Admiralty, or the mutineers?" As Flint spoke the band stuck up again, although this time it was considerably closer. "Fact is, they're asking for that what cannot be given; the Admiralty won't cave in, an' I can't see Parker an' his lot just meekly going back on watch. Talk is of blockading London, or sailing the entire fleet to France or 'olland. Government will send the troops in if either seems likely, then we really will be in the mire."

* * * * *

Soames lay in his cot; his face was puffy and bloated, with dark rims under the eyes, and a pallor of sweat that glistened in the dim light. Manning withdrew his hand from the man's forehead, and looked back at Mr Doust.

"The temperature is still high, I'm afraid."

Doust nodded. "It is to be expected. He came down with the fever the second day you were away. I found your notes, though I would have been a happier man had they been copied into the proper record."

"I did leave in something of a rush," Manning said lamely.

"You had been treating him for quite a spell, Mr Manning. There is no excuse for such sloppiness." Doust voice was firm, and Manning felt shamed.

Soames began to mumble slightly, but they took no notice as he had made little sense for some while.

"I do feel guilty, sir, for not involving you before." Manning continued. "If any of this is my doing, I will stand for the consequences."

The surgeon shook his head. "No, this is not on your account, laddie; indeed the mercury might well have alleviated the condition to a great extent. I would suggest that our friend here has the final phase of syphilis; what we know as the tertiary stage. It usually comes on with no warning, and is invariably fatal," he waved the glim in front of the man's open eyes, but the pupils did not react in any way. "There is little that can be done for him now; the mind has gone, and we can expect the body to follow shortly."

Manning nodded quietly. "I should have asked you from the start."

"Aye, it would have been proper, but not made any difference in the end, I fear. There are many so called cures, and some might have been successful for a while, but yon man would have reached this conclusion for himself in the end, whatever was done for him."

* * * * *

"We appear to have visitors, Mr Caulfield," Banks said as the sound of the band drew closer. Caulfield peered over the starboard rail, and looked down. Sure enough a longboat was heading for *Pandora* as she lay against the quay, her larboard quarter gallery enmeshed in wooden staging. The lookout hailed the boat as it drew near, although no answer could be heard above the din of ungoverned brass and woodwind, and the erratic beating of an innocent drum.

Banks looked at Caulfield pointedly. They clearly intended to board through the starboard gangway port; that which was reserved for officers and important visitors. He could bar their way, of course, and even order round shot to be dropped into the boat, but there seemed little sense in escalating an already volatile situation. Besides, the memory of the Spithead rebels, and their mature and reasoned outlook, was still strong enough to persuade him that he should at least give the courtesy of an audience.

Without a word both officers walked forward and watched as three men were grudgingly admitted through the port. One, clearly the leader, was dressed smartly in a tailed blue coat, with britches and boots. He carried an officer's sword, and a small pot house pistol was stuffed into his waist band. King was at the gangway port to meet them, but the visitors stepped past him, and the leader waved at the seamen who had gathered to watch.

"Brothers, I welcome you in the name of the Committee of the Delegates of the Fleet." The smile was genuine enough, but Banks was pleased to see no answering response from the men of *Pandora*. "For some while we have been demanding that your rights as men be recognised and..."

"As captain of this ship, you will address yourself to me, before you presume to speak with my people." Banks' voice rang out with authority if not volume, and the visitor turned to him as if in surprise.

"I will speak with you, sir, in good time," he said. "When I have finished addressing my brothers."

"You will attend me now, or be removed." Banks turned and walked back towards the taffrail; Caulfield followed with rather less certainty.

"See, the work progresses well," Banks said, turning suddenly, and pointing to where two carpenters were planing a short piece of oak. "Belike we will be free of the dockyard before so very long."

Caulfield paused, taken aback at the sudden change in his captain's manner. Why, the man was even smiling at him as if they were in casual conversation.

"Indeed sir," he said, hesitantly.

"Then we will be back at sea, back to our proper business" Banks continued, pleasantly. "And it cannot be early enough for me, that is certain!" Caulfield smiled weakly in return, and then noticed that the visitor was standing alone, and apparently ignored, on the quarterdeck. Banks also deigned to become aware of him at the same time.

"Ah, I see you have chosen to join us, Mr, ah?"

"Parker. Richard Parker, I am the president of the Committee of the..."

"Yes, yes, that has been said 'though I must confess it meant little to me. I assume you represent the mutineers; what business do you have with me?"

"I have no business with you, sir," Parker continued, although Caulfield noticed that his face, which was deeply tanned, had lightened several shades. "It is your men, your men and their welfare that concern me."

"Indeed; why, that concerns me as well," Banks continued lightly. "You will explain further?"

"I request the election of two delegates from your number" Parker was clearly becoming angry, and stammered slightly as he spoke. "They will join me in *Sandwich*, and speak for the men of *Pandora* in negotiations with the Admiralty."

Banks smiled easily, and held his hands wide. "There is no red flag on this ship, Mr Parker. She sails under true colours, and is manned by loyal hearts who stand for the King, and are ready to fight his enemies."

"We are all loyal men, sir!"

"No, I think not." Banks' tone was still casual, although Caulfield noticed an edge had crept in which grew as he continued to speak. "I think not, I think you are rebellious dogs who seek to sell your country and destroy its people." The attack was both vehement and unexpected; Parker took one step back as the captain advanced upon him. "I think you are an evil man, Mr Parker, a man who pumps himself up to be respectable and honest, but inside is nothing but a lousy traitor. There are no friends for you in this ship, and you will leave now, before I have you thrown over the side, do you understand me?"

Banks had spent his life dealing with insurrection on many levels, and was happy to benefit from the experience. Parker's anger was equal, but he lacked the skill and bearing of one used to command, as well as the authority that the captain had been born to.

"Brothers," he shouted suddenly, turning back from the confrontation. "I appeal to you all as fellow seamen!"

A murmur of disapproval erupted from about the ship, and someone blew a loud and vulgar sound that drew a ripple of general laughter.

"You will appeal to no one in this ship," Banks continued. "You will leave her now, and not return. Your presence, your ideals and your traitorous ways are not welcome and shall not be tolerated."

The cheers that followed Banks' words were enough and, red faced now, Parker spun on his heel and stomped towards the gangway while the sound of derisory hooting and jeers grew about him. At the port he paused suddenly and, just as suddenly, the noise subsided.

"I am sorry to evoke such a reaction," he said, looking about him. "Sorry and disappointed. I seek only to improve the seaman's lot. It is why I was elected, and why I came here today." He paused and ran the back of his hand across his forehead. "We will be victorious, but not without a struggle, and if it is my fellow man we have to fight, then so be it." The silence held as his considered his words. "I would see the men of *Pandora* join in our glorious venture, and will welcome her into the fold, where she and her people might stand united and defiant. Should that not be the case, then I must consider her our enemy and as such to be fought against, rather than for." He turned back briefly to the quarterdeck where Banks and Caulfield regarded him. "A red flag, a red flag at the main," he continued, addressing the men once more. "And a cheer from you brave lads, and you will be among us. I will see both tomorrow, or you will feel our disappointment. Do I make myself perfectly clear?"

CHAPTER ELEVEN

IT was midnight. Both cutters and the launch had been lowered in almost complete silence and now lay manned and ready at *Pandora*'s bows. The staging to the larboard quarter gallery had been released, and stood rather uncertainly on the quay. The ship had been singled up to a solitary bollard, and waited for the start of the ebb, due in approximately seven minutes. Throughout, all spoke in hushed tones, united by a common goal, and the irony of sneaking like brigands from a British port was lost on very few.

They would have no pilot; it would have been impossible to request one and still expect to maintain any degree of confidentiality, and it had been agreed from the start that Fraiser would lead the boats. Of them all, he was the most experienced and, since the incident with the French frigate, Banks had felt strangely confident both of the man and his abilities. Their charts were simple in the extreme, as local pilots were inclined to carry their own. These would be updated to reflect any recent silting or shifting of channels or alterations in currents and buoys, and usually heavily annotated with the owner's notes and observations. Fraiser's was dated ten years before, and could only be trusted for the most basic of information. He would have to rely on instinct, experience, and not a little luck. By the dubious light of the boat's binnacle lamp he was apparently examining the chart now; he bent low, and traced his route with his finger. His eyes were tightly closed, however, and his lips moved without a sound as he spoke with the one he considered knew and understood him better than any.

They would round Garrison point and head for Barrow's Deeps; he had decided that long ago. It would be a tight squeeze past Long Sand, but he felt that preferable and more predictable than taking the Southern passage with its sandbanks and less foreseeable depth. He would have to avoid the Red Sand, of course, and the shallows at the westerly edge of the sandbank called the Knob. Despite the growing rumours, all were currently buoyed and, even with the minimal moon and lack of any other form of light, a few reliable eyes in the boats should keep them in position.

But first they would have to pass the Nore, where further trouble might be expected, possibly making all his prayers and preparations redundant. As light was falling, the big two-deckers were clearly preparing some form of action. The noise of guns being run out came across the water, and the captain had even arranged for the jolly boat to row guard, lest the mutineers entertained thoughts of cutting *Pandora* out.

A British ship, cut from her moorings, by British seamen in a home port; the idea was incredible, although nothing, compared to the goings on of the last few days.

"Are you ready, master?" Banks' soft voice carried down from *Pandora*'s forecastle, and Fraiser looked up.

"Aye, sir. I reckon it's time."

He ordered the boats out and the strain taken up. The rowlocks had been muffled with slush soaked canvas, but still there was a low growl as the oars bit deep into the black water, and the ship's bow was eased from the quay and out into the stream. The two cutters would be towing on either side, with the launch between, and slightly ahead. King and Lewis were in the cutters. They had dark lanterns lit and ticking with heat, although the shutters remained tightly closed. It would be their responsibility to sight the marks and relay the information back to *Pandora*. It also fell to them to carry out any fine manoeuvring. Under tow and on a following tide *Pandora* would be lucky to even make steerage way, and her rudder would be of doubtful assistance. The ship must be guided through the narrow channels by carefully adjusting the pull from either cutter. The jolly boat, with Dorsey in command, had already abandoned its guard duties and was secured to the stern, where it might be of use should desperate measures be necessary.

Banks returned to the quarterdeck and looked about him. "Cast off, if you please, Mr Caulfield."

The first lieutenant nodded to the remaining hand on the quay. The tie was slipped and the man clambered up *Pandora*'s stern as the ship began to drift away with the freshening tide.

There was no sound or signal from the anchored fleet as the strain was taken up and *Pandora* gathered momentum. The clatter of a falling plank came from the abandoned staging, but no more; it was as good an exit as they could have hoped for.

"Nor-nor east," Caulfield muttered to himself, although all on the quarterdeck knew where the ship was heading. He glanced at his watch, three minutes on that course should suffice to see them past Garrison Point, any longer and they would run into difficulties, and possibly aground on the Flats. They had a leadsman in the longboat, and were also carrying sounding rods. But the latter were cumbersome in the extreme, and the need for absolute silence meant there would be little chance of taking regular soundings.

The faint gurgle of water from the stem told how the speed was increasing. Fraiser looked back and was surprised to see their old berth had disappeared into the gloom of night. Ahead the blessed light on Garrison Point was glowing brighter; he took a quick bearing and passed the message back that they were to take the ship round. The lines groaned, but *Pandora* was behaving herself admirably, and Fraiser drew a sigh of relief as the marker off the Flats swept by to larboard. They were up with the fleet now; their lights were a welcome guide as well as an indication of how close *Pandora* would have to creep to the heavy guns.

A shout, far louder than anything heard for some hours, echoed about the estuary, and was immediately taken up by others. Ship's bells began to ring in alarm, and a yellow light appeared high in the top of an anchored vessel, picking out the others in an eerie, spectral, glow. The officers on *Pandora*'s quarterdeck breathed out as one. That was as far as it went; there was no further need for secrecy or silence. Orders were bellowed on the decks of the warships, and the clank of a capstan was unmistakable.

"They're bringing *Inflexible* round on her spring," Banks' comment was unnecessary, all knew that arrangements had been made to allow the two-decker to be manoeuvred at anchor; the sweep of her broadside could be adjusted to follow *Pandora*'s course, simply by tightening a line. There was little wind, it would be down to the boats to pull her out of danger.

"Come on, backs into it!" King, in his cutter, peered forward into the gloom, watching for the marker that would tell when they were approaching the next sandbank. The familiar squeak of gun trucks was heard; it could only be a matter of moments before the first broadside rolled out. He assumed the mutineers would be aiming for *Pandora*, although, if the truth be known, the small craft were far better prey; without their forward pull, the frigate would be dead in the water, and only a couple of lucky shots would be needed to put them out of action.

On the quarterdeck Banks was sharing King's train of thought, and had also decided that the ship itself would be the target. "Tell the men to secure themselves," he said, the distaste evident in his voice. British seamen firing on their own; the very idea was an obscenity. Clearly the men mirrored his feelings and they gave free vent to their anger as they took dubious shelter behind the few solid barriers that could be found in a light frigate.

The waiting was almost unbearable; at any moment the night would be split with the crack and flash of gunfire; men would be killed and wounded horribly, the ship broken apart by round shot, and confusion and terror let loose amongst the waiting seamen. Someone began to giggle uncontrollably, and there was the unmistakable sound of fluid running from a piss dale. But no broadside.

"Back water starboard," King's voice rolled out and the larboard boat began to take *Pandora* round. He had almost missed the starboard mark, and had to take action before reporting it to Fraiser. He did so now, and watched as *Pandora* allowed herself to be guided passed the Knob. "Carry on." Stroke oar took up the pace, and again King felt he had left it too long; the breath dying in his lungs as he watched the ship slowly respond. The sound of an argument came from the anchored ships, and once more the clank of capstan pawls on whelps could be heard, but he had other matters to consider, and could give no further thought to the threat.

On the quarterdeck, Caulfield was following their track, and nodded appreciatively as the course corrections came through. The men in the boats were doing well, although they would have to be wary now; it would require nice timing to clear the sandbank, and get *Pandora* safely into the clear channel.

Banks peered back at the anchored shipping. The yellow light had gone, but battle lanterns were being lit, and *Inflexible* could be clearly seen, her deadly broadside following *Pandora* as they made their escape. They would be clear in less than ten minutes; three broadsides from a well set up ship; whether *Inflexible* could be described as such was debatable, although with the guns now bearing on the light frigate's vulnerable stern, it was probable that just one well aimed salvo would account for them.

Then the night was cracked apart with the blinding flash of high explosive that all but blinded eyes long accustomed to the dark. It was not a simultaneous discharge, nor the steady control of ripple-fire; for some time random shots screamed overhead, separated by intervals of up to five seconds. Clearly *Inflexible's* guns were in poor practice or not under total control. The aim was consistently high, and soon blocks, lines and other pieces of top hamper were raining down amongst the men on *Pandora's* deck.

In the launch Fraiser was keeping his eyes fixed ahead, determinedly not looking back at the gunfire, but using the reflected light to gather as much information as he could about their present position. The boat wobbled slightly as the sounding rod was lowered; there was depth enough, but he knew they were barely feet from grounding. A larboard buoy was suddenly visible almost directly ahead, signalling the edge of the channel and start of the sandbank. He called back the mark and rough bearing to Lewis and King, before ordering all three boats two points to starboard. They were making reasonable speed, and *Pandora's* bow began to creep over to the middle of the channel as the sound of firing gradually eased and the last of the shots passed overhead.

Seconds later the larboard mark was visible again as they passed. Noting it, Fraiser smiled to himself; if it hadn't been for the gunfire they might have missed the buoy and be aground on the sandbank by now; it was not the first time that the worst of situations actually turned out to work in his favour, and he continued to scan his chart and peer into the deep dark distance as confidant as any member of the crew that he, and the ship he guided, was in safe and capable hands.

In *Pandora,* Banks looked about him. Despite receiving a full broadside from a two-decker there were no casualties, other than a member of the afterguard who had been struck and knocked cold by a falling block. Possibly the broadside was a warning and might even be the first of several more deadly barrages to come. But Banks did not expect further trouble; instinctively he felt that the point had been made and now they would be left alone. Clearly the defiance *Pandora's* men had shown had angered the mutineers, although their annoyance was not sufficient to allow careful aim. Still, to have been the target of fire from British guns and British gunners had brought out reciprocal anger in his own people and Banks was quite sure they would have manned their pieces and returned the compliment, possibly with far greater accuracy, should he have been capable of giving such a dreadful order. As it was the grumbling and swearing took several minutes to die down, and it wasn't until Jenkins had yelled 'bastards!' and received a round of appreciative laughter that the mood began to change, some degree of order was restored, and *Pandora* was left to grope her way out of the estuary and on towards the open sea.

* * * * *

Sure enough, dawn found them clear of danger. The wind had risen with the light, and Caulfield ordered the boats in as the freshly set topsails began to fill and the ship leaned over to the stiffening breeze. With a reduced crew most of the able hands had taken a turn at rowing, although one night without sleep, made doubly worse by backbreaking exercise, was no reason for the usual routine of the ship to be interrupted. The sound of ho-lystones scraping across the deck echoed about *Pandora* but there was also smoke from her galley chimney signalling that breakfast, and blessed rest, was not too far away.

Banks was once more on the quarterdeck, although he had slept for three straight hours once the immediate threat was over. Caulfield, who had remained on deck throughout, touched his hat respectfully as the captain joined him.

"Master reckons we'll be clear of the estuary afore long, sir."

Banks noticed that Caulfield was looking decidedly seedy; clearly he would have benefited from a few hours rest. He glanced up to the taught sails to hide a slight awkwardness.

"I've spoken with the bosun, sir," Caulfield, misinterpreting the captain's look, added hastily. "Say's he'll have everything straight aloft afore noon."

"Yes, I just sent for the carpenter," Banks removed his hat and wiped the back of his hand across his forehead, before replacing it. "No damage from last night's little escapade in his department, and he regards the repairs to the quarter gallery as pretty well finished; they were going to take the staging down this morning, we just made it a little easier."

Caulfield smiled politely, "'t'will be a pleasant surprise for them."

Fraiser approached and touched his hat. Banks noticed the dark lines below his eyes, and once more felt mildly guilty for taking his rest.

"You'll be wanting a course, sir?"

"I will, master. But first I have to thank you for your assistance last night; it really was a splendid effort."

Fraiser nodded seriously. "Thank you, sir but I in turn had excellent support. Now where would you be aheading?"

"Yarmouth, Mr Fraiser. We should run in with Admiral Duncan and the rest of the North Sea Fleet there; let us hope Norfolk has a different set of problems to those of London."

* * * * *

Lieutenant King knocked lightly on the deal door to the cockpit that, until a few months ago, had been his own berth. Manning looked up from the table and beamed as he entered.

"What cheer, Robert? You don't mind me dropping by?" King asked, rather awkwardly. "Just wanted to wish you joy of your warrant."

"Pleasure to see you," Manning stood up from his chair, reached inside his coat pocket, and withdrew a sheet of paper. "Almost as good as seeing this." King accepted the document with the reverence it was offered, and nodded wisely as he looked it over. It was printed on paper, whereas his own commission was parchment, but such niceties counted for little, and he knew full well what the recognition would mean to Manning, and was genuinely pleased for his friend.

"How was London?" he asked, looking over the paper.

"Noisy, crowded, and smelling of horses, apart from that I couldn't say, didn't see much more than the front office of Surgeons' Hall, and an upstairs room in Mrs Suggett's boarding house."

King considered him quizzically. "I hear there were others recently arrived in town; you were not tempted to wander further?"

"Never could keep much from you, could I?" he grunted. "Yes, I did call at Lombard Street, but could not tell where she might be.

There was no word of her father at the hospital neither; methinks that one might have been snapped up by another."

"It would be sudden if so."

Manning sighed. "I fear not, Tom. The captain had designs on her from the start."

"The captain – *our* captain?" It came as a genuine shock to King.

"Aye, that's the one; an' who can blame him?" Manning's laugh was short and without humour. "And who can blame her, now I thinks of it. I mean, given the pick between Captain Sir Richard Banks, with estates, income and position, and Surgeon's Mate Manning, with nothing, why, there ain't much in the choosing, is there?"

"I would be sorry, but still think you might be mistaken."

"Well, whether I am or whether I am not, it is hardly a subject I can discuss with my captain, is it?"

"'t'would be an interesting conversation, to be sure."

"Oh, I could write; her father's business must be registered I think, but for what reason? She was quick enough to go and, were she wanting to be with me, there would be little obstacle."

King pursed his lips and nodded seriously. "Except you are at sea, and she would not know where *Pandora* is bound. And were she even to try and join you, women are not officially sanctioned aboard a man of war. Besides, she has an ill father to attend. Apart from that, I agree, there is nought to stop her."

Manning grinned despite himself. "Well, what do you think I should do?"

"It is no good asking me. My problems with the ladies are roughly equal to that of money; the lack of both galls me greatly. But I should not count this a lost cause, Robert. You clearly went well together, and I will not have it that the captain, whatever his position or intentions, could seriously alter that."

* * * * *

They sighted the squadron just after three bells in the afternoon watch. The wind had stayed strong and constant, and *Pandora* was well into the North Sea, heading north-north west; roughly following the English coastline that was close enough to larboard to be seen. A group of local men from the watch below had gathered on the forecastle and were pointing out landmarks and towns as they passed, and when the cry came from the foremast lookout, they greeted the news with obvious interest. King had the watch, and immediately sent Dorsey aloft with a glass to confirm the report. The men on the forecastle switched their attention to the sighting, and began to chatter and speculate amongst themselves to the extent that the master at arms had to order them quiet.

"Liners, I'd say, sir; at least three, and what could be a frigate," Dorsey had descended and stood in front of Caulfield and King as he made his report. "Can't tell the number rightly as they're sailing in close order and still hull down on what looks like a reciprocal course."

"Colours?" King asked, as Banks joined them. Dorsey shook his head.

"Couldn't say, sir. Pen'ants, to be sure, but nothing I could distinguish."

The likelihood was strong that any group of warships sailing as these were would be British; almost certainly some of Duncan's North Sea Fleet heading for the anchorage that *Pandora* had so recently departed.

"But you think they're on the opposing course to us?" Banks asked.

"Near as I could tell, sir. They're a point off the starboard bow, an' probably a mile or more further out to sea."

Banks nodded. "Very good, Mr Dorsey; kindly return, and keep me informed." Dorsey saluted and made for the shrouds as Banks turned to Caulfield. "Take her two points to starboard."

The first lieutenant touched his hat as he gave the order and the ship began to alter course. The yards creaked as the braces kept them in the off shore wind, and soon *Pandora* was heading away from the coastline, gathering up precious sea room should the squadron prove hostile. But there was certainly little to concern them for now; were this to be the full scale invasion that all England feared, the seas would be littered with transports and barges. And even if it did turn out to be an enemy force bent on attacking London, Banks could not believe that Parker and his cronies would be able to maintain control over the average British seaman in the face of such an outrage.

"I can see British colours now, sir." Dorsey was once more at the maintop and his voice brought a modicum of relief to the quarterdeck. "Though they look to be ensigns of the red."

The officers looked to each other in confusion; as an admiral of the blue, any ship under Duncan's command would fly the blue ensign.

"You should be able to see them from the deck any time." Dorsey continued, and sure enough a small forest of masts came into view, followed shortly afterwards by faint, fuzzy outlines, that soon grew into the hard and sharp hulls of warships bearing down on them.

"They're making a signal!" It was fortunate that Dorsey was also in charge of communications. All waited while he rifled through his book, and reported the correct private recognition code for that day.

"Make the reply with our number." Banks muttered to Rose, Dorsey's deputy, then stepped forward and began to examine the ships carefully with his personal glass. It was just possible that they were the escorting force of a convoy, and might not be aware of the chaos they were heading for at the Nore. Were that the case it was his duty to warn them. After several minutes inspection he was still uncertain, and finally lowered his telescope, before bellowing once more to the maintop. "Are you certain of the ensigns?"

"No, sir," Dorsey replied, after a pause. "No, I was awry. They appear to be plain red flags, like what we saw at the Nore."

A sigh swept about the quarterdeck; and Banks and Caulfield exchanged glances. So the problem had spread; it was yet another case of mass mutiny, although this time the ships were actually at sea.

"Ford here thinks he recognises *Lion*, sir - wait, there's another signal." Dorsey's voice cut into their thoughts with an edge that made every man shudder. "They're ordering us to alter course and await a boat."

"I'll be damned if I do!" Banks snapped back. "Take her a further point to starboard and add all the sail she will carry, Mr Caulfield. I want us as far from those traitors as we can be!"

Caulfield touched his hat again, and soon *Pandora* was cutting a cloud of mist with her stem as she powered through the rising waters of the North Sea.

"There's a gun sir!" Dorsey's voice again; and all on the quarterdeck turned to catch the brief cloud of smoke before it was dissolved by the wind. It came from one of the leading ships, but they were still considerably out of range. Presumably it was nothing more than a blank charge to call attention to the signal, although all in *Pandora* had experienced enough British shot in the last twenty four hours to want for more.

Banks thrust his hands deep into his pockets as unreasonable anger welled up inside him. They had been at war with France for over four years, throughout that time other enemies had joined the fight against Great Britain, but to have had to run from their own ships twice in a day was quite intolerable.

Then he felt the welcome sting of spray on his face as *Pandora*'s speed increased further, and his ill temper began to ease. She was a fast ship, and he prided himself in how he handled her; certainly no vessel under the doubtful control of mutineers would be able to catch them, and he could roam the high seas with relative impunity. But even one set up as she was; well commanded and manned, if not by a full crew, at least by men with loyal hearts, even she would need supplies and support from the shore eventually. And he was ordered to rendezvous with Duncan; he might evade this squadron, possibly keep at sea for many weeks, but eventually he must approach a British port again, and once more *Pandora* would have to face the menace of the mutineers.

CHAPTER TWELVE

THE officers met in the great cabin that evening, Banks sitting in the middle of the table with Caulfield and King to either side of him and Fraiser and Newman opposite. They had all dined recently and the decanter of port and sweet biscuits that Dupont had left went untouched.

Banks cleared his throat. "Gentlemen, we have important matters to discuss and, considering the circumstances, I felt it better to call a meeting, so that all would be equally aware of the situation."

King glanced down at the table. Clearly Banks was considering a deviation from normal routine, and wanted to be sure he had the backing of every officer; he might also be trying to protect his own neck in a later enquiry or court martial, if what he was planning went terribly wrong.

"It would appear that the ships we sighted this afternoon are continuing south, to London, or possibly Portsmouth. What happens to them there is not of our concern although, considering our reception and recent departure from the Nore, we have to assume that port is effectively closed to us." There were general nods of agreement as Banks continued.

"The carpenter reports the majority of repairs complete. He was still to carry out some minor finishing to the quarter gallery, but I think we will survive very well with the ship as she is." In fact the major item that needed replacing was his personal privy, but this was not the time to mention such matters.

"As regard to men, we are more than twenty down on compliment, which is a fair number to be adrift. However, what we do have are almost exclusively trained hands; moreover, they have proved themselves loyal – something that cannot be valued too highly in the current climate."

"Sir, the surgeon reports the purser unfit for duty," Caulfield interrupted.

Banks raised an eyebrow. "Anything serious?"

"He declined to say, but felt he should be exchanged at the earliest opportunity."

"Very well; I think Mr Soames' duties, important though they might be, need not concern us for the time being. I am sure a replacement can be found who will stand for him."

King hurriedly scratched his nose as a wicked thought occurred; Soames' position should be easy to fill; there must be cheats and swindlers a plenty in *Pandora*'s crew.

"Has something amused you, Mr King?" the captain asked suddenly.

"No sir." King said, the attention effectively suppressing any remaining humour.

Banks reached for his notes and studied them for a moment before continuing. "We are now approximately twenty seven miles into the North Sea, with a wind in the west that is blowing strong. Without that last point, I would be inclined to return to England, and make contact with the nearest semaphore station. It is conceivable that Admiral Duncan still retains loyal ships at Yarmouth Roads. However, considering our position, and the favourable weather, I intend to continue to the enemy coast and reconnoitre. It is possible that no British ship has been in the vicinity for some while, and I feel that our current situation should be taken advantage of," he sat back from the table and considered them. "So, what think you?"

There was silence for a moment, and then Fraiser raised his eyes.

"As I understand, we were instructed to meet with Admiral Duncan off Yarmouth," he looked to Banks, who nodded briefly. "Clearly conditions have changed somewhat since then."

"For all we know Spithead has risen up once more." Caulfield interrupted. "There might be no Channel, nor North Sea Fleet protecting Britain."

"Indeed," Fraiser continued. "But surely the salient point is that we were instructed to meet with Admiral Duncan. To my mind he is as likely to be at sea as at anchor, and might just as easily be found off the enemy coast. Besides, if we continue to the east it would only need a slight change in the wind to see us back to England, should we deem it necessary."

"And that very change would favour the Dutch; they must be considered a major concern," Newman this time; the marine officer took a scholarly interest in politics, and of all of them, was probably the most up to date with current affairs – an important attribute, and one Banks had considered when asking him to the meeting. "Since the declaration of the Batavian Republic, Holland has been almost as great a danger to us as France. It is only speculation, of course, but there have been numerous independent reports of a French army assembling near Texel; *The Times* ran a piece on it, so we must consider it public knowledge. It appears they have been amassing transports of every description there for some while, and the Dutch fleet are also on hand."

"The Dutch build sound ships and man them with professional seamen," Caulfield commented. "Their entire force might be a good deal smaller than ours, though most are centred in one place. Like as not they would be more than a match for anything Duncan has, even if he were in complete control. With the current state of mutiny..." he shook his head, unable to continue.

"The North Sea Fleet is a relatively new force," Banks continued. "Certainly the ships are not the best, several are captured prizes yet to be completely refitted, and the rest mainly older vessels that are not up to the rigours of foreign service."

"I understand the intention was to reinforce the fleet," Newman again. "Probably one of the reasons we have been assigned to them; who knows, there might be more ships detailed, but with the problems at the Nore and Portsmouth, I dare say the system has been under strain."

"Which brings us back to the point." Banks tapped the table firmly, and looked once more at his notes. "We could continue on this heading and raise the Dutch coast off Zeeland tomorrow. Then continue north, keeping a wary eye on the enemy as we go, finishing at the Texel. Admiral Duncan could be there, or we might meet him on our way. But in any instance we can show the flag, and see what's about. Master, have you any further comments about the area?"

Fraiser shook his head. "Shoal water's always a problem thereabouts, sir. And there are sandbars a plenty at the edge of the Broad Fourteens, but happen we can weather those. I might add that the wind is favourable at present, but will not remain so when we are facing an enemy lee shore. The prevailing winds for that area are from the south west, and there is a strong counter clockwise current, but we cannot count on either."

"*Pandora* has a shallow draft; certainly less than a seventy-four."

"Indeed she does, sir. But I would not be confident of our charts, and the bottom thereabouts is unpredictable."

Banks nodded. "Thank you, Mr Fraiser. Does anyone else wish to add?"

No one caught his eye in the silence. "Well, I have caused enough trouble in the last few days to worry about creating more. Therefore I propose that we do not make for Yarmouth as instructed; instead we continue with our present heading until we raise Holland, and follow the Dutch coastline north. I gauge that the information we obtain will be worth our disappearing for a few days; if not the fault will be mine, gentlemen, I will not ask for any of you to back me; it is a decision I willingly take on my own."

He looked about the room, conscious of mild relief on several faces. "So, let us continue, and see what the morrow brings."

* * * * *

It brought the enemy coast, first sighted as dawn was breaking. *Pandora* had been sailing under topsails alone throughout the night, and as the first sign of a misty headland was reported, King altered course to the northeast, as the other officers joined him on the quarterdeck.

"I'd say we were off Walcheren Island, Fraiser said, as the hand at the deep sea line called nineteen fathoms. "There are banks here about that might not be showing on the chart." He looked up at the wind. "I'd suggest a point further to the north to be the safer."

"Very good, Mr Fraiser," Banks said without hesitation. "Make it so, and I'd like the lookouts doubled, with each man replaced hourly, alternating a bell apart."

It was a sensible precaution when so deep into enemy waters, especially with a wind eager to press them closer. Caulfield gave the orders as the light slowly revealed more about their landfall.

Fraiser was right, a small church and a semaphore station that woke as soon as *Pandora* came into sight, confirmed his dead reckoning, and for the rest of the morning the British ship cruised slowly up the Dutch coast, with the doleful chanting of the leadsman continually checking their depth.

Small craft a plenty could be seen sheltering in the numerous inlets, and were scrupulously noted, although none appeared to be anything other than light coasters, with the occasional larger merchant laid up in ordinary. When the Batavian Republic had been declared, just over two years before, the Dutch fleet had numbered more than thirty line-of-battleships, with at least another forty frigates. But none were to be seen, and *Pandora* continued up the enemy coastline with total freedom.

Noon, with sightings and the start of the new navigational day, also brought the first warning of a change in the weather. The wind, which had held strong and constant, now grew fitful and the glass dropped alarmingly. By the time the hands had returned from their meal the first drops of rain had begun to fall, and as four bells in the afternoon watch struck, a solid layer of heavy cloud was bearing down upon them, reducing visibility and instilling a feeling of impending doom amongst the watch on deck. It was then that the wind returned with a vengeance.

"I'd say we would be wise to stand out, sir." Fraiser warned Banks, as the two stood on the quarterdeck, with watch coats gradually gaining weight in the heavily driven rain. "There's no telling, with the sea bed as it is."

"Very well," Banks bellowed in reply. The conditions were worsening by the moment, and he didn't think they would miss anything in the next few hours.

But he was wrong. Within minutes the masthead reported a sail between them and the land. It was a small ship, off their starboard bow, and the lookouts could have been forgiven for missing it completely, as the blurred image almost merged with the dark coastline that itself could barely be defined against the heavy sky.

Banks studied it through his glass as they crept up through the thick grey afternoon; it was a ship rigged sloop, probably carrying less than twenty guns, but it flew the Batavian flag, and was prey as far as he was concerned. Presumably she had spotted *Pandora* some while ago, and was hoping to find shelter in the shallows; it was a plan that had gone horribly awry for the small craft. The low draft that meant she could sail closer to the shore than a frigate was also a disadvantage, as she had little resistance against the wind which was now driving her hard against her own coast.

He glanced up at the fully reefed topsails, it would be reckless to enlarge the sail area in such a storm, but the enemy were off his starboard bow and he needed to increase speed in order to hold them. Caulfield touched his hat briefly as the order to shake out a reef was given. A swarm of topmen flew up the weather shrouds, and spread along the topsail yards, fumbling with the soaked reefing lines and battling the straining canvas that threatened to knock each from their perilous perch and down into the dark waters where only death awaited them. *Pandora* heeled further to starboard as the wind found the fresh sail and began to creak alarmingly as she dug her forefoot deep into the crusted waves.

"Clear for action, if you please, Mr Caulfield." The increase in sail had done the trick; the sloop was slowly being caught and should soon be in range of *Pandora*'s long nines. The Dutch Navy did not carry carronades: the large calibre lightweight guns that the Royal Navy considered an ideal armament for small craft. This ship would have conventional long guns; it was even possible that she also carried nine pounders, although less in number and her firing platform was bound to be far less stable. Besides, even a sixth rate, never a type known for stout timbers or sturdy bulwarks, boasted a stronger hull than any kindle-wood constructed sloop.

Banks watched the small ship as she gradually came into his field of fire. If he had been in the enemy captain's position he might have considered tacking; it was unlikely that *Pandora* would be as nimble in stays. But then the other commander knew these waters better than he did, and might have reason to keep his course.

The previous casting of the lead had been considerably shallower, although *Pandora* still had several fathoms under her keel. A sudden cold dread ran through his body, "Master!" he shouted to Fraiser, standing less than three feet from, him. "Are there any major hazards in the area?"

Fraiser shook his head. "Nothing charted, sir. The seabed shelves regularly enough though."

Banks nodded; that was consistent with the grey coastline they had been following all day; but still an inner feeling remained, warning him that the enemy might be leading them to disaster.

Caulfield announced the ship cleared for action as the sloop entered *Pandora*'s extreme firing range. Banks peered forward again; this might still be an elaborate trap, or simply that the enemy crew were too inexperienced to manoeuvre in such weather. Then he saw her topsails quiver, and noted with strange relief that the sloop was attempting to turn.

She had chosen to wear; not surprising in the circumstances and also reassuring, as it meant there must be more depth than Banks had expected. Fraiser also noticed the manoeuvre, and collected the speaking trumpet from the binnacle. *Pandora* would follow her round; they would lose some sea room, but the apparent confirmation that there were no major obstacles beneath was worth any delay in the action.

Pandora whipped about in the strong wind, and was just taking up speed once more when it happened. The sloop had also settled on her new heading, although both ships had been swept further inshore. For the sloop, it was slightly too far.

The first sign that she had grounded was the snap of tophamper, as her masts collapsed about her in a tangle. One moment she was a beautiful, lithe creature, battling the elements on equal terms, the next: a waterlogged lump, bestrewn with a snarl of lines, timber and canvas that seemed destined to all but drag her under.

Banks immediately ordered *Pandora* two points to starboard; if it were too shallow for a sloop, they were probably in equal danger, but the British ship beat her way out to sea safely, leaving the stricken enemy immobile in her wake.

Once a reasonable amount of sea room had been won back, *Pandora* wore once more, and returned to the grounded ship. The wind had eased slightly, although the waves were still fringed with a white crust, and spray mingled painfully with the rain. Much of the wreckage of masts and yards had been cut away, and it appeared that the Dutch crew were trying to re-float the vessel. King, peering at them through the deck glass, could make out men on her deck, struggling with the guns, clearly attempting to lever them over the side to lighten the ship. The sloop was still a good mile or more from the shore, which appeared deserted in the gloom of late afternoon.

"We'll pass and wear again, have the red cutter ready and manned." Banks said, gauging the waves professionally. "I'm looking for volunteers, both amongst the boat crew and whoever is to command."

Lewis, one of the master's mates, stepped forward along with King. Banks considered them. "I'll take Mr Lewis first," he said finally. "Though I can't afford to lose either of you. Choose your men from those who offer, and be ready on the larboard side." He turned to King. "We'll drop the larboard cutter, then continue and wear as before. Prepare the starboard cutter with a crew, we might need you yet."

Pandora turned about for the third time, and swept down upon the grounded ship. Backing sails, the cutter was deposited into the water, and soon was heading toward the sloop under oars. King watched its hesitant progress intently, aware that he would be in a similar position shortly. The boat was at an ideal angle, with the stern taking all of the wind and waves square on. Lewis looked entirely soaked, although that hardly distinguished him from any other member of the cutter's crew, or *Pandora*'s come to that. They were equipped with masts and sails, but Lewis had apparently decided oar power to be more predictable, and they certainly seemed to be closing with the sloop, that would soon be a wreck, quickly enough.

The cutter passed by the hull, and came about on the leeward side, gaining what shelter there was. King strained to watch what was happening but the wind was taking *Pandora* on past the scene. Doubtless they would be wearing again shortly: then it would be his turn to take to the water.

The return trip took longer, the cutter being heavily laden, and the men were rowing in the very teeth of the gale. Fraiser delayed the frigate's manoeuvre until the cutter had started back towards them, a group of men lying huddled beneath her gunwales. Lewis was sensibly steering for a position roughly in line with their drop off point, and as *Pandora* resumed her course once more, it was obvious that both men's calculations had been about right.

"Scrambling nets and falls," Banks looked about. "Mr King, are you prepared?"

King touched his hat and was turning to the boat crew that had assembled when a cry went up. The wreck had shifted, and was now bottom up, and turning slowly in the storm. *Pandora's* crew watched in horrified fascination as the hull eventually righted itself, and was momentarily afloat, with one figure clutching valiantly at the remains of the main shrouds. Then she tipped once more and plunged under only to emerge again, empty of life now, and began a slow leisurely roll towards the distant beach.

But there was no time to delay further; the cutter was nearing *Pandora's* hull, and Fraiser ordered sails backed to protect her.

"Abandon the cutter, Mr Lewis," Banks bellowed. It was a shame to lose a perfectly good sea boat, but not worth the risk of life that would be necessary in attempting to save it.

Soon men began to appear; exhausted and half drowned, they were eased over *Pandora's* side by eager hands, and allowed to slump onto the gloriously safe and stable deck where they were scoured warm and dry with rough canvas sailcloth, and given swigs from a bottle of Hollands that Doust had deemed appropriate, and produced from his store.

"Take her out to sea, Mr Fraiser." Banks ordered as soon as the last member of the cutter's crew was safely back in *Pandora*, and their boat had been left to fare in the tossing waves. The captain looked back at the remains of the sloop, now lodged against the beach and all but consumed by the hostile waters that continued to pound it.

Another ship to ship engagement and another victim had fallen to him and *Pandora*. It was a record he should be proud of; certainly he was of his men and the way they had behaved in rescuing the crew of the sloop. He mopped at his forehead with a handkerchief and pressed his damp hat back more firmly on his head. This was not the first time he had experienced the strange feeling of anti-climax at the end of an action. He supposed it was a normal symptom; the rush of excitement that sent men into battle must fall away at some point, leaving that strange emptiness he now experienced. Possibly it was something he would get used to in time, although he knew that a good deal of luck had been involved, and inevitably luck must run out. Certainly the chances of *Pandora* continuing to be successful must dwindle with each fresh encounter.

* * * * *

"Mr King, I do not need to remind you that nothing must be said about the mutiny." Banks' words had been spoken softly but they stayed with King as he and Fraiser prepared to meet with the prisoners in the sickbay. There were two seamen and a midshipman. King had been told that all could understand English, although only the young *Adelborst* seemed willing to speak. Banks and Caulfield were currently interviewing another officer, a *luitenant*, and what appeared to be a soldier, or possibly a marine. King and Fraiser had been detailed to talk with the lower ranks. The storm was dying slowly, and the ship had returned to cruising stations as King entered the sickbay.

"Come to visit our guests?" Manning asked, genially.

"Are they well enough to talk?"

"As far as I am concerned; there are no physical wounds, though I'd chance they have seen enough of the North Sea for a spell." He indicated the three men who were currently sitting companionably on the bunk so recently occupied by Kate's father.

"I present Wilhelm van Leiden: Lieutenant Thomas King and Sailing Master Adam Fraiser." The junior officer rose as King and Fraiser approached, and mumbled the names of his men as they all shook hands.

Van Leiden was roughly the same age, but slightly taller than King. Certainly above average height, with closely cropped fair hair, a tidy chin-tip beard and moustache, fine white teeth and a ready smile. He was dressed, as the others, in new slop clothing, although his bearing and manner singled him out as the natural spokesman. "I wanted to give you thanks for your very brave work," he told King, earnestly, as Manning brought in a wooden bench and the two groups of adversaries sat to face one another. "I have already spoken with the man who sailed the small boat, but I know that all in your ship try hard to save our lives, and we are most in your debt."

King paused, uncertainly. "I am sorry that such a deed was necessary."

Van Leiden smiled in return. "I also; the English and the Dutch are not the expected enemies; not like the French, eh?"

The Dutchman's smile was infectious, and King found himself grinning back.

"It is a shame that all men cannot live in harmony," Fraiser said, stiffly and van Leiden turned to him and nodded, suddenly serious.

"Indeed, sir; it is as much our wish as yours."

King leant forward and brought his hands out wide. "Can we offer you some refreshment?"

Van Leiden shook his head. "Thank you no, we have been well cared for already," he turned to the older seaman on his right, and King noticed a vaguely distant look in the unfocused eyes. "That which your doctor provided proved very acceptable to my *collega*. More would be an *overvloed* – ah... too much." Van Leiden gave a half nod. "You will forgive me; it is some while before I spoke English."

"You do so very well," King replied, adding the *cliché* of so many Englishmen: "I'm afraid I have little knowledge of your language."

"For many years my family traded with your Michaels Brothers company of Harwich. My father is a seller of clocks; I spent many happy *vakantie* days with the owner, Mr William Michaels and his family. They taught me your language, some English popular songs and how to catch and cook the sea bass. That was before..." he waved his hands vaguely.

"Perhaps you would like to send them a message?" Fraiser asked. "I would be glad to have a letter delivered for you."

"Ah, it is not a problem; our families do write with each other most regularly. They are doing well, and looking forward to the day that we can continue to do business, as are we all."

"You write?" Manning asked, amazed.

"It is no difficultly to send letters, even though we are at war. We read your papers as well; as I am sure you do ours."

King stirred uncomfortably in his seat. "Of course, I have read *Le Monitor*," he said. Indeed several of the French news sheets were published in conveniently translated editions, and available in major towns.

Van Leiden beamed again. "Ah, but the French papers are not worth the reading; it is all *fictie* and *onwaarheid*. – I'm sorry, I..."

"We know exactly what you mean," Fraiser assured him and all smiled again, although King, who usually read the officer's edition of *The Times*, wondered how much damage was being caused by the press, especially the lower deck newspapers, such as *The Sun* and *The Star*. Their treatment of the goings on at Spithead and the Nore must make interesting reading for the enemy.

"May I ask," van Leiden continued. "It has been mentioned that we are heading for Dan Helder; what are your intentions for us?"

"You will be exchanged," King said quickly, happy to guide the conversation away.

"Thank you, it is good, but I wonder if we have men to give to you in return."

"Then you will be asked for your word, laddie," Fraiser replied with fatherly authority. "If you agree not to fight or work against Great Britain until such a time that a suitable exchange can be made, your word will suffice."

"I understand, it is a good system."

"It is one that your Admiral de Winter has respected in the past, and it is right that we should continue."

"The *admiraal* is a good man."

"He is a gentleman," King agreed.

Van Leiden responded in mock horror; "Ah, he might not like it when you call him so, but would understand your meaning I am sure. Your *admiraal*, Duncan; he is a good Englishman also."

"And he might not appreciate ye calling him that," Fraiser replied, his accent slightly more evident. "But again, would be grateful fur the sentiment."

"They are both good men," van Leiden smiled. "Let us just say that."

The laughter was general and the drunken seaman came alive suddenly and flopped his arm about his officer's shoulder. "We are all good men!" he said, thickly. Van Leiden smiled at him briefly before turning back to the British officers.

"It is true, we are all good men" he said, his smile slightly faded now. "And yet we must fight."

* * * * *

The storm abated entirely the next day, and the following morning they approached the Dutch coast in bright early sunshine. *Pandora* was cruising a good two miles off the new harbour at Dan Helder, with Texel Island clearly visible in the distance. Deep within, masts of warships could be seen and Banks would not normally have missed such an opportunity. Despite the danger of shallows and enemy fire they could creep quite a bit closer, and make a good assessment of the shipping; valuable information that Duncan would certainly welcome. Even noting the position and size of the inevitable shore batteries would be useful. This was a delicate mission, however; his own men would be landing on enemy soil, right under the eyes and guns of the combined French and Dutch forces. To venture too close under a flag of truce might be considered as taking advantage of the situation; besides, there were to be two midshipmen and a master's mate in the cutter, and all had excellent eyesight.

King had the watch and smiled easily as the other Dutch officers and seamen made their appearance. He greeted van Leiden with a smile and a handshake as the blond Dutchman mounted the quarterdeck steps.

"You are keen to be back with your family, Wilhelm?"

Van Leiden nodded. "Yes, they will probably be worried; it will be good to reassure them. Although I have bad news to give to many; that is not something I like."

"I understand: such things are never easy."

"We are to enter the harbour by small boat, is that correct?"

"Yes, the captain has allocated our remaining cutter."

"You could come closer to the shore, with a white flag your ship would not be harmed, and our *luitenant* is familiar with these waters." He indicated the short, slightly stout officer that was now talking affably with Banks and Caulfield.

"I appreciate that, and know the cutter will be safe."

"You think, perhaps, we would suspect you of the spying?"

"That might be a consideration."

Van Leiden laughed, and slapped King hard on the shoulder. "No, my friend; we do not think you would bend so low. Maybe you send some men with the clever eyes in the boat though, eh? That would be expected, and I would also be looking for *Pandora* to return tomorrow; the best time for *verspieden* is when the sun is in your face and the moon at your back, no?"

Fortunately King was spared the need for reply by the approach of Caulfield, who noticed the humour on van Leiden's face with a look of mild concern. "If you are ready, gentlemen?" he asked, cautiously.

King followed van Leiden down to the gangway port and paused to shake hands with him. "I hope we will meet again in friendlier times," he said. There were further handshakes from other officers and members of the crew and, as the last of the Dutch clambered awkwardly through the port, King had a vague memory of a similar departure.

"Strange exit for an enemy," Lewis said, joining him and mirroring his thoughts. "Richard Parker left us in just the same manner not so very long ago."

"Aye," said King. "An' that was 'midst an atmosphere of threats and intimidation."

"Week or so later we say goodbye to our enemies," Lewis mused. "And there is friendship and camaraderie all about."

King nodded, and gave a brief wave to the cutter that was just setting sail, with a white flag of truce and a courtesy Bavarian tricolour flying to starboard.

"Times like this it is hard to know friend from foe," he said.

CHAPTER THIRTEEN

THE next day Pandora was heading back for England with all speed. Their return to the enemy coast that morning had confirmed all the cartel boat's crew had reported. The main Dutch battle fleet was certainly at anchor there, but it was the vast array of barges and small merchant shipping that caused the greater concern. Clearly preparations were advanced for an invasion; whatever the state of the British fleet, Duncan should be made aware of the danger without delay.

Crossing the Broad Fourteens, the regular sandbar running parallel with the north Dutch coast, Banks glanced up anxiously at the sails. The wind had shifted and was in the north east; ideal for them but equally so for an invasion force; it was vital they made their passage quickly. *Pandora* was set with topsails, topgallants, jibs and staysails, and all fiddle string tight. The strain was evident; the very masts and spars groaned in mild protest as her stem cut into the green, grey sea, sending a fine mist of spray back as far as the quarterdeck and, with a slight heel to larboard, she was a magnificent sight for anyone with the time to notice.

Flint, Jameson and Jenkins were on watch, although little had been called for from them for some while. They sat on the main deck, between two nine pounders, in the lee provided by the starboard gangway, as the ship blasted through the chop.

"Never known him to push her like this," Jenkins commented. Of them all he had been aboard the shortest time, although he was quite correct; the pace was punishing, and could not be maintained for long. "Lesser captains would have piled on the royals," he grunted. "Miserable job for the topmen in this breeze, and there'd be no gain in the 'aving of them."

Flint, who had not been listening carefully, shook his head. "Too strong for royals."

"I didn't say he should set 'em," Jenkins bristled. "I said lesser captains would have."

"More canvas means more speed though, surely?" Jameson peered up at the hard grey sails that appeared to have been sculpted from solid board.

Flint pursed his lips. "Not necessarily. Wind's on our quarter; too much press from aloft, she'll be turned to a hefty heel, and most of the hull'd be pushed under. There'd be a lot more splash, but no gain in knots, an' the masts and lines would be under a deal too much pressure."

"Too much pressure," Jenkins repeated. "That's just what I was saying."

"Times are when the fore t'gallant is set and the ship sails slower." Flint went on, ignoring Jenkins. "See, that's a burying sail; if the wind's not right it can set the bows under and cause more harm than good. Take it in, the helm eases, and your speed goes up."

Jameson nodded wisely; he had been at sea for nigh on three years, but there was still so much to be learnt, and he suspected there always would be.

"Wind falls off, now that's the time for royals," Jenkins added, still trying to regain his position. "Might even keep this speed up, an' with less of a blow."

The call from aloft interrupted their conversation.

"Sail ho, on the starboard bow!"

All eyes went up to the masthead, although few could see Ford as he clutched at the topgallant mast, and peered into the distance. The regular but violent movement the seamen were experiencing on deck was magnified several times by the height of the mast, making his platform describe vast circles in the sky. Ford was a seasoned hand, however, and well used to lookout duty. Despite the speed, the wind, and the wild movement, he had spotted the oncoming ships just as their masts had shown above the horizon.

"What do you make, there?" The captain's voice: this was clearly important, nevertheless Ford could not resist an inward smile. It was his job to report any sighting as soon as it was visible, but the very moment he did, they wanted further information. If he now came up with the size, speed and heading of the ships the officers would probably be satisfied although only thirty seconds before he had been trying to decide if they were indeed ships at all, or just another patch of cloud.

"Looks to be two, me'be three ships," Ford reported cautiously. "An' heading this way." The last point was a total guess, but one backed by many years of experience. With *Pandora's* current speed the sighting might be slower vessels being overhauled, but Ford thought not; the images were clearing by the second; much too fast for anything other than approaching craft. The alternative was that they were stationary, and this seemed unlikely as the royals appeared stiff and in the wind, so a move in their direction seemed the most obvious.

"I have them!" That was Wright on the fore, and Ford drew a slight sigh of relief that the sighting had been confirmed. He stared again. The collection of masts was more clearly defined now, with two together and the third, possibly smaller, but closer. There was also the slightest hint of something else; possibly an unrated vessel; maybe two. The chatter of conversation came up from below, and Ford looked down to see Rose, one of the midshipmen, just starting to leave the maintop beneath him. He had a glass slung over his shoulder, and would doubtless hog all the news and glory from now on. Ford moved to the weather side of the mast as the lad joined him. It was usually Dorsey who was sent aloft: Rose had joined as a volunteer, and had only recently been promoted to midshipman.

"Want me to take a line about you, Mr Rose?" Ford asked. The lad, who was still panting slightly from the climb, shook his head. "No thank'ee, Ford, I'll be safe enough." He wrapped his right arm about the mast, focussed the brass deck glass on the sighting and gave a generous sniff. Ford followed his gaze. The upper sails were in clear view now, with all ships apparently on the same course, which appeared to be to the southeast.

"Course east sou-east," the lad bellowed with absolute certainty.

"You sure of that, Mr Rose?" Ford asked; the lad grinned and shook his head.

"No, but there's two large, one smaller and at least one tiddler; they're sailing as close to the wind as they can make, so it's a fair guess." The seaman nodded; it was a good enough answer, and certainly in line with the usual protocol of masthead lookouts.

Caulfield's voice came from below. "Any sign of colours?"

Rose snorted at Ford. "Colours, he says!" then he bellowed back. "Too far off, sir. We'll know presently."

Sure enough, with *Pandora*'s great pace added to the speed of the approaching squadron, topsails were soon in sight, followed in no time by courses and the occasional glimpse of upper decks.

"They're warships, sure enough," Ford confirmed quietly. "Got a fair deep roach to the courses. Yer see the bottom edge of the lowest sail?"

"I see them," he said doubtfully.

"They're cut high: makes the sail less strong, but the better to avoid catching alight from gunfire on the deck. But that don't tell where they're from."

Rose treated Ford to his worldly look. "They're from the west," he said.

"I meant, what country." Ford was quite content with his lot, and happy to instruct younger men for as long as they were willing to learn. "See the sails are good and dark. Frenchies takes their time in harbours, an' they tend to have fresh white canvas."

"So you'd say they was British?"

"I would, 'though they might be Dutch, an' 'ave been at sea a while," Ford cautioned. "Think about where they're heading."

"Dutch is possible," Rose conceded.

"Mind, if it's a bunch of squareheads we're going to have to do some pretty fancy sailing."

The lad stared for longer this time, before finally bringing the glass down and glaring back at Ford. "It's no good," he said, the frustration obvious in his voice. "There's a perfectly good ensign on the leading ship, an' I can see blue, and white, but not no more: nothing I can safely report."

Ford was about to tell Rose that blue and white were prominent in both British and Batavian flags, but stopped when he saw anxiety in the young man's eyes.

"Give it a moment longer," he said finally. "You'll benefit from it."

"Anything, Mr Rose?" The captain's voice this time, and Rose went to raise the glass once more, but Ford stopped him.

"Not now, a spell longer," he told the young man. "It's all very well guessing the small things; no one's gonna care if the course is a point or two off, but you report that lot as the enemy an' it turns out false, they're gonna thank you for the trouble of clearing for action. An' if it's the other way about..."

Rose lowered the glass and looked down. They were still tearing through the water, but Ford could see the lad take several deep breaths and knew he was composing himself.

It might well have been the brief rest, combined, of course, with the dwindling distance, but when Rose looked again, the ships were properly hull up and he was able to make a complete report.

"British warships in sight, fine on the starboard bow, heading east sou-east. Two liners and what looks like a frigate, sir. Then there's a sloop and possibly something smaller, and a cutter. One of the liners is flying Admiral Duncan's flag, an' they're making what looks like today's private signal."

He brought the glass down, sighed and smiled at Ford. The seaman gave him a toothless grin in return. "Very good, Mr Rose," he said.

* * * * *

They met in the middle of the North Sea, with the wind still blowing strong but having backed to the north. Duncan's flagship, the seventy-four gun *Venerable*, and *Adamant*, lighter at only fifty guns, hove to while the frigate *Circe* bustled importantly about them. Banks ordered his gig away; it was a short passage to the flagship, and he was fortunate that the starboard side, the side reserved for officers, was in the lee. *Venerable* was an elderly ship, some said the oldest seventy-four in service, and her sides had the steep tumblehome usual in line-of-battleships. However the seas were still running high and Banks was not subjected to clambering up the entry steps: a boatswain's chair was lowered down to the boat. Before he manoeuvred himself into the thing, he slipped off his sword and belt, passing them back to the midshipman in the sternsheets. The lift came just before he was truly ready and, snatching the sword back, Banks grabbed on to the line like a child on a swing. He instinctively ducked his head as he was plucked from the tossing boat and swept up and round in a neat arc, before being deposited in an undignified heap on *Venerable*'s upper gun-deck.

With a barked command and the simultaneous slap of palms on muskets a bank of marines snapped to attention and presented arms, while Banks slowly staggered to his feet, trying to free himself from the canvas and line contraption, and make some sense of his sword and belt as he did. A midshipman came forward to assist as a chorus of ear numbing whistles broke out and a line of smartly dressed side boys soberly paid their respects. Banks had just about freed himself when Fairfax, Duncan's flag captain, stepped forward, a grim smile on his haggard face.

"Glad to meet with you, Sir Richard. We'd heard you was a-coming, but didn't expect to find you in the middle of the North Sea."

"I could say very much the same, sir." Banks shook the proffered hand.

"There's no end of stories about *Pandora*'s time at the Nore," he cleared his throat. "Since your rather hurried departure, she hadn't been reported by any of the shore stations. In fact you was starting to take on the trappings of a mystery ship when we left Yarmouth."

Banks wondered if now was the time to explain about the last few day's adventures. Clearly Fairfax had followed his thoughts though, and took charge. "Well, we won't go into that now. May I present Mr Clay, my second lieutenant?"

A younger man stepped forward and Banks shook his hand as Fairfax continued. "The admiral will see you in his quarters. Mr Clay shall show you the way; I'll probably join you later but you understand; there's much ado about the ship at present, and we must be underway immediately. You've no objection?"

"No, no of course not."

"I'll send your gig away; you can return to your ship once we sight land."

The reception party began to break up as Fairfax looked up towards the quarterdeck and raised one finger. Immediately the boatswain's pipes started to wail and ready men began heaving at braces. A signals party ran up a prepared hoist, presumably to *Pandora* while Banks re-affixed his sword and, as Clay led him up the quarterdeck steps and on towards the poop, he had the unusual experience of watching his own ship take to the wind.

Duncan's cabin was plain, dark, and furnished very simply, with serviceable fittings and several solid lines of leather bound books, packed into tightly secured bookshelves. The ship creaked as she gained speed, shifting to a slight heel when the wind drew her sails taught, and Banks felt the very deck beneath his feet flex slightly. He glanced down and noticed the canvas deck covering was damp in several places; clearly *Venerable* was in urgent need of a refit.

"The admiral is with his chaplain, sir." Clay explained. "He will not keep you more than a moment."

Sure enough a small man in clerical cloth entered directly, accompanied by Duncan himself.

But the chaplain could never have been considered undersized; it was Duncan that caused the illusion. Banks turned in time to see the admiral ducking beneath the lintel, his vast frame seemingly out of proportion with the narrow door and frail bulkheads.

"Ah, Sir Richard; good to see you, if an unexpected pleasure," his voice was soft, but with an inner strength that was heightened by a strong Scottish burr. He extended a massive hand that gently encompassed the younger man's, while his look of quiet understanding seemed to stare straight into Banks' very soul. "You won't mind accompanying us in *Venerable* for a spell? I am sure we have much to talk about and time really is not our friend at present."

Banks' reply was slightly mumbled; he had not felt so intimidated by a fellow officer since his first captain had interviewed him as an aspiring midshipman. But then Duncan's presence was the stuff of rumours; when young he had been known as the handsomest lieutenant in the navy; stories were told of crowds following him on land and Banks, who had instinctively dismissed such tattletale, quickly revised his opinion. Even now, in his sixties, the man's bearing, along with his incisive gaze and forthright eyes, gave an indication of the strength of character within. Banks had met with Nelson, but Duncan was of a different mettle. There was nothing of the showman; no vanity, no pretence, no airs. Duncan was clearly born to greatness, but equally clearly he had no interest in the trappings that accompanied such an earthly attribute.

"Mr Clay, I wonder if you would ask Menzie to prepare some refreshment?" The admiral turned back from the lieutenant, who promptly left the room with the chaplain. Duncan indicated a sensible upright chair opposite his desk, and Banks quickly settled himself, finding the hard oak surprisingly comfortable.

"We're not long out from Yarmouth," Duncan told him as he was seated behind the desk. "'though it will be a little while afore we're that way again, I fear. Yarmouth is following the Nore: there is mutiny and dissent where e'er you look. Not a happy situation for anyone."

Banks shifted himself uneasily. "We are somewhat down on compliment in *Pandora*, sir," he said. "I had hoped to supplement my people, as well as exchange a junior officer."

Duncan nodded, "Aye, I had feared as much; took a lot from you at Portsmouth after that regrettable incident, did they not? And there would have been no chance of making up, what with the problems at the Nore." His eyes flashed and his face came alight. "That was a happy escape, I may say; well handled, and none too soon, either."

Banks expressed his thanks. *Pandora* had yet to officially join the North Sea Squadron, and yet it was clear that Duncan had been following her progress.

"There is little worse than sailing with an incomplete crew, Sir Richard. I will be sending a cutter back with news as soon as we sight the Texel and shall include a request for men. If there are loyal hearts to be had, I am sure they will be sent at the earliest opportunity. Tell me, your sailing master, he is not the one to be exchanged?"

"Adam Fraiser?" Banks was surprised. "No, sir."

"He serves you well, then?"

Banks paused, remembering the incident with the French frigate. "Sir," he replied hesitantly. "Mr Fraiser is an excellent seaman, and a first rate navigator."

"But not a fighting man?" Duncan's face revealed a degree of humour that, combined with the unexpected subject, confused Banks.

"No, sir," he said, instinctively choosing his words carefully. "Mr Fraiser has strong views about fighting, but they do not affect his abilities as a sailing master which, I repeat, are most satisfactory."

"I am glad of it." There was definitely an amused twinkle in the admiral's eye, and Banks longed to know more, but the conversation was moving on. "Leave me note of the numbers you require, and I will do all I can to see they are available when times are more favourable. And the junior officer?"

"A purser, no more."

"I cannot help with that from *Venerable*; a bond will be needed, as well as a deal of accounts. But I shall ask when I send for more men. You are well provisioned?"

"We have water for two months, sir."

"That is good; there should be a resolution by then." Duncan smiled suddenly, and it was a pleasant expression. "That, or all will cease to matter!"

The door opened and the steward entered. Without a word he set a small wooden tray containing a pewter coffee pot and china cups upon the desk. Duncan looked his thanks, and stood to pour the coffee as the steward left them. Banks gratefully accepted milk and sugar, although the novelty of being served by his commander in chief was disconcerting.

"You might have met some ships from my squadron already?" The cup that Banks was passed seemed larger than most, and held a good deal of strong coffee.

"Yes sir, a group of liners were spotted off the Essex coast."

Duncan nodded. "And you spoke with them?"

"No, no sir we did not." It was going to be slightly awkward explaining that he had been frightened of closing with his admiral's own ships, but fortunately Duncan understood.

"Rebel vessels: you were right to give them a wide berth. We lost a deal more not twenty four hours ago." He sipped at his coffee, before sitting back and holding Banks with his gaze. "I tell you now, Sir Richard, I had expected this uprising for some while. Indeed my correspondence with the Admiralty goes back to the time that I accepted the North Sea command. British seamen have been poorly used for many years, and we cannot afford to ill treat them further. The settlement at Spithead was fair, though too long in the coming. And it should have ended there; if it had we might be on a better footing to continue this accursed war. As it is, the new disorder at the Nore has gone much too far and made the average Jack no friends in the process; last I heard Master Parker and his committee were threatening to blockade the very city. Such an action could never serve the seaman's cause; indeed it is difficult to see it as anything other than the work of revolutionaries. Frankly I am ashamed that the people have allowed themselves to be hoodwinked so."

"It is a sorry business, sir. Especially when we are in such peril."

Banks felt himself being studied.

"You have looked in at the Texel, I imagine?"

"Yes sir; twice in two days: the last not seven hours ago. On the first occasion we were able to land a cutter at the quay."

"Indeed?" Duncan's eyebrows rose slightly. "How so?"

"After meeting with the squadron I decided it might be safer to divert across the channel," he hurried on, unwilling to emphasise the fact that Duncan's own ships had been the danger. "There we followed the coast of Zealand north until we fell in with a Dutchman; an eighteen gun sloop: the *Gunther*."

"You fought her?"

"We ran her into the shallows, and she was wrecked. Some of her people were collected; two officers and there was a *Luitenant-Kolonel* who was being carried as a passenger, and two ordinary seamen."

"You have them aboard *Pandora* now?"

"No sir, I decided to take them in for exchange as it would give us reason to look in at the enemy."

Duncan frowned. "I would have preferred to have spoken with them myself. Where did you land them, at Walcheren?"

"No sir, we were well past by then. I continued north, and took them into the Helder under a flag of truce."

"I see, and did you discover much?"

"There were a considerable number of transports: we returned earlier this morning but could learn little else as the shore batteries are well sited. But it must be nigh on a hundred."

"And Admiral de Winter's fleet, they are still there?"

"Indeed, sir. We made it nineteen ships, but could not be certain. Topmasts set up and ready to go."

Duncan nodded. "It is what we expected, but good to have it confirmed. Our intelligence puts no less than thirty-five thousand French troops stationed nearby, with some Batavians and possibly others, all under the command of General Hoche."

"A sizeable number, sir; but not enough for England, surely?"

"With command of the Channel, it would suffice." Duncan stroked his chin as he considered the matter. "More troops could be brought across at will; there is a French army at Brest just awaiting such an opportunity. And should London fall there would be little left to oppose them."

Banks was silent: not much could be said in reply to such a statement.

"So, we will have to blockade the Texel, and see they do not sail." Duncan mused. "Although that might not be as straightforward as it appears." He sighed, and some of the life seemed to drain from his face. "I have to tell you that the ships you met, together with the ones we lost so recently, are the bulk of my force."

It was what Banks had suspected. "And they are at the Nore now, sir?"

"Doubtless, but under the supposed command of that fool Parker; the last I heard they were squabbling amongst themselves. The men say they will fight if the Dutch fleet comes out, which is laudable enough. But they will not sail to keep them in; that task must be down to us."

"What ships have we, sir?"

Duncan waved his hand dismissively. "What you see about you; there are no more."

"This is the entire force?"

"I'm afraid so, until my Lords of the Admiralty, and Richard Parker can come to some sort of a resolution."

Four ships, and two of those frigates; were hardly enough to stop a Dutch fleet of over a hundred.

"Keeping them in might be difficult." Banks said, lamely.

"Maybe so, Sir Richard. Difficult, but not impossible, I think."

In fact impossible was exactly the word Banks would have chosen.

"First we must ensure they do not realise how little opposes them. To that end, it is vital that that no ship is allowed out of harbour."

Banks shifted his weight uncomfortably. "We interrogated the prisoners before their exchange, sir. They seemed well aware of the problems at Spithead and the Nore."

"Oh, I do not doubt that; they will know about our predicament, but not the full extent. Were they to realise that just a handful of ships stood between them and success, they would leave harbour straight away, and our small force would be swept aside like so much rubbish. We must convince them that to do so would not be in their best interests. Make them think that as soon as they commit themselves, they will have an entire battle fleet descend upon them."

Banks' brief look of confusion seemed to inspire Duncan, who moved his massive frame forward in his seat.

"If we behave as if we wish for them to sail; tempt them out, as it were, it might have the opposite effect."

"It will be a bold bluff, sir."

"It will, and one we cannot afford to have called, but with such a small force I can see no other option," he sat back. "The French have made several attempts to invade in the past, and all have come to naught. They will be conscious of the risks they are running, and doubtless will remember the results of previous ventures. If we can instil enough doubt into the minds of General Hoche, and Admiral de Winter, we might just hold out long enough for the Admiralty to arrange for loyal ships to join us."

Banks sipped at his coffee as the thoughts began to tumble about his mind. Duncan's enthusiasm was infectious; history was full of similar bluffs that must have seemed as outrageous and unlikely when first put forward. Misrepresentation and trickery were major weapons in the art of war, and by hiding their true force the British would be doing nothing that had not been done a hundred times before, and in almost as many different ways. But of all the tricks played in the past, few, if any, carried quite as much importance as this; the very future of Great Britain, and with it Europe in general, was at stake. For millions of ordinary people it would be the difference between freedom and tyranny. And all was to depend upon one elderly man, his small group of worn out ships, and the deception he was about to attempt.

"We will meet with the other captains this evening," Duncan continued. "Doubtless Admiral Onslow will have an opinion; Richard never was one to hold back. But unless anyone can come up with a workable alternative, I would say we have no choice."

CHAPTER FOURTEEN

IT was a bright morning, with just the barest hint of haze that would soon be burnt off by the sun; one of many such days that were steadily building a hot summer. And now the wind was from the east; perfect for enemy shipping to leave harbour and cross the North Sea. Back once more in *Pandora*, Banks watched as Duncan's flagship beat slowly towards Texel Island and the narrow entrance that formed a gateway to the open water. The sea was relatively calm, although the numerous shallows discoloured the water, making it brown and murky. These were more than simple sandbanks to be spotted and negotiated; rather a complex tangle of banks and channels that seemed specifically designed to lure ships into their grasp. Even *Pandora*, being slightly further out, and with her lesser draft, was taking soundings while Fraiser kept a constant eye her course; what Patterson, Duncan's sailing master, was going through was anyone's guess.

Banks had met with him the previous night in the council of war held on board *Venerable*. He was a wizened, but solid, older man who had the look of one who had seen most things, and survived them all, although the plan that Duncan had put forward seemed likely to alter that.

Vice Admiral Onslow, who currently had *Adamant* after losing his own ship, *Nassau* to the mutineers, had been for putting back and taking shelter at Leith Roads on the River Forth. Duncan, of course would have none of it, blithely saying that to retreat to

Scotland would only invite comment that he was keen to get back to his wife and children in Lundie. The next few hours would tell much, and Duncan might be in line for censure of the worst kind, but it was certain that no one would be able to accuse him of running away.

"Flagship's signalling, sir." Dorsey's voice broke into the captain's thoughts. Sure enough a flurry of bunting had broken out on *Venerable*. "It's to *Circe*, sir. Asking if the final ships are in contact."

Further out to sea the thirty-two gun frigate acknowledged, and began to tack. Turning her back on the shore, royals and topgallants were set as she sped towards the horizon. Banks had spoken with Hackett, her captain, the previous evening. It seemed that his ship was not completely clear of mutineers; indeed parts of her lower deck were actually closed off to officers, and he and his first lieutenant were accustomed to carrying loaded weapons at all times. And yet she was being entrusted with a vital part of Duncan's plan – it was a measure of their desperation.

"They must be getting pretty close by now," Caulfield said, looking back to *Adamant* and *Venerable* who indeed were less than half a mile from their target. As they watched, the ships began to take in sail, and launches were swung out and lowered into the water.

"Less than five fathoms under us now, sir." Fraiser this time; it was expected, but it was also the signal to turn north where *Pandora* was to take up her station.

"Very well, we'll tack, if you please, Mr Fraiser." Banks watched with curiosity as his sailing master automatically touched his hat, and proceeded to bellow out orders. Both were Scots, so he supposed it was quite natural for Duncan to take an interest in the man, although he was by no means the only one aboard. There might be a family connection that Fraiser had not mentioned. Banks smiled to himself. It would be just like Fraiser to say nothing. With so many officers having achieved their rank due to connections, either family, friendship, or professional, he would naturally conceal such an important fact.

Pandora came round after the briefest moment in irons, and slowly began to follow the coastline north, where her role would be to keep watch for any small shipping that might attempt to break out. For Duncan's ruse to be effective the Dutch must truly believe there was a large fleet waiting in ambush just over the horizon.

One small vessel making a return trip would be enough; the arrogant façade that was now being built so carefully would crumble, leaving Britain open to invasion. *Stork,* an eighteen gun sloop, was to take up a similar post to the south, although it was part of Duncan's plan for the two ships to put out to sea, and return at the other's station on a regular basis.

The sun had started to gather heat and warmed the men standing idle on *Pandora*'s decks. A sense of lethargy seeped through the ship; it was as if time had ceased to matter, and everything that needed to be done would be, but in the slowest possible time. Barely three miles away a large and professionally run fleet lay at anchor. Properly handled, the ships could be out of harbour within the hour. Within two, three at the most, the meagre British force would be totally wiped out, and yet Banks felt himself drifting into a stupor as the heat, combined with the excitement of the last two weeks, began to tell. In desperation he took a turn or two along the quarterdeck, but it was too hot for exercise, and before long he found himself gazing languidly at the fort on Texel, while *Pandora* made a slow but stately progress north.

"They've picked up the buoy!" Caulfield again, and sure enough the flagship was now directly over the outer buoy, and was impudently securing herself directly opposite the harbour entrance. Still under tow, *Adamant* came up just behind, and dropped anchor. Then there was more work with the boats; clearly Duncan had ordered springs to the cable, allowing both ships to manoeuvre at will.

Fraiser shook his head in wonder. "They're right slap in the middle of the channel." he said, his navigator's instincts mildly affronted.

Caulfield sauntered up next to him. "Aye, like Horatius at the bridge, nothing can get out, lest they feel our guns, and if sunk, they'll be a danger to shipping for as long as they remain."

"Signal from the flagship," Dorsey's voice cut through their conversation. "Enemy anchored Deep Mars, number unchanged."

"Must be like a red rag to a bull," Fraiser grunted. "Looking in through their front window, they've even tied up to the Hollander's own buoy."

"Aye," Caulfield agreed. "If anything is going to goad them into a fight, it will be that."

Fraiser nodded. "Well then, we must hope that it doesn't." he said.

* * * * *

The Dutch craft, a *botter*, was slightly longer than thirty foot, with a large gaff mainsail, twin raised leeboards set level with the single mast and a highly raked bowsprit. The hull was low and flat; ideal for working in shoal waters, which was just what it was doing, and just what *Pandora* must bring to an end. The wind, still in the east, was in the small boat's favour; if it could evade the British frigate it should have a clear run at the open seas. Lewis, standing on the starboard gangway, studied the craft through his own small glass. Despite the late afternoon sun, the man at the tiller was heavily clad in a full-length coat; three more, similarly dressed, were engaged further forward, and there was a smaller man, possibly a boy, attending to the foresail. All wore large, floppy hats, and seemed to take little notice of *Pandora* as she bore down on them. Lewis guessed they were fishermen, and consequently considered themselves neutral, and he felt slightly embarrassed that they were about to be introduced to the realities of war in such an abrupt manner. The likelihood was strong that the boat intended staying in coastal waters, but while a chance remained that it might head further out to sea, it was their duty to apprehend and, if necessary, destroy.

Pandora was roughly a mile off the coast of Vileland, a small island north of the Texel, heading north-northeast with the wind on her starboard beam and closing fast on the small craft. Although it would not be fast enough; Lewis estimated that on her present course the boat would pass *Pandora*'s bows just short of half a cable ahead. From the forechains a leadsman was monotonously chanting the depth, which was adequate at just over six fathoms, and holding steady. Lewis guessed they were in one of the many small channels that follow the coast. He watched as Donaldson, the gunner, was called up to the quarterdeck to be given instructions, and moved aside for him as he trotted past, on his way to the forecastle. Clearly Banks wanted a couple of shots from the bow chasers to warn them off, although he might equally be planning something more deadly. Sure enough both forward guns, were cleared away, run out and Donaldson himself bent down to the larboard piece.

The brief dull report brought no reaction from the small boat's crew. Lewis guessed it was a blank charge, as there was little recoil and the angle meant it would have been all but impossible to lay the gun to bear directly on the *botter*. Donaldson glanced back at the quarterdeck before moving to the starboard piece and taking a more careful aim. This time the shot was obvious as it skipped a few yards in front of the boat's bows, making all on board start and turn to look at the British frigate in a way that was almost humorous. The man at the tiller waved, and was clearly shouting, although little could be heard above the whine of the wind through *Pandora*'s shrouds, the steady, regular slap of waves against her bows, and the monotonous chant of the leadsman that had already become tiresome. Donaldson fired the larboard gun once more, this time there was a proper recoil; Lewis did not catch the fall of the shot, but assumed it had also fallen wide.

The Dutchman continued, while *Pandora* closed on her. Donaldson moved back to the starboard piece, which was just about ready. From his vantage point Lewis reckoned the gunner would have just one, or maybe two more chances, then the *botter* would be within the arc of *Pandora*'s broadside. Again a shot rang out, and this time a hit was clear and evident. The small boat's larboard side was struck, her leeboard disappearing in a cloud of splinters and dust. She slew round to starboard, the sails flapping wildly, as the men struggled to control the tipping craft. Still *Pandora* bore down, although now it seemed the race had been won. Banks ordered the mizzen backed, and her pace began to slow, as the *botter* completed her involuntary turn and, with her one remaining leeboard down to give a measure of grip, began to slowly beat back towards the coast of Vileland.

Lewis looked back toward the quarterdeck. The captain, apparently satisfied, seemed about to leave the deck, as was King, who would be sharing the next watch, the second dog, with him. They had less than half an hour until then, and the sighting of the *botter* had robbed both of their meal. But there was time enough for a bite of biscuit and cheese, and Lewis was just turning to go below when it happened.

The cries from the leadsman had been droning on continuously; most had been all but ignoring them, but when the depth suddenly dropped from just over six fathoms, to barely four, the seaman in the forechains had the undivided attention of all of the officers and most of the men aboard *Pandora*.

* * * * *

On the quarterdeck Fraiser looked up from where he had been making a small prick in his chart. The channel should have been widening, and gaining depth; he was sure of his positioning having taken bearings from the shore only a few minutes before, and this abrupt decrease in depth was alarming. The next cry came at just over three fathoms; suddenly they had less than six feet of water under their keel and they were close to an enemy shore. Banks looked across.

"A course, master?"

Fraiser shook his head. "We had better stay as we are, sir," he said. "This channel continues for just on a cable, then widens, and the bar to larboard disappears altogether."

The captain nodded. With the wind as it was they would have no problem in turning, but with a bar running alongside they would have to continue, or risk almost certain grounding. The mizzen was still backed, and *Pandora*'s speed was barely enough to allow steerage.

"But the bed's shoaling."

"Aye, sir; it is, and according to the chart it has reason to, though not as severely as we are finding."

"It's a falling tide," Banks prompted, feeling instantly foolish; Fraiser was well aware of the state of the tide, and had gone as far to remind him, not ten minutes ago, when he had insisted on continuing after that *botter*.

The splash from the leadsman came, followed shortly by his call. Three fathoms. The next was the same; then the depth increased slightly, to nigh on four.

"Ready yet, master?"

Fraiser shook his head. There seemed little need to rush, as an early turn would apparently run them aground. The chart might be inaccurate, but it was all they had, and it indicated deeper water ahead, deeper water that would last a good half a mile; better to stay as they were a spell longer.

The next call was still just below the four-fathom mark. Room enough, although the chart gave the depth as almost twice as much. Then it started to shelve.

"By the mark three!" every officer on the quarterdeck held their breath, and Banks felt his fingernails dig into the palms of his hands. He glared at Fraiser, but the Scotsman shook his head. They had still to reach the point where the larboard bar began to decrease; any chart, however poor, was likely to detect shallows more reliably than depressions.

"I'd give it a while longer, sir," Fraiser said, quietly. "The bar is still marked, but starts to fade in less than half a cable."

Banks nodded, although all his instincts urged him to order the helm across and head for open water.

"By the mark three." The waiting was starting to tell. King was fidgeting like a midshipman, and even Caulfield, usually the most solid and composed of men, had started to shift his weight from foot to foot as if eager to break into a dance. Fraiser looked at the enemy coast, so close on their starboard beam. The island of Vileland was passing them by. There was a spell of clear water before the next, Terschelling, he told himself hurriedly. Presumably tidal streams passing between the two landmasses caused the deep water they were seeking. In which case it would be further than the chart showed, at least another cable, possibly more.

"Are we ready to turn yet, master?" The captain appealed to him, like a child might a father, but it was no good; Banks' instincts certainly led him seawards, but Fraiser's just as firmly kept them on their present heading.

"I'd not wish to alter course, sir. I think the depth we seek is further ahead."

"But the chart?"

"The chart shows us to have sufficient water here, sir."

"Do you want us to heave to, launch a boat and take soundings to larboard?"

"The tide is settling fast, sir; I fear we do not have the time."

"Then what do you suggest?"

"I suggest we continue on this heading, sir."

Then there was a pause, and all were silent as the leadsman's cry was heard again.

"By the mark three." They were holding their own, but only just.

Banks was also looking across at the enemy coast. It appeared to be lacking any form of military installation, but there might well be shore batteries concealed in the grass-fringed dunes about the entrance between the two islands. If not, and *Pandora* did run aground, they were likely to be within the range of any field artillery the Dutch chose to bring to bear on them, while they attempted to refloat the ship.

"Take her to larboard, quartermaster," he said suddenly. Fraiser looked up but was silent; Banks turned to him. "Mr Fraiser, I take full responsibility: we are in a dangerous situation, and have to try for deeper water."

"Very good, sir, but I would suggest waiting. Fifty feet might see us out of the channel."

"The channel could have shifted," Banks said determinedly.

The helmsmen were turning the wheel and the afterguard slowly pulled on the braces, keeping the sails drawing in the wind as *Pandora* slowly responded. Soon she had her bows pointed towards the early evening sun, and all seemed to breathe a collective sigh of relief as she began heading away from the enemy coast.

"By the mark four!"

Fraiser nodded to Banks. It appeared as though the captain was right; more than that, he had the moral courage to follow his belief and overrule the advice of others: it was a talent Fraiser respected more than most. But still the manoeuvre went against all his instincts as a sailing master, and he found it hard to fight down a growing inner tension as the ship sailed deeper into the dark seas. Then, with the gentlest of jolts, followed by a slight lurch to starboard, *Pandora* grounded.

* * * * *

The air was filled with a thousand sounds; boatswain's pipes called the hands to obey the flurry of orders that seemed to come from every officer. The thud of horny feet echoed on the deck, and creaking spars and shrieking blocks added to the cacophony, which encouraged panic and made logical thought almost impossible. But order remained; sails were gathered in, and the one remaining cutter was lowered from its davits. The launch was lifted from its cradle, and swung out from tackle attached to the main and forecourse yardarms, while Fraiser diligently took bearings from known locations on the land, and carefully marked their position; probably one of the few accurate points on the entire chart. Banks himself ran to the forecastle, dodging the seamen surprised at seeing one so mighty in what was considered their space. He leant out over the bower anchor, and peered down to where King was manoeuvring the small boat below.

"What bottom have you?"

"Sand, sir," King replied. "We seem well set. I'd say just under half the hull has taken ground. Cribbins here is a sound swimmer; he's volunteered to go over the side to confirm."

Banks shook his head; they would learn little from a visual examination, and he felt that *Pandora* had not suffered any great damage. The main problem was the falling tide.

A fresh squeal of blocks drew his attention to the launch, which was now suspended precariously over the heads of men working in the waist.

"Take a cable from the stern," he shouted down at King. "Mr Caulfield will join you shortly; with luck we might be able to pull her off, and still get out before the tide settles. Otherwise it will have to be the anchor." He moved on, not waiting for a reply, and ducked under the swinging launch as it hung overhead. Once back on the quarterdeck he approached Fraiser.

"Master, you were quite correct, and I am sorry to have doubted you."

Fraiser nodded his head politely, but said nothing.

"I'd be obliged if you would attend to the stores. We've taken at the bows: see everything that can be moved sternwards is shifted without delay. Caulfield approached him, touching his hat.

"The guns, sir?"

Banks shook his head, "I'll not lose the armament at this point, thank you Mr Caulfield."

"We could buoy them and collect later, sir."

"No, not yet," he repeated firmly, and moved back to stare across the taffrail at the nearby coast.

It was slightly less than a mile, and there were an assortment of small dwellings, larger buildings that might be warehouses and what looked like a church. No flags were flying, however, and no masts stood out in the small natural harbour behind the inlet. Were there active shore defences he would doubtless have learnt about them by now, although their predicament would be obvious and it would not take so very long for field pieces to be brought up from the nearby Fort on Texel. He turned back, looking for Fraiser, but finding him gone. Caulfield caught his eye.

"What time is low tide?" he asked the lieutenant.

"Just gone eight, sir."

That was good; a little over two hours, so in slightly more than four they would be in the same position but on a rising tide. Beneath him came the sound of the stern windows being forced open in his quarters. The cutter came into view, and a light line was thrown out to it. In no time a thicker cable was secured to the sternsheets, and the men began to row. He turned back, the launch was now in the water, and being brought round to join the cutter. Every rowing station was double banked in the larger boat's thirty-foot hull, and it had soon joined King's cutter, and taken up the strain.

The sound of casks being heaved about came from below, and there was the gurgle of water; presumably someone had ordered the well to be pumped dry. If it came to it he might have to start some fresh water barrels, but again, that could wait.

He turned back, and thrust his hands deep into his pockets; a vice he had tried to avoid since being repeatedly reprimanded for it when a midshipman. He looked about; everyone was working furiously, intent on saving the ship, for the longer she stayed as she was the more certain her fate would be. No one took any notice of him, and no one spoke. It was one of the privileges of command, he supposed. If he chose he could halt the work; a single, lunatic, order from him would see all plain sail set, anchors dropped, or the ship abandoned. Ultimately he could even have the colours taken down, should he so choose. It was up to him as captain to make decisions, although he was also expected to make the right ones. On the occasions when he failed, a measure of latitude would be extended, as was currently the case. Presumably, should he continue to slip, he would very soon stop being in command, but for now it would seem he had earned the right to have made the present error. It might even be a good sign; past actions had apparently won the men's regard, and he was now drawing on the credit accrued. But that was little consolation; he would have given every ounce of respect he might have amassed to relive the last ten minutes. And he wished, oh how he wished, there was someone with enough pluck, temerity and time to call him a purblind fool.

* * * * *

It had been a hot day, but as the afternoon gave way to evening, and the evening grew into dark night, King began to shiver. He and Lewis were in the cutter, off *Pandora*'s starboard side, taking regular soundings, coordinating their position from bearings taken on the land, and marking the depth on a rough chart that was gradually becoming filled with small dark inky figures. When they found a depth of more than four fathoms, they buoyed it, with a lengths of weighted line tied to pieces of painted wood. Looking back there was already a trail leading away from the stricken ship that should take her to safety and the open sea. But that was depending on two things; getting *Pandora* afloat, and no undiscovered obstructions halting her on the way. They might well have exposed a wide and deep channel, but could they be certain there were no odd promontories or even a rogue rock that would take the frigate's bottom from her? Behind him the crew of the launch were collecting the stream anchor. It was a delicate manoeuvre, securing the half ton lump of iron to tackle in the bows. If released suddenly it could easily flip the boat over, and they would be sunk for certain were some dreadful accident to occur, and the anchor be allowed to drop whilst directly overhead. They were taking the weight now, and King watched as the hull sank several inches in the water, and remained listing to larboard, with the bows far lower than seemed possible.

"By the mark four," the leadsman chanted. King nodded at Lewis, and another small marker was let over the side. Caulfield was in the launch, and was now supervising its passage along the side of *Pandora*, towards her stern. They would continue away from the ship, finally dropping the stream anchor a good hundred and fifty yards nearer the shore. Then, when the tide had risen to the extent that should make the manoeuvre worthwhile, the cable could be wound in. With luck they would gradually pull the ship back off the sand bar. Otherwise, if the anchor slipped, it would have to be raised again, transferred to the launch once more, and taken further back in the hope of finding solid ground before the benefit of the tide was lost. It would be a long and laborious business, although the end result should be a frigate free of the seabed, and ready to return to deep water.

"Three fathoms." The depth was falling, although as King took bearings he and Lewis agreed that they were finding the edge of a channel, rather than a proper reduction in depth. King made yet another mark on the chart, and the leadsman retrieved his fourteen-pound weight and marked line. King glanced at his watch; it was just before ten – roughly four bells in the first watch. The light was almost gone, however; the sun had been swallowed by the beautifully empty North Sea some while ago and every minute the darkness took a firmer hold, making all of their duties that much more difficult.

He heard the first gun but it did not register; they were returning to the ship to take another row of soundings, and King was making certain of their line and angle. They actually saw the result of the next however; a series of splashes that came straight towards them, finally ending fifty feet from *Pandora*'s hull, but less than twenty short of theirs. A moment later the dull report of a cannon reached them.

"Gun fire!" Lewis said, unnecessarily, and King nodded. They looked across to the nearby land; little had changed, although clearly a battery had been established ashore. As they watched a stab of light drew their eyes, and soon another shot landed, this time much further out, at least seventy-five feet off their beam, although the range was almost perfect. If the piece had been directed a few degrees to the left, it would have hit *Pandora* or sunk their small boat.

"Dutch don't intend us finishing the job in peace," Lewis grumbled. King nodded, but felt in his heart that the enemy would not be content just to take pot shots—not when there were other ways to ensure their destruction.

* * * * *

Banks and Newman also heard the gunfire, and from their vantage point on the quarterdeck, they had a far better view.

"I make it three, sir," Newman said cautiously after several shots had been sent hurtling towards them.

"Are you sure that wasn't the first firing again?" Banks asked.

"No, sir, they are taking longer to load than that, although of course I could be wrong."

Yes, he could be wrong; people were wrong. Frequently. Although seldom did they have to pay for their mistakes as Banks was doing now. The launch had almost reached the ideal position, and should be ready to release the anchor shortly. Then, providing the flukes bit into the soft sea bed, they could start to winch *Pandora* free. With luck they should be clear of the area within half an hour, so the prospect of enduring small calibre gunfire from field pieces did not seem so very dreadful.

Caulfield, standing in the bows of the launch, raised his hand, and Banks waved in reply. The boat tipped, then rose up and began to wobble alarmingly, but the anchor was safely deposited over the side, just as another round shot came close enough to drench the boat's crew with sea water. Its job done, the launch withdrew, as the men at the capstan began to wind the cable in. Banks beckoned to Caulfield to return to *Pandora*; if the anchor did slip, they would have to collect it again from the ship; for them to stay where they were was a senseless risk of human life. He watched as the slack was gathered in, before another sight distracted his attention.

Newman heard Banks catch his breath, and looked in the same direction. Something was happening on the shore. Lights could be seen and, by their faint glow, a small crowd were making their way towards the sea. There were masts moving amongst the figures; clearly they were launching boats. A flash from further off; possibly a signal; then an eerie blue light lit two more craft further out on the water. These were under sail as well as oars, and just emerging from the inlet between the two islands. Presumably the Dutch had gathered together enough heavy boats to launch an attack on *Pandora*.

"They must hold a goodly number," Banks said, his tone flat and dry.

"I'd say there were five in total, sir," Newman commented. "Say fifty men in each; mind not all will be seamen."

"Not all will have to be, providing they can reach our stern."

Banks' estimate was nearer to seventy-five per boat, but even going on Newman's figures, *Pandora*'s depleted crew would be outnumbered.

"We can rig stern chasers in the great cabin, sir."

But the captain shook his head; unless *Pandora* could be freed from the sea bed, anything they did would only prolong the agony.

The clack of the capstan's pawls slowed slightly, as the cable rose up from the sea and began to tighten. The gentle trickle of drips told how water was being squeezed from the hemp fibres as the strain increased. There would be no time to retrieve and reset the anchor; the boats would be on them long before they were even half way through. This attempt would have to work. Otherwise *Pandora* would be lost, and every man in her, taken.

CHAPTER FIFTEEN

"BELAY heaving there!" Banks' shout was unexpected and caused every man on the quarterdeck to look to him as he strode across to where the launch and cutter were just arriving alongside *Pandora.*

"Mr Caulfield, I'd be obliged if you would secure your boat to the stern; you also, Mr King." Even the addition of the six oared cutter would make some difference.

With the shore boats heading toward them, time was even more vital. A line secured to an anchor and pulled tight by a capstan was far more mechanically effective than any tow powered by oars. Adding the cutter and the launch to the pull would endanger them and their crews, for no great additional effect, although any increase would mean that much less pressure on the stream. And if the anchor's hold was to shift, *Pandora* would be lost for certain.

The boats were manoeuvred into position, and fresh cables attached at their stern sheets. Banks rejoined Newman and they both peered at the faint smudges of grey that were slowly becoming identifiable as oncoming boats.

"Still a fair way off, sir," the marine said. "But the artillery has ceased."

That was true, so much had been going on that Banks had almost forgotten about the sporadic, but constant, barrage they had been enduring from the shore guns.

"Ready, sir!" Caulfield's voice came from below, and Banks immediately bellowed for the marines and afterguard manning the capstan to continue to wind in the cable.

"Pull! Pull!" Caulfield was setting a staggering pace but the men in the boats were equal to it, and rowed for all they were worth, causing the waters to boil about them as the boats remained stubbornly stationary.

The capstan's pawls clanked once, and once again, then were silent. The strain must now be at the highest; it was just a question of what would shift first, *Pandora*, or the anchor. "Pull! Pull!" King was joining Caulfield now, the two officers all but screaming at the men who were already sweating as they dug deep into the cold waters of the North Sea. Another clank came from the capstan and another, almost grudgingly, after that. Then, with a flurry that made everyone think the line had parted, the cable began to roar in.

Banks looked back at Fraiser. The darkness meant there was no vantage point on shore to take accurate bearings. Either the anchor had lifted, or they were finally free of the sea bed.

"Cease rowing!" Caulfield's voice; Banks glanced down to the boats, to see his second in command waving back at him.

"Ship's free, sir!"

He released a long pent up sigh; *Pandora* had been brought off the bar with no discernible jolt: certainly it had been a far sweeter removal than their arrival. "Very good, get all back on board as soon as you can; we will have company shortly." Banks turned from the boats, there was little need and no time to explain further. "Mr Fraiser, you have Mr King's chart?"

"Indeed sir." Fraiser spread out the notes that Lewis and King had made in front of him.

"Then prepare us for getting underway, if you please."

The boatswain's pipes shrieked; many were still engaged with the boats there was a shortage of hands, but all on board knew the danger they were in, and made for their stations without orders, urging or protest. The launch would have to be hauled in first; men from the capstan went automatically to the yardarm tackle, while King manoeuvred his cutter beneath the quarterdeck davits.

"Abandon the stream," Banks ordered; in truth there was not the time for it to be raised; the cable was released from the messenger, and wormed noisily out through the stern gallery, finally flopping into the sea just as further shots began to rain about them.

"They must have light guns mounted in their bows." Banks shouted at Newman. "Can you return?"

Newman touched his hat. "I can get my men to fire at the flashes, sir. But it is devilishly long range, and we will be giving them the mark."

"So be it; they might be slowed."

At a word from Corporal Jarvis six of the marines formed up along the taffrail and began sniping at the boats while the launch was swayed up. The cutter was next, and was almost empty of men; King had sent the crew aboard *Pandora* as soon as they had attached the falls. It would only need to be winched clear of the water, and *Pandora* could be underway.

"Make sail!" Banks bellowed; courses and topsails were set, and instantly began to fill in the offshore breeze.

"Thank goodness we still have the wind," Banks muttered at Fraiser who nodded; he too had been giving thanks. Slowly the ship took life as the water began to mutter about her stem.

"Starboard four points." Fraiser said in a soft, steady voice. The helm was put over, and *Pandora* began to follow the course that King and Lewis had marked out.

The firing from the quarterdeck had slowed now, as the boats were being left behind, although the Dutch continued to take pot shots at *Pandora* as she eased her way back to deep water. One hit the cutter; a crack was heard, followed by the clatter of splinters, but no one on the quarterdeck paid it any great attention. It was only a ship's boat, and could doubtless be repaired or replaced. Besides, the Dutch craft would be unlikely to carry anything larger than four pounders, and the range was lengthening all the while.

"Very well, Mr Newman," Banks said. Newman touched his hat and Jarvis ordered the marines to cease-fire. The deck was suddenly still, seemingly for the first time since *Pandora* had run aground, so many hours ago. The ship slowly gathered way until she was once more racing through the water, as if glad to be back to her natural element. The wind blew through the shrouds and stays, making the sweetest, most welcome music Banks had ever heard. Fraiser smiled gently at his captain, and Caulfield finally joined them on the quarterdeck. The captain shook his hand. "Gallant effort, Michael," he told him. "My thanks and the thanks of all on board."

"I think you will find it a joint effort, sir." The lieutenant said, slightly more stiffly, and his expression was surprisingly serious. "But I fear I have bad news."

"Really?" Banks could think of little that would diminish the feeling of elation he was currently experiencing.

"Yes, sir. The last shot hit the cutter as we were moving off. Mr King was apparently knocked over the side. Cribbins went as well; he's a strong swimmer, as I think you know."

"And..?" Banks felt the disgrace and shame of the past few hours returning, now to be joined by a sickening dread; if anything had happened to King he would never forgive himself.

Caulfield opened his mouth but said nothing for several seconds.

"Come on, man," the waiting was just too hard to bear. "Tell me what happened!"

"I'm afraid we lost them both, sir."

* * * * *

The wind stayed in the east for three days and nights. For the most part *Pandora* dodged the shallows to the north of Texel island, putting out to sea at pre-arranged times, to return less than four hours later, beating back to the south, to patrol *Stork*'s station for a spell. On most occasions she would have changed her appearance in some subtle way; her ensigns switched from blue, to red, to white, a predominantly marked topsail was replaced, only to be re-set hours later and on one occasion she proudly flew a commodore's pennant. Meanwhile, still anchored in mid channel, *Adamant* and *Venerable* kept up a meaningless conversation with ships just beyond the horizon, ships that, if the Dutch had any knowledge of British signals, were increasing in number and strength on a daily basis. *Circe* was the most energetic of all, constantly departing with orders and requests, only to reappear hours later, carrying answers, and further questions from commanders of various squadrons in the fleet. To anyone on shore the appearance was that of an egotistical enemy, dead set on luring the gullible Dutch within the range of their guns. If the enemy warships anchored just inside the harbour had been from France or Spain, the plan might well have backfired. But the Dutch, even under the banner of the French run Batavian republic, were professional and calculating. Many years of sailing the same waters had given them a natural understanding and respect for the Royal Navy: a professional service, very similar to their own, and one they would never have believed capable of such outrageous deception.

And so with a well run fleet and an army and transports prepared, and with Britain effectively defenceless, the enemy remained in harbour, held back by an old man, two antiquated warships, a couple of small frigates, and some false flags.

Banks remained extremely active throughout; indeed it was his example that kept the crew of *Pandora* as busy as they were. Despite being short-handed, no officer spent as long on the quarterdeck as he did; being there for all of the day, and most of the night. He even took to eating scratch meals while standing next to the binnacle and talking with the officer of the watch. Lewis was brought up to act in King's place as watch keeper, and the other officers did what they could to cover his remaining duties. The continuous activities were such that there was no time for formal meetings; no grand dinners eaten at the gunroom or captain's table, nor any real chance to reflect and consider what had happened and, in Banks' case at least, who ultimately was to blame. But they all missed him, and the captain, whose hurt was heightened by regret and not a little guilt, missed him more than any.

News came on the fourth day, just as the wind had finally shifted. Banks woke from an hour's sleep; one of two he had allowed himself that night, and came up and on to the quarterdeck as dawn broke. They were to the south of the Texel, at the end of the Schulpen Gat and about ten miles from the spot where *Adamant* and *Venerable* were thought to be continuing their vigil, when the flagship's topmasts were first sighted. By six bells in the morning watch they had made contact and were heaving to, with *Circe* and the cutter *Rose* in attendance. Banks was transferred to his gig and prepared to visit his admiral.

Once more the bosun's chair was swung towards him, but this time Banks thought better of it. The sea was relatively calm, and he opted for the gangway port and a more dignified arrival. There was just a momentary feeling of doubt as he reached for the damp steps; to miss his footing now must result in a dunking and then the subsequent interview, spent sitting wet and steaming in front of Duncan, would be far more discomforting than any lift. But he had made up his mind and, in his present mood, cared little if such an indignity should occur. In fact, as he clambered up the side and pulled himself in through the port, he realised that secretly he would almost have welcomed such a public humiliation.

Fairfax and his second lieutenant were there to receive him, and along with Hackett, captain of *Circe*, and Brodie, the lieutenant in command of the cutter *Rose*, Clay led the visitors through to the admiral's quarters.

Duncan was there when they arrived; he looked up from his desk with a smile of genuine pleasure, rising to meet them and shaking each by the hand before indicating the waiting chairs.

"Gentlemen, be seated please, Menzie will bring refreshments presently. You've had a busy time of it?"

None of the commanders were over thirty, and it was hard for them to regard Duncan as anything other than an affable and supportive father. He listened to each report with attention, commenting approvingly on specific points, but not missing a mild censure when everything was not quite as he would have liked. When it was Banks' turn there was respectful silence. Of all of them, he was the only one to have actually engaged with the enemy. Shots had been fired, and taken in return; damage had been done to his ship and... And men had been lost.

The admiral nodded gravely, steepling his hands when Banks had finished; nothing was said for a moment. Then he drew a deep sigh, and his expression lifted just a little.

"It is a sorry tale, Sir Richard. Mr King was a promising officer, and I am sure we all regret his loss. However he died doing his duty and I am certain none of us would deprive him of that, nor wish to go in any other way."

"Sir," Banks persisted. "I feel I was at fault."

"At fault?" Duncan's expression was one of genuine confusion. "Because you ordered your boats to assist the men at the capstan? They ran a risk, to be sure, but it was a risk well justified by all accounts. Better to expose the crews of a cutter and a launch to occasional fire than risk the loss of your ship. And you did everything necessary to get those men back on board; you could hardly have abandoned both launch and cutter: I seem to recall you having lost one boat already," he smiled suddenly. "And a frigate without amphibious abilities is severely restricted in her usefulness."

Banks opened his mouth to say more, but Duncan stopped him.

"Or is it because you overruled the advice of your sailing master? Yes, I thought that could be weighing heavily upon you," he turned to the others. "Perhaps this should be said in private, but I feel we are all experienced officers, and some might benefit by Sir Richard's situation," he looked at the younger man. "You have no objection if we discuss this matter?"

"No sir." Indeed he had not. There was a lifetime's command experience stored up in Duncan's ample body, and recent events had taught Banks just how little he knew.

Duncan considered the officers in front of him. "Tell me is there any one amongst us who has not done the same in such conditions? I'm not necessarily talking about events that caused loss of life, but taking a slight risk, using your intuition, or instinct; something that would be called brave and inspired were it to succeed and rash or foolhardy should it fail." Banks looked about the cabin, and noted the shy smiles and nodding of heads. "Hindsight is a wonderful thing, Sir Richard." Duncan had turned back to him now. "'tis the pity we do not have it prior to an event." The general laughter broke the spell a little, although the admiral's expression remained serious. "You were concerned that Mr Fraiser was being slightly too careful; it is understandable, and one of the attributes of a good sailing master. You, however, are a frigate captain, and not expected to choose the safer course; indeed it is almost against your nature, or should be.

"I might remind all present that you do not command East Indiamen full of wealthy and cosseted civilians; what you have are warships: and warships are crewed by fighting men. You have a duty to risk those ships – and those men. And on occasions they might come to harm; but that is not necessarily your fault. No one regrets the death of Lieutenant King and the seaman more than me, but I would find it far harder to bear if Sir Richard's action had been truly slipshod, or were he wanton in his ways." The smile returned, and he fixed Banks with his eyes. "And were that the case, I doubt that you would be feeling quite so full of remorse."

The admiral drew back. "I tell you to think no more of it, sir. And that, if you like, is an order." His expression was deadly serious again. "I speak to you all, and mean what I say with my heart. An officer who does not concentrate his energies on defeating the enemy is of no use to me, nor the British Navy. You must forget the incident and continue as if it had not occurred; there is not the time for self recrimination or regret: we do not have the luxury of such elegances: do I make myself clear?"

The silence hung about them for several seconds; then Duncan spoke again. "Gentlemen, there is more to say. I have not left the Texel completely unattended. At first light we were joined by *Russell* and *Sans-Pareil*, both seventy-fours, as I think you know. *Russell* brought word from Captain Trollope that things are moving on a pace at the Nore. They have yet to reach a settlement," he added quickly, raising his hand. "But I think we might look for one in the near future. Henry Trollope is more than confidant of his own people; tells me they are doing all they can to make up for what passed before, and he is ready to trust them in battle." Duncan smiled. "Four capital ships and your own assistance will not hold the Dutch, but I feel we can be slightly more confidant than we were a few days back."

His attention switched to Banks. "Sir Richard, I am pleased to tell you that *Russell* has a replacement cutter for you, as well as a draft of twenty-five men. The Admiralty will be making arrangements to replace your purser, although that might take slightly longer. I have also secured a suitable man to serve as second lieutenant; he is currently on my books in *Venerable*, although he has been ashore as his father passed away. Rather than take him back I will lend him to you for a spell. Duty aboard a frigate might wake him a little which, between ourselves, would be no bad thing."

Banks nodded. "Thank you sir, we have been considerably undermanned."

"Then I trust that will make matters a little easier. Now, if we have nothing else to discuss, I propose that you all repair to your ships and return to the Dutch coast without delay. *Venerable* and *Adamant* will remain here for a spell, and probably join you in a day or two," he gave a quick smile. "You can expect us to be wearing different ensigns and, who knows, maybe a change of paint?" There was the murmur of shared laughter as the young men left the great cabin. Duncan watched them go in silence before returning to his seat behind the desk.

Setting himself down, he stroked the long white unpowdered hair back into order. The commanders who had just left had been given the charge of ships, and might even be considered made men, but he found it difficult to think of them as anything other than sons; and as a man whose family was central to him, there could be no finer compliment. Richard Banks was even a knight of the realm, and yet he was going through the anger and self-doubt that so often accompanied loss, in the same way as anyone of his tender age might. In time the feelings would diminish, and, were a similar situation to recur in the future, he should be all the better prepared for it. It would make him a man, even though now he felt nought but a boy. It was a lesson Duncan himself had learned in the past, and should be doing so again now for, in truth, a similar hurt to that which haunted Banks was now plaguing the elderly admiral.

Duncan was no card player, and his strict Presbyterian upbringing had made him one who spoke his mind, and suffered the consequences. He had always been entirely straightforward and direct: too much so, according to Henrietta, his wife, but that made little difference. There had certainly never been any room for subterfuge in his life, and the hoax that he had practised on the Dutch over the last few days was totally against his principles, beliefs and very nature.

Some commanders thought nothing of hoisting false colours; of deceiving the enemy into thinking their ship, or force, was from an entirely different country. There was nothing actually wrong in their actions; in fact the rules of war specifically allowed it, and yet never before had Duncan felt able to use such a ruse himself. But now he had fooled the enemy in just such a way, and was about to do so again. Indeed, he was even prepared to joke about it. Everything had been done with a greater good in mind, and as such might be considered excusable, but the feeling of guilt still stayed with him and, he feared, would do so for the rest of his life.

* * * * *

The launch was returning from *Russell* fully laden. Banks, pacing the quarterdeck, as had been his habit of late, glanced up as the forecastle lookout hailed their own boat.

"Aye aye." That meant there was an officer aboard; probably the replacement for King, although the very idea was repugnant to him. King was dead; he himself, by all accounts, had killed him, and yet the world went on the same, and here was another young man sent to take his place. Another who would risk his life, confidant that his superiors would support him, another who might be killed just as easily as Banks had killed the last. For a moment he recalled Duncan's words; the admiral had made sense: he had spoken sincerely and with the best of motives. But no one else could truly understand the situation, and Banks felt that it was yet another instance of 'the better the advice the harder it be to follow.'

A mild consternation at the gangway port brought him out of his self indulgent melancholy. There was laughter and banter: the hands were chatting and taunting like lads and the atmosphere was suddenly lighter. Drawn by the pull of simple pleasures, Banks continued his forward pacing until he paused by the fife rail. He peered down to the waist where new men were joining the crew. In a navy where few are without history and acquaintances, the newcomers clambered aboard, recognised friends and foes as one, and were rapidly absorbed into the cosmopolitan society of a small warship.

"There's 'Poacher' Elliot!" a lowerdeck hand shouted, loud enough to wake the Dutch. "Ain't seen him since the '*anibale*! You still got that pheasant tattoo, matey?"

Elliot grinned sheepishly, and found cover in his fellows as more streamed aboard to recognition and derision. Banks watched them without a trace of patronage or contempt. In the last few days he had learnt much about being in charge of men. It was one thing to make the decisions and give orders; quite another to live, and live comfortably, with those made by others. The men he watched now would have little control over their destinies, and yet there was a defined hierarchy that was as important to them as any that applied to commissioned officers. More so, in fact, for no rules governed their status; they would attain respect and position through trust and honest endeavour, rather than gimcrack badges and invented ranks.

All his life Banks had been a privileged person; born to govern and licensed to command. Now, for the first time, he was feeling the repercussions of his position and, as he watched the men beneath him shake hands and swap insults, he could not help but be jealous.

But he was forgetting himself; there was an officer on board. He moved away and stood to wait expectantly. The new man would be bound to be presented to him shortly, and he must stop philosophising over the hands and assume the correct attitude of a captain. He had known countless senior officers who had grown old and crusty, and guessed that such a change was now happening to him. Maybe it took a few mistakes to effect the transition. They probably would not give him a frigate next time, even if he asked for one, more likely a stately ship of the line, to sail in the midst of a mighty fleet. A position where order and procedure ruled, and there was none of the raw dash and danger associated with frigates. But he would be a better officer, of that he was certain. Whatever the mistakes he had made in the last day or so, he would learn from them; it was the least he could do for King.

* * * * *

"Lieutenant Timothy, it's a pleasure to see you again, sir!"

Timothy followed the first lieutenant out of the gunroom and looked about. The warrant officer facing him was certainly familiar, and yet he could not quite place him.

"I'm sorry, I..."

"It's Lewis," Caulfield told him. "Masters mate, though he should forereach on us all an' make admiral, rate he's going!"

"We was shipmates in the old *Vigilant*. I was a regular hand then, of course," Lewis added disparagingly.

"Lewis, yes of course, I remember," Timothy's face lit with happy recognition, and he twitched the lapels of the warrant officer's uniform. "Done proud for yourself, I sees, an' well deserved I'm certain."

"Had some help from good men," Lewis mumbled, suddenly remembering exactly who had helped him, and why Timothy was now in *Pandora*.

"Will you take Mr Timothy to meet the captain?" Caulfield asked. "Seein' as you're already acquainted?"

Timothy shook hands with the first lieutenant before moving off with Lewis. "Are there any more from the old barkie aboard?"

Lewis nodded, as he turned to lead the new man towards the quarterdeck. "Some hands, sir. Clem Jenkins, you'll remember him. And Flint, Jameson, Wright; few more probably, can't always recollect."

Timothy understood entirely; old shipmates soon became current, and it was hard to remember sailing with them in any other previous vessel.

"And Tom King," Timothy's voice rose slightly as the recollection came to him. "Did I not hear he was with *Pandora*?"

Lewis glanced down rather awkwardly as he stood aside for Timothy to mount the quarterdeck steps. "Mr King?"

Timothy stopped and beamed down at Lewis. "Yes, I'd heard he'd been made – what joy!"

"I regret, sir, he was killed; you're his replacement."

CHAPTER SIXTEEN

"THOMAS, it is you?"

King woke with a start, and turned awkwardly on the thin straw mattress.

"Will! I'm sorry, I..." It had been a long cold night; King had only managed deep sleep for the last hour or so and his brain felt as bleary as his eyes.

"No, no; it is I who must apologise; coming here and waking you, it is not the right thing to do at all."

King heaved himself up on the bed and threw off the single light blanket. He was fully dressed, and his legs moved stiffly as his stockinged feet reached for the stone floor.

"Give me a moment, and I will be more presentable," he said, as he padded across to where a tin bowl and jug awaited him. Splashing his face with the cold water did much to wash the sleep from him, and as he rubbed himself dry with the canvas towel, he smiled at Wilhelm with genuine pleasure.

"It is good to see you."

"And you also, although the situation is reversed now, no?"

"Indeed; you are the captor, and I your prisoner."

"But it makes no difference. I think we can still be good friends, and perhaps be very rude to each other sometimes, like good friends should be," he smiled beguilingly. "You have no injuries from your encounter with our marine corps?"

King shook his head. "No, I swallowed a good deal of your excellent sea water though."

Van Leiden nodded seriously. "But we will have had it back by now, I am sure. You are comfortable here?"

King looked about the tiny room. Small and stuffy, it grew unbearably hot in the daytime, and cooled to almost freezing at night. The one small sealed window, which was thickly glazed, but without bars, was all that stopped it from being a cell.

"It suits me well enough," he said simply.

"I will try to arrange for better, or at least for anything you might want. Your food is all right, I think?"

"The food is excellent, Wilhelm." As indeed it was; though the diet of fresh, pickled and smoked fish with very few vegetables was starting to become tedious.

"Well, I have spoken to my commander; you will be meeting with him later. He is happy to accept your parole, and agrees that I take you away for a while."

"Away?"

"I am quartered near to this place, and my wife is going to cook for you one evening. You would like to meet my family, perhaps?"

"That would be fine, Wilhelm. If I'm not causing you too much trouble."

"It will be no trouble," van Leiden beamed. "And my family would so much like to meet with one of the men who is trying to kill me; they are looking forward to it also."

King grinned in return, then both men became more serious. "These are dangerous times," he said. "We are aware of your shipping, and the plans for invasion."

"Indeed, but not what we propose to invade, I think. But yes, you are quite correct; dangerous times. And really it is difficult to see a way that matters will not end in much fighting."

* * * * *

The new men made a difference to *Pandora*. They had come straight from Yarmouth, and were volunteers, and volunteers of the finest kind. Not just trained and experienced seamen, they had been caught ashore during the most unpleasant mutiny anyone in the navy could remember. When the news that *Pandora*, known as a loyal ship, was looking for hands the regulating captain had been hard pushed to keep the numbers down to the twenty-five that had been authorised. And so she had benefited from a draft of men whose only wish was to prove their loyalty. It was even possible that some were not truly at liberty, and might even be on the books of other ships currently moored at the Nore, but a lenient attitude had been adopted. There were no delegates or malcontents; just professional seamen who could not care less about political rebellion or revolutionary ideals and only wanted to ply their trade. They would do little good kicking their heels in ships at anchor, while Parker and his cronies continued to prevaricate and annoy; better by far that they should be actively employed in a fighting ship, where their fidelity and enthusiasm could be proven and all memories of discontent and insurrection sweated from them.

Pandora was several miles south of the Texel, heading north-northeast and hugging the coast to starboard as close as the leadsman's chants would allow, when Banks came up on deck. It was morning, the new watch had just been set, and he nodded at Lieutenant Timothy, who touched his hat respectfully in reply. Timothy had been aboard for several days now, and yet Banks was still mildly surprised to see a fresh face. But then *Pandora* was such a closed community; it had been the same when Marine Lieutenant Newman had been appointed to replace the fallen Martin.

"All straight, Mr Timothy?" he asked. Of late he had been inclined to keep his fellow officers at a distance, even Caulfield, probably his closest friend as well as second in command, was suffering from this slightly aloof treatment. But Timothy was new and consequently noticed no change in the captain's manner. He was as experienced in the ways of commanders as he was the sea, and accepted the reserve without comment or surprise.

"Yes sir, we sighted a couple of fishermen at the turn of the watch, but they put about when they sees us, an' it's been quiet ever since."

"Very good." Banks supposed that their recently acquired reputation for firing on any vessel, whatever their size or purpose, had spread, and it was no bad thing, as far as he was concerned; certainly they were saved a lot of trouble. For a moment he even went to voice his opinions on the matter, before pulling himself up short and turning away to pace the quarterdeck in silence.

"Sail ho, sail to the west." Banks stopped his exercise as the masthead shout broke into his thoughts. How often had that call been made in the last few weeks? And most times it had brought more trouble than it had good.

"What do you see there?" Timothy had a good strong voice, Banks noted; something of an attribute in any officer.

"Four ships, at the least; reckon there will be more, sir." The sanguine delivery betrayed much. Clearly the lookout was in no doubt of the squadron's nationality. Coming from the west it was most likely to be British, but the wind was also from that direction, and Banks quickly decided that there was no need to be caught on a lee shore.

"Take her to larboard, Mr Timothy; as close to the wind as she'll hold. Mr Dorsey, I'd be obliged if you would confirm the sighting."

Again Timothy touched his hat, and began bellowing orders as Dorsey collected the deck glass from the binnacle and made for the shrouds. *Pandora* responded, like the well run concern she was, and soon they were heading away from the enemy coast, and roughly in the direction of the sighting.

"I make it seven." Dorsey's voice came down from the masthead when he had settled himself. "British by the looks, though I can't see no colours plain. An they're heading," he paused, considering, "north east, I'd say sir."

So, Texel bound, and likely to be big ships. It sounded as if they were getting proper reinforcements at last. Fraiser had been roused by the change of course, and stood waiting patiently in case Banks should require him. On her present heading they would intercept the new arrivals before they reached the Texel. They might be sent back to their former patrol area, or asked for news, and ordered to accompany them to join Duncan, but it would do no good to just watch the ships pass by.

"We'll keep her as she is, master," he said simply. Banks would normally have been happy to share his train of thought; the man had been an exemplary sailing master since the incident with the French frigate. And long before that, he reminded himself hurriedly, remembering also his own record, and lapsing once more into his thoughts.

"*Prince, Formidable, Caesar, Bedford*," Dorsey slowly began to real off the names of the British ships that were joining them, but the words flowed over Banks, and he was apparently lost to all as he resumed his solitary pacing.

* * * * *

Vice Admiraal Jan Willem de Winter was younger than King had expected, not quite forty, or so he would have estimated, although the thin, receding grey hair gave the illusion of age. And his dress was sombre in the extreme; a dark long coat that, although emblazoned with red and gold on the collar and cuffs, still imparted a look of rather stuffy respectability. But there was no mistaking the eyes; they had a young spark that revealed a lively mind; and they were inspecting King now, as he stood uncertainly to greet his visitor.

"You are the British officer who was pulled from the sea?" the *admiraal* asked shortly, his eyes still searching him for any signs of deception.

"I am, sir." King replied, and he had the strange sensation that he might have to prove his answer in some way.

"What ship are you from?"

King opened his mouth to reply, but the older and equally severely dressed officer on de Winter's right spoke first. "It was the British corvette *Pandora*, sir."

De Winter spun round like a cat, and there was a brief explosion of Dutch that King could follow perfectly well, despite having little knowledge of the language. The sorry officer muttered something apologetic in reply, and took a step back. De Winter turned his attention back to King.

"Forgive, me, sir," he said, a brief smile flashing across his face. "I should have made the time to meet with you the sooner. Perhaps we can sit?"

There was a table and one chair to the side of King's room. De Winter gave a sharp order, and the junior officer fled from the room, returning seconds later with another wooden chair, before leaving once more. The two men sat rather awkwardly opposite each other across the table, although both moved their legs to one side so that they were not quite face-to-face.

The *admiraal* smiled again, and pulled out a small silver case. Snapping it open, he proffered it to King. There was a neat line of dark cigars. They were short, very regular; and perfectly round;

quite unlike the heavier, ovoid examples that King had known in the past.

"Thank you, no, sir."

De Winter nodded, and selected one for himself, lighting it from the single dip that guttered on the table between them.

"I know your ship, and I know too that you were good enough to return my men," he puffed on his cigar thoughtfully. "You also will be exchanged. In fact it might please you to learn that *Adelborst* van Leiden's name will be taken from those who have given their parole, directly upon your release. It is a bargain, no?"

"There's a certain poetic justice," King said, then instantly regretted it, as de Winter's eyebrows dropped suddenly, and King hurried to explain himself. "I mean, it seems a fair exchange, sir."

"Indeed, indeed it is so. Two young men will be free to fight again. A splendid arrangement. Splendid."

King waited while the *admiraal* puffed at his cigar again. Clearly there was more to say; possibly he was having trouble with his English, or maybe it would be a difficult speech in any language.

"So, you will be pleased to return to your ship, and your men? You will take your seaman with you of course."

"Thank you, sir."

"First, perhaps, we should talk a little about the situation we find ourselves in."

King remained silent, uncertain of what was to come.

"We know, of course, that you do not have the fleet you wish for. We see that your admiral is very bold in his moves, and quite clever, sending messages, and disguising his ships, but it is *klaarblijkelijk* – I am sorry, it has become clear that you are trying to fool us."

Still King remained silent, more than that; he was actively trying to set his face into a fixed and neutral expression that would give nothing away.

"We are not so easily deceived, although our friends, the French, they are more so." Again, the sudden smile. "But that is of no matter. It might interest you that we know about your ships, and the state of their efficiency."

King did his best to maintain his poker face, although de Winter did not seem to notice or care.

"Let me give you an example; your HMS *Glatton*; she will be joining you shortly." That was news to King, although he was aware that *Glatton* was attached to the North Sea Fleet. "She has fifty six guns, and is a new ship; new, that is to you: the Royal Navy purchased her from your East India Company just two years ago." He drew on his cigar, considering. "We too have a large fleet of merchant vessels, but we do not wish for them to be warships. The design and the construction is very different. I notice that your *Glatton* is not armed with the conventional gun, but has carronades, the smaller pieces, that throw a heavy shot, but not very well, I think. We too have experimented with these guns, we found that they were not reliable, and we do not use them. Putting them on a merchant ship like *Glatton* might be a good idea because they are lighter, and she will not be so solid, but do not try and call her a warship, because clearly she is not." De Winter paused to smoke again. "There are three other ships in your fleet like *Glatton*; ships that really should be carrying cargo and passengers, and yet you try to use them for fighting your battles. Foolish, Mr King. Foolish in the extreme."

The eyes of the older man fixed King with his stare as he inhaled once more.

"And your own *admiraal*'s ship," de Winter continued. "One of the oldest of her kind in the navy; she is badly needing repairs, yet I can walk to my window and see her sailing outside my harbour in every state of weather. Once more, many of your ships are as she is; out dated, requiring repair, or replacement, and I am expected to be frightened of them? No, I do not think that I am.

"We also appreciate that you have the problem with your men at the harbour. It is understandable; sailors the world over have hard lives, and sometimes they have to tell about it. They ask for money, that is usual, but they also ask for food. It is strange that your country, an island, relies so much on the sailors, and yet you cannot feed them. Do they fight better when they are hungry? Or do they fight at all?"

King was not certain where this was leading, and felt totally out of his depth; supposing de Winter offered him a proposition? He could not speak for his admiral, let alone the British government. Something of this must have been conveyed to de Winter, and he leant forward and addressed King directly.

"I do not want for you to worry; I am telling you this so that you can talk to your *admiraal*, Mr Duncan, is it not? I feel it fair that we should be true with each other." He leaned back and drew briefly at his cigar, then shot the smoke out in a thin jet, and continued in a louder voice. "We do not sail because there are difficulties ashore, not because we are frightened by your ships and the games they play. There is much planning that has been done, and I will not bore you by telling how far we have come, but you will do me the honour of passing my message to Mr Duncan."

King nodded dumbly.

"Tell him we are not fools, and we are not to be fooled, and tell him when the time is right - that is, right for us - then we will be pleased to meet him on our ocean, and fight him and his frail old fleet, should he be misguided enough to require us. Tell him that I do not look forward to that day, but have all confidence in my ships, which are of the very best, and my men, who are true sailors, and not troubled by lack of money or food or poor equipment. We have met with your ships on many occasions in the past, and we have been successful.

"Tell him we know. We know everything, and we are not worried. Should he wish to postpone our fight that would be an honourable course, and one we would fully support. We can talk as men, and trust as officers; it is better than fighting, I think we all must agree on that. You will be able to pass that message to your *admiraal*?"

"I am sure it could be done."

"I would hear your word, and I wish for you to speak to Mr Duncan personally, that way there can be no mistake: it is in both of our interests that we understand each other."

"I give you my word."

"Good. That is good. I hear much about Mr Duncan, and know him to be an honourable man. Perhaps what I say might make him change his mind; and many lives can be saved." Again he drew on his cigar, which was starting to get so small that King wondered how he did not burn his fingers.

"Now, we must make arrangements to get you back to your fleet, and all can be well. I shall speak with the authorities in Paris, so it will not be today—maybe a week, maybe slightly longer. *Adelborst* van Leiden, he is a friend of yours, I think. He has asked for you to be granted a parole, and I see no harm in that. You may go in his care, and I am sure that he will be certain you come to no harm." The smile appeared again, although this time it seemed genuine, and he actually gave a small laugh. "I think if it was that you did escape, he would not be able to be exchanged, and also I could not promote him to *luitenant*, in my ship. It is something I have promised, and which he had been very glad to accept." He pressed the end of the cigar down into the candle's sconce, and smiled again at King.

"Go and eat with van Leiden, he is a fine man, and will be a good friend for you. Enjoy your stay in my country, and have a safe journey back to your ship. Send my compliments to Mr Duncan, and pass on my message. Should we meet again, I trust that we will be allies, and not fight each other." He paused and fixed King with his stare. "It is my sincere hope, and maybe it will be his also?"

* * * * *

"Well some of you will have known him, and some of you won't, but it's pretty clear that John Cribbins, formerly of this ship, has lost his number, so we're going to do the right thing by him, and his family."

Flint looked about at the crowd of faces that considered this with various degrees of interest. It was the second dogwatch, and some were almost ready for sleep, while others would be joining them in four hours or so. It was also the best time for an auction; the end of the day when all were fed and sound and the last grog ration was several hours away, so none could say they were too drunk to notice what they were paying.

"Let's start with the rules; coin, ticket or promissory note, but if the last the goods stay in hold until you gets the means to pay for them. All monies go to Cribbins' wife, if he had one, or woman, if he had one, or family, if he had one. If he was the solitary bastard he appeared, we passes it on to Greenwich, so we alls benefits. Agreed?"

A muttered chorus of concord came from the assembled group, and Flint continued.

"Right, let's cast off. One clasp knife; a true pusser's dirk. British made, and nowhere near sharpened out. What am I bid?"

"A groat." It was Jameson's voice. Jameson had first kitted out several years ago when joining *Vigilant*. He had been a boy then, and a lot of what he had bought had been for a boy, He was likely to be a major buyer that evening.

"Groat it is," Flint looked quizzically at the group. "Any advances?"

"Got to be worth a tanner."

"Make it a shilling."

"'alf a crown!" Jameson's voice again, firm and determined, and for a moment there was silence.

"Half crown I'm takin'..." Flint held the knife a little longer, although, in truth it was a generous price and he was happy for it to go to the lad. His eyes flickered briefly about. "Bought!"

Jameson felt inside his shirt for his purse and dug out a silver coin, which he tossed across to his friend, who threw the knife back in exchange. He examined it; bone handle with a good-sized fid for splicing, and a single blade that came out easily. He ran his thumb along the edge; it was even and sharp, although the end had been purposefully blunted to comply with the regulations. There was a copper ring set into the handle; he could thread a line through that and wear it about his neck and look every inch a topman. He clutched the purchase in his hand, more than pleased with himself, as Flint continued.

"Razor, strop and metal mirror, wrapped in a canvas housewife." He held the thing aloft, glancing over to Jameson, who smiled but shook his head. There were no other takers.

"Come on, good turtle handle to it, and the blade's fresh as a daisy."

"I'll give a cartwheel!" Jenkins voice rolled out.

"A penny, he says!" and there was general laughter.

"It's a fair bid," Jenkins turned on the mocking crowd. "Anyone want to offer more, they're welcome."

"Yes, but you got to pay!" Greenway reminded him, arousing further mirth.

"I'll pay when we gets finished, like Flint said."

There was a pause while everyone digested this. "I think you might be owing Cribbins a touch already." Flint reminded him delicately.

"All debts cancelled by death," Jenkins said empathetically. "It's the law."

"That's only if *you* dies!" Greenway again and again there was laughter, as well as several cries of 'pay up or peg out'!"

Flint looked about the group. "I'm aback here," he said. "Anyone know what the drill is?"

"He owes the money, fair and square." A voice came from the side. "Give it to 'is wida, that's the right way."

"He's dead," Jenkins insisted. "All bets off: all debts paid."

A cacophony of argument and discussion broke out, with Jenkins shouting louder than most. Flint looked about uncomfortably; there were petty officers a plenty in the crowd, one would have to put a stop to things soon, or else an officer might turn up. It was an established right for a crew to barter for a dead shipmate's possessions, but no one liked uproar, and it wasn't the best of starts for the new draft.

"Come on, come on, let's have some light here," he said; they paused, and looked to him expectantly. "As I sees it, Jenkins might still owe the money, but that don't stop him buying a razor."

"But how's he gonna pay?" someone called out.

"Straight, 'is money's all spent, everyone knows that."

"All right," Jenkins said defiantly. "Tells you what I'll do; I'll toss him, double or quits!"

"Toss him double or quits?" Greenway was appalled. "But he's dead!"

"If he's dead, and I can still owe him money, then he aught to be able to gamble," Jenkins turned to Flint. "'e was keen enough on it when 'e were alive."

"Are you serious?"

"Aye, and I'll play it straight, which is more than that lousy bastard ever did for me."

"Come now," Flint was bitterly regretting having started the auction. "It don't do to speak ill; he ain't with us no more; show some respect."

"Sounds to me like dead men get all the privileges round here," Jenkins grumbled.

"Fine, we'll do it," Flint said, and reached for Jameson's half crown. "I'll toss this in the air, Jenkins calls. If he wins, he owes nothing, otherwise it's double – and we're only doing it the once," he added quickly. "You're all going to witness?"

The crowd nodded, very satisfied with the evening's proceedings. This was far better entertainment thn a boring auction. There was silence as Flint placed the coin on top of his clenched fist, then a muffled growl as he flipped it in the air with his thumb.

"Heads!" Jenkins called, as the coin reached the zenith, before falling noisily to the deck, and rolling to a stop. Jenkins bent down, and was silent for a moment. Then he spoke. "It's heads," he said.

* * * * *

The house where van Leiden took him a few days later was outside the fort. Set in a small street of similar dwellings, it was low, with a large ground floor and a smaller upper level set deep into the long pent roof. A neat square front garden held a selection of immature vegetables and a ragged white goat, tied to a post. Van Leiden took King past the latter quickly, explaining that she was a fine animal but did not care much for men or strangers in particular and, seeing that King was both, he should be most careful. The front door was narrow and low, forcing King to duck down as if entering a midshipmen's berth, but when he straightened up he found the room inside to be spacious with a generously high ceiling. The girl that van Leiden embraced was very pretty; she wore a neat long cotton dress and her fair hair was tied back behind a red headscarf. She turned to him with a pleasant, but slightly wary look, and extended her hand.

"This is Thomas, the dreadful Englishman I told you so much about: Anna, my wife."

Her touch was warm and friendly, although King could not help but notice how rough her pale hand was. "You were very kind with my husband, I am grateful."

"He has more than repaid the debt," King replied awkwardly, before a scream erupted from the far end of the room. King jumped as a small animal burst through the back door and charged straight at van Leiden, knocking him backwards in a blur of flailing arms and legs.

"Joseph, Joseph, *zich houden!*" the boy continued to fight, although he soon noticed King's presence, and slowed a little. "Do not be so bad for our guest!" Now curiosity had the better of him, and the child stopped, hand held high, in the act of pounding his father, and considered King with a sidelong glance. King had been dressed in slop shirt and trousers when the Dutch had collected him from the sea. Now a prisoner, he was required to wear uniform at all times, so they had found a British senior captain's jacket for him. It fitted him tolerably well, although King had felt uncomfortable wearing it from the start, and was doubly so now.

"This is a very important English officer. He is in the Navy, as I am." The child continued to stare at him. "You will say hello, perhaps?" van Leiden looked up at King. "We are teaching English, French and German, although it can be hard, he tends to get them confused."

"How old are you, Joseph?"

The boy looked at him, but made no attempt to reply.

"He is eight." It was another voice, a woman, slightly older than Anna but very similar in looks, had entered the room unnoticed.

"Ah, this is Joseph's aunt, Juliana. She lives with us and helps her sister care for me," van Leiden assumed an air of self importance. "I need to be looked after very carefully."

"He is a lazy pig," Juliana added evenly. "My sister only tolerates him because she was raised on a farm." She looked at King in a very direct manner that he found quite disconcerting. "So, you are the Englishman. I am pleased to meet you; we have lamb tonight in your honour, and that is good."

"Come," van Leiden reached out for King's arm, and lead him gently towards the back of the house. "We will sit in the garden and maybe drink some beer, and you can tell us all about your dreadful country. We have heard much from our newspapers: the many troubles you have and how you are all starving; you can inform us more. Then we will eat."

* * * * *

"Blimey, it's a woman." Jack Dusty looked up from the ledger and peered through the gloom of the steward's room almost unable, and certainly unwilling, to believe his eyes.

"A mark for observation," she swept into the small space, automatically touching three of the surfaces as she did. Studying her fingertips, she pulled a wry face before switching her attention back to the elderly man sitting on a stool in front of her. "Worse than that, I am a woman, and I am in charge."

"I'm sorry, ma'am..." In fact, the clerk was also confused and not a little cross. With Mr Soames incapacitated, as he had been for a considerable time now, the work of the purser had naturally fallen on him. The ship's accounts were not in perfect order to begin with; he had tried to make sense of them, but knew in his heart he had not improved matters, and now it appeared he would have to admit the fact to this female.

"That's right," she insisted. "I have been sent to sort out the accounts for HMS *Pandora* in lieu of your Mr Soames, until a more permanent replacement can be found."

"But, a woman; I never expected..." Just what the clerk did expect was not clear or ever revealed, although apparently it was not what stood in front of him.

Her eyes narrowed, and even in the poor light he knew he was being examined. "It is not totally unheard of, or so I believe."

"No sir, ma'am." Then he remembered himself and clambered off his stool. "No, you are most welcome, I am sure."

"I suppose they call you Jack Dusty?" she asked, almost absent mindedly. It was the traditional name associated with his duties.

"That they do, ma'am."

"And would you want me to call you so?"

"I'm sorry, I..."

"I mean, do you wish to continue to be known as Jack Dusty, or would you have your own title back? I have no preference either way, 'though it has always seemed a strange rule for a man to inherit a job, and lose his name in the process."

"Jack Dusty will do fine, thank you, ma'am." He appreciated her consideration but actually was rather proud of the title.

"Now then, I need to see your journals. I understand Mr Soames is not in a position to explain matters, indeed he is to be returned to England at the first opportunity, so you will have to go through them with me. Shall we start with your day book?"

The clerk turned to the ledger on the desk in front of him.

"I was just attending to that when you came in, ma'am," he said, indicating the large fat volume that lay open on the counter. "Mr Soames had not made a complete entry for some time, just stuck these notes in the pages. I have been trying to set things right, but could not make head nor tail of some."

The woman looked over his shoulder, and picked up one of the small pieces of paper. It had a brief scribble and some numbers that could mean stock in, or stock out.

"Well, you can tell nothing from that; we will have to carry out a complete survey, and continue from there."

"A survey?"

"You do carry out surveys?"

The man looked at her blankly.

"Well, I shall not be held responsible for Mr Soames and his lax practices. As far as I am concerned I take over from this day, and we will need to know exactly what the ship holds. Later we can go back and see how much was paid, and some sort of valuation can be achieved."

"I can call the stewards, an' the holders, if you wish ma'am; 'though some might be at rest. We work a three watch system."

"Do you?" She eyed him carefully. "When all the ship runs to only two watches? I find that strange."

"Mr Soames preferred it."

"I dare say he did, but I do not." She sighed and rested her hands upon her hips. "Perhaps you had better assemble everyone, and I will address them together; that might be easier."

"Very good, ma'am." Jack Dusty bustled out, leaving the woman to look about her. The room was kept well enough, although it could use a decent clean, but first she had to get the accounts straight. A half open sack of flour was next to Jack Dusty's stool. She peered inside, and then closed it properly. There were plenty of things that needed tightening up, and doubtless she would have to introduce a few new practices, but she was very used to that; in fact she relished the challenge. And it was good to be back in a ship again. A sound came from the entrance, and she looked up expecting to see the stewards, but was only mildly surprised when Manning entered.

He stood in the half-light, a cautious smile upon his face. "Hello, Kate," he said.

CHAPTER SEVENTEEN

"I just didn't expect to see you back on board Pandora."

"No," she smiled at him. "Well why would you? I was out of your life, or so you thought."

"It wasn't what I wanted."

Her finger tapped playfully at his nose. "Nor I."

He found his face had set into a permanent smile as his eyes followed her about the small room.

"So, how did you get to be our new pusser?"

"Well I'm not, not officially, that is. My father has taken a turn for the worst, I'm afraid. The injury healed well enough; when they examined him at St Bartholomew's they felt there was little to add. The fracture was curing and you had relieved him of the pressure. However it seems that harm had been done and he was continuing to deteriorate: deteriorate in other ways..."

Manning's smile faded. "His mind?"

"Yes, I'm afraid he has been admitted to the Bethlem." She hurried on quickly not looking at him, "It is a very good hospital in the City of London and it specialises in those suffering from lunacy."

"I know," he said. "I am sorry."

"No, don't be, you did what you could and, to put it bluntly, he isn't dead. And it would do little good for me to sit a-watching him, and so I am here."

He looked at her quizzically: it seemed a poor explanation.

"While trying to settle my father's business affairs, I met with one of his former partners; he represents a major victualler. It seems your Mr Soames has been rather amiss with his returns, and they were starting to have doubts about him. Johnson, my father's associate and I, have worked together in the past. He introduced me to a member of the Victualling Board and said I was the very person to untangle a mess. They spoke to the Admiralty, who dithered about a bit as those in authority are inclined to, but I usually get what I want and before I knew I was being sent off on the next available ship."

"But we are at war: you are a woman..." his voice trailed away as the familiar foolishness that Kate seemed to evoke took him over.

"Yes, Mr Manning, I am aware of both those facts, but find them of little relevance." She began to flurry about the room, rearranging lines of bottles and generally putting all she could into a different order. "There are hundreds - thousands of women at sea, and not just officer's wives and passengers; quite a few are serving now before the mast, 'though the Navy would rather it were not known. And as for being at war, if I am acting as a purser I feel I am perfectly safe, lest I consume too much of what Mr Soames acquired, that is. Should we see action I am sure a place could be found for me in the cockpit." Her eyes suddenly found his. "We go well together, Robert; and this is where I belong."

"I'm glad," he said.

"Well let's see how things turn out, shall we? Who knows, if I take to it, I might even apply for the bond, and you will have me for permanent."

"And do you think you will?"

"Take to the work? Really Mr Manning, you hardly give a girl a chance. I have met but Jack Dusty to date, and he has failed to impress. I requested that he bring the stewards and holders back here for me to address, and where is he?"

"Explaining why they will be answering to a woman, I would chance."

"Well they will be, and tardiness will not help their position any; that is certain."

There was a pause as both eyed each other.

"I thought you had gone with the captain," he said, feeling instantly foolish once more, but she was gentle with him.

"I know you did, and I know why, but it was not the case, nor never would it be."

"It is good to see you again."

"Likewise you," she smiled at him again and a strange hunger grew in his chest as she continued. "As I said, I usually get what I want."

* * * * *

King had dined several more times at the van Leiden household; on each occasion he had become more comfortable and at ease amongst the family. It was a feeling he had not known for many years. The child, Joseph, soon passed through his initial shyness to view this strange and exotic officer as something between an object of wonder and a punching bag. The food was good, a different meal on every occasion, although they had the same basic ingredients of fish, lamb, smoked or otherwise, and cheese. And on most nights there had been a strange porridge for dessert; oats boiled in milk, probably goat's, and served with what had tasted like preserved cranberries. It was all miles away from lobscouse, sauerkraut and the duff and suet puddings he was used to, but none the worst for that. King's young appetite soon adjusted; so much so that, when walking back with Wilhelm on the last night before his return, he felt positively sleek. The food, the warmth and comfort of a family, and the strange detachment from war, even though he was still a prisoner—it had all had been quite overwhelming. He felt as if he had been sucked up into a different world; one where items that were previously considered important suddenly ceased to matter. It was a world where people led ordinary lives, and lived in rooms that were larger than cupboards, and did extraordinary things like bringing up children, and sleeping in warm, dry beds, and for more than a few hours at a time. It was a world he could become accustomed to if he allowed himself.

And there had been Juliana.

It was a subject King had felt unable to bring up until that last moment; after, in fact, he had said goodbye to her for what he was sure would be the last time.

"What of her husband?" he asked.

"He died about two years ago," van Leiden replied, as they walked slowly through the empty nighttime streets. "It was the war, you know."

King said nothing; there was little that could be added to such a blunt statement. From the first evening Juliana had taken control of the kitchen, and it was soon established that they would both wash up the dishes at the end of the meal. It had been an important time for King and, he suspected, for Juliana. They had talked as friends and, as friends, come to know each other well, although he had always been careful to steer their conversations away from her late husband. The joke had been that clearing up in the van Leiden household took longer than cooking, but no one seemed acutely bothered, and King had always returned to the late night coffee and Wilhelm and Anna with a mixture of regret and fulfilment. These were certainly novel surroundings; as a prisoner in a foreign land there could be fewer more so. He told himself that, after some time at sea, any available woman would be bound to take his fancy, and the only one doubly so. And he supposed now that there was irony in the reason she was available, which would also seem to rule out any possibility of their friendship developing further.

"I have spoken with my commander," van Leiden continued, seemingly unaware that King's carefully hoarded question had been more than casual interest. "He is happy for me to return with you."

"Excellent, you will take me out to sea?"

"Indeed, it is the first time I was on the water, since my release; maybe I have forgotten how to sail?"

"Maybe you have; you should ensure there are a number of other officers in the boat with you to be certain."

"With the sharp eyes do you mean?" he gave a wicked smile. "Yes that is a very good idea; one that I must adopt."

They were nearing the fort now, and a uniformed guard emerged from his post ready to challenge them.

"So, when I call for you on the morrow; you will be ready, no?"

King nodded. "I will be ready."

"You have my address if you should wish to write to me, and I will contact you also."

"That would be good, Will; I'd like that."

"Maybe you should write to Juliana as well." Even in the darkness he could detect a faint look of amusement on the Dutchman's face. "She is happy in our house, I think, though it must become boring looking after another family when you have had thoughts for your own."

"I would like to write," he paused, uncertain in the warm summer night. "But her husband, I thought, as I am an English officer..."

"Oh, she thinks the same of the English as we all do: you are nice enough people in your way, just misguided, both in your politics and your food. There is nothing she would like more than a letter from you once in a while. It will make her feel superior, and I am sure she will write back, and teach you the error of your ways."

"But her husband?"

"You need not write to him: he will not reply."

"I know that, you imbecile!" The sentry, who had been lounging by the gate, suddenly became alert and considered them both suspiciously. King lowered his voice and whispered urgently at his grinning friend.

"She's hardly likely to want letters from me, I am from the same country that killed him!"

"But it was the French," his smiled had faded now. "When our home was overrun there were many, such as him, who did not want the rule from another land. Several small battles were fought, and Dirk was killed. It was unfortunate: he and I did not agree on many matters, but I know he would not have enjoyed living under another government. Some say that to die for an ideal is a good thing; I am not so sure, but in his case it was right. For Juliana it is sad of course, but they had not been together long, and I am certain she would appreciate your friendship."

King nodded silently in the darkness. "And I her's."

"But now we must sleep, and I call for you at *middag*."

"Thanks, Will; for all you have done."

"Oh I have liked getting to know you better; maybe I have a different idea of the English now."

"And I the Dutch."

"It has been excellent for us both, but you must remember that not everyone in my country is as good as I am."

* * * * *

"I say, the mutiny's over." Newman was staring at the newspaper, and looked up at Fraiser as he entered the gunroom.

"Over, do you say?"

"Collapsed some while ago; complete stand down; mind it's *The Times*, so there is bound to be bias."

"Last I hears the delegates were all for blockading London."

"Belike they did. It says that sea trade to the capital city is now able to continue," Newman shook his head. "Blockading London, what mischief!"

"Och, that might have been their undoing; with the country at war any who take such a step in favour of their selves wouldna retain the public's heart."

"Aye, the mob is fickle, sure enough."

"With bairns to be fed they maybe have the right. But good news, none the less; good news for all."

"Not for those who took part."

"The ringleaders, d'you mean?" Fraiser handed his jacket to Crowley and seated himself at the table.

"I think they called themselves delegates, but no, I wasn't just thinking of them."

"Ah, the men in the ships?"

Newman nodded. "Aye, anyone serving in a vessel that flew the red flag is liable to a charge."

"But they canna hang all the seamen, it would be worse than the mutiny itself, an' no purpose would be served."

The marine set the paper down. "Well it ain't a problem I'd like to solve. Oh and we have post, by the way. But I fear there is nothing for you."

"No matter; that would be the new arrivals, then?"

"Yes, the battleships that joined us yesterday." Newman pushed the coffee pot towards Fraiser. "They brought post, provisions and a successor to Soames."

"Ah, well he will be very welcome, I'm certain." Fraiser poured a measure of coffee into a cup. "It might be the fault of his illness, but he were slipping badly towards the end; the scran they've been serving of late has been less than appetising."

"Well, let's hope things start to improve."

"Aye, I'd rather not have another like Mr Soames." Fraiser said firmly as he raised his cup.

Newman returned to his newspaper and smiled to himself. "Oh, I think you will find his replacement to be different enough," he said.

* * * * *

There was no wind, and King and van Leiden sat next to each other in the stern sheets of the cutter without speaking. The stroke oar, who was dressed as any other seaman except his hair was well cut and his face impeccably shaven, was keeping a careful eye on King as the small boat left the harbour and pulled steadily toward the three warships that stood watch in the open seas beyond.

King was staring at them, partly to avoid the eyes of the Dutch seaman, and partly because two of the ships were unfamiliar. They were both seventy-fours; apparently the North Sea Fleet had received support, and these heavy war horses had come to add force to Duncan's blockade. The other stood out as a craft built for speed and daring; she was a light frigate, and one he knew well.

"New ships?" van Leiden asked.

"No, they are part of our fleet," he said dismissively. "A very small part – it is a very large fleet."

"So you have seen them before?"

"Oh yes," King found it surprisingly easy to lie to his friend.

"Then you must have very good eyes; five British ships arrived only yesterday, and these are two of them. I know you cannot view the sea from your quarters. Maybe you can see through stone walls?"

King nodded seriously. "The English have many talents," he said.

They were drawing nearer to *Pandora* now, although the two liners had also closed with them. Van Leiden muttered an order, and one of the seamen stood up in the small boat and held the large white flag out in the still afternoon sunshine. King could see Banks on the quarterdeck, and next to him Fraiser and Caulfield. And there was Dorsey as well. He felt the need to wave or cry out, but he was an officer, and could not give in to such behaviour. Cribbins, in the bows, had no such inhibitions however, and began to bellow at his shipmates as they crowded the forecastle.

"Boat ahoy!"

"Aye aye!" van Leiden shouted back, giving King a sidelong grin as he did. The boat drew nearer, until it bumped against the hull just below the starboard gangway port. There was no man rope rigged, King turned to look at his friend, who gave him an off hand salute. He smiled, nodded, then reached for the nearest ledge and pulled himself upward. Fortunately *Pandora* had a pronounced tumblehome, and he was soon past the slippery steps, and reaching for the side of the port. Someone grabbed his arm, and he was surprised to see Caulfield beaming down as he dragged him aboard. Then his hand was being heartily shaken; it was Fraiser, who was saying something he could hear, but not understand. Lewis slapped him on the back, and shouted in his ear, but again he missed the exact words. Cribbins had boarded after him, and was being greeted by seamen on the gangway. King looked down to the small boat that had already pulled away, and was returning to harbour. Van Leiden was still in the stern, looking straight ahead. King's gaze rose to the harbour and the buildings he had grown to know so well: he could see the fort and the spire from the church that was at the end of the road, the road where van Leiden lived, lived with his family, and Juliana. He tore himself away; the commotion was still carrying on about him, although now he seemed able to make out actual words, and give halting replies. His hand was still being shaken; Manning this time, and what looked like Katharine Black standing next to him, but of course that was impossible. Then he saw Banks.

Standing almost alone on the quarterdeck, the captain seemed far older, and more dignified than he remembered; or was it just the contrast between his steady reserve and these lunatics who were trying to burst his eardrums? He broke away, and began to walk towards him, as the cheering slowly died down to almost nothing. Banks smiled, and held out his hand.

"Welcome aboard, Mr King," he said softly. "It is good to have you back."

"It is good to be back, sir." he replied. "Thank you."

* * * * *

Cribbins had been lecturing long and hard and for most of the afternoon, but that evening on the berth deck he seemed more than willing to continue. Sitting on a sea chest with a blackjack in one hand he gave forth to the assembled company, taking questions whenever possible and ignoring the dry comments that were becoming more frequent as he exploited his position to the full. The trials and dangers of being a prisoner of war were combined, oddly, with the benefits; of which there seemed to be a surprising number and variety. The other men, though initially pleased to see him, soon remembered his type and though most listened with the interest of those who receive singularly little social stimulation, they became increasingly ready with a barrack, or smart rejoiner, whenever the opportunity presented.

Now, with the evening meal digested, and the four o'clock rum fully spent, the novelty of speaking with one they had believed dead was gone and they were starting to become bored by him and his stories.

"So I say, I'm sick of fish; tells them straight I did. Sick of fish and sick of the ways they cooks it; some of which weren't natural. Give me good British beef, I said. And a fair spread of British onions to go with it."

The pause was slightly too long, before someone felt obliged to ask the obvious question.

"Well, it weren't beef," Cribbins replied. "That was for sure; it were mutton, and good enough, if you've not tasted the stuff for a year or two."

But as far as interest was concerned, he had reached the bottom of the barrel, and Cribbins became aware of several conversations starting up amongst his audience.

"So tells me then," he said, speaking in a rallying tone as he tacked. "What's been afoot in *Pandy* whilst I were adrift?"

There was another pause, before Greenway finally stumped up.

"We've had a few more joining us: several liners, and we gets a regular cutter and transports from home."

"Aye," another added. "No shortage of news, nor mail come to that. And we're pretty well victualled."

"Never better since 'er Ladyship took control." Greenway again.

"Her Ladyship?" Cribbins asked.

"Aye, th' bint we collected from that merchant earlier in the year. She's back now, standing in for the pusser."

"I remembers," Cribbins mused. "A comely looker: an' no longer a passenger, so fair game, eh? I'm partial to a bit of female company."

"You've told us," Flint said bluntly. "But you don't want to go messing with this one."

"She's fixed with the Surgeon's Mate, right enough," Greenway confirmed. "But even if she weren't; we never had such good victuals, not since she joined. Sent a whole load back she did; first two transports took as much away as they brought. Don't know how she managed it, but what we're getting' now is top grub; all fresh an' lovely, it is."

"An' she has a fair hand in surgery. Fixed me leg up proper," Piper told them. "Split right down it were, but her an' Mr Manning spliced it like good uns. You want to see the scar?"

"You've shown us the scar," Jenkins cut in. "But Piper's right, a fair face, a good hand with the food, and she can sort you up when you're crook; there ain't many women I'd want aboard, but this one can stay as long as she wants."

"Her and your Rosie, eh Jenkins?" Cribbins asked, a wicked grin on his face.

"What's my Rosie got to do with it?"

"Still planning on seeing her when you gets in?"

"Planning that, an' a wedding an' all, if that's any o' your concern."

"If I gets in afore you, it might well be my concern. *And* I've got the coin; come to that I got yours an' all!"

There was an awkward silence, which no one felt inclined to break.

"Actually, we settled that while you was away." Flint said eventually.

"Settled?" Cribbins had been enjoying being the centre of attention once more, and was clearly surprised. "How so, when I was rotting in some Dutch prison?"

"Well that's just it, we didn't know you was in a prison, we thought you was dead."

"An' we settled it," Jenkins said urgently. "Like Flint said. Once an' for all, so there would be no going back."

"'fraid you've lost me there, boys."

"We tossed for your debt," Flint explained. "Jenkins agreed to pay you double if he lost an', if he won, you'd be square."

"Double or quits? I'd never take a gamble like that!"

"No? I seems to recall you doing that very thing not three months back," Flint said evenly. "It seemed a reasonable enough answer to the tangle."

"So Jenkins here tossed?"

"I tossed," Flint said.

"An' let me guess," Cribbins looked cynical. "He won?"

"Straight up," Flint confirmed. "It were legal, right an' in front of everyone." He turned to look at the sea of faces. "Any here not happy with the way we did it?"

Cribbins' eyes swept about the group of shaking heads, and he began to grow angry. "Well, it's good to know this is a tight ship; that the men you serve with will look after you, even when you've been captured by the enemy."

"We thought you was dead." Jenkins reminded him.

"All the worse for that: rob a body, why not? Even though it be a shipmate."

"Now there's no cause for that," Flint cut in. "Like it or not, we was protecting your interests. If Jenkins 'ad lost, you'd have earned double, for your family, I mean."

"I ain't got no family, and it appears I ain't got no friends, neither."

There was an awkward pause; no one knew exactly what to say, although it was clear that Cribbins did not have the sympathy he expected.

"'mazin' what happens when a man goes off for a spell; strange what you discover 'bout your friends an' shipmates."

"Sounds like being dead ain't all it's cracked up to be," Jenkins said, dryly.

Cribbins turned on him: "An' you can keep it stoppered; I didn't agree to no double or quits; far as I'm concerned, you still owes me, and I'm looking forward to collecting."

"Now back up, there," Flint again. "Like I said, we fixed it fair and square. Jenkins don't owe you nothing, and you'd better forget about it from now on."

"That's right," Greenway confirmed.

"We all saw it," another added.

"Well I think it stinks rotten, and I'm not happy. Not happy one bit."

Again there was a pause, and again the sympathy was definitely against Cribbins.

Jameson, watching, hated to interrupt when men were talking. But the sight of Cribbins, who had certainly been through a bad time and now seemed totally let down by his mates, was too much for him and he summoned up the power of speech.

"If it will make you feel better," he started, and was horrified to notice every eye fall upon him. "I'll help you out."

"You?" Cribbins looked both surprised and disgusted in equal measure. "You're not but a lad, 'spite what it might say on the books. How can you help?"

Jameson felt suddenly foolish; Cribbins was right, this was out of his league and not of his concern. "Well, I was thinking," he paused, uncertain how to go on, yet very aware that the entire group was waiting upon his every word. "If it makes any difference... I could let you have your knife back for half a crown."

* * * * *

The dinner in the great cabin was as lavish as any Banks had hosted in *Pandora*. It was a joint celebration; welcoming King back from death, and a send off for Timothy, who would be returning to *Venerable* the next day. Banks felt slightly guilty about the last point; a commission in a frigate was every young officer's dream, and to be given such a posting, only to have it snatched away after so very brief a period, must be galling. The more so when *Venerable*'s current dilapidated condition was remembered. *Pandora* might stay with the North Sea Fleet for a number of years, or she could be despatched to any of the world's seas or oceans; maybe rejoin Jervis with the Mediterranean Squadron, or be sent off on an independent cruise to snap up privateers and enemy merchants. That way led to excitement and danger: prestige, prize money and promotion. But *Venerable* would be lucky ever to sail beyond home waters and, even if she maintained her present role, a substantial and time-consuming refit would be needed. Were he retained, as junior lieutenant Timothy could expect to be employed in all the mundane tasks of shipboard life. He might slowly mount the ship's internal promotion ladder as his betters retired, exchanged, or died, and in five, ten, maybe fifteen years he could expect to be a first lieutenant, although it would be to a different commander, as Duncan, and probably his successor, would have gone years before. Luck and a following wind might see him retire a commander, but without that he was heading for an undistinguished career, and one that might so easily have changed if his time with *Pandora* had been longer.

On the morning of the meal Banks had gone over the arrangements for the final time with Dupont; he was particularly concerned that the event went well and he knew that the questions he asked, and often repeated, were starting to annoy his steward. There was no doubt he was becoming a bit of an old woman; nit-picking points that the young, devil-may-care, mischief maker he had been would have simply ignored or trusted to luck. But when three o'clock came, and the first of his guests started to file into the coach, he felt he had done all he could, and that knowledge enabled him to enjoy the next few hours in a way that the lad who had begun the commission would have found impossible.

"Gentlemen, help yourself to a drink, if you please," he shook hands with Caulfield and Doust who both took a small glass, and Newman who politely declined. A moment's small talk, then he turned to meet King, who was looking especially smart; somehow he must have managed to get hold of a fresh uniform. And there was Fraiser, oddly relaxed and with a genial smile on his face. As Banks shook his hand he realised how much they all meant to him; more than just his officers; they had become friends. In the past he had always assumed such a thing to be impossible between a commander and his men but now he readily accepted that they were as much to him as any family. Timothy was next and looking slightly awkward; Banks did all he could to put him at ease, pressing a second glass of Madeira into his hand as soon as he could, and laughing heartily whenever possible.

And here was Manning, newly promoted: cause for another celebration, although he was aware that the gunroom had already feted the event. And Katharine; Katharine was on Manning's arm, but looking as desirable as ever. Banks had only met with her a couple of times since she had come back on board, and on each occasion it had been strictly business. She was there to audit and correct the ship's accounts and stores, not to be impressed by his achievements, his position, and certainly, as he had previously discovered, him.

And she was doing a splendid job; splendid. The food had improved; and he told himself he was pleased to see her now. Pleased that she had so clearly found a friend in Manning, and delighted that there was to be some female company to enliven the afternoon. As a person he had gone through so many changes since they had first sighted the Dutch coast and, if he was just a little sorry that she had so politely spurned his advances, then that was simply one more subtle adjustment for him to make.

They sat at the long table which had been fully extended to cover almost the entire length of the great cabin, with Banks at the head and the officers gradually descending in rank until it ended with Dorsey and Rose, the youngest midshipman on board, at the foot. Each took their place, self consciously looking to their neighbours and fingering the silver cutlery, little knowing the amount of brick dust and spit that Dupont and his assistants had used to create such a mirror finish. Then the air was filled with the smell of a robust onion soup as a tureen was brought in, and soon there was silence other than muttered comments and the clink of metal on china.

When nearly all the courses had been served, most had at least three glasses of wine inside them, and sudden bouts of laughter had started at the midshipmen's end of the table and gradually worked their way up, it became the merry occasion that Banks had so wanted. Cheese and fruit were served, and it was time for toasts; Banks tapped his knife against his glass and looked pointedly at Rose, the junior at the table. The lad, just recovering from a story Dorsey had been relating about a sheep, pulled himself up to his duty and, red faced and slightly stumbling, toasted the King. The gentlemen stood, but remained slightly bent to avoid the deckhead as they drank, then relaxed into their seats once more.

"We're sorry to be losing you, Mr Timothy." Banks said in the pause that followed.

"And I shall be sad to go, sir. But pleased for the reason, of course," he beamed at King who was seated next to him. "Still, I am also glad to return to *Venerable*."

Banks nodded, it was polite of the young man to be so loyal to his ship.

"You'll stay in touch, I trust," Newman, though an abstainer, was slurring his words ever so slightly, and his face was a credible shade of red. "It would be good to hear the gossip from the admiral's table, what?"

"'tis rare that he confides in me," Timothy said when the laughter had died. "But be sure, you will be informed." There was a slight gap, which Timothy felt obliged to fill. "In truth, it is the admiral that attracts me," he continued, a trifle awkwardly. Dorsey, who was just in the process of sipping some wine, choked and apparently took some in through his nose, an act that clearly amused Rose, although it was pointedly ignored by the others.

"Pray, tell us more, Mr Timothy." Fraiser said, with unusual attention.

Timothy held his hands wide. "He is an inspiration to be with. In the brief time I have spent under his command there is so much I have learnt."

"Indeed he is a fine officer, and an excellent seaman." Fraiser again, but he was watching the young lieutenant keenly.

"Yes; yes to both." Timothy went on. "But as a leader, a commander; I have never met the like, nor never expect to do so again."

The company digested this for a second before Caulfield cleared his throat.

"We were under Jervis, you know," he said rather stiffly. "Fine man, you could go a long way and not have a better leader."

"Aye, and Nelson has much to offer." King added. "He was with us at St Vincent; some of our number briefly served in his ship."

"The Mediterranean Fleet is certainly a prime command," Banks added. "And Admiral Jervis a man worthy of it."

"Duncan was offered the Med. Squadron." Timothy said quickly.

"Really?" Banks lowered his knife in the act of peeling an apple. "I had no idea."

"Oh yes. But he turned it down," The lieutenant continued. "His physicians told him to avoid hot climates, unless he wanted a relapse; you know that the fever nearly killed him when he was serving under Admiral Kepple? He recommended Admiral Jervis

– or Lord St Vincent, as I suppose we should start to call him, in his stead."

"Then, indeed, it must be good to serve with such a man," King said. "Though his deeds have not been notable."

Timothy nodded. "He might never have commanded a fleet in battle, although he has been in attendance, and completed some notable shore actions. But it is his strength of character that comes across; any man can teach you to splice, or navigate, Admiral Duncan has something far more valuable."

"You must tell us," Banks said, after the pause, and indeed he was fascinated.

"Well, you might take the recent unrest. We had trouble aboard *Venerable*, as did most ships, I fear." There was a hushed nodding of heads and a few whispered comments. "Captain Hotham was also bothered in *Adamant* and suffered an uprising; Duncan got to hear of it, and had himself rowed across to meet the disturbance head on. I followed him to the ship, and in truth I would rather have been boarding a Frenchman." He paused and his eyes fell to the table as he remembered. "The men were up in anger; ready to fight; eager, like before an action." The officers nodded; they knew the signs. "And the lieutenants, midshipmen, master's mates, they were all together on the quarterdeck, swords drawn, and blood as high as any. The marines had been called, bayonets were fixed and both sides ready for mischief: all was to erupt." He looked up suddenly. "And Duncan walked between them, cool as you could wish. He bade the officers to put by their swords, stood the marines down, and looked at the men like they were just so many folk who had happened to pass by, and he smiled as he spoke to them.

"But when he did it was in a mighty voice that seemed to cover the entire ship; it was like a father talking to his sons. He had a presence and standing that I have never before encountered; called them 'his lads', in fact, and said how he had looked after their interests, which was true, they all knew that. Then he explained that, if he were to continue to do so, he must maintain his authority, and he was not going to give that up easily. Then he asked them straight; 'is there any man here who disputes my right to command?'."

"No one spoke, and I thought he had done enough, then this fellow steps forward. Well, he was no lightweight, and 'twere clear the men would listen to him. It was a bad moment; and one that could have grown far worse; but Admiral Duncan was equal to it. He steps forward and reaches out to the man. I thought he was going to shake hands, but he just gets hold of his shirt, pulls him toward, and lifts him straight up."

Timothy looked around him, noticing he had the undivided attention of all at the table, as well as the stewards and the marine servants standing behind. "Picks him off the deck, no word of a lie, then he carries him to the starboard rail, and swings him over. 'Here is the man who would deprive me of the command of my fleet', he bellows, and I reckon all at anchor would have heard him. He turns to the ship's company and says; 'will any of you follow him, should I let go?'"

There was a smattering of laughter from the table, although all were impressed by the tale.

"So something that could have ended in carnage did so in mirth. There was a shout from one of the seamen: 'give a cheer for Old Adam!', and suddenly the troubles were gone and forgotten." A collective sigh spread about the table as Timothy continued. "I might remind you that *Adamant* was the only battleship to stay with Duncan and *Venerable* when the mutiny spread."

Banks cleared his throat. "Well said, Mr Timothy; the admiral is certainly a worthy man, and lucky to have one such as yourself under his command. But it still does not alter the fact that you will be missed."

"Thank you, sir, and I have valued my time in *Pandora*, for sure she is a different vessel to *Venerable* which is inclined to show her age, as you might be aware. But even with a worn out ship, and the backwater of stations, I would prefer to see the war out with Duncan than any other commander."

"And it does you credit," Fraiser said simply.

"Besides," Caulfield added. "The Dutch fleet might sail at any time, and we at last have the ships to meet them. Who knows, it could be that the North Sea is not the remote posting that all might think."

CHAPTER EIGHTEEN

KATE had made the uniform, but not from scratch; she had taken some of the panels and facings from two of King's old jackets, and combined them with further cloth and several buttons from one that Caulfield had donated. King had been getting decidedly scruffy of late, and she had offered to sort him out, after a uniform she made for Manning had been so much admired. The end result was not perfect; it appeared best in low light, as some of the colours did not match exactly, but it had already served a purpose at the captain's gathering, and now, as King and Banks were being rowed across to *Venerable*, it was doing so again.

The air was still, and it was a long pull; King always felt mildly guilty on such occasions as the eyes of the rowers naturally fell on him, sitting opposite them in the sternsheets, and doing precisely nothing while they sweated away. *Pandora* had been running low on some surgical supplies, which *Venerable* was able to provide, so the journey would have two uses. The second was far more important to King than a couple of cases of portable soup and some potions.

His initial inclination had been to say nothing of the meeting with de Winter. This came from a mixture of adolescent reserve and slight embarrassment as to the nature of their conversation, and the message he had agreed to convey. Besides, it was hardly customary for junior lieutenants to request to talk privately with their admiral. But then he had given his word, and recent experi-

235

ence had taught him that no good came from holding information back; perhaps if he had been a little more forthcoming when Crowley had approached him, the unpleasantness at Spithead might have been avoided. And so he had spoken to Banks shortly after rejoining the ship, and formally requested an interview with his commander in chief as soon as time allowed.

The captain, who had already read his written report, took his request seriously; for a British officer to have spent any time with an enemy commander was consequential in itself, and if he had a personal message to convey, one that he felt could not be sent by the usual means, then so be it. Unfortunately Duncan's time was limited, and further additions to the fleet meant that *Venerable* and *Pandora* seemed fated to be on different stations, so it was only now, several weeks after King had been released by the Dutch, that an appointment could be kept.

King had never met Duncan, although the admiral's reputation was well known throughout the fleet. He seemed to enjoy universal respect; stories that circulated about his exploits were probably greatly exaggerated, but there would be enough truth in them to mark him as a man of note, and King was looking forward to the meeting with nervous anticipation.

They were finally nearing *Venerable* now, and King noted the fresh, heavy paint on her prow, clearly covering a good deal of plaster filler. The ship itself seemed to squat lower in the water than was usual; possibly due to her outdated design, although there might be other, more sinister reasons.

"Boat ahoy!"

The coxswain looked toward Banks and replied with a hearty "*Pandora!*" to signify Banks' presence.

The sea was as calm as the weather and they mounted the starboard entry steps without incident. King was pulling himself through the gangway port as his captain acknowledged the customary compliments due to him, and they both turned and saluted the quarterdeck. Fairfax was there to meet them, but it was Lieutenant Timothy who led the way aft to the great cabin where Duncan would be waiting.

"Happy to be back?" King asked as they followed him through the ship.

"Aye, 'tis good to be at the heart of things once more."

"Beats life on a frigate, then?"

Timothy grinned and whispered, "more headroom," before announcing himself to the marine sentry, and taking them into the great cabin.

* * * * *

"Kind of you to spare me the time, gentlemen," Duncan said when they were seated, and King had had all his expectations confirmed. "I must apologise for not being available earlier; there were other matters in the fleet that rather took my attention. I'm afraid it is one of the perils of a command close to government; they cannot leave us be."

Banks sipped at his coffee. "How are things ashore, sir?"

"You know of course that Parker is hanged?" he asked bluntly.

"Yes, sir; I read the report. At the end of June, was it not?"

The admiral nodded. "From the fo'csle of *Sandwich*, his late ship. There was never any chance of reprieve," Duncan looked up suddenly, and King was struck by his clear eyes and direct gaze. "Were you also aware that he had been an officer?"

"No sir, that is news indeed."

"Served as a midshipman, a masters mate, and even acted as lieutenant for a while." The older man sat back. "Strange to reflect; he had a strong ability to organize, and the men liked and respected him well enough. And no lack of courage, though terribly misplaced, of course."

"Of course. But properly channelled..."

"Indeed. But I have more news" Duncan said. "And I regret it is in a similar vein. Your late fellow, Scales, is it not?"

Both officers nodded.

"He is also to hang, although in his case there might be clemency; that has been rather the habit of late, and I don't say that it is a bad one."

"I was not called."

"No, Sir Richard, at the time when his court martial was being prepared *Pandora's* position was not certain. But there was your written report, and witnesses enough to see it through. The fact that the marine made a good recovery will work in his favour no doubt."

"A sorry business, nonetheless." Banks said after another pause.

"Indeed, but one, like all that has happened of late, that we must put behind us. I will not say the men had cause, and certainly do not agree with the behaviour and temperament of those at the Nore, but there is a fairer system now and, I gather, the people are keen to make up for what has gone before. That is an important point, gentlemen: one we should remember in the days to come."

He looked at the two young officers in front of him, and smiled benignly.

"And it seems Mr King has been in contact with the enemy; spoke with Admiral de Winter himself, or so I hear."

"Indeed sir, I had one interview with him, and spent some time on Texel."

"I have your report; it makes interesting and valuable reading; you are to be congratulated; very astute observations."

"Thank you, sir."

"But I surmise there was more?" his eyes flicked across to Banks for a moment. "Something you were not able to put into your despatch?"

"It was the detail; the content of my conversation, sir." King felt suddenly awkward; he had asked for this meeting, and yet how could he tell his commander in chief that the enemy were well aware of the dilapidated condition of his fleet? "It might not be to your liking, but I gave my word," he added, rather feebly.

Duncan nodded. "Then you must honour it, my boy. And be assured that I will not judge you by what is said. Make it accurate; I would hear my opponent's words, and shall not consider them to be your own."

King drew breath. "Admiral de Winter seemed well aware of the problems we had encountered at Spithead and the Nore," that was no surprise; Duncan acknowledged the fact with barely a nod. "And he was quite disparaging about the type and condition of our ships, sir. He said that several have been converted from merchants, and in the main are outdated and in need of refit. He went on to point out that the Dutch fleet is not large but well maintained. The main bulk of it is at anchor in the Mars Deep; he has the cream of his seamen and they have not recently been in mutiny. In brief, he feels we are no match for him, and he is anxious to avoid bloodshed."

"And does he suggest we stand back and watch whilst he escorts a fleet bent on invasion?"

"I think he was hoping for a dialogue with you, sir, although that was not stated in so many words."

"I see." Duncan passed his hand through his long white hair, and King noticed a massive gold ring that seemed to pin two of his fingers together. "Thank you, young man. Thank you for what you have told me. None of it comes as a great surprise, but it is good to know what the enemy considers to be our weak spot. In the main he is right, but it would not take any great intelligence to discover that our fleet is not as modern as, say Lord St Vincent's. And the mutiny; that is hardly something easily kept quiet. But I have had word from the Nore and Yarmouth very recently, and flatter myself that I can feel the tenor of the fleet. It is as I have said; the lads are ready to move forward, and would welcome a chance to prove their loyalty. To be blunt, I think they will make a better showing in action now than they might have this time last year."

Duncan placed both hands on the desk in front of him and King could see that the ring did indeed extend to cover two fingers.

"And yes, it would be good if wars could be solved by talking, although I fear that the admiral is being a little naïve in this instance. By all accounts he is a man of honour, but I do not feel his French masters have the same concern for gentlemanly conduct, so there would be little point in entering into negotiations with one who could not be sure that any commitments made would be respected." Duncan paused and considered again.

"He also might boast of the Dutch fleet which, I understand, is indeed a powerful one. But it's all they have. He would need to risk everything were he to take us on, so has double the reason to come to another resolution. And finally, he might be doubting himself; Admiral de Winter has the reputation of a fine seaman, but as an officer he has yet to prove himself. I understand that he only reached the rank of lieutenant in the old Dutch Navy; his elevation to flag rank has come through political pressure, rather than ability or experience. He has yet to command a fleet at sea: yet to have grown used to thinking for a number of ships, rather than the one beneath him. In fact he has never commanded a true ship at all, so there will be further lessons for him to learn; hardly an enviable position when we would hope to bring him to battle within days of his leaving harbour."

Duncan sat back and half closed his eyes as he thought. "But it is interesting, none the less. Interesting and illuminating; I feel I know my opponent a little better now, and am strangely reassured by his attitude. Not the hothead I had feared, no not at all; clearly a man who wishes to avoid unnecessary carnage, which is commendable. And, possibly he is not quite sure that he can destroy us, otherwise why would he have bothered to speak with Mr King?" he smiled suddenly. "So there we have it, valuable information: very valuable indeed. The summer is heading to a close, we would have expected the enemy to move by now, indeed they have barely three months before winter storms and shorter days will threaten a second debacle like Bantry Bay. But we know a little more of their thinking, and we can use that to the good. I have had an idea in mind for a while, and what you have told me confirms my thinking," his eyes suddenly flashed at Banks. "Tell me, Sir Richard; how is *Pandora* set?"

Banks bent forward slightly as he spoke. "In fine shape, sir. We have made minor repairs following those undertaken at Sheerness; I would say she is good for a season or more."

"I am glad of it, but there are many of us not so well prepared. We will stay at sea, at least until the end of the summer. After that we can consider invasion unlikely; the army would have grown stale and, even if it were used, would be less effective. I feel they will stand down, perhaps to try again the next spring, perhaps not, but the immediate danger will have passed. By then some of our number will have been at sea for many months, sadly it is too long for the majority. A programme of refitting will be in order; we will take one or two ships at a time, and put them in for major refit. And the others, those who would not fare well in the autumnal storms, will also return to port."

Banks was in the act of sipping at his coffee, and very nearly coughed; for several months they had been without sufficient force to meet the Dutch, and now that ships were available again, Duncan was talking of withdrawing.

"It is easier to undertake the smaller repairs when at anchor, rather than scrapping off this coastline." Duncan switched his attention to Banks. "What say you?"

"But the enemy, sir; you would not be leaving them totally unattended?"

"Indeed not. Your ship and some others that are better set up will remain on station. The Dutch can make of it what they will.

With luck they might even think us more the worse for wear than we actually are; that we are sheltering in port out of necessity rather than prudence. I will see to it that you have enough small craft to keep up communications with England. When I am not on station I expect to be informed of even the smallest movement. And obviously I shall require you to advise me as soon as the Dutch sail."

"So we should not attempt to detain them?"

Duncan smiled. "No, captain, indeed you will not. Send news to me, and shadow the fleet; as I have said, there will be more than enough small ships to maintain a chain of communication. We can be across in a day or two, and will be relying on the observation squadron to have advised us of the enemy's course. If, as we expect, it be south there should be no difficultly in finding them. With luck they might even be trapped betwixt ourselves and the Channel Fleet; otherwise I will take them on alone. But one thing is certain, Admiral de Winter and his fleet will not go away; previous attempts to destroy them at anchor have failed: it is clear that they can only be defeated at sea. And somehow I feel that they will not be sailing while I am waiting outside their front door."

* * * * *

"I'm sick of being called a pusser," she said as she closed the ledger. "I know it is the tradition, and I don't think for one moment that anyone is going to change, or consider my feelings, but pusser - it sounds like some sort of cat!"

Manning grinned and looked up from his book; he loved these little rants of hers. "Purser sounds more like a cat," he said, after considering the matter. "A cat that is, well... purring."

"I'd prefer it; at least I would if I *was* a purser."

"You could always apply; the bond need not be a problem; Mr Doust's brother put up for Soames, and if someone such as he gets backing, anyone can."

She shook her head. "I'd have to serve as a clerk for a year before I could even make an application."

"Then you're earning your sea time now; if what you have been doing for the last couple of months ain't clerking, I fail to know what is. Besides, you have clerked for your father for more than a year."

"In the merchant service, though."

"It is counted the same; I'd say there was little to stop you applying now."

"But even then I doubt the board would agree." She pouted in a way that he found particularly attractive. "A woman might be given a temporary job, she might be used to clear up a mess and sort matters right, but to actually give her a position, an official rank; that surely would be pushing things rather too far."

"But a pusser—sorry a purser—even that ain't a rank in the normal manner of things."

"How so?"

"Oh it has status, a uniform, and a cabin in the wardroom in most ships, but a purser is a civilian officer; they would never be expected to fight; not unless they so wished, nor are they really subject to naval discipline as such. Even the distribution of the stores is down to the master. Pursers just have to keep accounts and make sure everyone is fed, watered, and clothed on a regular basis, and to the best standards that can be kept."

"Sounds more like a mother." Manning was always vaguely troubled when Kate used words like mother.

"Think of it as a glorified shop keeper," he said, recovering quickly. "But were they to make you a purser, it would not be like being a lieutenant or a sailing master. You'd still be a civilian: in essence, rather like a surgeon."

"Do they have women surgeons?"

"Er no, not officially, though there are some who act as such, especially in shore bases and hospital ships."

"It is a thought."

"You've done a good job in *Pandora*; everyone says that."

"Everyone calls me pusser as well."

"It's a compliment."

"Well I don't like it."

"If you were to be a purser," he said, emphasising the word carefully. "You would have to get used to it. But it would also mean that we could sail together."

"We are sailing together now."

"I meant..."

"I know what you meant."

There was a moment of silence while he waited for the reaction. They were close, but he had yet to be certain exactly how close, and this was the first time he had taken a true sounding.

"It is a consideration," she said at last. "Though were you a proper surgeon, I could always ship as your wife, and not bother with being purser at all."

Now it was her turn to gauge the reaction and it was swift and decisive. He put his book to one side and swung round to face her directly.

"Kate, I'd like that more than anything. Do you think it possible?"

"Eventually, yes I do. You would have to study, mind; passing a surgeon's examination is far more taxing than that set for an assistant. And you have to serve a while in your present capacity I believe, I'm not sure exactly of the time, but..."

"I meant you becoming my wife," he cut in. "Is that in your mind?"

"Robert, it has been in my mind since the day we first met, it has just taken a little while for everything to come to fruition."

"I see," he said, feeling suddenly helpless, and not a little manipulated. "So you can envisage a time when we are both living together in the same ship?"

"It is what we are doing now, surely?"

"I meant as man and wife."

"Oh yes, eventually."

"Eventually?"

"Yes, we would have to be married first, I would insist upon it; I think any decent woman..."

"But then?" the frustration gave his words extra emphasis. "When I became a surgeon, you would marry me?"

She looked mildly surprised. "When you become a surgeon? Robert, do you honestly expect me to wait that long?"

* * * * *

Banks was pacing the quarterdeck; it had become something of a habit with him. It gave exercise and aided thinking; it was also an opportunity to be on the spot should anything of import occur. He had dined with Hackett in *Circe* the day before, Fayerman of the *Beaulieu* had been present and they had all agreed that having Duncan off station, even temporarily, was rather akin to being in a house without a father. But on that afternoon enemy action seemed unlikely. The sun was still impressively hot for September, hot enough to calm his usually forceful pace to a slower and more considered stroll. And Caulfield was playing his 'cello below; it was difficult to rush while the measured, thoughtful sounds emanated from the depths of the ship. The first lieutenant had started with a series of scales and arpeggios, but was now plodding through several short pieces. None were known to Banks, but they made a welcome, if slightly exotic, accompaniment to the Sunday afternoon's 'make and mend'. And while the sun shone, while Caulfield played, and while he paced, Banks found his mind beginning to wander to other matters, matters far, far away from the immediate and impending battle with the Dutch, and the possibility that his country could be overrun.

A few months ago his aim had been to transfer from *Pandora*, into a larger, stronger and more important frigate. So much had happened since then, although his instinct was still to move when the possibility presented. He had to forward his career, the career that had been planned by his parents so many years back, when his first years of official sea time were being accrued as he lay in his cradle. A powerful frigate had been the logical aim, one big enough to make a difference, yet not tied to the apron strings of a fleet or some cautious admiral. A cruise would be ideal; to be given a ship, the time and an area to wipe clean of privateers and merchant traffic. Little opposition, independent command and an opportunity to put something back into the funds that had so readily been spent on his vocation so far. There might even have been the chance of a cutting out operation, maybe taking an enemy ship from under the guns of a shore battery, as he had done on one occasion already. That would do his status no harm at all, as well as filling the coffers. And successful frigate captains were known to get on; he might be a commodore by the time he was thirty. Acting as a minor admiral, he could command his own squadron or fleet, and make both an impression on this war, and his reputation within the navy.

But that ambition had changed; he had changed: in the few short months he had been stationed with the North Sea Fleet, Banks had undergone a transformation he would never have believed were it not as obvious as the weathering on the strakes beneath him. He had enjoyed his time as a frigate captain, but now needed something more: something different. Not the rash excitement of a light ship, a ship where action and danger were part of the territory and all else became expendable. That was not the way of wars; few matters of importance were ever decided by a ship-to-ship engagement. It was the larger warhorses like *Russell*, currently in sight, as she lead the small squadron on yet another tack towards the Dutch coast, it was the powerful ships of the line that were the true contenders. A group of ten, twenty ships could make a real impact, whether it be a fleet action, or a proper amphibious assault. *Russell* would carry almost three times the compliment of *Pandora*, twice the capacity in boats and four or five times the fire power. *Pandora* was a splendid ship, fast, sleek and agile, but she could not deliver a knock out blow. *Russell*, or any other third rate, was an entirely different proposal. She might lack *Pandora*'s grace, speed and panache, but did it really matter if she was slower in stays? So she would be inclined to wallow in any sea, and would be hard pushed to keep up with the faster merchants, did that make any difference to her importance as a seventy-four, a ship powerful enough to stand with her peers in the line of battle? And now, now they were beating against a contrary wind, scratching once more about the shallows of an enemy coast; *Russell* was leading a group of three frigates, *Circe*, *Beaulieu* and *Pandora*, while the little *Martin* scampered about between them. All could show her a turn of speed and agility and yet they were following dutifully in her wake. She was by far the slowest, the clumsiest and, when it came down to it, the ugliest, yet *Russell* would last far, far longer in action than any of the fine and dashing beauties that now paid attendance on her.

"*Russell*'s signalling, sir," Dorsey's voice cut into his thoughts, and he stopped his pacing to watch. "Our number, *Beaulieu* and *Circe* to tack."

Banks walked across to King, who had the watch. "Looks like *Martin*'s being sent in for her daily reconnoitre," he said.

"And maybe give the Dutch a touch of target practice, sir." King was finding it hard to keep his mind on his duties that afternoon. He had received a message from Juliana the day before. It was currently thrust into his jacket pocket, even though he had read it several times and could have recited the whole thing from heart if he had wished. "All hands prepare to tack!"

"Signal's down."

"Ready about!"

Pandora went into the well-worn routine as the little sloop threaded her way close hauled, and still on the port tack, between her larger consorts. Drawing considerably less than the frigates, she piled on further sail, until she was fairly skipping over the shallows, and right up to the Dutch defences.

"There's a gun!" The forecastle lookout saw the cloud of smoke that was gone as soon as it had appeared, although there was no sign of the shot. A dull thud rolled across the water, but *Martin*, now coming onto the starboard tack, seemed to take little notice. Several more shots were spotted, but the little ship darted about with impunity while her lookouts inspected the Dutch fleet, moored inside the harbour, at their leisure. They might as well try and knock a fly from the air with a musket ball, Banks thought as *Martin* gathered speed once more. Charlie Paget certainly knew how to get the best out of his little ship.

King chalked up *Pandora*'s change of course on the traverse board. The letter had come *via* a tortuous route from a family in East Anglia. He supposed he could reply in the same manner and had in fact begun to write the night before.

He looked up and watched the sloop as she weaved in between the flashes of gunfire. He knew the area well, and had actually walked in front of those gun emplacements quite recently. Beyond them he could see the steeple of the small church that stood at the end of the road where Juliana lived, where she would be now; it was a strange thought: he was within a few miles of her and yet they were so very far apart.

"She's signalling, Dorsey." King spoke, but Dorsey was ready with the deck glass, and began reading off the numbers as they broke out.

"Enemy situation unchanged."

"Very good, repeat to *Russell*." In fact Trollope's ship would probably be able to read *Martin*'s flags, but Duncan was keen for as much communication between ships as possible, and soon the Dutch would see *Russell* repeat the signal once again. It was up to them to work out if the British ships beyond their horizon existed or not.

Banks turned away from the brief excitement, and started to pace once more. Yesterday Hackett had put forward an idea; it had not reached the stage when it could be called a plan, besides, it was totally unworkable from the start. A landing party made up of marines and seamen from the current observation squadron would make a night time surprise raid on the Texel, cause a bit of damage, then away, leaving the Dutch with a bloody nose and far greater respect for the British. A year ago Banks would have been all for it, they could have thrashed out the details then and there, and Trollope in the *Russell*, might be looking over the proposition at that very moment. But Banks had been negative; a similar venture had been planned the previous year, although that had required a far larger force. The plan had been abandoned, and he felt it to be a bad omen. King had given a remarkably full report on the defences on Texel, and they were by no means light. It was quite conceivable that Hackett's force would not even land, and Duncan might well return to find his observation force greatly depleted in officers and men. Hackett had been surprised by his reaction, and not a little disappointed. Banks had been accused of growing old; it was in jest of course, but the afternoon's party had broken up shortly afterwards, and the thought stayed with him now.

But he wasn't too old; he ceased his pacing and stared back at *Martin*. He was surprised to see her still so close to the land; possibly she had spotted something that needed further investigation, or Paget had the devil inside him and felt like taunting the Dutch. As he watched she began to turn, a long sweeping arc that would eventually see her running back to rejoin the squadron. It was a beautiful sight, and *Martin* was a well-found craft, but Banks was growing tired of small ship antics; he wanted a larger, tougher vessel under his feet. One that could deliver a harder punch and one, he had to admit, where a band of officers would do more to look after the minutiae of running a ship and crew. Throughout his time in the navy he had met with countless crusty old captains; the kind who stuck by the rules, and managed their commands like small businesses. Captains who would not shirk from taking their ships into the fiercest danger, but, in turn, would not personally lead a boarding party, or cutting out expedition. They would maintain a fine table, however, and any officer serving under them would be certain of a sound education, if not the chance for valour. Yes, he had met with many like that, and had sometimes wondered why they joined the navy when an army career would have seemed more logical. But here he was, not yet thirty and the signs were well in place. He would stay with *Pandora* a while yet; certainly the North Sea Station seemed far more interesting than it had at first appeared, but when the change came, a seventy-four would seem the logical step.

"My god, she's hit!" Kings voice jerked him back from his day-dreams in time to see *Martin*'s tiny foremast tumble sideways and collapse amid a tangle of canvas and spars. She was a good way off shore, probably just under a mile, but still well within range of the gun emplacements that protected the harbour. Worse, as the wreckage slewed her round and began to act as a sea anchor, she would no longer be a moving target, and could be pounded to pieces by the land-based artillery.

Banks looked about the deck. "Mr Fraiser?" Fraiser was just appearing at the quarterdeck steps, hatless, and without his jacket, he had clearly heard the commotion and had come up from the gunroom.

"Mr Fraiser, what depth do we have there?" Banks pointed at the spot just over a mile off where *Martin* was even now starting to wallow in the swell.

"Insufficient for us, sir. There's a bar running right up to where she lies. I can take us a wee bit closer, but not much."

"Very good, see to it," he turned to King. "Summon all hands." On a Sunday afternoon's 'make and mend' there was effectively no watch below. "I want both cutters and the launch manned, and double bank the launch. Small arms for the crew; midshipmen for each of the cutters, and..." he paused, looking at King, conscious for the first time of what he would be doing.

"Yes sir?"

"Mr King, you will command the launch."

"Very good, sir." King touched his hat with nothing in his ex-pression other than a desire to be off, turned away and began to shout orders.

Banks caught Fraiser's eye. "Take her in, master, but be pre-pared to back as soon as the boats are ready. Mr Lewis, start a hand in the forechains with a lead if you please." *Pandora* was the nearest ship to *Martin*, and she had the shallowest draft. He glanced across to *Russell*, a good deal further out to sea and head-ing away; Trollope would be bound to signal to him soon, but time was of the essence. Even if the shore batteries did not account for *Martin*, there would be gunboats despatched within minutes and, with the wind behind them, they would be raking her with deadly fire in no time. To continue his earlier metaphor, the fly had now landed; indeed it lay rooted to the ground, and was just waiting for the swat to finish it off.

"Red and black cutters ready to launch." The crew were all seamen and had formed up on the quarterdeck. Pistols and cutlasses were loaded on board; it was unlikely that they might actually get to grips with the enemy, but better to be prepared, and the men would be reassured if they had the means to defend themselves. King pushed his way into the crowd and collected a boarding cutlass from the arms chest for himself, before making for the waist. He passed Caulfield coming up on deck with a slightly bemused expression on his face; clearly news of the emergency had only just reached him and he had yet to return to the real world.

"*Martin*'s been disabled, and is under fire from the shore. I've to see to the launch." The first lieutenant peered across to the sloop as King made off. "You have the deck, sir!"

"Ah, very good, Mr King."

"Back main tops'l!" *Pandora* creaked at her apparent mishandling, and slowly lost momentum. The cutters hit the water almost simultaneously, and were heading for *Martin* as the heavier launch was being swung over the side.

"Signal from *Russell*, sir," Dorsey reported. "Our number to give assistance." Banks nodded, and watched the launch fill with seamen and set off in the wake of the cutters. King was in the sternsheets, he could see the lad as he adjusted his cutlass and settled himself down in the boat. For him to choose anyone else for the mission would have been wrong; besides, Caulfield had not been on deck, and he could hardly have gone himself. But Banks was aware just how hazardous the mission was. King would be trying to tow a ship whilst under fire, and it had been just such a situation, and the result of Banks' own incompetence, that had almost accounted for him last time.

CHAPTER NINETEEN

THE wind was in his teeth but as King leaned forward in the launch, urging the boat through the gentle waves, he knew the pace was good and they were travelling fast. The lower vantage point meant that he could not make out much detail on *Martin*, although he would expect the wreckage to have been cleared by the time they reached her. Then it should be nothing more than a steady pull to tow her out of range of the shore batteries, and back to the safety of the squadron. Ahead Rose and Cobb were speeding through the water; he could hear their adolescent shouts to the men, interspersed by the regular bark of gunfire from the shore. There had been no sign of shot yet, although King supposed that the sloop would be the target, and remain so for as long as the emergency continued.

"Pull, pull, yer blighters!" It was the voice of Flint on stroke in the launch, already setting a cruel pace, but now subtly upping the tempo as the rowers came properly into their stride. *Martin* was growing nearer by the second then, as King watched, a series of splashes to larboard showed where the Dutch artillery was finding their range. Rose, in the new red cutter, had reached the sloop and was shouting something up to the men on board. A line was tossed to them, and quickly secured. King noticed another small boat off *Martin*'s counter; clearly they had launched their own cutter, and were about to take themselves under tow. Cobb, in the black cutter, was with them now and *Martin*'s bows began to come round as Rose's boat took up the strain.

"Right then, I'm taking her about," King told Flint as they were within striking distance; the pace slowed, and the men began to rest on their oars as King pressed the helm over, ready for the sloop to catch them up.

The other two cutters were rigging their masts and sails now. "There're gunboats heading from the harbour," Cobb shouted, as Flint stood up in the launch to accept a line. King tried to peer past the sloop's hull, but could see nothing. Then Flint snatched at the light rope that was thrown from *Martin*'s forecastle, and began to haul the towing hawser in. Meanwhile three of the hands in the launch had rigged the boat's two small masts. The sails were sheeted home and immediately began to fill. A heavy shot skipped past, as Flint secured the tow, before clambering back to his rowing position. *Martin*'s cutter was without masts, but its crew began to row enthusiastically, and slowly the sloop became a moving target once more.

"All right, on my count; steady." King took control, setting a sensible pace as the slack was taken up. Clearly the hands in *Martin* were awake, and had allowed a good length for the launch's tow, enabling them to take the lead, with the three smaller boats following, fan like, behind. He glanced over to *Pandora* waiting a mile or so off, so in deeper waters. It would be time consuming and totally futile to try and measure their speed, but by now the boat's crews were considerably experienced at towing ships, and *Martin* was certainly lighter than their frigate.

Cobb was pointing behind him and shouting something. King looked beyond the sloop and saw the reason for his excitement. Pulling toward *Martin*, and powered by oars and far larger sails, two heavy gunboats were now in plain view and creeping up on the sloop. They were keeping off her counter, just out of the arc of her broadside guns. A single cannon was mounted in the bows of each craft, and as King watched, one was steered round until the muzzle was pointed directly at them

The gun fired as he watched; the unexpected flash and loud report that followed forced King to duck down, bending double in the small boat. The shot had passed overhead and to one side, splashing into the sea less than forty yards from their larboard bow.

"Pull! Pull, you sods!" Flint's voice this time, and he had increased the pace. All in the launch could see the gunboats, and knew themselves to be targets. King glanced up to the sloop, where they were in the process of rigging the little used spritsail. His attention switched back to the gunboats; presumably they intended knocking out the towing force, before turning their fire on to the sloop; a sensible course, for once *Martin* was stationary and at their mercy, they could both stand off her stern and steadily shoot her to pieces. He might try a sudden turn in an effort to place at least one gunboat within the range of *Martin*'s broadside guns, although any manoeuvre carried out by four towing boats would be a slow, and obvious process; the Dutch craft, infinitely more manoeuvrable, would be more than able to maintain their position. *Pandora* was almost stationary dead ahead, clearly she had now gone to the limit the shallows allowed, but while she was at right angles to their bows, they could not benefit from her support. He would have to manoeuvre, but it would be a slower, more considered process. He looked back at *Martin* once more, and indicated to larboard with his hand, then bellowed to the men in the other boats.

Cobb and Rose nodded and someone in the other cutter raised a hand. Gradually he eased the tiller across, and even more slowly the sloop began to follow. The gunboats stayed locked on to *Martin*'s quarter, and for a while would even be sheltered from *Pandora*'s broadside by her hull. The range was shortening however, and if they could keep moving for long enough, until the time when the frigate's nine pounders would be truly effective, the Dutch would be well within their scope, and extremely vulnerable. Clearly they had guessed his intentions in *Pandora*, as her bows came round and she began to work slowly to the north.

"Pull! Pull!" The tow had straightened now and King increased the pace once more. The frigate would be in long range soon and could start to fire on the gunboats, although he sensed that Banks would not risk broadsides while his own men and boats could so easily be hit by a stray.

Another shot passed close by, sending water into the boat, and there was the sudden crack of breaking wood.

"The sweep's broke!" Jackson, pulling larboard bow with Bankhead, held the ragged end of their oar up in disgust."

"Carry on, the rest of you," King shouted. "Pull! Pull!" They carried no spare oars, but it was better that the launch continued out of balance than lost the power of four rowers.

"Pull! Pull!"

They could expect the next shot from the first gunboat at any moment. King glanced back to the sloop, and was in time to see the flash. Again he instinctively ducked his head, looking up to see Rose's cutter dissolve in their wake. One moment it was intact, with six men straining at the oars, the next the boat had totally disintegrated, almost plank by plank, and the water was full of bobbing heads and waving arms.

"Carry on, Mr Cobb!" King bellowed. It was his decision, and he came to it instantly. To divert the other cutter from the tow would lessen their power by two boats, with the additional problem of Cobb's continuing while crowded with survivors. The sloop was bearing down on them; the men on board would be able to throw lines to those in the water even if there wasn't the time for a scrambling net. Those that were left behind, well, the gunboats might pick them up; worse things had happened after all.

"Pull! Pull!"

The loss of Rose's cutter had certainly made a difference, and the men at the oars, who had been working for some time now, were starting to tire. Beyond *Pandora* King could see the other ships of the squadron further out to sea; they might well have launched boats that were coming to his aid, although there was no sign: besides, he felt in his bones that this would be settled within the next few minutes.

Another crack of gunfire; was it his imagination, or had the gunboats crept closer? This shot fell amongst the oars of the sloop's cutter, forcing the rowers to miss a stroke. *Pandora* was now comfortably in range and coming to the wind to offer her broadside to the enemy. A puff of smoke from a forward gun, and the shot landed between *Martin* and one of the gunboats that dogged her.

"Starboard!" King bellowed; now was the time to make the most of the earlier manoeuvre, as well as shorten the distance between them and safety. He waved his hand frantically, and the remaining boats slowly responded, dragging the useless lump of a hulk that seemed to grow heavier with every pull, until they were back to their original course, but with *Pandora* off their starboard bows, and ready to take out the enemy.

The British ship began to fire steadily; a discharge every two or three seconds; too fast for Donaldson, the gunner, to be laying each piece individually. Splashes from *Pandora*'s guns were erupting regularly about the gunboats, but they remained determinedly off *Martin*'s counter, and could be expected to fire again at any moment.

The shot that destroyed Cobb's boat came at almost the same time as the one that hit one of the Dutch craft. King watched as the British seamen struggled in the frothy waters; he could see Cobb, hat off and bellowing as he gathered the men together. They were in the lee of the sloop, and the tow had slowed considerably. With luck, any that had not been injured would be recovered. The Dutch were faring slightly better; their boat had simply been holed, and slowed to a halt as she settled in the water; the other craft had reluctantly followed, and was taking on survivors. King found he was holding his breath, and consciously expelled the air from his body, just as a flash of light caught his eye. *Pandora* had released the remains of her broadside on the Dutch. None of the shots hit and quite a few were well to the stern of the enemy; presumably the British gun captains were laying to the left to be sure of not striking any of their own craft, but the stunning concussion of the gunfire made a dramatic impact on them all.

"Pull! Pull! Pull!" Flint continued, but even he seemed slightly mesmerised, and the pace began to falter as the weary men gradually relaxed. *Pandora* had the enemy in range; a further broadside was due in a matter of minutes; there was nothing the Dutch could achieve now; their only course was to run. This they did, collecting as many men from the water as was possible, and turning their bows for the shore. The second salvo came as they were underway, and most shots hit the sinking gunboat, rolling it over in the water, and sending it straight to the shallow bottom.

Unordered, Flint unshipped his oar and rested forward, breathing heavily. The other rowers followed his example, muttering brief comments, curses and occasionally spitting over the side. The boat began to rise and fall without power or control in the gentle swell. King, who had not been involved with any form of physical exercise, still felt remarkably weary, and settled himself down in his seat, placed his head between his hands and gave one almighty sigh. It was over.

* * * * *

On the quarterdeck, standing where he had been for some while, Banks reached down and rested on the hammock packed netting, and also relaxed. From his higher vantage point he had watched the destruction of both cutters and the enemy gunboat, and had seen his officers and what appeared to be all of the men, rescued by the sloop. The sound of rhythmic movement and shouting came to him; he looked up to see two further cutters and a much larger launch come past *Pandora*, heading for *Martin*. They would be from the squadron; too late, but at least the reinforcements could carry the sloop back the rest of the way.

"King did well, sir," Caulfield said as he cautiously approached. His captain, whom he still regarded as a friend, had been decidedly distant for some while. Aloof and sometimes just plain rude, he was clearly affected by some private and personal matter, and displayed all the traits of a troubled man. Now, as he stood at ease by the quarterdeck bulwark, he seemed to have shrunken slightly in size; his head was bowed, his shoulders drooped; anyone would think King's rescue had been a failure. "Shame about the cutters," Caulfield persisted. "But it appears no one was hurt."

Banks turned his head and gave a weak smile. "You know I had rather a curt letter from the dockyard when we lost the first two? The dear knows what they will make of it when they discover I've accounted for another brace."

"It is rather becoming a habit." Caulfield said seriously, and then stifled a laugh as he noticed that Banks, standing upright now, was also attempting to control himself.

"Do you think they'll trust us with any more, Michael?" the captain asked, his eyes delightfully alight.

"Belike we'll be tested with one, and allowed another if we do not break it."

Then they were both laughing heartily. Fraiser watched as the two grown men standing near to him, began to giggle like schoolboys, slapping each other on the back and snorting as if they had just carried off some incredibly devilish prank.

"She's a fine ship, *Pandora*," Caulfield said stiffly. "But she just don't take care of her boats!" Banks spluttered, and the laughter was renewed again. Fraiser looked away and gave his full attention to the chart. He made a careful mark of their soundings, and cross-referenced the bearings with those he had taken earlier. The officers had almost controlled themselves now, and were mopping their eyes, with only the occasional outburst taking brief control. Fraiser had also noticed a change in atmosphere in *Pandora*, although he could not accurately place the time or reason for it. That the feeling had lifted was obvious however, and none the worst for that. He felt a slight chill on the side of his face, and glanced up to the weathervane; the wind was backing and apparently gathering in strength; his natural seaman's instincts went on to calculate the difference it would make when *Pandora* was under way again, but as he did so, and completely without his knowledge, he too was smiling.

* * * * *

"Gentlemen, please!" Kate said, as she swept into the gunroom. King and Newman had half risen, and sat back into their chairs rather guiltily. "I appreciate the compliment," she continued as she pulled a chair out and joined them at the long table. "But I think it wrong that you can not enjoy your private room without having to consider me at all times."

"Purser's a wardroom rank." Newman said 'purser' slowly and especially carefully; he had been warned: they had all been warned. "You have every right to be here; indeed you are most welcome."

"Well I cannot see how it can remain that way if you keep having to leap up from your chairs whenever I enter; poor Mr Caulfield banged his head yesterday." King and Newman exchanged looks, although neither of them dared to laugh out loud. "Besides, I thought this the gunroom; am I amiss?"

"Wardroom in a frigate's known as the gunroom," King explained. "On account of the actual gunroom not being large enough."

"To hold the guns?" she asked innocently.

"Er no, not exactly. To hold the junior officers." The silence that followed was as awkward as his answer.

Kate smiled. "Why don't you just say; 'it's the navy'?"

"It's the navy," King and Newman replied in unison.

Crowley appeared with a pot of coffee, and she stood to pour for both men and herself.

"I have your jacket mended," she said as she passed a cup to Newman; she knew he always took his black and without sugar.

"That's kind of you Katharine." he gave his ready smile and took the drink in return. "My man Adams has a pig's foot when it comes to the needlework."

"Oh, it were not me but Powell in the sick berth; a rare hand and a good eye."

"I was not aware."

"Very neat stitching; I think you will be pleased. Are you writing, Thomas?"

Caught, King looked up suddenly. He was indeed trying to write, but had not progressed very far.

"Yes, just a letter."

Kate considered this; in the time she had known him he had failed to mention living family or friends outside of *Pandora*, and certainly had not communicated with them.

"It is someone I met," he continued foolishly. Now both she and Newman were interested; there were few chances of a casual meeting in a blockading frigate.

"One of the hands on a lighter?" the marine asked, beaming.

"No," King replied crossly, then looked about the otherwise empty room before continuing in a softer voice. "Someone I met on land; when I was a prisoner."

"That van Leiden chappie?" Newman was more serious now. "He's an officer in a hostile force; I should be mindful there."

"His sister in law, actually."

Newman shook his head. "Still technically the enemy."

"Her husband was killed by the French; I fail to see how..."

"Killed by the French?" Kate interrupted. "So she is..."

"A widow, yes; I met a young widow ashore and now I am writing to her: if that is square with you both?"

Newman grew thoughtful. "Is she pretty?"

"Very."

"Then it seems an admirable pastime," he gave another of his regular beams, before adding: "You won't mention the war, of course?"

"She is hardly aware we are having one."

Kate toyed with her cup. "And is the letter going well, Tom?" she asked.

"No, but I have little need of assistance, thank you."

"Oh, I would never presume," but her eyes were a-twinkle and a smile was not very far away.

"Then I shall continue." But he did not; it was impossible with the two watching him in silence from across the table. For a moment he even considered writing any nonsense in the hope of boring them, but they knew him well enough. Finally he looked up in desperation.

"You will ask us," Kate smiled, supportively, "Should you need a hand with spelling, punctuation or, perhaps... construction?"

* * * * *

September went, to be replaced by a far harsher October with rain, strong winds and earlier evenings. As the second dogwatch began, with darkness barely minutes away, *Pandora* was once more cruising off the enemy coast. And once more the wind came off shore, ideal for the enemy to venture out, and ideal for the fleet of small craft still holed up beyond the harbour defences, to finally take to sea.

Of late the threat of invasion had started to diminish however; no army can stay in one place for so long without growing restless and suffering a definite lowering of morale. Men must be fed; fed, exercised and, to some extent, occupied, and after several months of apparent listlessness, there had been reports of divisions, brigades and even entire regiments dispersing to other French held territories. There were also rumours that one of the generals in command had died although nothing that could be substantiated. But the Dutch fleet remained, as powerful and menacing as ever and for as long as they did *Pandora* and her consorts, would stay, tentatively feeling their way amidst the shallows, teasing the enemy who sat safe, but impending, in their lair. For, even if the risk of invasion had lessened, the mighty force was a danger in itself, and had to be kept under constant observation. On good days, when most of Duncan's elderly warships were at sea, they were outnumbered. On the bad, such as today, the single ship of the line, and a cluster of frigates and small fry would make almost no impact on the fleet they so readily taunted.

Despite, or maybe because of her earlier mishap, *Pandora* was close inshore again, and the monotonous drone of the leadsman in the forechains was once more becoming just another of the regular sounds that haunts every sailing ship. It had been a gloomy afternoon and a thick layer of blanket cloud still sat heavily over the ship as she eased her way through the grey waters. The new watch had been set fifteen minutes before, and Caulfield, who had the deck, was just settling down to the two-hour stretch before he would be relieved. Then a bite of supper, and eight glorious hours of sleep, before he took the morning watch. He glanced at the traverse board, and went to pass a comment to Fraiser, who had been on deck for as long as they had been taking soundings, and would probably remain so until they ceased. Then came the call from the masthead, and their lives, the commission and the entire war, changed forever.

"Deck there, lights on the enemy fleet." For a moment all was still. Caulfield paused, his body, turned to address the master, becoming rigid as he waited for more. "A lot of activity, and I can see small craft in the waters outside the harbour. One ship is moving, although not under sail. Wait; there are topsails on two; maybe more..."

Fraiser and Caulfield exchanged looks, then the latter turned to the midshipman of the watch. "Cobb, the masthead for you, and tell me what you see." The lad was off and racing up the shrouds with the deck glass slung over one shoulder, but there was no time to wait for his report. Caulfield glanced around at the darkening horizon; they had been plying this coast for months, waiting for the enemy to sail. Now it appeared that they had, there was no denying a distinct feeling of vulnerability. "Send for the captain," he said, and was about to summon the watch below when he thought better of it. The Dutch might be merely rearranging the anchorage; it would be foolish to react needlessly, although an inner feeling told him that early evening could hardly be the best time to move ships. But, with the wind as it was, and darkness steadily falling, it was the perfect time for the enemy to attempt to leave harbour unseen.

Banks appeared just as Cobb had settled himself and was starting his report. Caulfield touched his hat respectfully but no one spoke as the midshipman's voice reached them.

"They're sailing." he said simply. "Seem to be leaving in line ahead, the first is just at the harbour entrance, and will be a'sea in no time."

"What of the small craft?" the captain asked.

A pause, while Cobb considered. "It appears to be warships, sir; the transports are still moored."

"Mr Fraiser, what depth have we?" In the months they had been patrolling the Dutch coast Fraiser, like any good sailing master, had developed both an excellent memory for the various sandbars and shallows, as well as an instinct for where further perils might be expected.

"We cana' take her further in, sir, but might continue on this tack a fair while yet."

They were to the north of the harbour; their current course, which was south-southwest, would take them up to and past the very entrance, allowing any southward bound fleet to be followed. And should the Dutch turn to the north, there should still be room enough for Pandora to precede them.

"Is *Circe* in sight?"

Yes, sir." Caulfield answered. "But a good way to leeward and we will lose the light presently."

"Then make a signal, tell them the Dutch are out."

It was impossible for such a statement to sound anything other than dramatic and all on board knew the repercussions were going to be vast. *Circe* would signal to *Russell*, and Trollope was bound to despatch a cutter or some other fast craft to Duncan at Yarmouth once the news had been digested. With luck Duncan should know by the morning after tomorrow. He would sail immediately, whatever the condition of his ships, and might cross the North Sea in a day and a half. If the observation squadron kept the enemy in sight and was able to signal their position, Duncan could bring them to battle. It would be the confrontation that everyone had been expecting for so long; in less than a week, it should all be over.

"Mr King," Banks addressed the lieutenant who had just appeared on deck. "It seems the Dutch have sailed. We will endeavour to give chase; I'd be obliged if you would join Mr Cobb at the masthead and remain for as long as I need you there." It was somewhat harsh, sending a lieutenant, but they needed an accurate assessment of the enemy's strength and possible course without delay.

King touched his hat and turned for the shrouds. The tension was growing as dusk closed in. Dorsey's voice was next.

"*Circe's* signalling, sir. Repeated from *Russell*; advise enemy heading."

"Very good." It might take a while for the ships to assemble out of the harbour, so a true course could not be given immediately. The despatch to Duncan would have to be delayed until this vital information was available, but far better to be sure than send the entire North Sea Fleet off on some wild rainbow chase. King was sound, and would report as soon as there was no doubt. Texel was coming into view now, and the lights that had first alerted the masthead were visible from the deck. Flags could also be seen, flying from the shore batteries, along with small pencils of smoke showing where the furnaces were alight for heating shot. Clearly the Dutch were taking every measure to ensure that their fleet left harbour without incident. And now those on deck could see the forest of masts as they slowly thinned out, and yes, there were two Dutch liners under topsails and jibs, actually outside the harbour walls, and heading on what appeared to be the same course as *Pandora*.

"Clear for action, if you please," Banks said casually as he considered his enemy. "But do not beat to quarters; I fear we might have a long night ahead of us."

* * * * *

Van Leiden was having similar thoughts in *Vrijheid*, the Dutch flagship. Since his promotion to *luitenant* and first boarding the ship only weeks before, his life seemed to have gathered speed at an incredible rate. He remembered, as a child, travelling to France with his family. There he had come across his first ever sizeable hill, and ran down it with all the enthusiasm of youth. It was soon after he had begun that he realised he was unable to stop. The hill had stretched on inexorably and his cries were only answered by amusement. Then a slip turned into a fall, and his light body had continued to tumble until he finally came to rest, panting and in an untidy heap, listening to the far away laughter of his family. It was much the same now; his position as junior *luitenant* meant that he had many responsibilities, most of which he knew little about. Each task he undertook seemed to lead to several more; he had learnt much through trial and error, and nothing from the stuck up prig who was his senior in the *luitenant*'s list, as well as the cause of many of his problems.

Van Leiden had been aboard the flagship for less than a month, and for most of that time had spent eighteen to twenty hours of every day trying to sort out his division and duties, whilst also learning the signal book, officer etiquette, and the difference between serving as an *Adelborst* in the *Gunther*, an eighteen-gun sloop, and a commissioned officer in *Vrijheid*, a seventy-four, and flagship of the fleet. He had yet to tumble, but if he did he knew he would not get away with a little gentle ribbing. Now, in a rare moment of peace, he stood at the break of the quarterdeck and watched as the leading ships snaked through the Schulpen Gat that led from the harbour, and out into the North Sea.

The sky was darkening rapidly, making the white lights that each ship carried stand out as *Vrijheid* passed through the harbour entrance, and began to roll gently with the swell. The wind felt stronger now they were at sea, and the ship began to take on speed, although a block had jammed and the fore topsail yard could not be adjusted. Van Rossem, the captain, was on deck, bellowing at the *bootsman* and his crew who were attempting to correct the fault. Earlier there had been problems with the main topsail; it was a brand new sail and the footrope had been too short so the sheets could not be brought home, even with the tackles clapped on. It was what was expected when a ship first took to the sea after months, years, in harbour, but at least they had a crew made up of trained hands; small adjustments to the ship could be made very quickly; it took far longer to create proper seamen.

One of the few exceptions was their *admiraal*; although a seasoned officer, everyone knew that he had never captained anything larger than a picket boat in the past. De Winter might have a forceful personality, with a size and presence to match, but they had yet to learn how he would fare when it came to commanding a fleet.

He had spoken to them only that morning, just after it had been announced that the fleet was to sail with the evening tide, and further communication with the shore would not be permitted. An assembly had been called in the great cabin, and the commissioned officers and some juniors were told exactly what was to be. They would be heading southwest, and their force would be the sixteen ships of the line, along with five frigates and five brigs that had shared their anchorage. There were further vessels waiting and ready in the mouth of the river Meuse; once these had been collected de Winter would be commanding a fleet far larger than anything that had been blockading them. The *admiraal* was operating under instructions given to him in July, when the invasion of Ireland had been thought imminent. De Winter was instructed to consolidate his force and then offer battle with the British if there were any chance of success; that had raised a laugh amongst the senior officers, all of whom were confident to the point of arrogance.

But then they had very good reason; the Royal Navy had fought and won several battles of late, but all against Spanish or French opposition; the last time they had met a fleet manned by proper seamen was when the Dutch had met them in 1781 off Dogger Bank. Then they had learned what a real navy was capable of, and it seemed destined that the lesson was to be repeated and maybe even improved upon. The *admiraal* had handled the meeting well, and all left feeling confidant and excited, with little thought to the fact that they would be leaving their home port to fight a battle without the chance to explain or say goodbye to those on shore.

Now they were well out to sea, and most of the other ships were clear of the harbour. An ironic cheer came from the forecastle, as the foretopsail yard was finally adjusted. *Adelborst* Cuypers, one of his signal's team and about the only true friend he had on board, went to make a comment but stopped as they both saw the doors under the poop open. The *admiraal's* large personality was matched by his size, although the he could never have been called stout, but as he swept out with his long hair tied neatly back and strode purposefully on to the quarterdeck, he was certainly an impressive figure. Van Leiden watched as he exchanged a few words with van Rossem, and then broke away to study the last of the fleet leaving harbour. He looked back again at the captain, and said something van Leiden could not catch. Then his own name was being shouted, and he jerked to attention.

"The British frigate to the north," the captain pointed up the coast. "Signal *Mars* and *Monnikendamm* to intercept!"

Cuypers was there with his book, flipping through the pages, while the two hands detailed to signals opened the main flag locker and stood ready. Van Leiden glanced back to where an enemy frigate, one of the relentless blockading force that had hounded them for the past months could just be seen. It was keeping pace with the fleet on roughly the same southwesterly course. Cuypers began to shout out the numbers, and the flags were attached to the halyards and sent skywards. They watched the two heavy frigates expectantly, and soon could make out the acknowledgement raised as the ships altered course and began to set further sail. Both carried over forty guns: each on their own would account for a British sixth rate if it were foolish enough to come within range; together the battle would be over within a couple of broadsides. He looked across to where the enemy was still blithely continuing to follow them; he wondered for a moment if it were Thomas' ship, *Pandora*. If it were, he hoped that the British would be sensible and run while they had the chance.

CHAPTER TWENTY

"IT's quite a sight," Cobb said, and he was right. The Dutch fleet was off *Pandora*'s larboard bow, and completely out of the harbour. They straddled untidily in a long line while individual ships trimmed their sails and sought to form a more regimented sailing order. Also at the masthead, King was making rapid notes in his pocket book, frantically jotting down as many details as he could before the light failed and black night swallowed them entirely.

"I make it seventeen liners, and four frigates plus some small stuff; what say you?"

Cobb shook his head. "Far liner looks more like a heavy frigate; can't see the ports though; too dark an' they ain't picked out."

"Twenty six in all?"

"Aye, twenty six is about it, and definitely heading for the south."

King made his report, and the signals flags were soon racing up; with luck *Circe* would be able to read them without Dorsey having to resort to the more cumbersome and less accurate night signals. But that was his problem; King and Cobb settled down to watch as the enemy ships jostled with each other to form two lines. Their course was certainly to the south—south-south west most likely—although even to be sure they were not heading north would be enough for Duncan to know where to start looking.

"Ask me, the far one's a frigate, and she's wearing out of station," Cobb said.

King peered through the glass. "You're right, and the nearer frigate's coming round as well. Better let the deck know." He waited as Cobb bellowed the news; yes, the two ships were definitely detaching from the main body. "Chance is high they're gaining sea room, before coming for us," he said, as the enemy settled onto the starboard tack. "They'll see *Circe* off, sure as eggs, and like as not, we'll be trapped against the Dutch coast."

King continued to watch as the ships began to fade into the gathering dark. They were certainly heavy, probably forty gunners, in which case they would throw a shot double the weight of *Pandora*'s main armament. And, being Dutch, they would probably be of shallow draft, so there would be no escaping into the shoals. The darkness was almost complete now, but in the last fragile wisps of dusk the enemy turned once more until they were as close to the wind as they could sail.

"That's it, they're heading back for us," King turned to Cobb. "Better nip down and tell the captain face to face." Cobb rolled his eyes; the journey from a frigate's masthead was not the simple exercise King had made it sound, especially as he was bound to be ordered straight back afterwards. "It is important," King said, and Cobb set off.

Left alone King watched as the enemy faded into the gloom of night. Banks would have to act swiftly; unless he altered course in the next few minutes, those ships would surely take *Pandora*. He glanced down and could just make out Cobb on the quarterdeck approaching the captain. Caulfield and Fraiser were called in, and there seemed to be a discussion going on, with lots of shaking of heads and pulling of chins, but *Pandora* did not alter course; instead she beat to quarters, the men taking up their battle stations, ready for immediate action. Banks must be determined to continue shadowing the fleet for as long as possible, and was willing to risk meeting any enemy that tried to stop him. To starboard lay the vast North Sea; there was still time; *Pandora* could wear, add sail, and find relative safety in the cold dark night. But instead she continued on her present course, with every yard taking her deeper into danger.

* * * * *

King's warning had not been easily ignored; Banks was sorely tempted to let the enemy ships chase him away from the fleet. He might even lure them as far as *Russell* and the others; that would be a fine action and, if carefully handled, should account for both with no loss to the British. However, *Pandora's* value lay in the information she could gather. The other ships of Trollope's observation squadron were aware that the enemy was out, but not their exact position. They might follow the coast in the hope of staying in touch, but could do little if the Dutch suddenly turned to the west, or even wore round to head northwards. If *Pandora* could avoid the attention of the two enemy heavies, and stay in touch with the fleet throughout the night, they would know their exact position and heading and be able to relay both in the morning. Information such as that would be invaluable when it came to Duncan joining them in battle, and was certainly worth risking the fragile hull of one light frigate.

It was quite dark now, and what moon there was would not rise for a good three hours. *Pandora*, sailing under topsails alone, was barely making steerage way and, with ports closed and properly darkened, would hopefully merge into the gloom. But then light played strange tricks at night, and for all Banks knew, *Pandora* could still be visible to the enemy. He stared out at the two frigates' last known position. They might be intending to face them; continue close-hauled, and attack from head on; or pass, tack, and come up on their stern, effectively trapping *Pandora* between themselves and the enemy fleet. The first course would merely drive them off; the second almost guaranteed their destruction. Either way it was likely to be sudden, with the enemy relying as much on their estimate of his position as he was on calculating theirs. It was simple; all he had to do was guess their orders and react accordingly; had they been instructed to chase off the annoying little frigate, or sink her?

"Four points to starboard." The order rang out in the still air, and for a moment no one reacted. "Four points to starboard I say!" Banks repeated, with a slight edge to his voice.

"Four points to starboard, quartermaster," Caulfield repeated, although the wheel was already spinning, and the braces were hauling the yards round as the ship began to turn. That would throw a fox into the hen house; whatever the Dutch might have planned, he had altered *Pandora's* course in a manner that had surprised her own crew: it only remained to see if the Dutch could be similarly confused. The frigates might well be dead ahead and bearing down on them; the new heading would be effectively playing into their hands. Large and powerful ships, each carrying a massive broadside, only the darkness and the fact that the enemy would not expect such a bold move would save *Pandora* from annihilation.

However the night was truly black, one of the blackest Banks had known and, if they could slip past undetected, *Pandora* would be free to continue stalking the fleet. Banks rubbed his hands together and blew on his fingers; he might be on the verge of graduating from a simple frigate captain to something far superior, but there was enough of the firebrand left, and he had an inkling in his bones that the ruse would work. He even felt slightly smug as *Pandora* settled on to her new course, and began to nudge her way out into the gentle waves of the North Sea. Then, with a chill, Banks remembered his premonition after the last ship-to-ship encounter. *Pandora* had been lucky, no one could deny that; but her luck had already been pressed a long way: perhaps, this time, he was pushing too far?

* * * * *

The order had been given for absolute silence and every light to be extinguished; the men squatted at their quarters with doused battle lanterns ticking softly behind closed ports. Lanthorns on the orlop deck were turned down to nought and the binnacle lights were put out. Slow matches, burning in tubs between the guns, were doused and, as the blackness flowed readily throughout the ship, even those lamps that shone so bright in the sealed off, magazine light room were extinguished and left to smoke in silence. And silence there was, a silence so complete that the gentle wind rasping through the shrouds sounded like a low, tormented moan, giving *Pandora* an uneasy, spectral feel, so much so that even in a hull tight packed with humanity, many felt alone and strangely vulnerable.

None more so than Powell, who sat in the area usually occupied by the junior warrant officers. If action were joined, injured and dying men would surround him, but now he was alone. Mr Doust, Mr Manning, Miss Black and the other loblolly boys were a good way off in the operating area. Normally there would be talking, the noise of sharpening tools and maybe the odd laugh as they waited for the dreadful work to begin. But then normally there would be light, movement and company. His was a sensitive soul, used to picking up the subtle signs in all things, be they the unspoken symptoms of a comatose patient, vagaries in the weather, or a superior officer's ill temper. Sitting silent in the darkness, while the ship headed slowly toward danger, and perhaps destruction, sitting below the waterline, and far from the hope of escape should she sink or explode, he felt his senses rise up to almost unbearable levels.

Apart from the scuttling of a rat in the hold below—a sound so easily magnified that it sounded like the crash of a round shot raking them from bow to stern—apart from the rat, the creak of timbers and the pounding of his own heart, there was no noise, and the ship was filled with an expectancy that hurt. He shuffled uncomfortably on the warm deck, shifting his position in an effort to break the tension that was almost tangible. He found his breathing had become shallow and frequent; he looked up, but in the absolute black there was no relief, no contrast, just a deep impenetrable obscurity. A slight groan escaped, making him jump and even further on edge. He was panting now, panting and starting to wriggle uncontrollably. It must end, it must end soon; he could not take the silence, the dark, and the waiting any longer, no longer, no longer at all; he knew that a scream was only seconds away.

* * * * *

The enemy fleet was just visible on their larboard bow; small pinpricks of light at their mastheads showed where they were continuing to vie with each other for position. And there was the very slightest lightening in the sky astern, over the shore that was fast receding as *Pandora* crept on. But there was nothing more, no star broke the heavy autumn sky, and her speed was not great enough to turn a wake. Certainly the frigates were out there, and probably still on the opposite tack and heading almost directly for them. Of course, *Pandora's* masts might conceivably be silhouetted against the lighter eastern sky, but there was no profit in thinking such thoughts; either they would be spotted and attacked, or missed and allowed to live, and fight another day. Next to King, Cobb stirred uncomfortably. They were perched as high as they could be, both with their arms wrapped about the main topgallant mast, and the tension, the uncomfortable position, and Cobb's constant fidgeting, was starting to tell.

"Get down to the crosstrees," King whispered. "You can see almost as much from there, and Ford might be getting lonely."

"You'll be all right?"

"I'll have better room, and a touch more peace without your inherent wriggling. Besides no one's going to steal me. Now be off, and quiet about it."

The lad gratefully clambered down, resting his stomach briefly on the yard as he sought for the ratlines with his feet. Then he was gone and King was left to his private and very black world. Even the foremast lookout, standing slightly lower, and not more than fifty feet away from him was only visible because he knew him to be there. Without the regular sounding of the bell, time had ceased to matter; King might have been up there for ten minutes, or half an hour, but when he first saw the flash of movement off the starboard bow, it seemed to stop entirely.

He stared out, keeping his concentration on the same bearing, as *Pandora* solidly plunged her way forward. Another glimpse, but no more; the ship, if it were a ship, was equally well blacked out. He was certain the second sighting was further off their beam, which meant they were converging on almost reciprocal courses. He glanced down and could just make out Cobb and Ford sitting companionably together on the crosstrees. Cobb was sweeping the larboard sector, and Ford the starboard, and both seemed oblivious to any actual sighting.

"Object off the starboard beam!" King muttered, his voice hoarse with the effort of shouting in a whisper. Ford immediately glanced up, then across to where the lieutenant was pointing. King looked also, and the sight came and went almost in the same instant. This time it was deeper on their beam, and he was reasonably sure it to be a sail, set a little lower than his own position. He glanced down again, but Ford was shaking his head; clearly he had caught nothing. Cobb was climbing up to join him; King stopped the midshipman as his head drew level.

"Down to the deck; quick as you can," he whispered urgently. "Ship in sight on the starboard beam; probably a cable or so off, and on the opposite course; got that?"

The lad nodded, and disappeared at once. The fastest way down to the deck was by a backstay, but the landing could also be noisy; Cobb was the best judge of that however. King had a history of being the only one to make a sighting and, as he stared out to sea, he almost wished that the enemy were more apparent.

* * * * *

"You're sure?" the captain asked.

Cobb shook his head. "I didn't see it myself, sir, but Mr King: he was positive."

Banks stared out to starboard in a futile effort to see from the level of the deck. But the dark was complete; he could hardly make out the lad Cobb, or Caulfield standing next to him.

"Very good, return to the top; ask Mr King to continue to watch. Send Ford out to the larboard royal halyards - larboard mind. If the sighting becomes clearer, he is to give three tugs; d'you follow?"

Cobb nodded his head in the darkness, adding a forgotten "Yes, sir."

"And if it is the enemy, and he alters course or there is little doubt that he has seen us, you are to call out as usual. Now off you go." Banks turned to where he thought Caulfield still stood. "With luck we will pass them in the darkness."

A ship on the reciprocal course would be gone in no time, even if she were travelling as slowly as *Pandora*. And, should the enemy have caught as brief a sighting as they had, there would be little likelihood of them opening fire. In the Dutch captain's position, he would continue on his present heading until *Pandora* had passed, then tack, turn back, and try to creep up behind and rake her.

"Aye, sir," Caulfield replied thoughtfully, his mind running on very similar lines. "But if they have seen us..."

"If they have seen us we shall know about it soon enough."

* * * * *

"David, David; it's me, Katharine."

Powell turned in his misery and stared in the direction of the voice. "Miss Black?" he asked, in a voice that was considerably above a whisper and must have turned a dozen heads.

"Quiet now," she came closer, and felt about in the darkness. "You seemed restless, David; are you all right?"

"Yes, miss," he said, feeling foolish. "I don't like the dark, but I'm all right."

"I don't like the dark, either. It's horrid; but it won't last," her voice was soft and strangely reassuring. "We're all here together. Mr Doust, Mr Manning, the other loblolly boys, they're all back there, not five yards away."

"I know."

"And Mr Everit, the carpenter, with the men that help him; they're hereabouts." She thought quickly. "And there is Mr Donaldson, the gunner, and the cook, and several more, in the magazine, just a bit further back." As soon as she had, Kate regretted mentioning the proximity of explosives to a frightened man, but he seemed to be taking it well enough.

"I just felt a bit... on me own," he had settled himself now; the touch of skin in the darkness as he reached out for her hand was balm enough.

"You might feel on your own, but you have an important job."

That was no exaggeration; Naval protocol demanded that the wounded were seen in strict order, regardless of rank or, in theory, degree of injury. Powell, who was charged with comforting those awaiting attention, knew the rules, but also understood instinctively when some would benefit from the surgeon's time, and some would not. Consequently a few of the more desperate cases might be deftly moved ahead of the less demanding while, for the truly hopeless, there was rum and laudanum a-plenty.

"But David, there is no need for us to worry about that now." He quivered slightly, remembering the last person to have called him by his first name. His eyes grew moist and then began to flow with silent tears. But she was still there, still talking in that soft reassuring way, still holding his hand, childlike, in the absolute black that had suddenly become a friend. "What say we keep company, David? See this wicked darkness out together? And if there comes a time when we do meet action, I'm sure there will be plenty to make us occupied."

"And no shortage of company then, miss." The pressure was easing now, to be replaced by a warm feeling of peace and a gentle smile.

"That as well," she agreed and smiled also as they sat together in the darkness while *Pandora* continued to creep through the night.

* * * * *

King had seen the sail twice more, and both times the sighting was further off, and towards the stern. If pressed he would have said the other ship was steering a point or so to larboard of the reciprocal; which might mean the enemy were searching for her further to the north. If that were the case every second was taking them further away from danger. Or *Pandora* could have been spotted already: the Dutch would have no mark to aim at, and might be gathering speed to tack, and come back on a closer heading. He continued to stare into the darkness; Cobb had returned and relayed the captain's instructions. He was with him now, sweeping the larboard sector, as King continued to peer out to starboard. Then, as he stared and strained, all darkness suddenly vanished, and the night was split into a thousand tiny fragments of deep, intense, almost torturing luminance.

The vision grew, rising up, up into the black sky, bringing strange colour, and savage contrast to all about. But most of all it brought light, blinding light that lit the sails, yards and lines about King making him feel stupidly exposed as he clung to the mast. He all but gasped as the rocket continued skywards, leaving a trail of yellow flame where it had been, and brilliantly picking out the two heavy frigates to stern of them.

* * * * *

They were several cables off and one, the nearest, had been King's mystery sighting. The second, further away and steering several points northwards, had fired the rocket. Clearly they had guessed *Pandora* would manoeuvre; they might even have caught the beginning of her turn, but they had thought she would pull back, away from the immediate danger of a hostile fleet. Had she done so the British frigate would have been trapped between the two and they would now be firing into her helpless hull. Banks nodded quietly to himself; no one would know how close he had come to that very decision; on another night it might easily have been so, and they would be suffering two deadly broadside at that very moment. But there was no time for further speculation; the Dutch would realise their mistake, and be mildly humiliated. *Pandora* was still close enough to be spotted, and now he could expect to be the subject of a lively chase. Both ships would have to tack or wear to catch them, however; he had to take advantage of the situation, and pile on as much speed as possible while he could.

"Make sail!" he shouted, his words sounding unusually loud, although the deafening bellows of Caulfield, Fraiser and the boatswain soon surpassed them. The men thundered into position, their horny feet on the deck sounding reassuringly familiar. Light from the rocket was fading, and the black swiftly returned, but months of exercise and practice bore fruit as the men continued to work effectively in the darkness.

The wind was growing fitful, although still held enough force for *Pandora* to pick up speed. "Light one binnacle lamp and below deck," Banks ordered. "And the slow match; but keep the ports closed." To travel at any speed in the darkness had been foolish; to do so now, while under full sail, would be reckless in the extreme. *Pandora* was already bucking and jolting as she ploughed through the waves, and soon they might have to call for some delicate manoeuvring.

"They're going about," King called from the masthead, he had seen a swirl of movement in the dark, and made the obvious assumption. Banks immediately turned his attention to the enemy liners, now some way off their larboard quarter. He might be trying to outrun the frigates, but to do so and lose the fleet he was shadowing would totally defeat the objective.

"Take her two points to larboard," he glanced at Fraiser who nodded his head in the dim glow from the binnacle and reached for the traverse board to chalk up the order. The sailing master did not need to consult his charts. They were far enough offshore to be free of any known shallows, at least for the time being; besides, the wind was not exactly constant and he had a suspicion it would start to fail before the night grew very much older.

"The wind is dying," the captain was clearly of the same mind.

"Aye, sir. An' I'd thought it set for the night," Fraiser nodded seriously in the darkness. "Belike there'll be a few out there who would wish they hadna' ventured out this evening."

* * * * *

But in *Vrijheid* the mood was still buoyant. The weather might be fickle and the night was certainly growing more cold but the ship, like every other in the fleet, was manned almost entirely by experienced seamen, and they were actually free of the land; something many of them had not achieved in several years. Better, they were sailing as a fleet, a mighty fleet, and in their own North Sea; the waters their ships had been designed for. Van Leiden was watching the tell tale lights that marked the position of each ship. One, he was reasonably sure it was *Beschermer*, a fifty gun fourth rate, was inclined to carry too much sail, and had twice almost overtaken the next in line. Were this to be daylight he would doubtless have been occupied, sending countless signals, and generally chivvying them into close order. But night signalling was a far more primitive art; one that would involve the use of coloured lights, guns and even rockets. The *admiraal* was reluctant to advertise their position by anything more than the essential but tiny masthead lamps, so van Leiden had been relatively idle for the first time since he had stepped aboard the flagship. Besides, they were making reasonable progress, even with the fluky wind; daylight was only hours away and there would be plenty of time for manoeuvring in the morning.

It was just past midnight; the quarter moon had risen, although the minimal amount of light it shed only made the night seem darker. The British frigate was still plaguing them somewhere off their starboard counter; occasionally she could be seen from the flagship's masthead, along with the two frigates that had been sent to deal with her. They seemed to be having less luck in spotting *Pandora*, as van Leiden had now decided her to be. Two more rockets had been sent up, but on each occasion the British were well out of range and had immediately disappeared into the darkness, apparently altering course as soon as they were enveloped once more. The rockets had achieved little, other than to reveal the frigate's own positions, and raise the *admiraal*'s anger. He had been keen to despatch a further ship to help the search, but the captain had prevailed upon him. To do so could only add to the confusion and it was quite likely that the first two frigates would find and fire upon the third; a dreadful start to any expedition.

That had been an hour ago, and de Winter had since retired to his quarters, obviously resigned to having his course and position monitored throughout the night. Things would change in the morning; with daylight there should be little difficulty in prising away their constant spy, and they could continue unseen to collect the other ships. Van Leiden was glad; what he had learnt of the officers in *Pandora*, and King in particular, reassured him that the

British were no fools, and would not risk an engagement with a superior force without reason. The wind might be fading, but it was expected to rise with the daylight when their frigates would have every chance of chasing the British away; faced with such a fleet as theirs, only a *dwaas* would do other than run.

The main course above his head flapped loudly, filled once, and then flapped again. From aft came the soft sound of a flute, the *admiraal*'s instrument; clearly he was still up and the music made an odd accompaniment to the still, dark night. Just a few more hours; tomorrow, and they would be free.

CHAPTER TWENTY-ONE

BUT as dawn broke upon the fleet the wind stayed low. Worse, for the Dutch; true to the vagaries of the North Sea, that which found *Pandora*, six miles off their starboard beam, was stronger and backing round to the west, giving the frigate a distinct advantage when *Mars* and *Monnikendamm*, her two frustrated adversaries from the night before, made for her. The heavier ships lumbered under full sail while *Pandora* skipped to the southwest, dipping in towards the fleet, round and away again faster than the Dutch could anticipate. The game continued until noon, when *Pandora*'s masthead sighted another vessel coming in from the north. It was *Circe*, and they were no longer alone.

Banks and Caulfield smiled at each other; both had spent the bulk of the night and all of that morning on deck, and now they knew the time had been well used.

"She's sighted us, and is altering course," the masthead confirmed. The Dutch were currently nine miles off *Pandora*'s larboard beam; had she not been there it was quite possible that *Circe* would have missed them completely. The frigate was within signalling distance in no time, and had called up *Russell*. Trollope's ship came together with two other liners that had intercepted the lugger sent to alert Duncan, half way across the North Sea. Now, with three proper battleships the British had a force that could really keep an eye on the enemy; one that would not be brushed aside by bluster and a couple of frigates. Trollope quickly organised the shadowing force so that *Pandora* and *Circe* could keep the enemy under constant observation, while the larger ships stretched out to sea in the hope of catching Duncan when he came looking.

Throughout the night, which passed without incident, and on to the following day the British stayed on station, matching any slight variation of heading, with *Pandora* occasionally sweeping in for a closer look, and to taunt the outlying frigates. Then, on the following afternoon, when the fragile day was giving in to dusk, the enemy made a distinct change of course.

"Two points to larboard," Fraiser ordered, and *Pandora* came round, following the fleet exactly as she had for all of the watch. Dorsey was on hand, and the signal flags raced up; within minutes all the ships of the observation squadron knew and Trollope had ordered the appropriate alteration. They were fifty miles or so from Texel; no distance considering the time taken, but now the enemy appeared to be heading for the coast.

"What land have we, master?" Banks had rested for most of the night, and all of the officers and men had stood down for a brief period, although there were few places of comfort in a ship cleared for action.

Fraiser busied himself with his charts and looked up. "We're just off the Hague, sir."

"Fair sized port," Caulfield added. "They'll find shelter there for certain."

"Belike it ain't shelter they're after." It was Newman's voice, and all looked at him in mild surprise.

"There is no need to take on so, gentlemen," he smiled. "I might not have your nautical talents, but I read the papers. The river Meuse empties hereabouts and is a holding anchorage; ask me, our friends won't be looking for shelter, but reinforcements."

That made sense, although it also worsened the situation somewhat.

"If it is the case," Caulfield said slowly. "We had better hope Admiral Duncan is with us directly, and that he brings a sizeable force along with him."

* * * * *

Van Leiden sat in the launch as it headed back to *Vrijheid*. Next to him de Winter was motionless and fuming. The meeting ashore had not gone well; he had never known the *admiraal* to be so angry. Their intention had been to call briefly and collect further ships. According to a despatch received only hours before they set sail there were three line-of-battleships ready to put to sea. Such an addition to the Dutch fleet would have made victory over the British an absolute certainty, and had been a major deciding factor when it came to the fleet leaving harbour. Since then the harrying force of British ships that stalked their every move had been annoying enough. Adding to that the fluky, meagre wind, and many stupid mistakes from both seamen and officers—men who were out of practice and, in a few cases, physically unfit—meant that any progress they made had been slow and frustrating. But to have crept, stumbled and staggered their way down the coast as far as this, only to face disappointment and incompetence had clearly been the final straw for de Winter.

Rather than a sizeable force, they had found only one solitary sixty-four, and she would not be ready for sea within the month. The *admiraal* was angry, and it was the cold, repressed wrath of a man betrayed; a man placed in an impossible position, a man who had been pressed into a command that was beyond his own experience but had risen to the challenge, only to find himself in turn controlled by forces far less competent, informed and honourable.

But now they were committed; they had put to sea and the British were shadowing. If they stayed in one place they could expect to meet with Duncan's ships within a few days. And if they travelled south the chances were strong they would find Bridport's Channel Fleet. Either way there would be a battle, a battle that, even when won and won decisively as was expected, would not be without cost. The ships that de Winter now commanded represented the greater part of the entire Dutch fighting navy and would be bound to require extensive repair and refitting before they could put to sea again.

The alternative, and there always was an alternative, was to head north, attempt to dodge whatever Duncan had sent to meet them, and return to Texel. The wind, which had backed further, was stronger now and would serve for a passage home. With luck they should be off port by tomorrow afternoon; tomorrow evening they might all be sleeping ashore, with the entire force safely back at anchor.

The *admiraal* swore suddenly, and beat the gunwale of the boat with the side of his fist. Van Leiden turned to him, then away again, trying to set his concentration on the flagship they were nearing, and avoid the probing eyes of Sweelinck pulling stroke oar. In a situation such as this it was not unlikely that the two men were thinking similar thoughts, and clearly de Winter was as much at a loss as his junior.

To return home was to do so with ignominy. The Dutch navy was a proud force, and with reason. Until so very recently it had been one of the strongest maritime powers in the world, and the main reason why the country's trade and empire had expanded. To the uninitiated, and those who had ordered them to sea naturally fell into that category, to them there was no reason why they should not meet the British. Only later, when they were asked for replacement spars, copper and timber, only then would the problems start, and the proud and victorious ships would gradually deteriorate into worthless hulks as they rotted at their moorings for want of supplies. Much might be made of their victory but, however decisive it turned out, the final cost would be the destruction of the Dutch fleet.

So north was effectively ruled out, and south. To the east lay Dan Hagg; they might put in there for a while, although there would be little benefit; at least at the Texel they were known, and had some power over the dockyard and victuallers. Besides, many men had family ashore; some might even desert if they were taken to a different port that was still relatively close to their homes. So it would have to be the west.

Van Leiden felt the excitement grow. It would have to be the west; they could beat out against the contrary wind and gain sea room. There may well be a good deal of merchant shipping about; entire convoys to be raided; their ships and cargoes taken and sent back to the republic where they would be of immeasurable value. Duncan might even have been delayed, and could be caught in harbour; how would it be if the Dutch were to set a blockade on the British: what would the world say to that? And if not, if they simply fell in with the enemy fleet; with luck they might be to windward of them. Then they could close and force the British ships against the Dutch coast: the entire fleet might be wrecked or run aground without a shot being fired. To the west: with all matters taken into consideration, it really was the only option.

He smiled smugly to himself knowing he had the answer, although equally aware that it would do little good. He was merely a junior *luitenant* and had to rely on de Winter; the angry man who sat next to him now as the *Barkas* neared the black hull of his flagship; he was the one who must have the fine thoughts and come to the great decisions.

The custom in the Dutch navy was the same as in many others; the most senior officer was the last to board a small boat, and the first to disembark. They were close to the entry steps now, and the *coxswain* was standing with the boathook. De Winter was also getting ready to leave, and pulled himself up from the thwart stiffly, resting his hand on van Leiden's shoulder. The *luitenant* looked up and was surprised to see the *admiraal* smile down at him. All traces of anger seemed to have vanished; he was as affable and relaxed as ever; it was the face of a contented man.

"I think I might have the solution, *luitenant,*" he said simply; and van Leiden found himself smiling in return; if that was the case they would all start to feel a great deal more easy. "We will sail to the west," he said, and van Leiden very nearly laughed out loud. Yes, the *admiraal* had it: the only feasible option; they would sail to the west.

* * * * *

In fact their actual course was roughly south-southwest for the starboard tack; or as near to the wind as they could come without pinching. The Dutch ships were making reasonable speed close hauled, and had formed into a creditable sailing pattern. Now, in the position of prey rather than predator, *Pandora* and her sisters were about five miles ahead of them, and spread out just within signalling distance to cover any further moves de Winter's fleet might make. But it was growing dark and soon they would have to move together and allow the enemy to close if they were to remain in touch. The hours of darkness would be tense, with the likelihood that the Dutch might change course at any time, or even forereach on them; were that to happen, and any of the British ships fell back amongst such a powerful fleet, they would be snapped up within minutes.

Pandora was still cleared for action and, although the hands had gone back to the usual watch routine, food was served cold and no one relaxed or slept for very long. King's beard had not been attended to for several days now, and was starting to grow rough and noticeable. He felt at his chin as he gazed back at the enemy fleet, a sight that had almost become commonplace. As he watched a trail of signal flags broke out on the nearest ship, her jib sheets suddenly eased and the forecourse started to shiver.

"They're tacking!" he yelled, just as the masthead lookout called to the deck. Sure enough the first two ships were preparing to come about.

"Enemy is tacking in succession," the masthead dolefully reported.

"Make to *Russell*, enemy is altering course to starboard," Dorsey touched his hat to Caulfield and began to raise the signal that he had already prepared. The nearest Dutch ships were in irons now with the braces on the main and mizzen masts set for the new course. Both payed off smartly enough, and soon the sails were trimmed and they were gathering way on the new tack, while those behind began to follow.

"Smoothly done," Caulfield said grudgingly as they watched. Indeed it was a distinct improvement on some of the evolutions they had witnessed before. "Make enemy course now nor-nor west, and prepare to tack."

"Strange they didn't wait until night," Fraiser commented, in one of his rare displays of spontaneity. "You'd ha thought they'd use the dark to try an' shake us off."

"Belike they didn't trust themselves," Caulfield mused.

"Or they were making too much to the south," King added.

"You mean they're purposely heading west?" Caulfield looked at King in surprise.

"Why should they not?"

The first lieutenant nodded. "Why not indeed? The admiral must have got word by now, and should be at sea, I merely felt they wouldn't be so keen to meet him."

King said nothing, he remembered the words of de Winter and despite all that had been said since, he remained convinced that the Dutch were ready to fight and totally confidant of victory.

"At least we should have some light tonight," Caulfield said, looking up at the sky, clear for the first time for many days.

"Aye, it will last the night, but not much longer," Fraiser added. "Be set for a light rain on the morrow; then it will clear a wee while, before rain again in the next day."

Caulfield was impressed. "Sure that is a bold and accurate prediction, Adam."

"Nothing less than what I have been told."

"What you've been told?" The first lieutenant eyed him with an amused twinkle. "Hear him, our fine and scientific sailing master, so fond of his instruments and charts, and yet he relies on hearsay!"

King grinned, but Fraiser apparently remained defiant. "There's not the reason for fancy glasses when we have one as gifted as Powell aboard. He says the rain will come and go, an' because he does, I believe it will."

"Well, he has been proven right in the past." King added.

"Aye, but can he tell us where Duncan might be?" Caulfield again, but Fraiser shook his head.

"Indeed he can not; neither would I listen if he said he could."

"There is a difference?"

"Between judging the actions of men against those of nature? Oh yes," Fraiser smiled enigmatically. "I'd say there was all the difference in the world."

* * * * *

In fact both Fraiser and Powell were correct. The night, though dark and seemingly endless, was starlit, and the moon had gained strength. The British remained just ahead of the Dutch, matching them with each and every tack and, as dawn broke, the situation remained essentially unchanged.

As it did for the following day; *Pandora* and her consorts kept pace with the Dutch as they slowly clawed their way to windward in the gentle rain, with each tack taking several hours, and gaining but a few miles of sea room. The watches were as tense as they were without incident, although all remained aware that it might only take the slightest mishap; a spar carried away by accident or freak wind, and they would be at the mercy of the oncoming enemy.

And that night it was truly dark once more; too dark to maintain a close watch without endangering the watcher. Trollope signalled a recall at the start of the second dog, and *Pandora* gratefully increased sail, leaving a deeper margin between her and the enemy. The following morning might show an empty sea; indeed they could have lost the entire Dutch fleet, but their luck had already been stretched far enough; to draw it further would be foolhardy.

Dawn broke slowly and with it came a few more spots of rain and a sea far more crowded than they had expected. As the first true light spread across the grey seas the Dutch fleet was revealed, about five miles directly to leeward; very much the position that Banks and Trollope had anticipated. But the enemy were divided; a group of five liners had detached themselves from the main force and were even now on the opposite tack, straining under optimistic sail and clearly intending to get to windward of the British.

Once more the signal flags went soaring up *Pandora's* halyards, although now there was more to report. In addition to the advance squadron, seven transports were approaching the Dutch from the north.

"Fortune out there in prize money," Caulfield grumbled as he stared at the merchants. "And all flying the Batavian flag."

"Part of an invasion fleet?" King asked, but Caulfield shook his head.

"You wouldn't find troop or army transports sailing without an escort, even if they had intended to meet up with the main Dutch force; my guess is they're traders from the north, and taking a chance."

"If they'd tried it a fortnight back we could have had them." A healthy convoy would bring a sizeable amount to any junior officer involved in the sharing of prize money; King had heard of some who had been set up for life, and the idea was not exactly abhorrent to him.

"You forget, we were tied up to the Dutch coast; who knows what has passed us by while we've been on blockade. Seems they've called off the hounds though," Caulfield pointed to the separate group of five ships now some four miles to starboard. They might have been within range by noon, forcing the British to pull away or offer battle, but it seemed they were being recalled. A stream of signal flags had been flying for some while from the nearest Dutch ship in the main fleet, and the separate squadron was starting to come back on to the opposite tack and take in sail. Meanwhile the transports were hove to in the midst of the Dutch fleet.

"Speaking with them," Caulfield commented. "Wonder what news they bring."

"Can only be from the north," Newman added, joining them. "Unless they have been in sight of a semaphore of course, then there is no telling."

They watched for a while in silence until King asked the obvious, unanswerable, question: "Do you think they know of Duncan?"

Caulfield snorted, "If they do, I would that they might tell us."

* * * * *

Breakfast on the berth deck was not a pleasant meal. For all the time *Pandora* had been cleared for action the galley had been quiet and the fire cold. The small amount of cooked salted meat that had been left was gone after the first day, since when they had been surviving on banyan provisions; cheese, pickled cabbage, onions and biscuit. Burgoo, the oatmeal porridge usually served hot and with molasses, became nothing more than horse feed when mixed cold. Hot tea, popular in the colder months, was also just a memory, and they were all back to small beer, with pressed water and not even the chance of stolen goat's milk to brighten the fare. Flint sat at the mess table stirring despondently at his wooden bowl with his spoon.

"I've put raisins and apple in mine," Jameson said brightly. "Don't taste so bad then."

"You're at the age when it don't matter," Flint grumbled. "Give you the sack it came in, and you'd eat it all an' ask for more."

"Try letting it get cold," Jenkins suggested.

"*Let* it get cold?" Ford this time. "But it *is* cold."

"I've not touched mine for a spell, nor will I." Jenkins continued determinedly. "An' I don't look at it, I don't think about it, an' I don't annoy it with me spoon." he looked pointedly at Flint. "I lets me mind wander over other things, then I turns to it as if it had been forgotten, tells myself it's gone cold, an' when I does eat it, well it don't taste quite so bad."

* * * * *

In less than five minutes the enemy came back to the wind, leaving the transports to continue to the south. Then the British officers watched in silence as the Dutch began to slowly turn their backs and head northeast.

"Well, there's a thing," Caulfield grunted, as King was ordering a signal to *Russell*. "Whatever it was they discovered it certainly made a difference."

"Heading for their coast." King returned and stated the obvious.

"Aye, but is it for home, or Duncan?"

"Much depends on when Duncan heard the news," Newman said enigmatically. "And I would suppose it better he was told later, rather than earlier."

Caulfield turned to him. "How so?"

The marine had the undivided attention of both officers.

"Were the fleet already at sea and already at the Dutch coast, we can expect them to be heading south."

"Heading south, and clinging to the coast." Caulfield nodded then sighed; he was following Newman's supposition and had already reached its dreadful conclusion.

"It would be the sensible course," Newman continued. "Duncan would not have expected the sudden turn to the west."

"Indeed, it took us all by surprise." Caulfield agreed.

"So you fear the Dutch know where the fleet is, and can see the chance to trap them?" King was also there now.

"You must grant it possible."

"And Duncan has no knowledge of the enemy," King added. "If he is to the east the first he will know is when the Dutch come down on him; we can give no warning."

The three men were quiet; for Duncan to be trapped on a lee shore, with a powerful fleet to windward and his force divided, was just as terrible as it was likely.

"Well gentlemen," Newman said wryly. "We can assume one of two things; that they are either heading home, after a little excursion, or they have been told of our fleet and are ready to squeeze them against the shore."

The captain came up on the quarterdeck, he appeared fresh and well rested, although King noticed that he also had a slight bristle to his face.

"What course?" he asked briefly as he touched his hat in acknowledgement of their salutes.

"The enemy have spoken with a merchant convoy and are turning to the north east, sir." Caulfield said, pointing back across *Pandora*'s counter.

"Any news of the fleet?"

"None."

Banks nodded. "Mr Fraiser?"

"He is below, sir: shall I raise him?"

"No," Banks shook his head in emphasis. "No, let him rest," he studied his first lieutenant briefly. "And you should do likewise, Michael. Mr King, you have slept I gather?"

"Yes sir."

"Then we can hold the deck together."

"*Russell*'s making a signal, sir," Dorsey had the book in his hand and thumbed through the pages as the seaman read out the numbers. "Ordering us to follow."

Banks nodded at Caulfield who touched his hat and left the deck, while King began to bellow the orders that would set *Pandora* on her new course. Once more the braces heaved her creaking yards about, and she turned her head towards the enemy.

"Where is *Circe*?" the captain again.

"Further to the north, sir," King replied, adding in a softer tone. "I think Captain Trollope is keen to raise the admiral."

"As well he might be," Banks was silent for a moment. Trollope had been carrying the bulk of responsibility for the last few days. To track an enemy force at sea was hard; given the difficult and changeable weather and a fleet seemingly wandering without purpose, he had done well. But to do well was only what was expected; it was one of those jobs that could not be excelled at: Trollope could either complete it competently or fail, and he had had plenty of opportunities for the latter.

The morning drew on, with the Dutch steadily heading to the northeast, and the British squadron doggedly following in their wake. At nine, Banks decided that they had endured enough and authorised the galley fire to be lit, although there was no relaxation in the constant tension that seemed to have become part of the ship's very fabric. In the past there had been times of 'make and mend', of mess nights, with stingo, singing and stories. Men had danced hornpipes on the forecastle, and all had known japes and tattletale, tournaments and a little unofficial gambling. But *Pandora* was a warship, a frigate currently engaged in tracking and signalling an enemy force, and nothing could be closer to her true role. The heady days of casual sailing, when men could sleep in hammocks and eat regular meals: banyan days and Sunday worship, all that had been swiftly brushed to one side; forgotten as if they had occurred in a completely different ship as she assumed her true *raison d'être*.

* * * * *

The race was on; the Dutch had settled to their new course and had set as much sail as they could carry. If they were intending to trap Duncan, clearly they must not delay. The wind was now in the north west and blowing fresh and constant. Banks had been able to add top gallants and staysails, and *Pandora* was creaming through the seas with the enemy square on her bows. By two bells in the afternoon watch they had regained their previous station and reduced sail once more. Most on board were more settled, having had their first hot food in days, although the thought that they were following a fleet destined to destroy their own, and would be able to do very little about it, still haunted officers and men alike. Then it was time for 'Up Spirits'; Banks glanced down to see Katharine in her usual dark long dress, wearing a warrant officer's blue jacket against the cold. She was standing just below him in the waist, to one side of the launch, and he noticed, with a pang of desire, how some of her long hair had been blown free, and was trailing charmingly in the wind. Two stewards carried a pin of rum, and a larger cask of water, which Katharine proceeded to mix in the usual manner. The boatswain's pipes called all hands and the men were assembling on the half deck ready to collect the freshly mixed ration when Dorsey's voice rang out.

"Signal from *Circe*, repeat all ships," his voice was bright with excitement as he trained his glass on *Russell*. "Flag in sight!"

The cheering and yelling went on, despite roars and threats from the petty officers, until Kate firmly replaced the stopper on the grog cask, and motioned to the stewards for it to be taken away. Suddenly order was restored, and the men returned to obediently queuing for their ration, although there remained a lightening in the atmosphere that nothing could have quelled.

"Where away?" Banks asked Dorsey, who was still studying *Russell.*

"There's another hoist, sir." he paused, counting off the numbers silently before giving the answer without reference to his book. "North west," he turned and beamed: "Coming down with the wind!"

The men's enthusiasm was infectious, and Banks found himself chuckling like a satisfied child as the officers began to beam and smack each other on the back. Duncan might be poorly equipped with worn out and obsolete ships, but he had come to sea without hesitation, and rather than being trapped against a lee shore, even now was bearing down on the enemy. There would be a battle now; that was for certain.

"Three cheers for Old Adam!" The officers grinned as the shouts rolled out, with Jenkins adding the obligatory tiger. Banks noticed the smiles and banter, the energy and optimism that had been so lacking. It was a different group of men to those who had spent the last few days in the presence of an overwhelmingly superior enemy. One slip, one wrong or misinterpreted order, and the Dutch would have had them; now they could hope to meet on slightly more equal terms. With Duncan in sight and an accommodating wind they should close by the following day. They had one more night to survive, although with the enemy neatly caught, there seemed little chance that they could escape battle. By tomorrow evening it should be settled and either the Dutch would be silenced, or the British North Sea Fleet would cease to exist, and the long threatened invasion could finally begin.

CHAPTER TWENTY-TWO

DUNCAN was on the quarterdeck of Venerable by first light the following morning. Like all in the British fleet, the flagship was carrying as much sail as the brisk wind would allow, as she headed for the Dutch coast and the enemy. On Venerable's starboard beam the frigate Circe could just be seen from the deck, as she shadowed the Dutch. Beyond her Russell, and the rest of the observation squadron, already augmented by some from the main North Sea Fleet, were heading to meet up; with luck they would join, or at least be within direct signalling distance, before long. It would have been better to have met with Trollope; a brief discussion with all captains before action might iron out any last minute confusions. But the officers knew each other well enough; more to the point, they knew him, and his intentions: Duncan would far rather have a group of informed, professional men under him and no pre-set battle plan, than precise instructions with every perceived eventuality covered, and a bunch of fools to follow them. The decks were steaming gently in the fresh early sun, although all on board knew that the fine start would not see the day out. Captain Fairfax had also breakfasted early, and was talking with Cleland, his first lieutenant. Duncan strolled across and acknowledged their salutes with a dignified raising of his own hat.

"Gentlemen, I trust all is prepared for today's activities?"

"We are ready, sir," Fairfax replied. "Carpenter still reports a fair amount gathering in the well, but we have cleared all for now, and two hours a watch is considered sufficient to keep it at bay until it can be attended."

It was unfortunate that the steady leaking *Venerable* had been suffering from for some while should suddenly have increased on the very eve of action; pumping was exhausting work, and both Fairfax and Duncan knew that it would take very little damage to *Venerable*'s worn out hull to make matters considerably worse. In fact the chances were high that, whether they met with success or defeat, the British flagship would be sunk by the end of the day.

"Very good, William, I am sure you have done all that can be," he lowered his voice slightly. "You are happy with the people?"

"Morale seems high, admiral. The men are eager for action."

Duncan turned to the lieutenant and raised his eyebrows enquiringly.

"I could not ask for more, sir. And I believe it is the same in other ships. It's difficult to believe..." Cleland left the sentence unfinished, not wishing to bring up memories of the mutiny on such a morning.

"Difficult to believe that we have a full fleet, and that seven of our number were actively against us barely months ago?" Duncan smiled briefly and nodded. "There were mistakes on both sides, but all is in the past. The lads will have every opportunity to show their worth today, and a glorious victory shall surely wipe the slate clean." He turned back to Fairfax. "Tell me, captain, there is nothing pressing for the while?"

"No, sir; all is quiet."

"Then be so good as to summon the men."

They came in silence, and stood waiting expectantly in the waist, the able and ordinary seamen, landsmen, boys, artisans, idlers, warrant and petty officers and supernumeraries. The officers gathered on the quarterdeck and the marines, brilliant in pipe clayed white, shining silver and rich red coats, formed in crisp ranks, seemingly becoming part of the fabric of the ship. Only those actually keeping the watch, the helmsmen, quartermaster and lookouts, remained at their posts, and there were no wry comments or grousing from the watch below; all knew why they had been called, and all, be they Christian, pagan or undefined, were willing, almost grateful, to be there.

Once assembled Duncan strode to the break of the quarterdeck, and looked down as a deep, uniting silence came upon them all. He stretched his hands out wide and seemed to gather all together as one, holding them with his very presence. Then, in a soft but penetrating voice that carried throughout the ship and into every man's heart, he called for approval on the day; committed them all to their God, and asked for protection in the coming battle. He spoke as one with certain knowledge, rather than faith, and his authority was such that the assembly was spellbound, finally breaking up without the usual chattering and jokes that seem intrinsic to seamen after any formal gathering. Duncan had known nearly all present for many years. For many years he had nurtured and guided; at times standing both for, and up to them. They were thought of as his lads; indeed there had been occasions when he had acted as their father, and all had been done so that they could stand together on this day. And now, unspoken, but universally acknowledged, he gave them his final blessing. There was nothing more he could do: nothing more that could be done, and yet all were content and supremely confidant that it was enough.

* * * * *

The observation squadron had been joined by several ships from Duncan's fleet with Admiral Onslow, once more back in *Monarch*, leading in loose order to the north east. The two groups of British warships were still several miles apart although, if the wind held steady, they were expected to be as one before noon. *Pandora*, to the south and closest to the rump of the Dutch fleet, was at the very end of the line, with *Russell* close by. The enemy was in plain view directly ahead with all sensible sail set, and heading for their own coast in three columns, on a course roughly north-northeast.

"Belike they've seen enough and are heading for home," Caulfield said. "Can't say that I've ever wanted a fight, but t'would be a pity to have come so far and still return disappointed."

"They wouldna be heading for home."

Caulfield turned back surprised. "What say, master?"

"They're makin' for the shallows," Fraiser looked up from his chart. "Keep the same course and they'll hit the coast roughly fifteen miles south of the Texel."

Caulfield sauntered across and peered over Fraiser's shoulder.

"So, what is there that draws them?"

A stubby, ink-stained finger pointed out the bleak coastline. "Nothing to speak of; a few small villages, no shore batteries, as far as we know; just shallows."

"The Dutch draw a good deal less than our liners," Caulfield continued. "D'you think they might be trying to avoid action by sheltering in the shoals?"

"The Dutch won't avoid action," King had joined them and was strangely confident. Even though he had done all he could to avoid spreading despondency, de Winter's words were still with him.

Caulfield looked up and at the enemy fleet. "So why do they not tack; our fleet remains divided, they could go hell for leather for one group and we would be the worse for it."

Fraiser nodded sadly. "The Dutch are no fools. Why should they fight a pitched battle on the open sea when they can choose the place, and a better one at that? These are their home waters; they know them as well as we do the Solent. Take us over to the shoals where we, with our deep hulls and inferior knowledge, have to keep feeling for the depth; they can run amuck atween us, and if any try to follow the chances are strong that we'll ground. Then they can pick us off at their leisure."

It made sense, but was not the most heartening of views.

"Signal, Dorsey!" King had spotted movement on *Beaulieu*. The frigate was stationed to the west of their small group, and repeated messages from Duncan's squadron.

"From flag, general signal, prepare for battle."

King and Caulfield exchanged glances; *Pandora* had been ready for almost a week. "Shall we beat to quarters?" King asked.

Caulfield shook his head. "The captain's still below, there'll be time enough for that."

By nine the position had changed little; the enemy fleet was still well out of range, although the British groups had closed upon them. Banks, who had breakfasted well in his screened off quarters, had appeared an hour back, and was now holding the deck with King, while Caulfield and Fraiser ate a hurried meal below. Another signal came from *Beaulieu* and Dorsey, who was squatting next to his flag locker sucking on a biscuit, sprang up to read it.

"It's to *Circe*," he reported after a few seconds. "Flag's ordering her to close up."

At that moment the masthead lookout bellowed from above. "Sail! Sail in sight on the larboard beam." Banks and King instinctively turned in that direction, but nothing could be seen past the ships of their own group.

"Colours?"

"Not as yet, sir, but we're closing fast. I'd say she were the *Triumph*; she 'as her rig: I knows her bowsprit, it's a high one."

Banks smiled at King. "Seems like we're nearing the admiral's squadron."

"There's more," Ford, at the masthead continued. "More behind, what look to be British, an' she's the *Triumph*, sure as a gun."

"Signal from flag to *Russell*," Dorsey again. "Close with the flag."

"I think we're there, Mr King," Banks beamed as if he had just been invited to a particularly pleasant social gathering. "Time to beat to quarters, I fancy."

The marine drummer mounted the quarterdeck and began to pound out a tattoo that resounded throughout the small ship as the hands made for their battle stations. Fraiser and Caulfield hurried up the companionway and joined the other officers.

"Get some breakfast, Thomas," Banks said as they arrived. "There's time enough for that, and to shift your clothes if you've a mind. Don't forget; britches and silk stockings are for a fighting man."

King turned to his captain.

"So much better for the surgeon if he comes to operate, don't you know?" Banks gave another boyish smile, and King left, wondering slightly.

At nine twenty-two Duncan signalled once more, ordering his fleet to form a line on a starboard bearing to allow the slower ships to catch up, but by ten it was clear that their speed was not sufficient and a general signal was made for all ships to make more sail. *Pandora*, one of the smallest in the British force, was still the furthest to the south. In a general fleet action there might be little for her to do, other than relay signals and possibly take possession of a prize. Few heavy battleships would waste their time or shot on her, when there were larger and more potent ships to face. But de Winter was sailing with several frigates and brigs, small stuff that would be in a similar position to *Pandora*, and Banks was silently hoping he might wage his own private battle.

By eleven the heaviest Dutch ships had formed into a single line of battle, with their smaller craft, the frigates, brigs and corvettes, to the lee. It was clear that the British would join with them to windward in two distinct groups, with Duncan leading seven line-of-battleships to the north in *Venerable*, and Onslow with nine that included two fifty gun fourth rates, to the south. By then the enemy's force had been correctly assessed and it was clear that the British were outnumbered both in ships and guns, although the fact was considered purely academic by all who knew it. For the next hour they crept closer. Texel, home and safety, lay barely twenty miles off, and Duncan knew that if the Dutch were to escape this time his force would spend the next ten years blockading them.

"General signal," Dorsey's voice rang out once more. "Bear up and sail large."

The officers on the quarterdeck exchanged glances; it would not be long now. King turned to Banks. "With your permission, sir, I will attend to the guns."

"Indeed, Mr King." The two men nodded briefly, not knowing if each would see the other again, before King turned and made his way down the quarterdeck steps.

"General signal," Dorsey's voice cracked this time. "Pass through the enemy's line and engage to leeward."

Banks glanced at Fraiser. "What depth have we, master?"

"A fair amount here, sir, but less than nine fathoms yonder," the Scotsman pointed just ahead of where the enemy were closing up to create a veritable wall of fire, not five miles from their own shoreline. "If we are to take them it must be soon; the shallows increase further as we near the Texel."

The captain stroked his chin contemplatively "Our line ships shall have to fight their way through as it is: there will be little room to spare."

Fraiser was still looking at the Dutch, his demeanour as dispassionate as ever as his mind calculated angles and positions. For the British to penetrate and break the enemy line they would have to approach at a steep angle. And the enemy were holding extremely close order; packed tight, they would present an apparently impenetrable barrier. The vast majority of the British guns would be totally useless until they had actually punched their way through. Then they might well create havoc, raking ships on either side, but to reach that position would entail surviving several unanswered broadsides. There could be no doubt: it would be carnage.

"The admiral means to close on their beams?" Caulfield had caught on now, and was looking suitably concerned.

"Aye, that would seem to be his plan," Banks voice was steady and considered. "Not an enviable role for the liners, though one, I think, that might stop the Dutch before they reach the shallows, and that is clearly what Duncan is about."

The first drops of rain fell just after noon, as *Monarch*, well to the fore, began to nose her way towards the tightly packed Dutch battle line. A puff of smoke came from the nearest enemy ship, followed immediately by a full two deck broadside, although Onslow's flagship seemed to weather the barrage as if it were nothing but spray and spindrift. Watched by all, the British ship edged closer. Another broadside rolled out from a Dutch seventy-four.

"They're aiming low, at the decks," Caulfield commented, his eyes glued to the action taking place not a mile from him.

"Aye, the Dutch don't follow French tactics," Banks was also watching fascinated. "They won't be happy with knocking away a few spars; expect them to fire on the downward roll, hit the hull and the men in it; destroy the ship, not merely force it to a halt."

"Why does the admiral not fire with his for'ard guns?" Caulfield asked.

"Maybe he thinks they might kill the wind, besides they would do little good, whereas if he can get through the line..."

Another broadside came, and another after that, but still the British ship continued. *Powerful* and *Veteran* were also approaching now, and starting to feel the enemy's wrath, but *Monarch* was so much closer and beginning to be obscured by smoke from the Dutch broadsides.

Banks looked again at the sternmost ship, up at the sails, and then to Fraiser, whom he considered just as carefully. "Master, I want us to starboard of the enemy." His tone was deliberate and flat.

Fraiser was taken aback, and turned to the captain. "To starboard, sir?"

"Indeed, we cannot pass through the line, but we might meet with those who have done so." Still he watched the sailing master with care. "Take us about the rearmost ship; we might even catch them unawares with a broadside to their stern, but once on the lee, we can meet up and fight it out with their frigates."

Caulfield turned, a look of concern on his face, as Fraiser considered the angles carefully. *Pandora* was approaching with the rear of the enemy line fine off her starboard bow, it would take no very great alteration of course to follow the captain's wishes. They might even make their approach in relative safety; the attention of the last Dutch ship would be on the British liners. But once past, the fun would certainly begin, especially if *Pandora* despatched her puny broadside into the fourth rate's tail. A twenty-eight gun sixth rate could never hope to silence a two-decker with one single rake, but the larger ship would be bound to take greater notice when the frigate had passed and rounded her stern. The Dutch starboard battery would be unfired and the small ship that had just inflicted such a painful blow would be a perfect target. Both Fraiser and Caulfield were in no doubt that Banks' plan was verging on the insane. Men would die, *Pandora* would probably be destroyed, and all in a futile attempt to join in an action fought by ships that totally outclassed a tiny frigate.

"Carry on, Mr Fraiser," Banks was still regarding the sailing master in a strange, almost impartial, manner that was totally lost on the Scot, who had greater matters to consider, and merely touched his hat formally in reply.

"Very good, sir," he said, and began to give the orders.

* * * * *

From *Venerable, Monarch's* course was plainly visible, and Duncan was also studying his junior's reactions intently, although in his case the vice admiral was a good distance away and deeply immersed in the mayhem of battle.

"Onslow does well to hold his fire," he said, as once more the British liner was enveloped in a hail of shot. "*Monarch* was a fine ship when I had her, and she is so now."

"Indeed, sir," Fairfax, Duncan's flag captain was also watching. His ship was heading for the Dutch line and at roughly the same angle as *Monarch's* approach, in fact the scenario playing out before them would be almost exactly what *Venerable* would be experiencing within a few minutes.

"Breaking the enemy line is all important, William," Duncan continued in a softer tone.

"Radical tactics, sir."

"Perchance, but then Sir Charles Douglas did the same at The Saints."

"That was Rodney, for sure?"

Duncan smiled. "Rodney's victory, aye, but t'were Sir Charles who ordered the line broke, and secured it for him. Besides, that fellow Clerk has been theorising about it for years, but even if it were not for any of them, there is no option for us now." He looked to the van of the Dutch line, and the coast beyond. "They have their home port barely hours ahead; if we do not stop them they will shortly make the shallows where we cannot follow, and then be back, safe in their lair, while we wait outside once more."

"Yes sir," Fairfax agreed, although his tone was flat. "But there is little order; I am concerned we might create nothing but confusion."

"There is not the time for planning, but my officers know what needs to be done, and my lads too; have no doubt of that."

Veteran, *Adamant* and *Agincourt* were following Onslow in, although it appeared that *Agincourt* was lagging behind slightly. Still, even if Onslow was unable to force his way through at the first attempt, the enemy's line would be halted. Duncan peered ahead, where their own target was becoming clearer.

"Mr Patterson, take us between the two flags, if you please." *Venerable*'s sailing master stepped forward at the mention of his name and followed the admiral as he pointed forward to the fifth and sixth ships in the line, each of which were flying admiral's pennants as well as the Batavian flag. "With luck one should be de Winter's."

"Very good, sir," Patterson replied, but made no move and gave no orders. Duncan turned to him.

"Beggin' your pardon, sir; in truth them Dutchmen are packed together closer than fish in a basket. An' if you rightly mean us to pass through the line, well there are shallows beyond; dangerous shallows: we might be aground afore we knows it."

Duncan smiled. "There is no doubt in my mind, Mr Patterson. I am determined to fight them, and will do so on land, if not at sea."

Monarch was closing with the Dutch line now, and would have to suffer one last broadside before she was in a position to reply. The officers in *Venerable* watched in silence as yet again Onslow's flagship was all but hidden in a cloud of smoke and flame, finally emerging once more, now less than eighty feet from the battle line.

"There is another ship yonder," Fairfax commented. Sure enough a Dutch heavy frigate was coming up to starboard of their line, clearly intending to block *Monarch's* passage. Then the British ship's bowsprit found a gap, and within seconds the seventy-four was scraping between the bowsprit of one enemy and the stern of another. *Monarch's* guns had been double shotted, and both broadsides were despatched almost simultaneously, raking each enemy with devastating fire.

"Do you wish to adjourn to the poop, sir?" Fairfax asked, looking back to the deck above. "'t'would give a better vantage point."

Duncan shook his head. "No, William, better to stay next the wheel, and where we may be reached if need be."

"Very good, sir," the captain replied. "We should be in range at any moment."

Duncan switched his attention to the Dutch ships they were aiming for, that were indeed very close now.

"The guns are ready?"

"As you ordered, sir—canister on round."

"Then there is little left for us to do," he looked about him at the men, his lads, who were about to fight the most desperate battle of their lives. "Gentlemen, you see a severe Winter approaching," he said, his eyes suddenly bright and with a spark that could even be called wicked. "I advise you all to keep up a good fire!"

The men at the nearest guns laughed politely, but Midshipman Neale, standing next to his signal's locker, looked mildly confused.

"An admiral's joke, son," Duncan told him kindly. "Not known for their humour, so be glad that they are rare."

"Yes, sir." The young man's face cleared, and suddenly was all concern. "'though it was really very good indeed," he said.

Then the Dutch opened fire and order was suspended, as *Venerable's* decks became a mass of raining shot and tearing splinters.

* * * * *

In *Vrijheid*, van Leiden saw them come. His signals section had been unusually busy throughout the morning but now that the *admiraal* had their ships packed tight, in a credible line, and sailing on a course that would see them home and safe by the evening, once more he was idle. From further forward came the regular shout of a man taking soundings; they were in good depth; most casts were more than seventeen meters, although the sea shelved steadily and they were as close as they dared come to the coastline, less than five miles off their starboard beam.

They had expected the British to form a line of battle: the time taken for this would have brought them nearer to the truly treacherous shallows at the approach to Texel island, but the *admiraal* seemed content with their position. Certainly if the British were foolish enough to try and burst through their line, they would find little water for their deeper hulls; there would be limited room to manoeuvre: some would be sure to fall foul of the shoals becoming stranded and an ideal target for the frigates to rake at leisure.

It was a British admiral's ship that was approaching, probably Duncan's, and she was clearly intending to come between them and the *Staten-Generaal* immediately to their stern. He heard movement from behind and turned to see de Winter and van Rossen moving towards the poop. They were probably going to speak with *Admiraal* Storey in the *Staten-Generaal*; the ship was close enough for his signals to be of little use. Probably they would be ordering them to close up further; although there was the smallest of gaps between the hulls. Besides, both Dutch ships were seventy fours. Duncan, if it were Duncan, must face tremendous fire from the combined broadsides and would be unlikely to even reach them, let alone penetrate their line.

Van Leiden looked again at the British ship; she was old, that was obvious. Her bows were of a style the Dutch had abandoned more than twenty years ago, and she was in urgent need of some paint. There was not one ship in their navy that appeared anything like as disreputable, and she belonged to an *admiraal*! He thought briefly of Thomas, and *Pandora*, the frigate he had visited twice; she was in far better order, but then that was to be expected: it was easier to build frigates than proper warships. The entire British fleet was in sight now, and he knew it likely that *Pandora*, and Thomas, would be amongst them. But he hoped not.

Now the *kapitein* had returned to the quarterdeck and was striding towards the *eerste luitenant*. There was a brief discussion; both men touched their hats and, strangely, shook hands quite formally. Then the *luitenant* moved away and faced down the length of the ship.

"Open fire on my order!" He had very good lungs and was fond of using them, but on this occasion the bellow must have carried to most of the other ships nearby. The men at the nearby guns had certainly heard him well enough and a ragged cheer went up as the *kapiteins* of each piece began to lay their weapons on the approaching ship.

"Ready!" the *luitenant* raised his hand and an eerie silence hung until every *kanon kapitein* had his hand up ready. Then, with a savage downward sweep: "Fire!"

The ship heeled slightly as the broadside erupted, with both gun decks despatching their charges within a second of the order. The smoke blew back across the deck, momentarily blinding van Leiden, but he stumbled towards the side to peer out, as the gun crews began to reload their weapons. The shots had found their mark, he was sure there were actual pieces falling from the British ship's rigging, and the bows themselves were showing signs of damage. Sails flapped wildly, but were soon taken under control, and the enemy flagship continued towards them, just as another broadside was despatched by the *Staten-Generaal*.

This time he had a far better view, with no smoke to confuse the issue. The British ship visibly staggered under the weight. Her starboard bow and side were peppered with shot that landed at almost point blank range, smashing ragged holes into the dried timbers and putting up such a cloud of dust that she might already be on fire. There would be time for three, maybe four such salvoes and on each occasion the enemy would be closer, and could be expected to be slowed, if not completely halted. The British were brave, but foolhardy; it was impossible to think that they could get near enough to cause real damage, let alone break the Dutch line. The battle would be over within an hour, two at the most, and there was Texel, not fifteen miles off, where they would shortly tow their prizes and find shelter for their own ships. Tomorrow night he might conceivably be dining once more at home with Anna and Joseph, and maybe even Thomas King. On a day when many would fall it was pleasant to have such a prospect; something positive to hope for; an agreeable meal in a better world, a meeting of friends who should in fact be enemies. Yes, he told himself, it was a good thought to have. And a prospect, he knew, that Juliana would like also.

CHAPTER TWENTY-THREE

ONSLOW'S *Monarch* was steadily pressing her hull between the two Dutch ships although the heavy frigate, previously spotted by Fairfax, was coming up to starboard of the enemy line and threatening any further progress. Having already despatched both broadsides into the liners to either side, the British ship would have to manoeuvre past the annoying forty-four that was attempting to lie athwart her prow. Onslow was not unduly worried however, the frigate would be dealt with in due course; it was more important that he had broken the enemy line. Now all he had to do was hold his position and the Dutch would be stopped. The deck heaved as a second broadside rolled out, the guns almost touching their targets, and smoke could be seen filtering up from the starboard Dutchman's lower deck where a small fire had started. *Monarch* edged forward, her bowsprit threatening that of the frigate.

"Take her a point to larboard, Edward, if you please," the admiral pointed forward and *Monarch*'s captain touched his hat. "The angle should allow for our for'ard pieces to cover our new friend," Onslow glanced about. "Whilst the others can be sure not to neglect the old."

O'Brien bellowed the order, and his ship continued with her last ounces of momentum. They were well placed; it would all be down to the gunners now, and who could fire the fastest, and continue to do so for long enough to secure victory. The captain took a sidelong glance at Onslow as he stood solid amidst the confusion of battle, apparently as comfortable as one spending a day at the races, and smiled inwardly at the man for whom two targets were not enough.

* * * * *

Meanwhile *Pandora* had closed considerably on the after part of the Dutch line; King, squinting through a larboard gunport, calculated they would be in accurate range in less than three minutes.

"Captain intends to rake her stern," he told Cobb, the teenager who would take his place in charge of *Pandora*'s main armament should he fall. "Don't expect much in reply until we have passed; the Dutchman will be too intent on beating off our liners. But once we are clear and are forereaching on their starboard beam we might get a measure of attention."

"Aye, an' then some."

King noticed that the youngster's grin was quite dispassionate. They were expecting to face at least one broadside from a two-decker, and yet to judge from his expression it might as well be about to happen to someone else.

"How are you loaded, Mr King?" The captain's voice came down from the quarterdeck.

"Double round, sir! Both batteries."

"Very good; change to single round after the first discharge."

"Single round, aye aye sir. Would you have the guns drawn?"

"No, just reload with single."

King touched his hat and Cobb began to pass the message along the line of gunners. It was strange, *Pandora* was about to take on a much larger ship; he would expect to continue with double shot; they were well within range, after all. He glanced again at the enemy, she was closer now, and noticed two heavy stern chasers that might do them a deal of damage. The ships of Onslow's squadron could also be seen, with *Monarch* still struggling to be free of the frigate that was locking on to her bows. *Montague* and *Russell* were on *Pandora*'s larboard beam, and advancing upon the Dutch line. Both had piled on an inordinate amount of canvas in an effort to reduce the time they would spend taking enemy fire. He looked particularly at *Montague*, the nearest to him, and a seventy-four. She was powerful enough, but hardly the fastest of sailers. Her captain was clearly aiming to come between the penultimate ship in the line and the last: *Pandora*'s target, although it seemed likely that she would not have sufficient speed. In which case...

No, it did not do to speculate. The captain had surprised him in the past, and there was every reason why he should do so again. The only thing King had to worry about was his guns; that they fired effectively and often: anything further was beyond his responsibility and concern.

* * * * *

Pandora was a fast ship and had speed in hand. Banks had shortened sail down to topsails, reefed topgallants and staysails, and she was still keeping ahead of *Montague*, currently on her larboard quarter with all plain sail set.

"I'd like to pass close enough for a broadside, Mr Fraiser." Banks said deliberately. "We're double shotted, so less than half a cable would be ideal. Is that possible?"

"Yes sir, though an increase in speed might be in order," Fraiser glanced back to where the seventy-four was straining to get ahead. "Yon ship is takin' our wind, but we might be impeding her if I make any further to larboard."

"Very good, master; make it so."

Fraiser collected the speaking trumpet from its becket; the noise of the battle was growing, this was not the time for a misheard order. The reefs were shaken out while the forecourse was set and *Pandora* surged forward under the extra power. Her heel increased slightly, forcing King's guns to be depressed to maintain their level, but there was no doubt that her speed had increased considerably. Caulfield smacked his hands together as the ship pulled comfortably ahead of *Montague*. "Captain Knight seems to be hogging the stern ship," he said. "I would have thought him better served pushing betwixt her and the next for'ard."

"Yes, I was rather afraid of that," Banks' tone was unusually flat. "It appears *Montague* cannot make the speed as well as the heading." Caulfield eyed him warily; there was definitely a slight twinkle in his captain's eye; he was planning something, although the lieutenant could not begin to guess what it was. Banks cleared his throat. "There's room enough now," he looked pointedly at the sailing master. "Take her in, if you please, Mr Fraiser."

Fraiser touched his hat once more before leaning back and bellowing through the speaking trumpet. The rudder bit, the sails were braced round and Caulfield very nearly laughed out loud as the frigate moved in front of the British two-decker, and Banks' ruse became clear.

None, save the captain, had foreseen *Montague* changing her objective; only he had been alert to the fact that the clumsy seventy-four would not have enough speed to gain the obvious position in front of the sternmost ship. Now she was heading for *Pandora*'s goal, to rake the Dutchman's stern, something that would have far greater effect than the little frigate's puny broadside but, more importantly, she would distract the attention of the enemy ship. *Pandora* was ahead and, with luck, would be past and in relative safety by the time the Dutch had recovered sufficiently to consider her. She might receive one broadside in reply, but by then the enemy would have a seventy-four on their starboard counter to worry about.

But there was more to Banks' plan than that. Caulfield now saw, with rare insight, that all orders for manoeuvring the ship into what was ostensibly a perilous position had been made through Fraiser. During their encounter with the French frigate, the sailing master had claimed to be equally concerned about saving their stricken enemy, as he was the safety of *Pandora*. Now Banks had tested him: checked to see if he had genuinely sought to avoid unnecessary slaughter, or was merely taking the moral high ground, whilst hiding other personal traits that were far less honourable. Caulfield, who considered himself very much a fighting officer, had not guessed Banks' ploy, neither had he foreseen that the British seventy-four would unintentionally give them an extra measure of protection, so he was reasonably certain Fraiser would have missed it as well. And there could be no doubt that the sailing master had conned *Pandora* into danger without question. His orders would have seemed to be placing her, her people, and himself in grave danger, yet he had not swerved or protested in any way. If Caulfield was right, and Fraiser had been the subject of an elaborate test, there could be no doubt that the Scot had passed.

Caulfield considered his captain with renewed respect, and Banks, clearly conscious that his second in command had smoked his plan, grinned and nodded once in return. Then there was a shout forward and, standing in the waist, King brought his hand up high. Caulfield consciously brought himself back to the real world; there might be the time for further study of human nature later, now they were drawing near to an enemy two-decker, and had other matters to concern them.

* * * * *

Although *Venerable* had survived several broadsides her pace had slowed. The damage was mainly to her hull, however; her masts still held, and she advanced relentlessly towards the Dutch line. Duncan and Fairfax had stayed on the quarterdeck, and were now watching with grim satisfaction as their ship came into a position where she could at last return fire. The name *Vrijheid* could just be made out on the transom of the ship on their larboard bow; the admiral had guessed correctly: he was fighting directly with de Winter. To starboard was another seventy-four; it remained anonymous, but was causing further problems. She had come forward in an attempt to seal the gap that *Venerable* sought, and now her bowsprit was threatening to clash with the flagship's, blocking her effort to break the line.

"Helm a larboard, if you please," Duncan said urgently.

Fairfax yelled at the quartermaster, who began to heave at the wheel, aided by the only helmsman left to him. *Venerable* responded, bringing the mystery ship into the line of fire from her broadside guns. Duncan nodded at Clay, the second lieutenant, and received a salute in reply. Then a call to be ready, a raised sword, and with a single shouted word the entire might of the starboard battery was unleashed.

Venerable's first broadside had been loaded with care before the battle, and caused more devastation than any she would fire that day. With the mystery ship less than fifty feet from her, each shot told, and could almost be followed on their course from the muzzles of the British guns. Splinters spun from the Dutch ship's sides, and her very hull seemed to wallow from the blows. Duncan watched, also noting with grim satisfaction that he was one of the few who did.

Steam rose from the lamb's wool swabs as they purged red-hot embers from the barrels. Fresh cartridges were inserted, to be followed almost immediately by further shot. The gun captains were probing with their priming wires, and lacing touch holes with fine powder and spirit, and soon the blocks began to squeal as the guns were heaved up to the firing position once more. It was fast, stunningly fast, considering the damage, both to man power and material, that *Venerable* had already suffered, but now she was ready to speak once more and, once more, the ship heaved as another broadside swept down upon the enemy.

"Ready larboard!" Clay had moved to the opposite battery; now *Vrijheid* would be the target. Again the old ship vibrated to the crack of the guns; men were deafened by the sound, blinded by the smoke and choked by the fumes, but their blood was up and they worked on, drawing on reserves of energy and nerve; reserves that, for most, would last out the battle and five minutes more.

The starboard gunners were signalling their pieces ready, and another deadly broadside rolled out. *Venerable* had yet to fully penetrate the line, although the ship on her starboard beam had been forced out of position. But another was coming on to her stern, and she was in danger of being raked. Duncan looked about; *Triumph* had made it to the line and was just releasing her first broadside into the ship that threatened *Venerable*. And there was *Ardent*, coming across *Vrijheid*'s bows, discharging her guns as she thrust her way through the tangle of line and spars that had been the Dutchman's bowsprit.

"The enemy are not as steady, nor as fast," Fairfax bellowed to Duncan during a rare break in the firing. They stood less than three feet apart, but both were already quite deaf. "Belike they feel the lack of carronades!"

The admiral nodded, but did not attempt to speak. Indeed, this was ideal work for the shorter barrelled gun; a heavier projectile could be used, fewer men were needed to tend it, and the reload rate was faster. Marines had formed up and were sniping at men on *Vrijheid*'s poop. Duncan noticed with surprise that *Venerable* had moved forward, and was now almost past the Dutch flagship. The ship they had punched out of line was now on their starboard beam, and another two-decker had crept across their bows. There was also a further ship, apparently a sixty-four, off their stern. All were engaging other British vessels at the same time, although Duncan knew that his tired old flagship could only take so much punishment and it was at that moment that the carpenter clambered up from the waist and approached Fairfax. The man had apparently lost his hat, but deferentially knuckled his forehead in the way of all seamen.

"Beggin' your pardon, sir, but I needs more men at the pumps. She's takin' water badly for'ard. We can stopper the leaks for now, but the well's nigh on three-quarter full, and is 'dangerin' the orlop."

Fairfax paused to allow the starboard broadside to speak once more before replying. "Go to Mr Cleland, tell him I authorise you to take anyone he can spare, apart from the gunners: no one is to leave a gun, do you hear?"

The carpenter nodded, touched his forehead briefly, before bustling off to find the first lieutenant.

Then a bright light from further forward drew the officer's attention. Contrasting vividly with the grey afternoon, the growing mass of yellow and red began to rise up with hypnotic majesty. A fire had broken out on one of the ships. Duncan watched with a falling heart; it must be *Triumph*, who had last been seen in that quarter. The flames leapt from the deck, and began greedily consuming canvas, line and spars. Within minutes the ship was nothing but a blazing wreck, incapable of further action other than to save herself, and endangering all about her.

"What of *Triumph*?" Duncan bellowed at Fairfax, who showed little concern, and pointed forward. Sure enough the British ship could just be seen emerging from around the bows of the enemy flagship directly ahead.

"See, Essington comes to relieve us," Fairfax shouted. "Sure, he is a welcome sight!"

Welcome indeed, the more so as Duncan realised the nationality of the stricken ship. The men who were desperately trying to save her must be Dutch, and as he registered the news, he noted that it was with an odd combination of relief and guilt.

* * * * *

On the orlop deck Doust, Manning and Black were also experiencing mixed emotions. *Pandora* had yet to come under fire, but they were ready, and strangely eager to be active. About them lay the tools and instruments that would be used to repair the broken bodies they were expecting. They had roughed out a plan between them; those who just required stitching would be the preserve of Manning, with Black on hand for bandaging and splints. Doust would handle all the amputations, as well as splinter and shot extractions, and any complex abdominal surgery, something at which he was considered exceptionally fast. That was the intention, but they all knew how easily it might degrade into mayhem.

There were four large lanthorns smokily burning over the operating area, and the atmosphere was already heavy. Manning brushed a lock of hair from across his eyes and smiled at Kate.

"First thing we do after this is get your hair cut," she told him briskly. He grinned; hair, and the necessity for cutting it, was something he always forgot about until the surplus of one and lack of the other became a nuisance.

"I'll bother John Donna in the morning."

"Donna?"

"Aye, foc'sleman; does all the haircutting in the ship, some of the officers' included. Fair hand at the tailoring as well, I hears."

Kate pulled a face. "I'm not letting no common sailor hack you about." She reached down and picked up a pair of small scissors and advanced towards him. He drew back in mock horror.

"Whoa, Katie: now's not the time, nor the place."

Doust snorted. "There's nothing else a happening, laddie, you might as well let the lady have her way."

Manning's eyes rose to heaven, but he squatted down obediently enough as Kate began to stroke his hair into a semblance of order, and took the first few tentative snips. Beside them a loblolly boy chuckled. Kate regarded him seriously over Manning's head.

"I'd hold my peace, were I you, Hobday; there's a fair thatch on your top that could do with attending: like as not we will even have the time."

* * * * *

Monarch had succeeded in ousting the Dutchman from her jib boom, and was now pouring successive broadsides into her hull. The frigate's steering gear had clearly been hit; she was drifting to leeward, and had long ceased to reply. To larboard a seventy-four flying an admiral's flag was also suffering the British ship's fire. There were no officers visible on her poop or quarterdeck, and she was expected to strike at any moment. Onslow had received a small cut to his right hand, but had staunched the bleeding with a handkerchief from O'Brien. The admiral turned from his position on the poop, and looked back. *Adamant, Powerful* and *Director* were directly astern; they had already dealt with one two-decker, which had struck, and were now sending a boat to take possession. Behind them another Dutch battleship was about to be engaged by *Montague*, with the spunky little *Pandora* coming past at break-neck speed.

"Signal Bligh in *Director*," Onslow's voice was raw from shouting, but O'Brien seemed to understand. "Tell him to lead any remaining British ships forward to relieve the flag. Onslow pointed emphatically, and the bandage slipped. Dutch battleships some distance ahead still heavily encumbered Duncan's flagship. O'Brien touched his hat and looked for the signal lieutenant, while Onslow took another turn about the bandage, biting the knot in his teeth as he pulled it tighter. Duncan might have to strike at any moment, but at least with a reasonable force coming up behind, they might be able to re-take *Venerable*, or at least see her loss avenged.

* * * * *

The wind was on her quarter as *Pandora* powered through the grey, rain filled day, and on towards the stern of the last Dutch battleship. In the waist King was ready; his guns run out and set for elevation, while Newman had the marines lined up along the hammock stuffed netting. The sails were drawn tight, and she was sailing fast, too fast, it was hoped, to receive much from the heavy stern chasers that were poised to return fire as soon as she came within their arc. Banks glanced back, they were now comfortably ahead of *Montague*, stumbling behind at a fraction of their speed. The seventy-four would deliver a far greater punch, however, all *Pandora* would do was send a softening blow, and hopefully distract the enemy sufficiently to enable the third rate to do her work.

"Fire as you will, Mr King!" The lieutenant acknowledged the captain's shout, and raised his hand high.

"Ready, lads; on my order, but only when you have her sighted!"

There was little point in a smart, simultaneous discharge if half the shots went wide or were ill aimed.

The range was closing: it was only seconds. Fire erupted from one of the stern chasers, the enemy had spoken; King's arm came down, and he bellowed in time with the first discharge. The smoke was blown away as soon as it had come, but the noise seemed to echo about the men as they attended to the guns, making their ears ring with a constant reverberation. The first shot from the enemy crossed their bows, but the second scored a direct hit on the forecastle puncturing a neat hole forward of the forechains, and taking out three men standing by number one gun.

On the quarterdeck, Caulfield had pushed his way forward, and was peering over at the enemy ship. Splashes fell to either side, but it was clear that the majority of shots had struck. Crown glass from the stern gallery shattered and disappeared in an instant, while part of the taffrail was beaten in. More importantly one ugly ragged hole appeared right next to the rudder; with luck the steering would have been disabled, or at least damaged; something that *Montague* would thank them for when her turn came. Caulfield caught King's eye, but there was no time for comment or congratulation; the men were slaving to haul the guns back into position for another barrage, although before that they could expect to receive at least one broadside in return.

Newman's marines were firing now, small snaps of sound, almost insignificant compared to the roar that had been, but their shots would disconcert the Dutch, and might buy extra time.

Caulfield returned to Banks and Fraiser; the latter was looking anxiously up at the masts; the enemy ship was on their quarter and blanking their wind, causing some of the sails to flap, and a definite decrease in speed.

"I'd be happier with a man at the lead," he told the captain. "But at this speed I take it that..." Fraiser's mouth was open to say more when a cry from Dorsey turned everyone's attention to the enemy.

She had fired, smoke was billowing from her two tiers of guns, and as they watched the shots began to tell.

One smacked next to *Pandora's* larboard forechains, almost alongside that of the previous hit, endangering the foremast and, in turn, the ships entire sailing ability. Another punched through her side, the entry point was well above the waterline although, with the ship heeling to starboard, it might cause greater problems later. Three marines went down as one; part of the hammock netting in the waist was blown apart, and number five gun, larboard side was hit and sent careering inboard, sweeping over its captain and one of the servers and killing both outright. Further shots flew through the rigging, parting a line here, and knocking down a block there, but the succession of splashes to starboard and across their bows showed that the firing had been rushed and, in the main, ill aimed.

"Well, that might have been far worse," Newman beamed at Caulfield, although his assessment was premature; he was no seaman and knew little of the consequences should the forechains be damaged. The boatswain was on hand, peering over the side and tugging at the deadeyes and limp lines that hung about him.

"Depends much on what our friend Peters discovers." Caulfield told the marine, "There'll be a measure of work a splicing if I'm any judge; captain will take us off the wind, as soon as he's able."

"Cannot they be tightened?"

"Oh a turn or two maybe for individual lines, but there will be some parted that needs to be spliced and if the mounting is weakened we can kiss goodbye to any plans for fancy sailing 'till we make port."

And it was then that Newman's smile finally faded: he looked concerned, confused almost, and fell forward as if bowing to the first lieutenant. Caulfield was taken unawares and caught him clumsily, although he quickly recovered and began to steer the body down to the deck as gently as he could.

"Alex, are you hurt?"

Newman registered Caulfield but said nothing as he was guided onto his back. Then his eyes emptied, his head fell to one side, and colour slowly faded from his face. There was a darkening patch spreading across the marine's tunic and Caulfield noticed that his own hand was sticky. He quickly wiped away the smear of blood onto his jacket as if to deny its existence, but as he laid his friend down on *Pandora*'s whitened strakes, the first lieutenant knew him to be dead. He looked about helplessly, but there were two privates and a corporal standing by, ready to claim their own. Within a minute of discussing the damage to their rigging, Marine Lieutenant Newman had left the deck.

* * * * *

Matthew Jameson saw him go, or at least he saw the red jacketed body being carried down to the orlop. He gave the matter little thought, however. Despite the fact that Newman had been one of the more popular officers on board, Jameson had problems of his own.

He tended number three gun, along with other members of his mess and this was not his first action. Indeed he had seen cannon fired in anger more times in his brief career than many seamen would their entire lives, and he considered himself as hardened to the horrors of battle as any man on board. There had been just one instant, many years ago in *Vigilant*, when he had lost his nerve. It had been a prolonged engagement, and they were hopelessly outnumbered. The terror of being in a two-decker fighting for her life; the sound, sight and smell of conflict, coupled with not knowing if he would be the next to die, had totally overwhelmed his juvenile senses. That had only been for a moment, however, and his friend and Sea Daddy, Flint, had been on hand to see him through. Flint was there now, but Jameson had an inner feeling he would not be able to help this time.

They had gone through the tense period of waiting, the nervous interval that always made the older men sharp and snappy, well enough. Then the first and, to date, only broadside had been fired; usually this would be the moment when the nerves stilled and all emotions were placed to one side until the action ended. Then the enemy had hit back.

There had already been the one shot that landed next to the larboard forechains, and that had all but taken off Matthew's head. He had felt the wind of it, a frightening sensation in itself as it was widely held that the air of a passing shot could be every bit as deadly as the ball that preceded it. They had been in the process of loading, and he had managed to think of little else other than sponging his own gun clear.

The enemy broadside followed, the broadside that had sent a gun two down from theirs crashing free of its tackle, and into Burt and Weir; men he had known well, and were now hideously dead. That had been bad enough, but again he had been familiar with others who had fallen in the past. What he could not come to terms with was the second shot that had landed in almost the same hole as the first; again he had been missed by nothing more than chance, and a rat's whisker, and instinct told him that where two had come, a third was sure to follow. He felt his heart racing so fast he could hear it in his head, and the hands that gripped the flexible rammer were locked on, knuckles white, steadily squeezing the rope as if he were determined to draw water from its very fibres.

The other men were sound enough, Jenkins had even made a joke, and Jameson had known it was a joke because he had seen the rest laugh; but though he felt he could remember every detail, not only did he miss the humour, he did not understand what the words actually meant.

He looked at Flint, cool as ever, as he watched them making number five gun safe, and wanted very much to talk to him, but the words that were forming in his mind would not come. He opened his mouth and made a strange guttural noise that he quickly changed into a cough after attracting the attention of the other men. His voice was there certainly, but he could not communicate: even now in his thoughts, he was not sure how he was actually thinking. Were these words and phrases that circulated about his mind? Or did a dog or a cat think in the same way, with emotions, senses, and feelings colouring moods and desires? Had he lost his mind, or merely the ability to pass on what was in it, and consequently was unable to interpret what they were saying to him?

As if to test this at that moment Flint did speak. Jameson relaxed slightly when he heard the well-remembered timbre of his voice, but still he could not understand what was being said. And Flint was speaking directly to him; the facial muscles moved, and there were the well-remembered expressions, but an inner feeling told him he could have understood as easily if his friend had switched to Russian. Flint was indicating the bucket at Jameson's feet, and he guessed he might be wanting a drink. The lad picked up the small tin cup, filled it to just under half full, so that his shaking hands would not spill any, and passed it across. Flint took it and laughed, as he had to all but prize Jameson's fingers free. It was taken as a joke however, and Jameson smiled back relieved. Flint said something more when he had finished drinking, but there was no change and Jameson remained effectively cut off from the world of language.

Inspiration had not deserted him, however, and he tapped at his ears and pulled a face. One of the penalties of working with the great guns was that, at the best of times, all the servers were slightly deaf and it would come as no surprise to anyone if the recent discharge of a broadside, coupled possibly with receiving the hit so close by, might have taken his hearing completely. Flint shook his head and grinned, he spoke slowly and in a tone that was as comforting as any bellow could be, but the individual words left Jameson none the wiser. The lad shrugged and pulled another face, and Jenkins muttered something that made them all laugh. They all laughed, laughed together and laughed heartily with a shared mixture of relief, fellowship and fear, and it was only Jameson who remained totally oblivious to the joke.

* * * * *

Onslow might have doubts about how long Duncan could continue, but in *Vrijheid*, there were no expectations of *Venerable* striking. Van Leiden was slightly wounded; a splinter had scraped his left cheek, causing blood to flow freely down the side of his face and soak deep into his uniform jacket. But as he stood on the quarterdeck, sword drawn more for reassurance than actual use, the cut was the last thing on his mind.

For some while he had been conscious of their own rate of fire. His men were working hard enough, and yet still they were receiving two, sometimes three British broadsides for every one they could send back in reply. About him many had fallen, and there were at least two guns left unattended, with several more working with less than half their usual crew. As he looked about the *luitenant* realised with a chill that, apart from de Winter, he was the only officer left alive on the quarterdeck. In fact the *admiraal* stood quite near to him, apparently in deep thought. Van Rossem had gone; van Leiden had not seen him fall, but knew that for the *kapitein* to have left the deck he must be either severely wounded or dead. And there were no other *luitenants*, or even an *adelborst* to be seen; his own friend, Cuypers had been dragged down to the surgeon with a wound to his chest some while ago, and the *eerste luitenant*, though still presumably alive, had left to take control of the lower deck after several officers below had fallen. Another British broadside swept across, the *admiraal* moved suddenly, and briefly van Leiden thought him hit, but he was making towards the ladder to the poop and at a pace that belied his massive frame. On an impulse van Leiden followed, clambering up the short flight of steps and on to the smaller deck.

There the scene was very much the same. De Winter was standing at the taffrail, looking to the south, where the rest of the Dutch ships could be seen. He turned as van Leiden appeared, and beckoned urgently for the *luitenant* to join him.

"Our ships have surrendered to the south!"

Van Leiden walked quickly across the deck. It was impossible of course: it would mean that a good proportion of the Dutch force had already been lost. The proof was there, however; in the dis-

318

tance he could see *Jupiter* and *Harrlem:* clearly they were no longer fighting, with British ships under sail passing them. And another ship, probably *Hercules*, was on fire, and drifting with the wind towards the shore and the deadly shallows. But there was *Brutus*, flying Bloy's flag and *Leyden* with others behind. They were apparently undamaged, and heading their way. De Winter seemed to spot them at the same time, and pointed excitedly, knocking van Leiden on the chest with the back of his hand as he did.

"We must signal. Ask for help!"

It seemed like so much wasted effort; surely the ships would see *Vrijheid*, and guess her predicament, but van Leiden dutifully made for the second flag locker. There were no *seingever* to assist him, although the code was simple: a single flag was the signal for assistance required and, when hoisted from the flagship, would be bound to draw the ships to them. Van Leiden had located the correct number, and moved across to a mizzen halyard. De Winter was already there, and snatched the canvas bundle from him, tying it inexpertly to the line so that the flag began to unroll before it was hoisted. A bullet sang next to them, causing van Leiden to duck instinctively. He looked across; there was a line of red coated British sea soldiers taking pot shots. He nudged at the *admiraal*, and pointed at the marines, but de Winter continued to fumble with the flag. Then another shot whined past, followed almost immediately by one that, by some lucky accident, actually cut the line. The flag and broken halyard dropped from the *admiraal*'s fingers, falling on the deck between them. There was a sudden lull in the fighting, for a moment the battle itself seemed oddly suspended as de Winter considered the small heap of canvas and line. Then he shrugged, drew a deep sigh and smiled ruefully at the *luitenant:* for the first time van Leiden realised that he was looking at the face of a defeated man.

CHAPTER TWENTY-FOUR

PETERS and his team had done well, and Banks was pleased to tell them so. Several shrouds had been replaced, although the ratlines had yet to be re-rove, which meant the topmen would have to ascend by the more dangerous lee side for the time being. The damage to the larboard forechains was not considered to be critical. Or at least if it was, as the boatswain had told them dolefully, they would all discover soon enough. Banks had returned *Pandora* to full plain sail and now she was once more cutting through the dark wet afternoon with a plume of spray flying from her prow.

Director with *Powerful* and *Circe* were off her larboard bow on the very edge of deep water. Near them a ship was on fire and drifting to starboard and the shallows, although Banks planned to pass them all within the next few minutes. *Venerable* was in sight, and still surrounded by Dutch ships, but the liners would relieve her; Banks saw his objective beyond the cluster of battling ships.

There were at least three enemy vessels heading away from their own stricken flagship and on towards the Texel and safety. The last of these appeared to be a frigate. A powerful one, Banks would guess she carried over forty guns, but none the less, potentially a match for *Pandora*.

The wind was lessening, but still whistled through the lines as he drove her on. They were passing the small group of British ships bound for *Venerable* now, and on a mad impulse Banks took off his hat and waved it at *Director*. William Bligh had her at pre-

321

sent; he had known the man back in 'eighty six when Bligh had been a captain in the merchant service, and Banks a fresh young midshipman sent to cover for an officer taken with the flux. Banks remembered him as an excellent officer, and had learnt much in the few weeks they were together. It was hard to credit some of the stories going the rounds since the *Bounty* incident. There was no response from *Director*'s poop, but Banks supposed Bligh had other matters on his mind.

To starboard the burning ship was still drifting steadily towards the coast, and would be on the shoals in no time. Caulfield was examining it carefully through the deck glass.

"Dutchman, a sixty-four," he spoke quietly, as if to himself. "If she takes the ground she'll be lost for sure, along with most of those in her."

"I was thinkin' of going for the frigate yonder," the captain said.

"Very good, sir. The liner's already accounted for," Caulfield replied in a level tone. "An' she might even last the hour, should we decide to leave her."

Banks tore his gaze away from the men desperately fighting the fire that would probably end their lives. *Pandora* was drawing level with *Venerable* now, and he could see *Triumph*, still sending thundering broadsides into a third rate, along with *Belliqueux* and *Veteran*, who had another enemy two-decker wedged between them. He turned back and caught Caulfield's eye. The frigate could be reached, he was sure of it, but she was a large ship, far larger than *Pandora*, and it must be doubtful as to what might be achieved if they did engage her.

"So, what think you, Michael?"

Caulfield shook his head. "She's a heavy ship, sir, an' we'd have no support. Were it my decision I think I would decline and," the pause was slightly too long. "Perhaps save the sixty-four?"

Banks switched to Fraiser, who still had the worried old woman look he always wore when they were travelling at speed across shallow waters.

"We'll be trying for the sternmost frigate, master," he said evenly. "Think we can reach her?"

Fraiser pursed his lips as he considered the matter. "She's making a fair rate herself, sir, but I can have us in range if that be your intent." His expression was now completely blank; he had told the captain what he wanted to hear and, like any good sailing master, was ready to carry out whatever order came his way.

Banks sighed. "Very good," he said, glancing back at the frigate for the last time before turning to his officers. "Take us about, and we'll head back for your burning liner."

* * * * *

In the cockpit they had done all they could. Two men had been moved to the wings and were lying with fresh stumps tightly bound, and a third was slowly dying from savage internal wounds that were hopelessly beyond anything Mr Doust might attempt. The others, those with minor injuries that had been attended to, lay on the dark deck, covered in canvas sheets. Periodically Kate would walk along the line dispensing advice, reassurance, and small sips of lemonade from a pewter jug. On one occasion, she had to pause to close the eyes of a young topman with a broken leg. It had been a simple enough fracture that set well, although clearly there were other internal injuries that had not been so easily diagnosed. He was swiftly taken away to await later burial.

And now they were waiting once more, listening to the distant sounds of battle, the faint moaning of those injured, and the steady creaking of timbers as the ship powered through the seas. There was no telling how the action had progressed; the distant gunfire seemed as regular as ever, although none could judge if it came from the British or the Dutch. Kate wiped her hands on a piece of waste cloth while Manning pulled away the stained canvas that covered the nearest sea chest, and they both sat down.

"It must be getting late," he said. Neither of them owned a watch and Doust, who had a handsome silver Thompson permanently tucked into his waistcoat pocket, was dozing quietly in the corner. "Texel is close by, we must be almost at their doorstep; this should not progress beyond nightfall."

She nodded, and leant to one side as *Pandora* heeled suddenly.

"They'll be manoeuvring," Manning reached out and wrapped his arm about her shoulder, continuing to hold her close as they sat, swaying gently with the motion of the turning ship. Movement from forward caught their attention; someone was talking with Powell. They both rose rather stiffly, as the loblolly boy approached somewhat diffidently with two seamen in tow.

"It's Flint," Powell said, by way of introduction. "Or rather his friend here." The backward toss of Powell's thumb indicated Jameson with a mixture of scorn and disbelief.

"What be the matter, lad?" Manning asked him gently; there seemed little visibly wrong, although they were all well aware how dangerous latent injuries could turn out to be. Jameson said nothing, but continued to stare at their faces.

"Are you injured?" Manning persisted. "Tell me where it hurts." There was slight recognition, but no comprehension or understanding; it was as if the entire world had moved on to a different plain, leaving Jameson behind, beached and very much alone.

"That's the problem, beggin' your pardon, sir," Flint interrupted, casting a beseeching look at Manning and Black that withered as it reached Powell. "He can't make no sense. He don't seem to understand nothing, not even who we are properly." Powell turned away, clearly disgusted, but Kate reached forward and touched Jameson lightly on the upper arm.

"Matthew, isn't it?" Flint nodded, but Jameson gave no response to his name, although he did glance down at her hand momentarily. "Matthew, come and sit with me for a while. Rest, you'll feel better shortly."

Jameson made no move; she pulled him slightly. "Come, come with me," she repeated and obediently he began to follow.

"Sit for a spell and we will see what occurs," her voice was soft and soothing. Flint looked helplessly at Manning as his friend was led away.

"It's nothing that 'as happened to him," he said, his voice rich with confusion and concern. "He weren't hit, nor injured in any way. He just seemed to go, all of a sudden." The seaman rubbed at the back of his head, and drew his hand down his neck. "It's like he ain't there no more," he continued helplessly. "Or rather Matt is there, the Matt we all knows, but we can't reach him." He sighed, and looked away from Manning as if ashamed. "It's as if he's lost his mind," he said finally.

* * * * *

Vrijheid was not alone in having her colours shot away; *Venerable* had been without any distinguishing flags on several occasions. The jack, as well as the admiral's personal pennant, had fallen, to be replaced as soon as was feasible. Finally Duncan ordered Crawford, an ordinary seaman, to climb up to the masthead and nail the flag back in position so that she would be able to continue to fight without interruption or confusion. It was one of many such incidents on that day, events that seemed logical at the time yet destined to be recalled and marvelled over for years to come. Duncan's only intention was to make it plain, both to the Dutch and his own men, that they had not surrendered.

Vrijheid had drifted apart from *Venerable*, as both had damaged steering; *Director* was currently heading for the Dutch flagship with 'Breadfruit Bligh' in command. She was one of the smallest British battleships, a mere sixty-four, although Bligh handled her in a way that would have been considered bold were she a first rate. After having fought and defeated *Alkmaar* and *Haarlem*, he brought her up to the van and, with *Powerful* in support, turned towards *Vrijheid*. *Director* opened fire when she was within twenty yards of the Dutch ship's larboard quarter, and continued to rain regular broadsides as she crept up her length almost within touching distance, finally reaching the bows, and delivering several raking shots, before rounding and continuing down her starboard side. Adrift and without masts, de Winter's ship had no means of surrender although, as her guns gradually fell silent, it became clear that there was no further fight left in her. The frigate *Circe* was near by and still had a serviceable boat aboard, and so it was that Richardson, Bligh's first lieutenant, was conveyed by *Circe*'s jolly boat to the side of the defeated Dutch flagship.

He boarded by the larboard entry port, and almost immediately met with de Winter, on the spar deck. The admiral, assisted by the ship's carpenter and van Leiden, was in the process of nailing a sheet of lead across the damaged hull of a small dinghy. On seeing the British lieutenant he stopped, and laid his tools down. Van Leiden helped him to his feet; he seemed frail, somehow wasted, and their eyes did not meet. Van Leiden nodded in sympathy, certainly neither of them, nor any other officer in the Dutch Navy, had predicted such an outcome. Other members of his crew came forward to pay their respects as Richardson diplomatically guided the defeated admiral from his ship, down the boarding steps, and into the waiting boat.

* * * * *

The wind had veered slightly and now blew light and from the north. *Pandora* was bearing down on the burning Dutch sixty-four, although Banks had reduced to topsails, forecourse, jib and spanker. The stricken ship was lying across the wind, with the flames from her poop and stern galleries still very apparent.

"We can only go so far," Banks spoke softly to the master alone. "If she blows I don't want us anywhere near abouts, and we keep to windward at all times, do you hear?"

"To windward, sir." Fraiser repeated earnestly, as if humouring a child. "I'll certainly not be taking us to the lee, there's no the depth. It can only be providence that has kept her from taking ground as it is."

Caulfield could see figures moving about the deck, a team was working one of the ship's pumps, and there was a steady stream of water flowing down to the seat of the flames under the poop. They had also established a human chain, with lines of buckets being lowered amidships and passed back. The blaze was apparently in check, but had taken hold of her stern, and would surely finish her if the shoals did not make their claim first. *Pandora* was drawing close now; close enough for all to notice the heat on their rain drenched faces. What those poor devils on board were feeling was unimaginable.

"Let us hope they have seen sense and cleared or flooded the magazines," Caulfield said, bringing his glass down.

"I think we can count on that," Banks reply was both optimistic and loud enough for all to hear; he wanted no fouls ups or slips just because men were frightened of being blown to pieces. "We'll start by bringing her off the shoals, and into the wind" he continued. "Then be ready with the launch and cutters. Pass the word for Mr Peters."

The boatswain was on the quarterdeck and saluting the captain within a minute.

"I want a line passed to that ship," Banks told him. "We're going to haul her off, is that clear? I want your best man with a throwing arm, and all needs to be in place before we reach her."

Peters was gone as fast as he had come, and in no time a light line was being fed up to the quarterdeck through the stern gallery.

Banks turned back to Fraiser. "We can only do this once, I propose to bear down upon the ship and pass her close. As soon as we are within throwing distance we will bear away, and come off close hauled and still on the starboard tack, do you understand?"

"Yes, sir." Fraiser's eyes were strangely alight, and he seemed in no doubt as to his duty.

"You realise that if the turn is misjudged there is every chance we will run aground, or aboard the Dutchman?"

"I understand that, sir."

Again the look of confidence was unmistakable, and Banks knew he could be trusted.

Jehue, a forecastle man blessed with an upper body that might have been carved from a chunk of solid mahogany, came up and onto to the quarterdeck with Peters. All watched as a deep-sea lead was attached to a light grass line; the seaman swung the weight experimentally, eyeing the distance and sniffing the breeze.

"We're about to turn, do you think you can reach her, Jehue?"

Light from the burning ship, now less than half a cable off *Pandora*'s bows, was reflected in the man's serious dark eyes.

"Aye, sir; I reckons I can."

Banks looked across to Fraiser. "Very good, then there is no time to be lost; carry on, master."

"Send a fresh man to the forechains with a lead; hands be ready to turn ship." Fraiser's call echoed about the frigate although all on deck were well aware of what was about, and ready to respond.

"Brace in the afteryards," he paused, timing his moment. "Up helm!" *Pandora* began to turn painfully slowly. He was cutting it fine, but soon the frigate was sweeping towards the stricken ship. It would be close; Jehue should have an easy job of it but, as Banks had said, there could be no second try. Now they were almost level with the wreck, and very nearly as far inshore as she had drifted. The leadsman called; there was less than two fathoms under her keel. Fraiser looked up at the coastline, still several miles off; two fathoms was little to play with so far from the shore. *Pandora* continued to bear down on the stricken ship. Heat from the fire became more noticeable, although the light rain that had plagued them for most of the afternoon was fast turning into a torrent. It soaked all about, but doubtless was welcomed by the fire fighters on board the Dutchman.

"Lay the headyards square! Shift over the headsheets!" Now their bows were passing the prow of the prize. Men were standing ready on the forecastle, and Jehue began to whirl the lead, eyes fixed on his target, barely thirty feet away. They drew level, and then the stern was as close as it would come. Banks choked back the order to throw; the man knew his business, and would certainly not benefit from prompting.

"Haul aboard, haul out!" *Pandora* was turning away and starting to pick up speed as the wind found her; now the distance was slowly increasing.

Jehue's taught body suddenly released, and the line snaked out with a rush as *Pandora* came to the wind. Eager hands grabbed at it as it fell neatly across the forecastle and soon a heavy towing hawser was being dragged across the widening gap.

"We'll keep the tow as long as possible," Banks said, relief evident in his voice, although the danger was by no means over. With the ship gathering speed it was quite possible that the hawser would not be secured in time and might even run out before the Dutch had properly anchored the tow.

"Brace up headyards!" *Pandora* was responding well, a perfectly timed manoeuvre, but the tow had still to be collected and secured. The officers watched in silence as the Dutch crew pulled the heavy hawser up from the sea, and passed it through the weather hawsehole, before fastening it at the bitts.

"Safe below, Mr Peters?" Banks asked the boatswain.

"Aye, sir. There's little left to be taken up, and I had to hold a measure back for freshening, should it become necessary, but I reckons they'll have it fastened b'now."

Banks nodded, they were heading back towards the battle once more, although the firing seemed to have died considerably in the brief time they had been distracted. Slowly the hawser began to lift and grow taught, and the Dutch ship's bows dipped slightly, before being pulled round. A deep groan came from below as the strain was taken up, and *Pandora*'s speed was steadily drawn from her, but there was no doubt, the Dutch ship was under way, and the flames that had been impeding the fire fighters were now raging off her quarter and could be approached with far more certainty.

"We'll send a cutter to take possession, and I dare say they could do with some help. Better make it volunteers, Mr Caulfield; for the officers as much as the men."

Caulfield touched his hat and left to attend to the boarding party. Banks continued to watch as the Dutch ship straightened, and obediently began to follow them. Then he became strangely aware of Fraiser standing near by. He turned to him.

"That was a job well done, master." The two men's eyes met, a lot had happened in the past few months: Banks certainly acknowledged the change in himself. "Thank you for your efforts; I am greatly obliged to you."

Fraiser nodded and Banks thought he could spot the slightest hint of a smile on the Scot's face. "'tis a terrible thing, a burning ship," he said.

The captain grinned readily in return. "Aye, it is, Mr Fraiser. A terrible thing indeed."

* * * * *

Duncan watched the small jolly boat as it headed through the dark, rain soaked afternoon with a feeling of immense, but unspeakable, relief. Already seven enemy ships had surrendered, and it seemed likely that more would follow. But crossing the short stretch of open water was the Dutch commander, and that spoke as much for the victory as any prize.

The boat approached the flagship and was allowed to rest against the side without the bother or indignity of a hail. De Winter was the first up through the gangway port. Wearing a large dark coat that ended just below the top of his black boots, he looked about him with an air of resignation. Duncan stepped forward and considered his opponent face to face for the first time. The Dutchman was younger than he had expected, although there was a poise and bearing in his stance, which was emphasised by his large, full frame. In fact he was almost as massive as Duncan, with square shoulders and a natural authority that shone out, even in this final moment of defeat.

"Do I have the honour of addressing the *Admiraal* Duncan?" his voice was clear but respectful, with only a slight accent.

Duncan removed his hat and held out his hand. De Winter reached inside his coat and drew his sword. His face softened slightly as he held it by the forte for a moment, examining the weapon as if for the first time. Then he stretched his arm forward and offered the hilt to the British admiral. Duncan shook his head and waved it away.

"I would much rather take a brave man's hand than his sword." De Winter paused for a moment, before smiling slightly and returning the weapon to its scabbard. He took one step forward and reached for Duncan's right hand with his.

"It was a hard battle, admiral," Duncan told him. "But now over, we must do all we can to make our ships safe."

"There is much to be done, and many wounded."

"Many wounded," Duncan agreed. Then his face relaxed and he chuckled slightly. "Indeed, it is to be wondered at, that two as large as us should have come through it all unscathed."

* * * * *

"He used to stammer," Flint told Kate earnestly. "When he were first taken aboard *Vigilant*, an' a youngster."

"I'd hardly call him old now," she replied, considering the prone body that had finally given in to Mr Doust's second draft, and was now soundly asleep. "This is not the first time he has seen action?"

"No, he's been in a fair few scraps and... and always held his nerve." He blushed slightly, there had been the one occasion in *Vigilant* when Matthew had done anything but, although Flint had hardly been a model of composure on that day, so he reckoned the lad was allowed one fall from grace.

Kate shook her head sadly. "I know little of such wounds, but wounds they be, even if there are no scars to show."

"D' you think they'll be able to sort him in England?" Flint's voice was hopeful, although inside he knew the likelihood to be bleak. When a man can lose both legs in battle, and be rejected by his ship, the navy and effectively his country for the same reason, he could foresee no bright future for one who had merely lost the desire to talk. And there would be those, like Powell, who would consider him a coward, and many more who had never even smelt the scent of battle, ready to agree.

"I can make no promise, but am hopeful it will not last for long." She bit her lower lip slightly, knowing that her wishful thinking might be giving Flint false hope. "The best we can do is allow him sleep," she continued hurriedly. "There should be further to be learnt in the morning."

"I'm obliged to you, miss; more than I can say."

She smiled and pressed her hand reassuringly against his shoulder, and Flint obediently turned and walked from the orlop. She hoped he was not to be disappointed; so much was unknown about injuries to the mind, but what she had said was in some way correct. Matthew could wake to a normal psyche, and continue through life as if the incident had never occurred; instances had been known, although the reason still lay undiscovered. Alternatively, and she knew that this was more likely, he would remain as he was, gradually becoming accustomed to communicating through the guttural sounds of an animal, while little lay ahead other than the life of a beggar. Then she brightened as an idea occurred, maybe a hospital might be found where he could live as an inmate, earning his keep clearing out the wards and tending to the less demanding patients? Or he might find a place working on a farm, or a workhouse; just because a man could not speak, it did not necessarily mean he was feeble minded. She looked at him once more, sleeping peacefully, many miles away from the real world that would be all too ready to face him when he awoke. There was only so much she could wish for, eventually reality must take a hand. And it spoke much that the Royal Navy had felt the need to build a specialist hospital for their insane; he would probably go there, or somewhere similar. Why, he might even be sent to join her father in the Bethlem.

* * * * *

"I had expected you to form the line of battle," de Winter told Duncan as the two admirals sat in the screened off remains of *Venerable's* great cabin. It was night, and the ship was still cleared for action, but Fairfax had found the time to arrange this small measure of privacy between securing his own ship, and mustering the prizes. De Winter sipped at his port and sat back. "Were you to have done so I would have had time to take my ships nearer to the shallows. Both fleets should than have been drawn into the shoal water; many of yours would have taken ground and I could have destroyed them at my leisure."

Duncan swept his white hair back into a semblance of order. There was little he could say in response; a defeated enemy was not the easiest of guests, and he had no need or desire to start an argument. He looked across at the younger man's face and noticed a look of contrition.

"I did not mean to appear the bad loser," the Dutchman assured him.

"I understand, admiral, and in your position would probably feel as you do. But it was a battle like few before, and neither of us should feel the need for regret." De Winter nodded, as Duncan continued. "You might wish to send a message to your government, I would arrange that."

"I would be grateful, sir. Thank you."

"We hope to be heading for Yarmouth some time tomorrow, and expect to see England in under two days. My ship has suffered considerably, and I think it better that you should precede us; I will have you transferred to a frigate. *Pandora* is relatively undamaged.

"*Pandora*? It is a name I am familiar with."

Duncan nodded. "You were good enough to repatriate two of her men."

"Ah, yes."

"Adam Fraiser, her sailing master, is my nephew and Godson: a fine man. She will have you there the quicker and probably in greater comfort."

De Winter smiled, "I am in no rush, sir, believe me. But I would send that message, if you would be so kind."

* * * * *

As the following dawn finally broke, the dark clouded sky gave little promise for the day ahead. Van Leiden followed the lieutenant up the entry steps of *Pandora* and raised his hat respectfully as his feet touched the deck. King had seen the boat approach, and was waiting to meet him at the entry port as soon as Caulfield had led the unknown British officer away. The two men shook hands without speaking, then embraced as brothers. *Venerable*'s master at arms, who had accompanied the prisoner, cleared his throat diplomatically, and they drew apart, awkwardly grinning and patting the other on the shoulder.

"Tom, it is good to see that you are all right."

"And you, Wilhelm; but your face?" the lieutenant indicated the large patch of cotton and diachylon plaster that covered most of one cheek.

"Oh, it is nothing," van Leiden's eyes twinkled mischievously. "But I am hoping it might leave a scar; it would be good, no?"

King shook his head, "If you say so, Will. But what brings you to *Pandora*?"

"It is your navy, they have made such a mess of our fleet, and so I come to complain." King raised an enquiring eyebrow, and the Dutchman continued. "The *admiraal* might be travelling to England in this ship. Mr Cleland has come to speak to your captain, and I was sent to ensure his accommodation would be acceptable."

"You will accompany the admiral?"

"Oh yes, I am about all that is left of his officers, but I think maybe it will not happen. Your Mr Duncan would need to come as well, and a small frigate is not quite right for two *admiraals*, even if the journey will be brief."

"*Venerable* must be badly damaged."

"They are making good progress; she should survive to get us to your harbour."

"Well, it is fine to see you, and I hope we will meet again in England, even if *Pandora* does not take you there."

"That would be good; maybe you can make me fat, as my family did you?"

"Ha! I cannot promise home comforts."

"No?" he pulled a sad face. "You do not have a sister who can cook?"

"I doubt that you will be our guest for very long."

Van Leiden grinned. "So it has seemed in the past."

"I will have a message passed back to your family. And I was writing to Juliana just yesterday evening, so you can send a letter to them as well."

"Ah, it is good that you write, she enjoys to hear from you."

"I have thought of little else since we met."

"And she you; it is fine, I think," he placed his hand on King's shoulder. "And soon it will be time for you to be my prisoner again, then maybe she can meet you once more. I shall tell her so in my letter, and she can start to save the dirty dishes."

* * * * *

Doust had transferred most of the patients to the re-established sick bay and, with the galley fire alight once more, warmth began to spread through the ship, along with the promise of a proper breakfast. Kate had slept little but now, as she mixed the warm burgoo in a small pewter bowl, she felt her eyes begin to grow heavy. One man had died in the night but the others had survived, and were likely to recover now. With luck they would be back in England within a couple of days. There was much to be done before then, and she would still have to present her accounts: something she had been secretly dreading, despite the fact that they had been brought up to her exacting standards. Kate played with the spoon, stirring the bowl; after a while the oats began to soften, and the burgoo was then considered fit to eat. She had added some raisins and preserved cherries, and supposed the mixture would do the men some good, although it would have been so much better to serve fresh eggs, or milk, or anything more appetising than gruel.

The first patient was Jameson, and she was particularly eager to see that he ate, and ate well. He lay quiet but awake in his hammock after a peaceful, though drug induced, sleep. She approached him with the bowl, and smiled into his eyes.

"Breakfast, Matthew?" His head stayed still and he made no attempt to talk. She placed the bowl down, and reached under his arms to ease him up in the hammock. The body was light and moved easily, but his eyes remained dark, blank and distant. "Just a little to eat," she soothed. "Make you strong again."

She picked up the bowl and loaded it with a little of the mixture.

"Come now, take a bite," his mouth dutifully opened, and accepted the spoon.

"There's a lad," he took some more. "Now you don't want to worry, just rest and relax." She gave him another spoonful and another after that. In her time, as a Mother Midnight, she had looked after many older children while her current charge was recovering from, or preparing for, the trials of birthing. And Matthew was no different, no different from any infant who needed reassurance, food and the promise of safety. He continued to eat until she noticed, with slight sadness, that the bowl was empty. She smiled at him. "That's all, Matthew. That's all until later. Sleep now, sleep, and feel better."

As if responding to her words his eyes did close and she got up quietly and left. They opened again as she went, and for a moment the lad looked about and realised he was quite alone. But still his lips moved very slightly and, in the subdued sounds of a ship at dawn, he muttered a faint "Thank you."

AUTHOR'S NOTE

Duncan's action became known as the Battle of Camperdown (after *Camperduin*, a village on the nearby coast), and was the second major fleet engagement of 1797. It resulted in ten enemy ships being captured, a figure that equals the total number of prizes taken at the Battle of Cape St. Vincent and the Glorious First of June combined.

The British victory was achieved with an inferior fleet, mainly comprising of vessels that were completely worn out, or requiring extensive repair. The Dutch ships were well maintained and designed with a shallow draft to suit the waters off their coast. The fact that they fought well has been universally acknowledged; their standard of seamanship was also considered markedly superior to that of the French and the Spanish at that time. They lacked two things: carronades, the shorter barrelled gun that took less men and time to load, and delivered a heavier charge in relation to its weight and, ironically, they had not just endured one of the largest naval mutinies in history.

There is little doubt that the British seaman had been treated badly, and some form of protest was inevitable. Much had been rectified by the middle of May however, when a resolution was reached with the men at Portsmouth. The uprising at the Nore, subsequently led by Richard Parker, was less justified; the delegates made extreme demands and sought to enforce them in ways that were directly against their government and country. By the time the mutiny collapsed there was both general ill feeling against the British sailor and a genuine and urgent desire to make amends, and prove their loyalty, by those who had taken part, most of whom were members of Duncan's North Sea Fleet. Certainly the victory did much to re-establish Jack Tar in the public's esteem and affection.

Crawford, the seaman who nailed the British colours to the mast, returned to England to be hailed as a hero. He was granted an audience with George III, a pension of £30 a year, and the people of Sunderland, his home town, presented him with a silver medal. He fell on drunkenness and hard times however, and was forced to sell the medal. When he died of cholera in 1831, he was buried in a pauper's grave.

Jan Willem de Winter stayed in England until the December of 1797, when he was exchanged and returned to his native land. For several years he served as ambassador to the French republic. He died in Paris in 1812.

Valentine Joyce, the 'leading spirit' of the Spithead mutiny was a veteran of the Glorious First of June and Bridport's action off the *Ilse de Groix*. Following the pardon, he continued in the Royal Navy, being rated midshipman in 1799. He was lost, and a promising career ended, when the sloop *Brazen* was wrecked during a gale on Ave Rocks, near Newhaven, Sussex in January 1800.

Richard Parker was one of twenty-nine hanged following the mutiny at the Nore. His body was buried at Sheerness, although later exhumed by his wife, who intended to take it to his former home near Exeter. She was apprehended on Tower Hill, however, and he eventually found a permanent grave in a Whitechapel churchyard. His death mask, taken at this time by John Hunter, an eminent surgeon, is still housed in the Hunterian Museum of the Royal College of Surgeons.

Following the battle Adam Duncan was raised to the peerage and created Viscount Duncan, of Camperdown, and Baron Duncan, of Lundie. He continued to command the North Sea Fleet, and was still in overall charge when Admiral Storij, who had escaped during the latter stages of the Battle of Camperdown, surrendered the entire Batavian force two years later. Duncan retired from active service shortly afterwards, although he soon became bored with civilian life. He died suddenly in 1804, returning home from canvassing the Admiralty for further employment. He and Admiral de Winter remained firm friends until his death.

HMS *Venerable* was repaired and returned to sea. She was lost off Torbay in November 1804, a few months after the death of her greatest commander. Her sinking followed a series of freak mishaps, and she is distinguished as the first ship of the Royal Navy to be lost while attempting to rescue a man overboard.

Alaric Bond
Herstmonceux,
East Sussex, England
2010

GLOSSARY

Able Seaman	One who can hand, reef and steer; well acquainted with the duties of a seaman.
Adelborst	*Dutch*. Junior officer, similar to midshipman.
Achterdek	*Dutch*. Poop deck.
Achtersteven	*Dutch*. Stern.
Ague	A fever, as from Malaria. Also a chill or a fit of shivering.
Apron	Metal, usually lead, touchhole cover on a gun.
Armstrong	Pattern of cannon designed in the 1720,s, very common earlier in the war, single button, no loop.
Azimuth compass	Originally designed to measure the position of celestial bodies, a sighting arrangement was provided, often used for taking land bearings.
Back	Wind change, anticlockwise.
Backed sail	One set in the direction for the opposite tack to slow a ship down.

Backstays	Similar to shrouds in function, except that they run from the hounds of the topmast, or topgallant, all the way to the deck. Serve to support the mast against any forces forward, for example, when the ship is tacking. (Also a useful/spectacular way to return to deck for topmen.)
Backstays, running	A less permanent backstay, rigged with a tackle to allow it to be slacked to clear a gaff or boom.
Bag, hammock and birdcage	*SL* Sailors possessions.
Banyan day	Monday, Wednesday and Friday; days when meat is not served in the R.N.
Bargemen	*SL* Maggots in biscuit.
Barkas	*Dutch.* Launch or long boat.
Barkie	*SL* A favoured ship.
Barricoe	Water barrel.
Base ring	Thickest part of a gun.
Beach-master	The officer in charge of a landing party.
Belaying pins	Pins set into racks at the side of a ship. Lines are secured to these, allowing instant release by their removal.
Bight	Loop made in the middle of a line.
Bilboes	Leg irons, or iron garters.
Billboard	A large piece of timber fitted under the channels to prevent the anchor damaging the ship.
Billy Blue	*SL* Admiral Cornwallis.
Billy Pitt	*SL* William Pitt. First (Prime) minister of state at the start of the revolutionary war.
Billy Pitt's man	*SL* A quota man, one sent up for naval service by a port or county.
Binnacle	Cabinet on the quarterdeck that houses compasses, the log, traverse

board, lead lines, telescope and speaking trumpet

Birds of passage   *SL* Those not staying on a ship for any length of time.

Biscuit   Small hammock mattress, resembling ships rations. Also Hard Tack.

Bish   *SL* Chaplain, (also Holy Joe).

Bitter end   The very end of an anchor cable.

Bitts   Stout horizontal pieces of timber, supported by strong verticals, that extend deep into the ship. These hold the anchor cable when the ship is at anchor. Also Jeer bits.

Blab   *SL* One unable to keep his mouth shut.

Black Dick   *SL* Admiral Howe.

Black strap   *SL A* poor quality port or any coarse red wine.

Black vomit   *SL* Yellow fever (or yellow jack).

Blackjack   *SL* Half-pint tin mug. Also a pirate flag or bubonic fever.

Blanket bay   *SL A* deck filled with slung hammocks

Block   Article of rigging that allows pressure to be diverted or, when used with others, increased. Consists of a pulley wheel, made of *lignum vitae*, encased in a wooden shell. Blocks can be single, double (fiddle block), triple or quadruple. Main suppliers: Taylors, of Southampton.

Blomefield   Pattern of cannon standard by 1794. identifiable by loop to top of button.

Bloody flux   *SL* Dysentery.

Boat fall   Line that raises or lowers a ship's boat

Bobstays   A line or chain that runs foreword from the cutwater of the bows, to near the end of the bowsprit.

Bolt rope/line	Line sewn into the edge of a sail, at the bolt.
Boom	Lower spar which the bottom of a gaff sail is attached to.
Bootsman	*Dutch*. Boatswain.
Bowline	Line attached to the middle of the leech that keeps the leading edge of a sail forward when sailing close to the wind.
Braces	Lines used to adjust the angle between the yards and the fore and aft line of the ship. Mizzen braces, and braces of a brig, lead forward.
Breach rope/line	Heavy line to stop the recoil of a cannon, (7" for 32 pounder).
Brig	Two masted vessel square-rigged on both masts..
Brilot	Fire ship.
Broach	When running down wind, to round up into the wind, out of control usually due to carrying too much canvas.
Broad arrow goods	That which belongs to the state (often marked as such). Rope is identified by a differently coloured strand running through.
Building a chapel	*SL* When a ship swings about 360 degrees at anchor
Bulkhead	A wall or partition within the hull of a ship.
Bulwark	The planking or wood-work round a vessel above her deck.
Bumboat	*SL* A shore based vessel that approaches large sea going ships to sell luxuries etc. Often contains money lenders (who will give a mean return in cash for a seamen's pay ticket). Frequently crewed by large masculine women, who employ far more fetching girls to carry out the bargaining with the seamen.

Bumfodder	*SL* Toilet paper. (Bumf.)
Bungs	*SL* Cooper.
Bunt	Middle upper part of a sail, next to the mast.
Bunting	Material from which signal flags are made.
Buntline	Lines attached to the foot-ropes of top-sails and courses which, passing over and before the canvas, turn it up forward, and thus disarm the force of the wind. Can be a minor obstacle to seamen when working on the yards.
Bursten belly	*SL* Hernia.
Burton pendant	Line from the masthead, rather like a shortened shroud, with an eye in one end. Can be used to attach the tackle for lifting boats, guns or other heavy objects on board.
Button	Top of a mast or extreme end of a cannon, on Blomefield model, carrying a loop to take the Breach rope.
Camels	Devise for raising the draft of a ship to allow it to frequent shallow waters. Barges filled with water or sand and barley, are securely strapped to the hull. The weight is removed, and the ship effectively floats on the barges. Also used for refloating ships sunk in shallow water.
Canister	Type of shot, also known as case. Small iron balls packed into a cylindrical case.
Cap-a-bar	The misappropriating of government stores.
Capsquare	Metal plate that holds the trunnion of a standard cannon. This is hinged at the rear to allow the barrel to be remounted.

Carrick bend	Knot used for joining heavy lines or hawsers.
Carronade	Short cannon firing a heavy shot. Invented by Melville, Gascoigne and Miller in late 1770's and adopted in 1779. Often used on the upper deck of larger ships, or as the main armament of smaller.
Cat's paws	Light disturbance in calm water indicating a wind.
Catharpins	Short lines fitted between the shrouds on opposite sides at the level of the futtock shrouds to tighten the shrouds, and allow more space to turn the yards into the wind.
Caulk	*SL* to sleep. Also Caulking, a process to seal the seams between strakes.
Chamber	Area in a gun where the charge is placed; this is the same as the bore in ordinary cannon, but smaller in carronades.
Channel	Projecting ledge that holds deadeyes from shrouds and backstays, originally chain-whales.
Channel Gropers	*SL* The Channel Fleet, when under blockading duties.
Charlies	*SL* Watchmen.
Checked shirt	*SL* Said to be worn by a man who has been flogged.
Checker players	The ships that Nelson commanded. Captains could paint their ships in the way they chose, but Nelson's ships used the yellow on black, called Nelson Fashion, that soon became the norm.
Chips	*SL* Off-cuts of timber, the entitlement of shipwrights. In theory small enough to be carried from the yard under an arm. Also *SL* Carpenter.

Cleat	A retaining piece for lines attached to yards, etc.
Clewline	Line that runs to the corner of a square sail, and used to haul it up to the centre of a yard.
Clews	Loops sewn into the lower corners of a sail. Also the free part of the sail. controlled by a sheet on a jib or staysail.
Close hauled	Sailing as near as possible into the wind.
Close order	In a fleet, sailing 1.5 to 2 cables apart.
Clout	*SL* Cloth.
Coach horses	*SL* The captain's barge crew.
Coal Box	*SL* The chorus of a song, usually ending with Hip Hip Hip, Hurrah! (seamen enjoy the chance to sing loudly).
Coaming	The ridge about hatches and gratings to prevent water on deck from getting below
Cob or Cobb	*SL* A Spanish dollar piece.
Cobbed across the table	Warrant officer punishment; a man is stretched across the table, secured by his hands and feet, and beaten by each messmate in turn.
Cockbill yards	Following the death of a captain it is customary to set the yards of his ship at odd angles on return to port.
Companionway	A staircase.
Course	A large square lower sail, hung from a yard, with sheets controlling, and securing it.
Crank	*SL* Description of a ship that lacks stability, having too much sail or not enough ballast. Opposite of too stiff. *SL* unseaworthy.

Crimp	*SL* One who procures pressed men for the service.
Cringles	Loops attached to the boltropes on the sides and bottom of the sail.
Crows of iron	"Crow bars" used to move a gun or heavy object.
"Cuddy" Collingwood	*SL* Popular Northumbrian Admiral, 2nd in command at Trafalgar.
Cutch tan	Brown dope used to treat sails.
Cutter	Fast small, single masted vessel with a sloop rig. Also a seaworthy ship's boat.
Cutting out	The act of taking an enemy vessel while it is in a supposedly safe harbour or anchorage.
Davy/Davy Jones' Locker	*SL* The sea bed. Also sailor's hell.
Deadeyes	A round, flattish wooden block with three holes through which a lanyard is reaved. Used to tension shrouds and backstays.
Deadlight	Small glass panel that cannot be opened in a hull, deck or gun port. (Also modern closure on skuttle.)
Dispart	The taper of a gun towards the muzzle.
Dogwatch	Short two hour watch that breaks the four hour cycle.
Dolphin striker	A spar that projects downwards from the head of the bowsprit, introduced in the 1790's.
Double stingo	*SL* Very strong beer.
Doxies	*SL* Shore based prostitutes or temporary wives. Usually very attractive, as by tradition they do not pay the ferryman's fare unless they find a "Fancy Man". (Also the officer allowing them on board will only admit pretty women for the honour of the ship.)

Driver	Large sail set on the mizzen in light winds. The foot is extended by means of a boom.
Drogher	*SL* A slow merchant ship.
Dunnage	*SL* Seaman's baggage or possessions.
Earing	Loop sewn into the upper corner of a sail for attaching rigging lines.
Eerste luitenant	*Dutch.* First lieutenant.
Eight bells	The end of a normal 4 hour watch. The bell is rung every half hour, the number of rings increasing with the passage of time.
Eyebolts	Bolts with a ring or opening to enable them to be attached to a hooking tackle.
Face	The end of a gun.
Fat head	*SL* The feeling one gets from sleeping below on stuffy nights.
Fetch	To arrive, or reach a destination. Also the distance the wind blows across the water. The longer the fetch the bigger the waves.
Fife rail	Holed rail to accept belaying pins.
Figgy dowdy	A sweet pudding made from suet and pork fat, flavoured with currents and alcohol.
First Luff	*SL* First lieutenant.
Flexible rammer	Gun serving tool made of thick line, with rammer to one end and sponge to the other. The flexibility of which allows a gunport to remain closed while the gun is served.
Forereach	To gain upon, or pass by another ship when sailing in a similar direction.
Forestay	Stay supporting the masts running forward, serving the opposite function of the backstay. Runs from each mast at an angle of about 45 degrees

	to meet another mast, the deck or the bowsprit.
Foretack	Line leading forward from the bowsprit, allowing the clew of the fore-course to be held forward when the ship is sailing close to the wind.
Founder	Verb, to sink without touching land of any sort, usually during bad weather.
Frapping/Frapped	When not in service the gun, carriage and breaching tackle are lashed together, or Frapped.
Futtock shrouds	Rigging that projects away from the mast leading to, and steadying, a top or crosstrees. True sailors climb up them, rather than use the lubber's hole, even though it means hanging backwards.
Gaff	Spar attached to the top of the gaff sail.
Gaff sail	Fore and aft quadrilateral shaped sail, usually set at the mizzen.
Gallouts or Guffies	*SL* Marines. Also Jollies.
Gammoning	Wrapping line about a mast or spar *e.g.*: the lashing that holds the bowsprit against upward pressure, to the knee of the head.
Gasket	Line or canvas strip used to tie the sail when furling.
Gewgaws	*SL* Trinkets.
Gig	Medium sized boat.
Gingerbread	Gilding usually to the stern of a ship.
Glass	Telescope. Also, hourglass: an instrument for measuring time. Also barometer.
Glim	*SL* Lantern.
Go-about	To alter course, changing from one tack to the other with the wind crossing the bows.

Goose winged	A sail set with the lower corners pulled down to the yard below, while the centre remains furled, an alternative to reefing.
Gore	The lower edge of a sail, usually scalloped, in the case of a main or forecourse. In warships the gore is deeper (more round). Also Roach.
Grape	Cannon shot, larger than case.
Grappling-iron	Small anchor, fitted with four or five flukes or claws, Used to hold two ships together for boarding.
Groat	*SL* Fourpence.
Grog	Rum mixed with water (to ensure it is drunk immediately, and not accumulated). Served twice a day at ratios differing from three to five to one.
Ground tackle	Anchors and cables etc.
Guard ship	Usually a third rate, party manned, armed and stored, used as the first line of reserve. Commissioned, and available for full service relatively quickly.
Gudgeons	Fixings on the stern post to pintles on the rudder.
Gunpowder	A mixture of charcoal, salt petre and sulphur.
Half deck	Area immediately between the captain's quarters and the mainmast.
Halyards	Lines which raise: yards, sails, signals *etc*.
Handspike	Long lever.
Hawse	Area in bows where holes are cut to allow the anchor cables to pass through. Also used as general term for bows.
Hawser	Heavy cable used for hauling, towing or mooring.

Head	Toilet, or seat of ease. Sited at the bows (head) to allow the wind to carry any unpleasant odours away.
Head braces	Lines used to adjust the angle of the upper yards.
Head rope/line	Line sewn into the edge at the head of a sail.
Headway	The amount a vessel is moved forward, (rather than leeway: the amount a vessel is moved sideways), when the wind is not directly behind.
Heave to	Keeping a ship relatively stationary by backing certain sails in a seaway.
Hogging	The sag in the backbone of a ship, where the bows and stern droop to lower than that of the middle. Often caused when a vessel has been at sea for some time.
Hollands	Gin.
Holy Joe	*SL* Chaplain, also Bish.
Holy-stone	*SL* Block of sandstone roughly the size and shape of a family bible. Used to clean and smooth decks. Originally salvaged from the ruins of a church on the Isle of Wight.
Hounds	Top of a section of mast, where the shrouds run from.
Hoxton	The Naval asylum in North London. Hopeless cases are transferred to Bethlem. One in 1,000 seamen go mad, (National average is 1 in 7,000) The constant banging of heads on beams is often blamed.
Hulled	Describes a ship that, when fired upon, the shot passes right through the hull.
Idler	One who does not keep a watch, cook, carpenter, *etc.*
Interest	Backing from a superior officer or one in authority, useful when look-

	ing for promotion to, or within, commissioned rank.
Jack Corse	*SL* Bonaparte.
Jack Dusty	*SL* Purser's steward, also Jack of the dust.
Jacob's ladder	Rope ladder (often used for boarding from boat).
Jakes	Privy, pot, or seat of ease.
Jape	*SL* Joke.
Jaunty	*SL* Master at arms.
Jeer bits	Stout timber frame about the mast, these extend deep into the ship.
Jeers	Thick lines which raise the lower yards. Supported by:
Jib-boom	Boom run out from the extremity of the bowsprit, braced by means of a Martingale stay, which passes through the dolphin striker,
John Company	*SL* The Honourable East India Company (H.E.I.C.).
Johnathan	*SL* An American.
Johnnie Newcome	*SL* A new member of the crew.
Johnny Crapaud	*SL* The French equivalent to John Bull.
Jollies	*SL* Marines. Also Guffies.
Jolly Boat	Small cutter usually with a crew of 7.
Junk	Old line used to make wads, *etc.*
Jury mast/rig	Temporary measure used to restore a vessel's sailing ability.
Kedging	To move a ship by pulling alternately on two anchors that are continually dropped ahead of the ship by the ships boats. Similar to warping (towing against solid objects).
Kelson	The inner keel, on which the mast step rests.
Kite	*SL* Sail.

Landsman	The rating of one who has no experience at sea.
Langridge	Shot consisting of irregular iron pieces linked together.
Lanthorn	Lantern.
Lanyard	Short piece of line to be used as a handle. Also decorative tassel to uniform.
Larboard	Left side of the ship when facing forward. (Later known as Port.)
Lasking	A variation of the attack in column, where each ship, instead of aligning its heading with the line of battle axis, steers slightly up wind, thus allowing its broadside to fire with effect, while permitting the wind to carry the ship down to a more effective range.
Lateen rig	Triangular sail attached to a yard hung obliquely to the mast. Commonly found on the mizzen in square rigged ships until the adoption of the gaff.
Launch	Large ship's boat, crew of 40-60.
Leeward	The downwind side of a ship.
Leeway	The amount a vessel is pushed sideways by the wind, (as opposed to headway, the forward movement, when the wind is directly behind).
Legs and wings	*SL* A surgeon's 'offcuts'.
Lifts	Lines that keep the yards horizontal, each lift leads from the mast, through a block at the yard arm, and back through another block at the head of the mast, and down to the deck, where it is secured.
Liner	*SL* Ship of the line – Ship of the line of battle (later battleship).

Lining	Part of a sail that is reinforced, usually at an important point, with a double thickness of canvas.
Linstock	The holder of slow match which the gun captain uses to fire his piece when the flintlock mechanism is not working/present.
Loblolly men/boys	Surgeon's assistants.
Long toggies	*SL* A young landsmen.
Lubberly/Lubber	*SL* Unseamanlike behaviour; as a landsman.
Luff	Intentionally sail closer to the wind, perhaps to allow work aloft. Also the flapping of sails when brought too close to the wind. The side of a fore and aft sail laced to the mast.
Main tack	Line leading forward from a sheave in the hull allowing the clew of the maincourse to be held forward when the ship is sailing close to the wind.
Martingale stay	Line that braces the Jib-boom, passing from the end, through the dolphin striker, to the ship.
Master-at-Arms	Senior hand, responsible for discipline aboard ship.
Men in lue	Men carried in press tenders to replace the sailors taken from homebound merchantmen. They are often pretty poor sailors themselves, thus avoiding the press. Also Ticket Men.
Neaped	A ship that has gone aground on a spring tide is said to be neaped. It may have to wait up to six months for another suitable tide.
Nettles	Lines to either end of a hammock.
Nippers	Light line which attaches an anchor cable, or any heavy line, to the capstan messenger. *SL* ships boys, (who tie and untie the nippers when raising anchor).

Oakum	Unravelled line fibres, mixed with tar to act as stopping between planks. See Caulking.
Old Nobbs	*SL* King George III.
Oldster	*SL* Midshipman who has failed to pass through to lieutenant.
One legged spider	*SL* Popular sailor's description of a marine climbing aloft.
Open order	In fleet sailing, 3 - 4 cables apart.
Ordinary	Term used to describe a ship laid up; left in storage, with principle ship-keepers aboard, but unfit for immediate use.
Ordinary seaman	One who can make himself useful on board, although not an expert, or skilful sailor.
Orlop	Deck directly above the hold, and below the lower gun deck - from the Dutch word to overlap. A lighter deck than the gun deck (no cannon to support) and usually level or below the waterline. Holds warrant officers' mess, and midshipmen's berth, also carpenters' and sail makers' stores. Used as an emergency operating area in action.
Over threes	*SL* Referring to a captain of over three years seniority, and entitled to wear both epaulettes (after the uniform changes of 1795)
Paddy's Reef	*SL* A hole in a sail.
Palm-and-pricket men	Sailmaker's assistants.
Parbuckle	The rig, consisting of two looped lines, used to drag barrels etc. on board without using a davit.
Parbuckle rails	Rails, often near the entry port, that aid items entering the ship, see above.
Pariah-dogs	*SL* Men who change mess so often they are forced to mess alone, or

	with others of their kind. They are usually unpopular for a number of anti-social reasons.
Parrels	Bread shaped pieces of wood that help to keep the yard against the mast, and allow for its adjustment.
Peak halyard	Line that secures the extreme end of a gaff.
Peter Warren	*SL* Petty Warrant Victuals, fresh food sent from the shore to ships staying in harbour for some time.
Pickthank	*SL* Teller of tales, causer of trouble.
Pinance	Boat powered by oars or sail. Smaller than a barge.
Pintles	Fixing on the rudder to gudgeons on the stern post.
Pointing the ropes	The act of tapering the end of a line to allow it to pass easily through a block.
Poop	Aft most, and highest, deck of a larger ship.
Pooped	The breaking of a heavy sea over the stern or quarter of a vessel when she is running before the wind. A common cause of foundering.
Popham's Code	The RN signalling code, using flags, usually four to a hoist.
Pox	*SL* Venereal Disease, Common on board ship; until 1795 a man suffering had to pay a 15/- fine to the surgeon, in consequence, many cases went unreported. Treatment was often mercurial, and ineffective.
Preaching Jemmy	*SL* Admiral James Gambier.
Protection	A legal document that gives the owner protection against impressment.
Provisions	Naval rations.

Puddening	The protective wrap of line about the shank of an anchor.
Pumpdale	Gully that crosses a deck, carrying water cleared by a pump.
Purser	Officer responsible for provisions and clothing on board.
Purser's dip	Tallow lantern allowed below deck.
Purser's eights	Term used to describe the purser's practice of only issuing 14 ounces for every pound of provisions.
Pusser	*SL* Purser.
Quarterdeck	Deck forward of the poop, but at a lower level. The preserve of officers.
Queue	A pigtail. Often tied by a man's best friend (his tie mate).
Quoin	Wedge for adjusting elevation of a gun barrel.
Quota men	Those who entered the RN to "relieve themselves of public disgrace" - usually sent by a magistrate. Also Lords Mayors, or Billy Pitt's men.
Ratlines	Lighter lines, untarred, and tied horizontally across the shrouds at regular intervals, to act as rungs and allow men to climb aloft.
Redbreasts	*SL* Bow Street Runners who patrol the rougher areas of a port or town.
Reef	A portion of sail that can be taken in to reduce the size of the whole.
Reefing points	Light line on large sails which can be tied to reduce sail in heavy weather.
Reefing tackle	Line that leads from the end of the yard to the reefing cringles set in the edges of the sail. It is used to haul up the upper part of the sail when reefing.
Reinforces	Bands about the barrel of a gun.

Rigging	Tophamper; made up of standing (static) and running (moveable) rigging, blocks *etc*. *SL* Clothes.
Roach	The lower edge of a sail, usually scalloped, in the case of a main or fore course. In warships the roach is deeper (more round). Also Gore.
Robbands	Lines passing through the holes in the sail, and tied over the top of the yard. The outer ends are stretched along the yard by the earrings.
Rondey	*SL* The *Rendezvous* where a press is based and organised.
Round houses	The enclosed (private) heads at the stem of the ship. Larboard side for midshipmen, warrant officers and mates, starboard for patients in the sick bay.
Round Robin	*SL* Means of complaint open to crew against their officers, a petition to the admiral commanding the station. The names of the petitioning seaman are written in a circle so that no man's is at the top to identify the ring-leader.
Running	Sailing before the wind.
Sailor's joy	*SL* A home made drink so potent that even men accustomed to drinking grog on a regular basis soon become maniacs under its influence.
Samson post	A stout wooden prop or pillar midway between the centre line and the bulwarks.
Sauve-tete	The netting rigged when in action to catch falling debris from above.
Scarph / Scarphing	The process of joining wood to build keels, masts and other major items.
Scavelman	One who works with ballast at a naval base.
Schooner	Small craft with two masts.

Sconce	Candle holder, made of tin, usually large and flat for stability.
Scrag	*SL* To be executed by hanging.
Scran	*SL* Food.
Scupper	Waterway that allows deck drainage.
Scuttle-butt	Bucket with holes for line or leather handles used for water for immediate consumption. *SL* gossip (the modern equivalent is chatting by the water cooler).
Seingever	*Dutch.* Signalman.
Selling before the mast	The act of auctioning off a dead mess mate's possessions.
Serving mallet	Mallet shaped instrument with a groove running opposite to the handle, used when serving a line.
Sew-sew boy	*SL* Seaman adept at needle and thread, often made and repaired clothes, in addition to the official tailor (Snips).
Shakes	Barrel staves.
Shakings	Line waste, common about blocks and tackle.
Shako	Marine's headgear.
Sheet	A line that controls the foot of a sail.
Sheet anchor	Heaviest anchor (although often not much bigger than the bower). Also slang for the seaman's last hope - if the sheet doesn't hold...
Shellback	*SL* An old sailor.
Ship fever	Fever common aboard ships usually, though not always, Typhus. Also jail or camp fever (for many years considered to be different illnesses). Carried by body louse infesting dirty clothing.
Shoe-boy	*SL* Lower deck nickname for a servant.

Shot rolling	The act of rolling a cannon ball at an officer, usually a sign that mutiny is about.
Shrouds	Lines supporting the masts athwart ship (from side to side) which run from the hounds (just below the top) to the channels on the side of the hull. Upper run from the top dead-eyes to the crosstrees.
Slab line	Line passing up abaft a ship's main or fore sail, used to truss up the slack sail.
Slatches	Large cat's-paws on the water, an indication of strong wind.
Sloop	Small craft, usually the command of a commander or junior captain.
Slops	*SL* Ready made clothes and other goods sold to the crew by the purser.
Slush	*SL* Fat from boiled meat, sold by the cook to the men to spread on their biscuit. The money made was known as the slush fund.
Slushy	*SL* The cook.
Smasher	*SL* A carronade.
Snips	*SL* Ship's tailor.
Snitch stitch	*SL* The last stitch when sewing up a dead man in his hammock. It passes through the snitch of the nose to ensure the man is properly dead.
Spanker boom	Boom attached to the driver.
Spindrift	Spray, from the bows of a fast moving ship, or skimmed from crested waves in a storm.
Spitkid	A small bucket or spittoon. If a man is caught spitting on deck, he may be tied to the ratlines with a spitkid about his neck, for the men to take target practice.

Spring	Hawser attached to a fixed object that can be tensioned to move the position of a ship fore and aft along a dock, often when setting out to sea. Breast lines control position perpendicular to the dock
Sprit sail	A square sail hung from the bowsprit yards, less used by 1793, as the function had been taken over by the jibs, although the rigging of their yards helps to brace the bowsprit against sideways pressure.
Squaring yards	The act of squaring the yards on the masts, usually achieved by marks on the braces.
Stag	*SL* To turn against your own.
Stag horns	U and V shaped structures inside of the bulwarks used to fix the braces and sheets.
Stay sail	A quadrilateral or triangular sail with parallel lines, usually hung from under a stay.
Step	The wooden support placed on the kelson, on which a mast rests.
Stern sheets	Part of a ship's boat between the stern and the first rowing thwart, used for passengers.
Stirrups	Lines hung from a yard to support the footrope.
Stood/Stand	The movement of a ship towards or from an object.
Strake	A plank.
Studding sail	Light sail that extends to either side of main and top sails to increase speed in low winds. Made of the thinnest canvas (No 8).
Study	A cooper's anvil.
Swab	Cloth, or (*SL*) officers' epaulette.

ALARIC BOND

Sweep	A large oar, usually used to move bigger vessels, such as brigs or cutters.
Swifter	Line (or man) stretched between two bars of a capstan to increase the power.
Swipes	*SL* Weak beer.
Tabling	A hem sewn around a sail.
Tack	To turn a ship, moving her bows through the wind. Also a leg of a journey; relates to the direction of the wind. If from starboard, a ship is on the starboard tack. Also the part of a fore and aft loose footed sail where the sheet is attached or a line leading forward on a square course to hold the lower part of the sail forward.
Taffrail	Rail around the stern of a vessel.
Tampion	Wooden bung, used to plug the mouth of a gun.
Tarpaulin	Tarred cloth or *SL* used to describe a commissioned officer who came from the lower deck.
Tattletale	*SL* Gossip.
Throat halyard	Line that holds the inner end of a gaff.
Thrumming	The act of using a sail, that has been half sewn with many small threads, to block leaks in the hull as a temporary repair.
Ticket men	*SL* Those protected from the impress, through some cause or other. Also men carried in press tenders to replace the sailors taken from home bound merchantmen.
Tiddley suits	*SL* Sailor's shore clothes.
Tight ship	In good order: watertight.

Toe the line	Midshipmen when being disciplined *en mass* are made to stand in a line behind a plank, (strake), seam.
Top/ toping the glim	*SL* To extinguish a lantern.
Topping lift	Line that secures the extreme end of a gaff. Also peak halyard. Also a line leading to the end of the boom to support it when not under sail.
Trick	Period of time served by a helmsman, usually an hour.
Trucks	The wheels on a standard carriage gun, small with heavy axles.
Trunnions	Gun barrel supports, on either side. Cast as one piece to the barrel.
Tumblehome	Describes the narrowing of a ships hull as it rises, making the beam of upper decks shorter than that of the lower.
Turnpike	A toll road; the user pays for the upkeep. Usually major roads.
Under threes	Referring to a captain of under three years seniority, and only allowed to wear one epaulette, on the right shoulder (after 1795).
Vakantie	*Dutch.* Vacation.
Vangs	Lines that hold the side to side movement of a gaff or boom, leading to rails on each side of the deck.
Veer	Wind change, clockwise.
Verspieden	*Dutch.* Reconnoitre.
Voorplecht	*Dutch* Forecastle.
Wadhook	Cannon serving tool rather like a giant corkscrew, used for removing debris, charges *etc.*
Wales	Reinforcement running the length of the ship, under the gunports.
Warm	*SL* When describing a person, rich.

Warping	To move a ship by towing it against solid objects, trees, posts etc. Similar to kedging (towing against anchors).
Washboards	*SL* The lapels of the uniform coat that denotes a Lieutenant
Watch	Period of four (or in case of dog watch, two) hour duty. Also describes the two or three divisions of a crew.
Watch bill	List of men and stations, usually carried by lieutenants and divisional officers.
Wearing	To change the direction of a ship across the wind by putting the stern of the ship through the eye of the wind.
Weather helm	A tendency to head up into the wind. A well trimmed ship is often said to have slight to moderate weather helm. The opposite of lee helm.
Windward	The side of a ship exposed to the wind.
Wormed, parcelled and served	Standing rigging, which has been protected by a wrapping of canvas and line.
Yellow Jack	*SL* Yellow Fever or Black Vomit.

ALARIC BOND

His Majesty's Ship
The Jackass Frigate
True Colours

Alaric Bond was born in Surrey, England, but now lives in Herstmonceux, East Sussex, in a 14th century Wealden Hall House. He is married with two sons.

His father was a well-known writer, mainly of novels and biographies, although he also wrote several screenplays. He was also a regular contributor to BBC Radio drama (including Mrs Dale's Diary!), and a founding writer for the Eagle comic.

During much of his early life Alaric was hampered by Dyslexia, although he now considers the lateral view this condition gave him to be an advantage. He has been writing professionally for over twenty years with work covering broadcast comedy (commissioned to BBC Light Entertainment for 3 years), periodicals, children's stories, television, and the stage. He is also a regular contributor to several nautical magazines and newsletters.

His interests include the British Navy 1793-1815 and the RNVR during WWII. He regularly gives talks to groups and organizations and is a member of various historical societies including The Historical Maritime Society and the Society for Nautical Research. He also enjoys Jazz, swing and big band music from 1930-1950 (indeed, he has played trombone for over 40 years), sailing, and driving old SAAB convertibles.

Lightning Source UK Ltd.
Milton Keynes UK

172509UK00001B/253/P